A Tattered Curtain
novel

ROUGE

GREER RIVERS

Blue Ghost Publishing, LLC
BGP Dark World

Cover Design: TRC Designs

Editing and Proofreading: My Brother's Editor

ASIN: B0BGQJNB9Y
Paperback ISBN: 979-8-9861242-7-8
Hardback ISBN: 979-8-9861242-8-5

ROUGE

GREER RIVERS

Rouge

The Garde values four ideals: The Truth we *twist*. The Beauty we *flaunt*. The Freedom we *grant*. The Power we *take*.

I believed their lies until Lacey O'Shea.

She's the only daughter of the Garde's leading family, and she was meant to be mine. But her father stole her from me to sell to another.

So I stole her back.

But there's more to the conspiracy that kept us apart, and we have to keep our relationship secret from her former fiancé, the Baron, to find the truth.

He wants to lock her away, but she's a bird desperate to flee her gilded cage.

I'll fight the Baron, the Garde, and the whole damn world to free her.

Playlist

"Boulevard of Broken Dreams" by Roses & Revolutions
"Play with Fire" by Sam Tinnesz, Yacht Money
"Where Are You?" by Elvis Drew and Avivian
"Cravin'" by Stileto, Kendyle Paige
"Colors" by Elvis Drew
"Revolution" by Bishop Briggs
"PLEASE" by Omido, Ex Habit
"Elastic Heart" by Sia
"Figure You Out" by VOILÀ
"Love into a Weapon" by Madalen Duke
"Hold Your Breath" by Astyria
"Take Me to Church" by MILCK
"Twin Flame" by EMM
"Dancing in a Daydream" by Roses & Revolutions, Weathers
"Fire on Fire" by Sam Smith
"Way Down We Go" by KALEO
"Angel By The Wings" by Sia
"Kryptonite (Reloaded) by Jeris Johnson
"Bird Set Free" by Sia
"you should see me in a crown" by Billie Eilish

Get the full playlist here:

A Note From The Author

In writing this book, I was lucky enough to get to work with someone from Ireland who helped me bring these characters to life. As Irish Americans, these characters' colloquialisms and mannerisms are a "wee bit" different than their Irish cousins, and certain Irish words and phrases are used metaphorically. That being said, I hope you fucking love every fecking thing about Kian!

The Tattered Curtain Series consists of complete standalones inspired by classic stories and stage productions with tragic endings. *Rouge* is a dark, modern-day, spicy reimagining that transforms classic tragedies, such as *Romeo and Juliet*, *Camille*, and *Orpheus and Eurydice*, into dark and twisty HEAs.

TRIGGER/ CONTENT/ TROPE WARNING

Rouge is a dark romance. It should only be read by mature readers (18+).

Protect your heart, friends. Reader discretion is advised.

To Mr. Rivers.
I choose you every day.

"If men knew what they can have for a tear, they would be better loved and we should be less ruinous to them."

Alexandre Dumas *fils*
La Dame aux Camélias

Prologue

T he love of my life is dying... and it's my fault.

Act 1

Scene 1

THE RED CAMELLIA

Three weeks ago

Thrusting deep inside her ignites an all-consuming fire underneath my skin and I have to dig my fingers into her thighs to resist collapsing from pleasure. Her loose, strawberry-blonde curls spill over my pillow as she gazes up at me through sky-blue eyes. I've only ever seen them on a screen, but they sparkle in person.

This isn't real. It feels too good to be real.

Her moans fuel me to shove reality away. She's rightfully mine and knowing I've finally captured her has blood, adrenaline, and ecstasy surging through my veins, pumping into my cock. One more thrust and I'll secure a McKennon heir—

A gentle buzz vibrates next to my head, wrecking the happy ending I'll likely never get from the woman of my dreams. The soft noise blares in my ears thanks to my splitting headache.

Last night I got lost in my frustration and stayed out way too late with my two best friends. Merek dipped out early, naturally. He treats his job as head of McKennon security seriously, which means the lad works twenty-four seven. But Tolie thrives in the nightlife. He knows the Vegas underworld almost better than I do.

thanks to the many jobs he's secured through O'Shea Entertainment, Las Vegas's largest employer, and going out with him is always a fecking adventure.

He and his castmates partied all night as a "pregame" for Halloween this weekend. After I made sure Tolie wasn't going to try to fuck one of the Greek statues again, I dragged him back with the rest of his friends to Rouge, the Las Vegas burlesque and male revue club where they dance. I crashed in his dressing room while they kept the debauchery going.

Thank feck Tolie has a rule against sleeping with castmates in his own dressing room bed or I'd have hauled my arse back to my suite. Then again, maybe I should've. I didn't drink, but the pounding bass that blared through the walls until six am made me feel like I did.

The night before the cast's Devil's Night performance was *supposed* to be easygoing, and it was by their standards. But I should've left as soon as they broke out the absinthe. Now, I'm still in my black button-down and slacks, reeking of cigarettes I didn't smoke and booze I didn't drink and suffering a migraine-like hangover I didn't even get to earn.

My mobile rumbles against wood and I blindly slap the bedside table until the aggravating device tingles underneath my hand. As I grab it, the folded playing card underneath it drifts to the ground.

I swipe the screen and press it to my ear without even bothering to open my eyes. If it's quiet here, it's too early in the day, giving away who's on my caller ID. None of my direct business contacts are up in the daytime. Only him.

"Dad, you're not supposed to call before noon." My voice sounds like I've been chewing rocks, and my throat doesn't feel much better.

"Jesus, Mary, and Joseph, Kian. It's 12:01, and this is bloody important. You're lucky I followed your stupid rule. You didn't break yours last night, did you?"

I grit my teeth, wanting to snap back, but the note of concern in his question has me biting my tongue. Out of habit, my fingers gravitate to the poker chip-sized coin in my pocket and I trace the raised design as I answer him.

"Of course not. Nuns drink more than I did last night."

"Good, because this party-boy facade has gone on too long. Kian... it's time to wake up."

My heart stutters in my chest as my exhausted mind tries to keep up. The adrenaline I felt in my delicious dream is actually thrumming through my veins now, helping me ignore the pain in my head.

"Is this about the Red Camellia?"

"It is. I confirmed the details at poker last night while you were off playing the part. I need you to ruin the Red Camellia."

My sleepy eyes finally snap open at the command I've been dying to follow for three years.

As soon as the last word is out of his mouth, I'm already putting my father on speaker so I can text Tolie at the same time. He's a crucial part to this crazy plan he helped me concoct. I could go try to find him in the cast's big rec room where I left him during the wee hours of the morning, but I'm not in the mood to see postcoital naked strangers right now.

> Practice ASAP. Tonight is a go.

I'm sure he's half-asleep, but he answers me almost immediately, albeit with typos.

> TOLIE
> Ill mak sre everthig is perfectionissimo.

The excessive emojis following one of Tolie's many signature words make me snort, but my father's phrasing finally registers and my brow furrows.

"*...ruin the Red Camellia.*"

As much as I want to object, the words fall from my lips out of habit.

"How do you want it done?"

I always ask the same question when it comes to jobs for the Garde, the secret society my family pledges our loyalty to. I'm a low-ranking card to these men, even though the McKennons were once poised to take the throne.

It was the Keeper, Charlie fecking O'Shea, who ruined us.

I was supposed to marry his daughter, Lacey O'Shea, according to the arranged marriage contract our fathers entered into years ago. My father and I thought O'Shea was one of the few good men left in the Garde, but after he withdrew that contract without explanation, he made me the black sheep of our society and he became my enemy number one. The fact that he's currently in jail and *my* family is the one being ostracized shows everything that's wrong with this organization.

Families have to buy into this society and once they join, their assets are tied up with the organization. We receive half of our inheritance after our parents die and we're only eligible for the rest once we get married to another Garde heir and have a child of our own. If we never do, our remaining fortunes get locked in with the Garde and distributed to the other families. It's how the founders ensure loyalty, but their rules have fecked me over and they've lost mine.

I've made my own connections, money, and business dealings without the Garde's help, but none of it matters. Since my father is still living, I don't report the wealth I've made independently from the Garde, so they think I have nothing. When the Keeper inexplicably deemed me unworthy, many in our society stopped doing business with McKennons, rendering me powerless in their eyes, too. Now, no Garde father will ever consider letting his daughter marry me. Not that I want their women.

I want *mine*.

"I could give feck all how it's done." My father's Irish accent thickens with every angry word. "From the wee bit we know about his decision, his daughter could've been the one to put him up to all this. Kill the girl and dump her in Lake Mead if you have to, or fuck her and ruin her in a way that no one else will want the precious O'Shea flower."

"Mam wouldn't have liked you talking that way," I tsk playfully, trying to calm him down. My mother passed away from a heart attack nearly four years ago. I can't have my father do the same.

She was the one who championed Lacey as my future bride, making the argument that the two most powerful families should unite to prevent divisiveness within the society. I've never met a member of the O'Shea family in person. Having all of us together in one room—especially the heirs—could lead to a brutal coup or mutually assured destruction. But Mam met Lacey when she was just eighteen, and after that one meeting, my mother was convinced we were a perfect match.

"Bah, she knew my flaws and loved me anyway. The woman was a saint. Your mam would've been able to fix all of this if she'd been alive when Charlie breached the contract."

She might've had a sixth sense about who her son should end up with, but I don't know how my mother, a woman, could've convinced the Keeper of anything. The Garde values a woman's beauty and nothing else about her. The lack of respect for my late mother in the role she played in the matchmaking has only made my father more furious about the betrayal.

But the McKennons have been clawing our way back to the top. We finally have the support to take back what's ours and the timing couldn't be more perfect.

"Charlie O'Shea might be my nemesis, son, but he can't stab our whole family in the back and expect us not to retaliate. This is your revenge more than mine. You deserve to do with his prized possession as you see fit. The Red Camellia was supposed to be yours, after all."

"You're goddamn right about that," I mutter under my breath.

I sit up and grab the folded queen of diamonds card from the floor as I open my social media app. Scrolling under my fake profile, the app proves it knows me better than I know myself, and Lacey O'Shea magically appears on my feed.

Her sky-blue eyes are dull, completely devoid of any intelligent thought or passion. Nothing like the ones in my dream. There's no smile as she stands beside her best friend, Roxana Muñoz, in a pose that thousands of other socialite influencers have adopted in an effort to look effortless. It makes me sick to see, and I'd almost believe the facade... if I wasn't also keeping track of her in Roxana's less curated profile.

Roxana has perfected the art of oversharing and constantly takes snapshots of her chaotic life. I scroll the feed to quickly find one of those posts as I try to stay engaged in the conversation.

"How did you confirm my tip? My contact wouldn't give me a definite answer on the timeline this week. I think they're skittish about what I'll do. Everyone in town knows Monroe is here for his wedding this weekend, thanks to his big-arse mouth—"

"He's 'the Baron' now, you know," my father reminds me with a harsh chuckle. "Monroe's father might've died from 'mysterious' causes, but it still made him the head of the household. According to our rules, that makes Monroe *the* head of his name."

"'Mysterious circumstances,' my arse. The only thing mysterious about the old Baron's death is that his son didn't off him sooner."

"I have no doubt he played a part. There was little 'old' about the man. He was fit as a fiddle. The coroner wanted an autopsy, but of course the Keeper couldn't allow that. We can't implicate another Garde member. Deaths are dealt with in-house."

"And deaths within families aren't dealt with at all. Just like the old days."

The Garde tried to distinguish itself from the Mafia that all but ruled the United States at one time. Instead of overtly entering lives of crime to slake their lust for money, they traded secrets, using them to gain positions in government and influential companies across the country.

It only took two generations of moral compromises for greed to dig its roots. The society brags about higher-minded ideals, but they've perverted them: twisting truth, flaunting the facade of beauty, granting the illusion of freedom, and stealing all the power they can for themselves. These days, the Garde is just like its Mafia counterpart. But because the Garde has infiltrated the government, they're able to use their authority to avoid getting caught.

Now the organization has a list of enemies longer than its membership and one of our own is being prosecuted for the first time. We should be sticking together more than ever before, but they've turned their backs on my family.

"It's the way it is. The Garde has rules, and he's the head of his family—"

"The man's a snake, Dad. I'd rather cut off his head than give him the distinction."

"You'll have to play nice a wee bit longer if you want to win this, Kian."

Fecking hell. He's right. But I refuse to acknowledge it with anything more than a grunt as I tug on my hair in frustration.

There's a long-suffering sigh before he responds, "Well, *the Baron* is indeed in town for his wedding, so I convinced an old Garde friend still loyal to the McKennons to invite him to one of our standing poker games. Of course the weasel jumped at the opportunity to schmooze."

"You're terrible at poker," I groan. "You didn't lose this time, did you? Last time you lost to a Baron—"

"I didn't lose!" He gives a wry chuckle. "Believe me, I've learned my lesson. I don't play for anything but money now."

I snort and shake my head, resisting the urge to tease him further about betting the deed to a hotel on the Las Vegas Strip in a game several years ago with Monroe Baron Sr. Losing the property wasn't a devastating blow. There are still plenty of businesses in Vegas with our name behind them, not to mention my own private holdings, so it's funny as hell now.

"You should've invited me. Maybe I could've won the hotel back."

"We don't need that hotel. One is enough. And you know I couldn't do that. I wasn't planning on playing, regardless. Just observe. Fortunately, the arrogant fool was so hammered by the time I got there that I was just another face to the bastard."

"Loose lips with the liquor, is he? *The Baron* should be a teetotaler, like his father before him if he knows what's good for him. They've never been able to hold their liquor."

"He thinks he's impervious to everything, including getting rat-arsed. I made sure he never had an empty glass. After a while, all I had to do to find answers was listen to him bitch and moan."

My father boasting about tricking the cocky son of a bitch should make my chest swell with poetic justice, but breath escapes my lungs as I study Roxana's most recent post.

With the other picture, Lacey's practiced, emotionless expression was front and center. But as always, without an audience, her performance ends.

In this photo, Roxana sticks her tongue out with her middle finger raised beside her cheek, her face so close that I can see where the filter has erased the pores from her deep-golden skin. She almost takes up the whole screen, but in the background, there's Lacey, enthralled with two street performers dancing on the Vegas Strip sidewalk.

Her smile is perfection, so pure I can feel the delight that's making her smooth ivory skin glow. She's untucking a loose strawberry-blonde curl from behind her delicate ear, as if she's trying to create a curtain of separation between her and the camera so she can enjoy the show in peace. The move inadvertently flashes the huge sparkling rock on her left ring finger.

Fuck.

I shake my head and want to exit the app, but I'm unable to peel my eyes away from Monroe Baron's diamond, flashing like a hazard light at me.

"Monroe bitching and moaning?" I scoff. "What does that

gobshite have to complain about? Charlie O'Shea's daughter is basically the future queen of the Garde. Once Monroe marries her, he's next in line to be Keeper. Then when he runs for office, he'll already have access to every single secret the Garde has *and* he'll no doubt use that advantage to secure the American presidency one day."

And Lacey will be his forever.

That near-constant, gnawing ache in my chest flares up again. It's gotten worse as the years have passed. Waiting in the shadows for the right time to get my revenge has nearly killed me.

My father insisted I grow up in Ireland away from all the Garde's backstabbing, but my family's crime connections got me mixed up in the fighting circuit. It was brutal—I've had to set my own broken nose too many times—but those skills have proven to be useful time and time again in helping me blow off steam and performing the odd jobs my father has me do to protect our business. They've been my only saving grace for the past year, but I'll never truly rest until I have my revenge.

I fiddle with the queen card in my hand and my eyes widen as an idea sparks. My father won't like it. As much of a softy as Finneas McKennon is with his family, McKennon revenge against everyone else is notoriously biblical: steal, kill, destroy. Anything less would be a failure in his eyes.

This all-or-nothing strategy has made him an excellent businessman but a terrible poker player. He's good at assessing what's in front of him but awful at reading the players around him, and he's notorious for placing big bets on bad cards.

But what if stealing the queen of diamonds is all I need to gain a winning hand?

"The Baron doesn't want Miss O'Shea to go to her bachelorette party at Rouge tonight, especially since she's refusing to have his bodyguards in tow. Seems that she feels safe in her hometown," my father continues, giving me the information I need about her security presence—or lack thereof. "He also believes going to the revue is a slap in the face the night before their *real* wedding."

"So they *are* supposed to get married tomorrow? My contact couldn't confirm."

"According to the man himself, they're meeting at the court-house tomorrow morning to get the legal part over. He even said she better not embarrass him tonight at the 'sinful' show or he might call the whole thing off."

"Let me guess, he was a good little boy and went home all by himself after the poker game?" I sneer, knowing good and bloody well that Monroe has a different mistress every day of the week.

"Of course not. He left while necking two of the waitresses from the casino floor. Barons don't have McKennon loyalty. That's what's wrong with the Garde. Arranged marriages don't have to be solely business contracts, even less so if it's a good match. Despite our families' differences, you and Lacey were a good match before she became a daft socialite. Your mam was never wrong. Blackmail and financial power may be the most important things to the organization, but nothing gives a man more strength than having someone he loves by his side. Just look at your mam and me. Once I set my sights on her, there was no one else. Garde men will never understand that, though. It'll take someone like you as the Keeper to change everything for the better and O'Shea made sure that could never happen."

"Careful, Dad. Don't let old age make you get all fecking romantic."

"Oh, trust me, there's still enough ruthlessness in me to get the job done. Speaking of which, Miss O'Shea maintaining her pure image wasn't the only grievance the Baron had. He's convinced she'll fall into trouble at Rouge."

"It's her own family's establishment. What trouble could she get into?"

"Ironic you'd ask. Hopefully your ruse tonight promises just that. You have to ruin the O'Shea name, Kian. If you do it right, the Garde may even wise up and realize you're the leader we need to overthrow that spineless traitor while he's in his jail cell. I'm counting on you and so are all the families who supported us when we were shunned. It's the only way to get back at the Baron and the O'Shea all at once. Ruin them and never look back."

My thumb grazes over Lacey's face on the screen, covering up the diamond ring, and a slow smile stretches across my lips.

"I plan on it."

Scene 2

THE GREEN FAIRY

"Lacey, dear, do you think that dress may be... I don't know, a little revealing?"

My future sister-in-law's comment makes me want to strip naked just to spite her. Instead, I act like the good "Garde girl" that I pretend to be and plaster on a smile in Maeve's direction. I tug down the tulle hem of my short white dress, even as my other hand balls into a fist.

The costume is admittedly ridiculous, but I didn't blink when my best friend, Roxy, insisted I go all out. It's an over-the-top, lace-and-diamond-studded, runaway-bride cocktail dress, complete with tennis shoes. It'll be great to dance in, but the glittering outfit plus the huge princess-cut rock on my ring finger makes me look like a walking disco ball.

"Try not to be so jealous, Mimi," Roxy tsks in my defense as she pours us shots, careful not to spill in the limo.

"My brother's the only one who's allowed to call me that."

"But the name Maeve is so... stuffy."

"Lacey, make Roxana stop! She's been mocking me ever since I got into the limo."

Roxy smirks, highlighting her perfectly applied bloodred lipstick. Her deep-brown eyes are covered with heavy eye shadow and her hyperrealistic fangs make her more intimidating than her personality already is. Not to mention the fact she's wearing an all-black leather jumpsuit that straddles the line between sexy vampire and dominatrix.

"Roxy... Maeve..." I warn, trying to get them both to cool it. "You guys have been hissing at each other like cats all night long and it's only the beginning. I just want to have fun."

"Alright, alright, jokes aside, Maeve, it's my bestie's birthday and bachelorette party. She deserves to look fucking hot, okay? Her outfit is practically tame for Devil's Night. Besides, everyone dresses like a slut for Halloween."

"It's just so short, especially when you fidget so much. And that plunging neckline is quite low-cut," Maeve argues. "Not to mention the fact that 'runaway bride' might send my brother the wrong impression. There's too much at stake for you to even joke about that."

She bends toward me to lift up the lace *V* of my neckline, but I jolt back and my fisted hand snaps open with the barely contained urge to slap her away.

"I like it." My eyes narrow before I lean closer to her so that my obliviously drunk friend can't hear my whisper. "And you don't need to remind me how much is at stake."

Roxy interrupts us by giving me a full-to-the-brim shot glass of Belvedere vodka. I quickly sip the top just in case the limo driver has to stop abruptly for a drunk pedestrian again. The crisp liquor is supposed to be smooth going down, but I still wince at the taste.

Maeve's eyes widen. "Brides shouldn't do shots. It's trashy!"

She reaches for the shot, but I pull away and take a big gulp despite the burn.

Roxy snorts. "You should've seen this girl shotgun a beer at a Saints game back in the Big Easy. I swear she had the guys at the tailgate ready to get down on one knee. We may have the Keeper's flower in our midst, but your brother's certainly not getting a shrinking violet."

Roxy's reference to the Garde's pretentious title, the Red Camellia, makes me squirm. When I was a child, I thought it was a cute nickname from my dad because I loved the pretty flower growing up. It wasn't until talks of marriage and proposals that I realized it's the Garde's name for the Keeper's only daughter and that pretty flower is destined to be plucked for the Garde's pleasure.

Neither of them notices my discomfort, though. Maeve's jaw hangs open, too horrified by Roxy's story to scold me for fidgeting. When my soon-to-be sister-in-law seemingly remembers herself, she smooths the all-black dress that serves as her nun costume and clears her throat before literally looking down her nose at me.

Why the hell did she even want to come if she was planning on critiquing me the whole time?

"You grew up in Sin City, so maybe you don't know, but you're *supposed* to leave that kind of behavior behind in college, like I did. I'm sure going to a New Orleans arts school was full of temptation, but hopefully you kept your legs closed tighter than you have tonight." She pushes my knees together so quickly I can't stop her. "My brother and the Garde have expectations, you know. Although I'm sure Monroe will be able to tame you."

I bristle as she glances up and down my dress with contempt.

"I'm not an animal meant to be tamed. But don't worry, I know what's *expected* of me." I knock back the rest of my shot without waiting for Roxy's toast.

The Garde may be in charge of my life, my body, and my future, but these small moments of rebellion get me through each shitty moment.

"Hey! We should at least say 'Cheers' or something," Roxy grumbles until I hand her my empty shot glass.

"Hit me again."

I'm going to need as much liquid courage as I can get if I'm going through with my final act of rebellion I have planned. There's a segment of tonight's burlesque show that's for amateurs only. My friend Tolie works for my family's entertainment company and he's organized a routine so that one of the dancers will choose me as the act. It's been so long since I've performed onstage and I can't fucking wait.

Roxy shrugs and refills the glass before pouring two more. "Here, Maeve, *dear*, why don't you take the edge off a little? It might be a long night."

Roxy's bloodred smile is saccharine sweet as she hands Maeve her shot. Maeve's pale skin is nearly translucent in the limo's LED lights, but her scowl is plain as day as she stretches across me to take the glass.

"Come on, now. Play nice." Roxy pokes out her full bottom lip, a move she perfected in grade school to get what she wants. "I'm the maid of honor, and Lacey insisted I invite you, even though sisters are always snitches on bach nights. Are you going to let loose and celebrate with us or prove me right?"

Roxy's microbladed black brow rises in question and Maeve's cheeks blush so furiously it gives her a purple hue.

"I'm not a *snitch*." Maeve raises the glass in the middle of the three of us. "To the bride, the prettiest flower in the Garde. May God bless you with many Baron babies."

Her toast makes me grimace, but she doesn't see it as she downs the shot in one gulp and slams it onto the leather armrest beside her.

"Okay, you guys have *got* to stop stealing my thunder," Roxy whines. "*I'm* supposed to be making the toasts. Now you have to do another."

Maeve coughs in response and narrows her light-brown eyes at Roxy. Her sour expression is almost funny, but even though Maeve is on her high horse tonight, guilt makes me want to give her a break.

"Maeve, you don't have to take any shots. She's just teasing you."

My future sister-in-law's disdain shifts to me. With her straight dirty-blonde hair slicked back by a designer headband and the disappointment on her face, she looks just like my fiancé. All she needs is a goatee.

"I won't be called a snitch. The Garde prides itself on keeping secrets and I've kept my fair share."

My forehead furrows at her pointed stare. I don't know what the hell she's talking about. Does she know how wild and crazy Roxy and I used to get on Bourbon Street and Frenchman Street back in New Orleans? That can't be it, though, right? We were so careful not to get caught.

Before I can ask her to elaborate, Roxy pours and shoves another full glass into Maeve's hand.

"Prove it. Drink up."

Roxy stares at her deadpan, but I frown slightly behind the lip of my glass. They're both up to something, although I doubt one knows the scheme of the other. Whatever their agendas are, I'm letting them sort it out. I'm much too on edge to deal with Maeve's condescension tonight all by myself. It's nice to have my friend defend me, even if she does have questionably toxic tendencies herself.

"No, you and Lacey go first. I just drank mine and neither of you have finished yours!"

"Jesus, Maeve, it's not like I'm force-feeding you Belvedere and Dom Perignon. I was supposed to do the toast, and you stole my shine. Now you get to drink another so I can do mine and we don't get bad luck."

Maeve pouts but takes the glass, surprising me. I don't know what her angle is. Like Roxy, I thought Maeve only wanted to come because her brother forced her to spy on me. He hates that I'm having a bachelorette party at all, let alone going to a burlesque show the night before I sign my life away for the Garde.

For my dad.

The thought settles me. He's the reason I agreed to this arrangement in the first place. So for his sake, I crack on a new fake smile and keep trying to make the best of things.

"I'll drink as many as you want, Rox."

"That's the spirit!"

"No, no, no. We don't want the bride to be a lush on her bachelorette night!"

"Speak for yourself," Roxy scoffs. "I can't wait to get my girl sloshed."

"She's kidding, Maeve. I'm not getting drunk, I swear."

I can't if I'm going to dance tonight. Granted, Maeve doesn't know what I have planned.

"Good," Maeve answers with an approving nod. "Tomorrow's an important day for you."

"Why? What's tomorrow?" Roxy asks and my heart stutters. "We already got our papayas waxed, her mom is taking care of the rehearsal dinner and wedding planning, and the actual event is Saturday. I thought tomorrow's slate was free?"

Maeve might not be a snitch, but she's definitely not as good at keeping secrets as she boasts. Only our families know that Monroe and I are signing the marriage license tomorrow morning. We don't want anyone interfering with the legalities of the actual marriage and the Baron's grand vision for a lavish rehearsal dinner party and a surprise, extravagant wedding—one that my mom has almost ripped her hair out trying to get perfect—is a flashing caution sign to anyone who might want to thwart our wedding to get a leg up in our society.

"Sorry, I meant Saturday..." Maeve rambles on, dropping secrets like a dump truck. "*Saturday* is important. As long as she doesn't embarrass my family by then, all she'll have to worry about soon is producing an heir."

The words smack me in the chest and land between the three of us like a brick.

It's no secret that the Garde treats its women like trinkets before we're married and broodmares after, but to have another woman accept that fact so easily makes me scared for the future of the Garde.

"I don't plan to sit idly by while my husband rules, you know. We don't have to be trophy wives if we don't want to be. Just look at my mom. While my father's been in jail, she's done a great job running his businesses."

Maeve scoffs. "Only the ones the government didn't seize for investigation. Good thing my brother is swooping in to save the day."

I'm careful not to react so Roxy doesn't notice that Maeve keeps revealing way too damn much with her drunken limo-ride confessions. I love Roxy, but her loyalty is to her family name, and the Muñozes have been unpredictable in their ties the past year. Garde men like her father are eager to barter—or even kill—for power whenever they sense weakness. As one of my father's financial managers, Monroe's testimony will be crucial to prove my dad's innocence. Our families have kept the fact that he's testifying a secret because we don't want rival families like the Muñozes finding out how important Monroe is to my father's freedom.

After my father's first arrest, the sudden lack of brownnosing and ass-kissing was a stark difference from what I'd grown up around. Two years later, my dad was rearrested on new charges and the judge sent him back to jail. Now, he's forced to stay there until his trial—which will be God knows when, thanks to the slow as fuck judicial system.

When he went away, there was a question as to whether the Garde would overthrow him, making my mom and I worry we might not even survive long enough to see the trial. If a patriarch dies without a son or brother to fill the void, the rest of the bloodline soon dies out with him under "mysterious circumstances" so fortunes are returned to the Garde and distributed among the remaining families.

But precedent said that death is the only way the Keeper position changes hands. Even behind bars, my father remains in full control of the Garde. Officers turn their heads when he uses his smuggled phone to negotiate alliances and the secrets he still protects keep me and my mom safe, too. Our society continues to thrive under his rule.

The only problem so far has been the McKennons, but nothing can keep them in line.

Even though we've never met, at one time, I was supposed to marry the heir to the McKennon name. I was nervous about the arrangement, but after meeting his sweet mother years ago, I got excited to marry him. When he broke our contract, I was devastated... at first. I soon learned he's just like everyone else in this society. They all think my family backed out of the deal, but my father told me the truth.

Kian McKennon didn't want me. He wanted power. And that made me furious.

He didn't care that my father was framed and when he discarded me, I finally understood why my family has always hated theirs.

Thankfully, Monroe Baron stepped up and asked to marry me. The Garde doesn't know he believes my father is innocent, so they think he's a saint for debasing himself with me, the daughter of an alleged criminal.

But that's what the Garde thinks, and Maeve knows better. Her loose lips have me boiling.

"I've done nothing to embarrass your family."

"Whether you're the embarrassment or your father is, it doesn't matter. Once my brother is Keeper, the disgraced O'Sheas will be forgotten, just like the McKennons."

"The O'Sheas will be *forgotten*?" Roxy's eyes widen to the size of golf balls. "You may be the future Keeper's sister, but Lacey's still practically the Garde's future queen."

"No, no. That's not what I meant." Maeve shakes her head quickly. "I mean, the O'Shea's *disgrace* will be forgotten."

"But you said that the 'disgraced O'Sheas' will be forgotten," I argue.

"Oh no. You just misheard me, silly. I wouldn't say something like that." She waves away the thought as if I'm the one who's out of line here.

When my and Roxy's faces don't soften, Maeve laughs

nervously and digs into her purse to retrieve a prescription bottle without a label.

"What're you doing?" Roxy asks. "Is that Valium?"

"Just a little pill for my nerves." Maeve pops the top skillfully one-handed.

"Wait," I interrupt. "You've been drinking. Is that a good idea?"

"I'll be fine. I've done it before."

"That's not necessarily the same thing—"

She ignores me as she tips the bottle back like the shot she just took. The pills slide down the see-through orange plastic before she swiftly takes a few sips of liquor and swallows both.

I can't tell how much she took, but when she's done, she drops the bottle back into her chic purse and smiles at me like she didn't just insult my family, pop sketchy pills, and chase them both with expensive vodka in a matter of seconds.

Roxy recovers more quickly than I do and slowly raises her shot glass between the three of us, stopping me from questioning Maeve further.

"On that disturbing note... to one dick for the rest of your life! And to the millions of dollars that will hopefully help you forget the one dick part. Cheers!"

Roxy clinks all of our glasses while I giggle and Maeve looks irreparably scandalized. Still, she knocks the shot back with us like a champ.

As soon as the liquid passes my taste buds, I hiss and shake my head, scrunching my eyes closed at the burn.

"Jesus, that'll hit you in the ovaries," I mutter, ignoring Maeve's permanent expression of disapproval.

"Oh, I forgot!" Roxy digs through her purse before pulling out a small stack of index cards connected by a silver ring and handing them to me. "For you."

My brow furrows until I read the curly pink cursive on the front written in Roxy's handwriting, "Bitch of Honor Kidnappings." I flip the paper cover to see a cutely decorated date card that says, "Waxed Papayas and Pedicures." When I flip again, I see a "Stupid Rom-Com of Bride's Choice," an "Ovaries Deep in Booze Night Out," and a "Wish You Were Still Single" card, followed by many more.

"You made this for me?" My chest twists at the thoughtfulness behind the gift.

Roxy shrugs and tries to put her best nonchalant Garde face back on. "You mentioned you were afraid we wouldn't be able to hang out. Anytime you want to use those, just send me a pic and I'll come kidnapping, no questions asked."

"Roxy..." Tears fill my eyes. "That's so sweet—"

Maeve snatches the cards from my hand and rips one out. "A 'Wish You Were Still Single' card? Really? I don't think you'll be needing this one. Ever."

Roxy grabs the coupon book back and shoves it in her tight bodysuit before waving the ripped paper in the air. "You know what, Maeve? I think this one will be perfect for our girl tonight. There's nothing like a bach party to make you want to be single again."

"No. Lacey's 'single days' were over when my brother arranged to marry her. He's been waiting a long time for her family to follow through with this arrangement. She shouldn't want to be hungover or do something stupid so close to the wedding."

I want to argue with her out of spite, but she's not wrong. It has been a long time. Years, in fact, but it's the Garde way. We're not supposed to get married until the birthday after our college graduation and not a day before.

One night. That's all I have left of my single life.

Having to wait to get married is a godsend in our world, giving us a tiny sliver of freedom before our responsibilities weigh us down like chains. It's soul-crushing to know I'm required to leave my passion behind while I stand by a man as he achieves his. Monroe has made it clear he only wants me for my name and my father's position. Once I have a Baron heir, he can gain his inheritance and secure the society's support for his political aspirations.

Women in the Garde are traded back and forth in exchange for power, like cards on a table, passing down dynasties and fortunes. Without a Garde-approved wife and heir, half of Monroe's inheritance will either go to Maeve if she marries and has a child, or it'll revert back to the Garde. The pay-to-play system is a ruthless and archaic practice, but that's all the Garde is. Ruthless and archaic.

And there's nothing I can do about it.

Yet.

The thought whispers seductively across my mind, but I shove it away. Dancing is one thing, but a coup-like rebellion is *not* the wisest thing to think about when I'm sharing alcohol with my uptight future sister-in-law.

The limo slows to a stop, and Roxy does an excited shimmy in her seat. With anyone else, it'd look laughable, but the girl was one of the best dancers at the Bordeaux Conservatory, the performing arts school we both attended in New Orleans. Every move she makes is fluid and perfect, no matter what.

"We're here!" she sings off-key and chugs some liquor out of the bottle. She sucks in an inhale and huffs before handing it to Maeve.

"Drink up, Mimi. Gotta loosen that stick up your ass."

Maeve frowns but still takes a sip. Years of being told what to do trains most Garde women to be compliant. Considering the heavy-handed way the Baron has insisted on controlling my own life even before we get married, I don't doubt that she'd jump off the glass wall of a nearby rooftop lounge if someone richer than her told her to do it.

"You too, future Mrs. Stick Up Her Ass." Roxy winks at me as she retrieves another bottle of Dom from the limo's cooler and hands it to me.

I chuckle as I lift it to my lips, wanting a sweet sip to take the edge off my anxiety, but my phone rings in the pocket of my dress.

"Shit." I shove the bottle at Roxy, interrupting her taunting Maeve. I swear she's getting her wasted on purpose. Roxy is notorious for drinking until she blacks out, and with the Valium in Maeve's system, I might be babysitting on my bachelorette night.

I pull my phone from my pocket and glance quickly at the screen before bringing it to my ear.

"Monroe? We're about to enter the club. Can I call you after?"

My fiancé scoffs back. He's been pissed about me going to a male revue ever since Roxy and Tolie came up with the idea. His sister watches me through drunken, interested eyes, so I resist the urge to roll my own. Maeve probably won't remember a damn thing about tonight, but it's better to be safe than blackmailed.

Roxy looks quite pleased with herself, and realization sets in. She *is* trying to get Maeve drunk. Maybe she's making sure Maeve won't be able to tattle to Monroe about my dance? I was hoping for a "get married first, ask for forgiveness later" situation with him, but her not remembering it at all would work so much better in my favor.

"I don't know why you have to go to this ridiculous show in the first place. It's a glorified strip club, for God's sake. It's embarrassing that my future wife is going."

"And where will your bachelor party be, hmm? A monastery?"

Monroe huffs. "Clearly not, but men are different. You shouldn't be out gallivanting across town in a dress like that."

I glance down. "How do you know what I'm wearing..."

When I look back up, I catch Maeve looking at everything but me.

Of course she ratted me out. She probably sent the group picture of the three of us to him as soon as we took it. I shouldn't have expected anything less, honestly, I just didn't realize she'd move so damn fast.

"Just remember, I have no problem postponing this wedding as punishment. I could even push it past your father's trial. What would happen then? Exoneration is a lot harder to get than a 'not guilty' verdict. Don't embarrass me tonight, Lacey."

The air in my lungs freezes at his cold threat. The O'Shea part of me wants to rebel against his cocky attitude. How the fuck dare he try to intimidate me and use my father's freedom against me?

But the reality of my situation calls for the fake, sparkly facade I reserve for the world that only wants to look at pretty things. Where I'm seen but not heard. And *that* part wants to cower in a corner.

My mouth chooses a mixture of both before logic kicks in.

"This is my bachelorette night, Monroe. I'm going to have a good time. Rouge is a Garde establishment. An *O'Shea* establishment, even. I'll be safe from the paparazzi. My father's people are loyal and I promise to call you after. Just like we negotiated."

Monroe grumbles on the other end of the line, but I can't quite make out what he's saying. When he finally responds, I bristle at his tone.

"Don't fucking bother, Lacey. I've tried to warn you. It'd be a shame if this whole thing falls apart because you got trashed like a bar slut. What will your father do in prison if he doesn't have you as a bargaining chip? Garde loyalty only lasts for so long."

I open my mouth to object but he hangs up on me. My heart races in my chest and I look to Roxy, prepared to beg her to just take me back home and end this night early.

"Maybe we can watch a rom-com or something instead—"

"Nope, here—" She shoves a shot of green liquid in my hand. "Drink this. A gift from Tolie."

I eye the color with suspicion and smell licorice from the glass even before I sniff it.

"Oh god, what is it?"

Roxy snorts. "The green fairy. She'll treat you right, babe. Don't you worry about a thing tonight. Tolie and I have it all covered." She tilts her head at a hiccuping Maeve, confirming my suspicions. "Whatever happens in Rouge, stays in Rouge."

She winks and the stone elephant sitting on my chest lightens.

I smile a little before tipping the shot back. It burns as it goes down and the strong licorice taste makes me grimace before I even swallow it. I shudder and fight the urge to cough it back up.

"Whew, that's strong!"

Roxy chuckles. "It does the trick, though. Now let's go throw ridiculous amounts of money at stunning half-naked men and women."

On cue, one of Roxy's bodyguards opens the limo door and the loud chaos that is Fremont Street echoes from both ends of the parking garage, bouncing against the wide walls and high concrete ceilings. We're in Las Vegas proper at the Montmartre Hotel and Casino, one of the businesses my family owns, and bright-red LEDs along the ceiling are our only light.

It's been ages since I've been in this part of town. I was in New Orleans for so long I'd almost forgotten what it's like.

As soon as I hop out of the limo, I lock eyes with an enormous three-dimensional mural of a devil's head spanning the wall from floor to ceiling. He's holding the rotating blades of a destroyed red windmill as if he's in the process of decimating the idyllic French village painted behind him. The art pays homage to both the underworld and the original Moulin Rouge cabaret in Paris. The club's door resides inside the devil's large, wide-open mouth and a red carpet rolls onto the stone sidewalk like a long red tongue. Music blares from the entryway and a shiver of excitement ripples through me.

"Don't worry," Roxy whispers to me once she climbs out of the limo. "I'll make sure that card gets put to good use tonight."

She loops her arm in mine and grins while pointing at the neon-red sign above the windmill's slowly rotating blades.

"Welcome to Rouge, Lacey."

Scene 3
DIRTY DANCING

"Welcome to Rouge!" Tolie's rich voice echoes over the music blasting from the speakers, giving the illusion that he's everywhere in the large venue.

The entryway opens up to cabaret-style seating with people grouped at tables in front of a stage. When it's not Halloween, the space is gorgeously decorated in rich reds and silver accents, drapery, and tableware. Its opulent design is perfect for my family and the Garde when they throw benefits and balls. But now, the entire room has been transformed to look like the fire and brimstone of the underworld, complete with the gaping mouth of hell stage right.

We've arrived in the middle of the first act. A chorus line of women dance a slow, erotic version of the cancan, another homage to the original Moulin Rouge cabaret that was known for the frenetic dance in the 1890s. Their glitzy fallen angel costumes have wildly colored feathers peppered in their Victoria's Secret-style black wings, and their midnight skirts flutter to their waists as they extend their thigh-high-covered legs in the air in a sensual *port d'armes*.

The move requires them to turn on one leg with the other

pointed to the ceiling, and their rotation is smooth even while they stretch to stroke their hands from their heeled ankles down to their thighs. Their core strength has to be stellar, especially considering they're able to hold their standing splits for as long as it takes the bouncer to lead us to our table.

Our seats are at the front and just right of center. As we pass through the audience, it's clear we're not the only Halloween bachelorette party in the room. The brides are easy to spot since we're all wearing white amid groups of women dressed in themed costumes. Of course my little party—a runaway bride, a vampire, and a chaste black dress masquerading as a nun costume—has no cohesion. Granted, it was barely a party to begin with, but hopefully the show will get us in the spirit.

When the dancers finish, Tolie suddenly appears from behind spooky, gray tattered curtains at the corner of the stage in a cloud of smoke. His spiked purple hair stands out against his black tuxedo, but an orange feather boa wrapped around his neck adds another pop of color to his emcee ensemble. As he smiles, his theatrical fake mustache curls from cheek to cheek across his olive skin.

"We may be in a drought, but it's always raining men in Rouge! And on this Devil's Night, be prepared to face..." He flings his arms out wide as the curtains open with a whipping sound. "Your demons!"

Wild, high-pitched cheers and screams explode around me, and I clap with the rest of the room when six huge men appear in black hooded capes that cover them head to toe. The music halts abruptly, quieting the women just enough to get us all to stop losing our shit over the clothed men. But when a new song begins, all bets are off. The exciting hip-hop beat has me squirming to dance, and I fist my hands in my lap to stop myself, so I can relax and enjoy the show before it's my cue.

The men move in unison as they glide across the floor to the edge of the stage. There, they wait for the bass beat to drop before lifting their black-masked heads and simultaneously stripping off their capes, revealing their muscular chests, oiled-up abs, and swollen arms. They still have their capes in their hands as they do stunts like backflips, back handsprings, and spirals in the air, making the fabric fly until each dancer discards it near the closed curtains.

While the dancers perform at the front of the stage, taking up the audience's visuals, my gaze catches the movement behind them. Stagehands sprint out with chairs and set them up in a line before disappearing. As soon as the last one vanishes, each dancer makes their way to a chair, some crawling backward on their knees, undulating against the floor, while others pelvic thrust toward the crowd.

Once they sit, the six demon-masked men execute their sensual stripteases. Even behind their masks, their eyes engage the audience, and the noise from the thirsty crowd makes my ears ring.

"Hot, right?" Roxy yells drunkenly over the blaring speakers and shrieking women and I nod in return.

"Kinda mad at myself that I've never watched a show before!"

"Of course you haven't! The Keeper's precious flower at a male revue?! The *scandal!*" She gasps in mock horror before laughing. "Let's live it up before you're stuck having a nepo baby and bored out of your goddamn mind for the rest of your life."

Roxy lifts her shot with a sloppy smile, totally unaware that her last statement churns the alcohol in my stomach. The girl's a socialite who flocks to a nightclub like a moth to a bug zapper, but she can't hold her liquor to save her life. It doesn't bode well that she's already ordered a tray of shots for the table even though we've only been here for half a song. Out of the corner of my eye, I see Maeve's head drooping to her chest. The two of them may be passed out before I even take the stage.

So much for me being the drunkest one tonight.

I'm glad I didn't pregame while we got ready like Roxy did.

The alcohol is affecting me, but so far, it's only buzzing through my system, giving me the courage to perform for the first time since I graduated.

Roxy takes the shot without me and knocks the glass back onto the table. She grabs another one from the tray and shoves it in my hand.

"Enjoy tonight while you can, betch. If the rumors about the Baron are true, it might be one of your lasht."

Her drunken, slurred speech almost makes her hard to understand, but her warning is crystal clear. Blood quickly drains from my face, making me light-headed and I empty the shot in one gulp. The fruity concoction isn't nearly as strong as the liquor Roxy had in the limo, but it does the trick. When I slam my glass back onto the table like she did, Roxy's smile turns sad.

"Ish too bad it didn't go the other way." The words roll from her mouth like she's trying to find them with her tongue. "The one with Kian might've turned out alright-y."

"Yeah, well that wasn't necessarily up to me, now was it?"

Even if he wanted me—if I wanted *him*—it doesn't matter now. He wouldn't be able to save my father.

I don't tell her that though. Instead, I forgo another shot of liquor and sip my champagne. I never planned on getting shit-faced tonight, but I might if she keeps talking this way.

"True. True. But tonight can be up to youuu! Who knowsh? Maybe you'll get laid if you play your cards right!"

My gaze cuts to Maeve to see if she heard Roxy, but my future sister-in-law's chin has officially made a bed on her chest and her eyes are shut. I think I'm in the clear, thank God.

The Garde has a misogynistic policy that the women remain "pure" before our wedding night, so we don't "ruin our beauty and worth." Literally, that's how my mom phrased it when she warned me against boys at age twelve. It's a disgusting double standard instituted by men who make millions off of strip clubs and don't even know that a tampon can "take our virginity" just as easily as a dick can. I rebelled as soon as I got to college.

That first night, Roxy covered for me with our bodyguards while I led the hottest tourist I could find into a bar bathroom. To date, it was the best sex I've ever had, not because it was romantic —it was far from it, and it wasn't even all that good—but it was *my* decision. My first big 'fuck you' to the Garde. If the Baron finds out I've slept with other people, though, it could screw everything up. Thankfully, Roxy's hidden agenda worked and Maeve is already out like a light.

The tension in my chest eases and my nerves light up at the realization that I'm actually getting to perform one last time. Roxy's screams of excitement fuel me and I turn back toward the stage to see her tossing dollar bills everywhere, yet somehow still missing the men.

Before long, I find myself grinning from ear to ear, letting go while I watch the performers dance and gyrate. They're more acrobats than exotic dancers, almost like watching one of my favorite Cirque du Soleil shows, but I'm not surprised.

Vegas performers are the best of the best. They have to be since the competition is so cutthroat. I catch myself studying their moves instead of ogling their physiques. That is, until they rip off the rest of their demon costumes, leaving only their revealing black speedos.

Of course, that makes the crowd go nuts and we momentarily drown out the music. Once we've quieted down a fraction, the tempo changes, prompting the men to suddenly line up in a row again and freeze at attention. Their positioning hides whatever is behind the curtain as it opens wide. The throbbing, deep bass music takes on an ominous tone and drives my pulse faster.

"And now..." Tolie's voice echoes over the sound system again and my veins thrum as I realize it's almost my cue. "The devil himself!"

The demons kneel in unison, revealing a giant of a man in an all-red cape. The devil in question raises his red scepter at the applause and sets it back down. With his horned mask taking over the top half of his face, the only defining feature we can see is his short, messy brown hair, a hard, scruffy chin, and grim lips set in a serious line. When he lifts his head, his intense gaze, hooded by the spotlight, is dark and focused. A hunter searching for his prey.

He stalks slowly toward the front of the stage in the same hypnotic cadence of the song blaring over the speakers, "Play with Fire" by Sam Tinnesz. The crowd's fervor is at an all-time high, and the devil grins like he can't help himself. With the way the women are cheering him on, those simple movements are all he needs to get a rise out of them.

Tolie warned me that the new guy needs more experience before he can be included in a real number. It's one of the reasons why my friend is letting me perform the amateur act. The new guy will get stage experience without the pressure of learning a routine and apparently crowds love when a secretly skilled audience member surprises them by taking over a segment. All the devil has to do is stand and look pretty while I have my way with him.

"The devil waits for no man... or woman," Tolie announces. "But on Devil's Night, and every night here at Rouge, the ladies *always* come first. And tonight, he's picking one of you!"

The women shriek with anticipation, and the devil lifts the scepter in his hand to command us. The room snaps into rapt attention and I shift to the edge of my seat, holding my breath. He strides across the stage, his body powerful yet graceful. Even though he's new to dance, his movement makes me wonder if he's trained in something else. Fighting, maybe? A lot of them are coached to be light on their feet. Either way, he's got promise and it'll be fun to see how good his reflexes are.

Tolie's voice echoes over the speaker again, but I don't see him at his podium, so he must be announcing from backstage now.

"Everyone knows the devil is bad but did you know... he's always loved a good girl?"

Roxy and I snicker at his cheesy line and I *swear* the devil scowls. The audience is eating it up, though, and "oohs" and "aahs" flutter around the room.

"He's been searching the realms to find the one who will sate his insatiable lust. The one he can... *pleasure* in this life and beyond. And lucky him, he has the pick of the crop, doesn't he, ladies? Now which one of you beautiful women shall it be?"

Once again, all the women around me lose their damn minds, including Roxy.

"Silence!" the devil's deep voice thunders through his headset microphone and straight to my clit.

Holy shit.

He travels away from my side of the stage, using his red scepter to point at each table, and my heart sinks at the fear that Tolie forgot to tell him the plan. But before I give up hope, he stops outside the mouth of hell decorating stage right, turns on his heel, and prowls back to me.

Every step closer, my muscles threaten to leap out of my skin, desperate to climb up and join him. I expect him to talk up the crowd like Tolie did, ham it up a little, but he's silent and the audience twitters with nervous energy.

When he finally gets center stage, feet away, he front flips onto the ground, making his cape whip in the air and shocking the hell out of me. The move elicits thrilled squeals from the tables around ours, everyone no doubt hoping he'll choose them. But when he straightens again, his broad shoulders roll back and I catch a glimpse of his sculpted, tanned abs as he lifts his scepter to point. At *me*.

Finally.

"You," he commands. "You are my chosen one. You are the one I claim."

My lower belly flips at the dark promise in his words.

"Me?" I know this was planned, but it somehow feels like a dream.

"Yes, you."

I vaguely register a mixture of disappointed groans and encouraging cheers. Roxy stands and claps, egging me on, while

Maeve shakes awake. She lunges for my hand, but the devil reaches for me at the same time—

As soon as he touches me, electric sparks zap up my fingers like I've been shocked. I can't help gasping as I instinctively clutch his calloused palm.

He moves the microphone away from his lips and leans in to speak so only I can hear. "We're going to have some fun."

There's something almost... sinister in the devil's smirk, but before I can question it, alcohol and nerves take over, reminding me that I need to put on my final performance.

Tomorrow I'll don the mask the Garde has designed for women like me. One that smiles and nods in support of a man I hate while he fulfills all of his dreams at the casualty of my own. I'll wear this bitter acceptance for the rest of my life and I'll never be able to rip it off. But tonight I can play a part that's all up to me.

It's a gift to know when you're doing something you love for the last time. I'm going to soak it up for all it's worth.

I press my hand against my thunderous heartbeat to try to calm the hell down. His eyes roam over me before flicking back up to meet my gaze. This exchange of glances lasts longer than I'd expect during a set like this, but the pause no doubt teases the hungry audience more. It's definitely doing it for me and my skin is on fire for his touch.

My heart skips at the way he looks straight into my soul. His hair has a red tint under the spotlight and his almost familiar hazel gaze shines. His hand grips mine tighter, making me feel like we're the only two in the room—

"Lay-she!" Maeve slurs drunkenly while tugging at the tulle of my dress. "You can't! What about my brother?"

She's been half-asleep since we entered the building, so it's just my luck that she'd wake up now. The liquor has hit me too—in the best way—destroying all inhibitions, but the thought of performing has me sobering slightly. My unused muscles are already springing to life and it's all I can do not to swat her hand away and leap up onstage.

Roxy rolls her eyes dramatically and pries Maeve's hands off me. "Ish a bashelorette night! Let her have shome fun. Take a nap if you don't want to wash."

Maeve pouts and tugs her phone from her pocket to start a text, but the devil growls into the microphone.

"Did we forget to mention putting away all phones?"

Roxy grabs the device from Maeve's hand and stuffs it in her purse.

"Hey!"

"Devil told me to." Roxy smirks as Maeve crosses her arms and slouches in her chair. Roxy turns back to me and shoos me. "*Go*. Have shome fun while you shtill can."

My eyes widen, reality crashing in. This might very well be my last night of freedom. Tomorrow I sign my marriage license and my life and body away with it. If tonight's going to be the last night I can live my life the way *I* want to, I'm going to fucking live it.

"Get on stage. Get on stage." The room begins to chant, not that I need the encouragement now.

"You've heard the people. Do you dare disobey them?" The devil's voice is like warm velvet. "Do you dare disobey *me*?"

The intensity in his gaze makes my core heat. I can practically feel all the liquor in my system evaporate in exchange for lust and adrenaline. Part of me knows I shouldn't be doing this, but the other part knows if I don't have this one final dance, I'll regret it for the rest of my life.

I glance behind me one last time. Roxy waves her hand like she's fanning herself and winks at me. Maeve is losing her battle with sleep again, the Valium and the alcohol concluding their tango inside of her with a lights-out performance.

My pulse eases in my chest, knowing that the Baron's snitch has checked out, and I decide to give myself over to the moment.

I turn around again and face the devil. The stage presence I cultivated at Bordeaux melts over me and I step within inches of his lips so I can speak into his microphone.

"No, Devil. I would never disobey you."

His hazel eyes widen before a dark sensuality takes over their golden hue. The carnal smile that spreads over his lips makes me shiver with need.

"Come then, my bride."

Scene 4

DANCING WITH THE DEVIL

W hen the curtains opened, it didn't take me long to find my runaway bride glittering like a diamond in the front row.

During my Male Stripper 101 crash course earlier today, Tolie instructed me to engage with the crowd, play the part, make the women go wild. But I couldn't be bothered, not when I'm this close to my goal. It's all I can do to stop myself from picking Lacey up and whisking her right out of here.

Everything has been in motion since I got word that the Red Camellia wanted a bachelorette party. Performing to seduce her was mostly Tolie's idea, and I was desperate enough to agree to it. I never would've thought my mother's insistence on cotillion and ballroom dance lessons could be remotely useful, but they and mixed martial arts made learning his routine a lot easier once I got over my ego.

This costume is absurd and this scheme even more so once I start dancing, but if it's the only way I can get Lacey alone, I'll try anything. She's had bodyguards nonstop for years, either hers or Monroe's, but tonight there's no one to save her. All I have to do is steal the Red Camellia.

My queen of diamonds.

But my strategy is already slipping through my fingers.

I had no way of knowing how I'd feel once she was right in front of me. I expected hatred because her family cast me aside or even the way I usually feel when I carry out a job, indifferent.

What I didn't expect was the literal shock I would experience at her touch. Or how I'd fall into her gaze, blue as the desert sky, so different than on a screen or in my dreams. Her eyes are wide and hungry, and I know she's been dying to come to me ever since I first walked out on stage. I've felt the same.

A gulp travels down her slender throat as she steps away from her seat. I tighten my grip before leading us to the stage, ensuring she won't slip through my fingers, and glance back at her friends for good measure.

Monroe's sister has already passed out again. I know Roxana will keep her mouth shut, and since she drunkenly snatched Maeve's mobile before the girl could feck things up, I'm in the clear. If the Red Camellia goes "missing" tonight, no one will suspect a thing until it's too late.

My mind and heart race when I pick Lacey up and set her on the stage. Placing my hands beside her hips on the edge, I push my feet off the ground to somersault over her and land in a crouch behind her. The crowd gasps and applauds, but I'm too afraid Lacey will run away to stop and soak in their appreciation. I pivot on my toes and grab her by her waist to stand us both up before she can escape me.

The dancers kneeling on stage hop out of their positions with grace as I hug Lacey from behind, holding her against my chest. My captive feels so good in my arms I almost miss my cue despite the thunderous percussion signaling it over the speakers.

Tolie said to let her dictate the dance since she's the professional. I'm just supposed to perform the few moves he taught me, so I'm not standing there like an eejit, but I have no idea what she's planning to do.

Stage right, a throne appears out of the gaping mouth of hell, positioned parallel to the crowd and facing stage left. The nearly naked demons exit the stage, dancing, thrusting and doing flips into the hellmouth, and I hand one of them my scepter before he disappears.

Remembering I can't feck this up now by getting lost in the moment, I twirl Lacey to make her face me, but instead of stopping, she spins on her own.

Alright, here we go. Show me what you've got, tine.

The tulle of her short dress lifts up, but not so high that the crowd can see what she's wearing underneath. I'm in awe of her toned thighs until the crowd's claps and cheers startle me back into focus.

Beyond pleased that she's showing the side of herself I've never truly experienced, I clear my throat and rumble into my microphone, making sure I don't reveal my accent.

"Ah, we have a dancer. I see I've chosen wisely."

I guide her to the throne, where she sits back with a beautiful blush rising up her cheeks. The music takes on a pulsing beat and pumps through my veins. I glide around the chair and reach over the back to slide my hands up her torso, grazing the lace and diamond corset pushing up her breasts. When her hands cover mine and her nails lightly scratch my forearms, my cock threatens to burst from my red breakaway pants. My fingers run over the bare skin along her neckline and into her strawberry-blonde hair.

"Turn up the music," I demand into the microphone as I pull away from her. "No more talking. It's time for the bride to dance with her devil."

The slow, sensual beats of "Where Are You" by Elvis Drew and Avivian blare so loudly it pulses underneath my skin, drowning everything else out. It's easy to pretend it's just the two of us as I prowl around the high-back wooden throne.

Using the throne to shield my movements, I covertly fix my hardened cock, careful not to catch the barbell. Underneath the breakaway pants, I'm covered by a scrap of fabric the dancers wear to keep the crowd from seeing them completely naked, but I make sure the tip hides behind my spandex waistband, too.

Once I've secured my raging hard-on, I flick my microphone
switch, whip it off my head in an unchoreographed move, and
send it skittering across the stage. Anything else I have to say will
be for Lacey's ears only. Her brow furrows at the microphone, but
as I reenter her vision, our eyes lock. We hold each other captive
with our gazes, making it easy to forget the rest of the room.

Fecking dangerous.

Stay focused.

Her family tried to ruin yours.

That last reminder helps me push through the hold this girl
has over me. I position my body at an angle so the rest of the
room can see as I point to the cloak's knot underneath my Adam's
apple. Without making me wait, she tugs eagerly at the string and
bites her lip as the cape unravels, revealing my oiled, tattooed
upper body. Her hands slide down my chest and my body ripples
with pleasure along the trail.

Feck, why is she affecting me like this? I don't cave for women.
Ever. Least of all when I'm on a job.

But apparently with Lacey, it's different. I try to tell myself it's
the promise of revenge floating in the air, but everything's
different.

Those blue eyes I've grown obsessed with are full of life as
they follow the hills and valleys of my muscles. My abs tighten at
her perusal and she bites her lip. A low groan escapes me from
deep in my chest, and her wide eyes snap to mine, no doubt
because she felt my need vibrate through my skin. Desire races up
and down my spine and I wish I could end this performance early
and just get on with my duty.

Will I be able to do it?

A year ago, ruining the O'Sheas seemed simple enough a
task. There are plenty of ways to cut a man off at his knees, and
with as much hatred as I had boiling in my blood, killing Charlie
O'Shea would've been easy. Lacey was the job, though. Despite
what my father wanted, my strategy for her was different. I
won't harm a woman, but I had no problem destroying the

reputation of the soulless, selfish creature that'd taken over her social media.

But *this* woman? Fuck, she's got a fire in her I'm not sure I want to snuff out.

I whirl around to the front of the chair and roll with the rhythm of the song. Her eyes bulge and she tries to cross her legs, but I kneel before her in one fluid motion, pull them apart, and shake my head.

"No."

The audience is to my left, so no one can see underneath her tulle, but I sure as hell can. She may be wearing a pure-white dress, but there's nothing but crimson lace and sin underneath. I can't help my wicked smile as my palms cover her inner thighs and slide up her soft skin. Her body shivers underneath my touch and rumors I've always dismissed briefly cross my mind.

Legend has it, as the precious daughter of the Keeper of the Garde, she's never been touched this intimately. But I can't imagine this firecracker sparking in front of me right now letting something as fecked up as the Garde dictate her life to that degree.

I push the thought away and continue the rest of my ruse. All the other sounds in the room drown out, leaving only the pulse of my heart and the steady bass of the music. There's no one else but her and me.

My hands skip over the tulle skirt as I rise from my knees. Every fiber of my being wants to take her backstage and have my way with her, forget my father's plan to get rid of the O'Sheas once and for all, and go with what I've longed to do for years. But I fight it, knowing I need to wait for the right moment.

I roll my body up hers, and she gasps when my bare pecs come within an inch of her flushed cheeks. Using my knees, I spread her thighs to kneel between them on the seat of the chair. Before she can shift underneath me, I grab her legs and press them against my outer thighs, silently instructing her to squeeze.

She obeys immediately and I try not to let the pleasure override my already struggling focus. Instead, I wrap my arm around her back, lift her onto my hips, and fall backward off the chair with my hand out to catch myself.

I land in a crab position with my feet wide apart on the ground. She hooks her nails into my shoulders to keep from falling off as I thrust and undulate underneath her, making her ride me. Her eyes widen, no doubt at the feel of my rock-hard cock against her warmth, and her head drops back as I find her clit with my shaft.

I thought I'd hate having to perform like this, but watching her pleasure take over makes it easier to play the part. Is this all an act for her? Or does she... does she know it's me?

While I'm mimicking fucking her, I feel the moment her impulses take over before I see the spark in her eyes. She arches backward, diving her hands behind her and between my legs. Her tennis shoes push off my chest as she uses me for leverage to perform a back walkover. I drop to the ground and roll backward myself to land in a crouch, trying to follow her lead.

By the time she's upright, I'm already there, chest to chest with her. She grabs on to my shoulders and arches her back deeply as she swirls around. I caress her throat with one hand and I band my arm around her lower back with the other, helping her dip lower, holding on to her as she takes control of the dance. When she comes back up, she pushes against my chest hard and twirls away from me into the middle of the stage.

Once she stops, she draws me in with a come-hither motion. A growl forms in my chest at the thought of her trying to command me, but with every low bass note, I prowl closer. I just need to finish this act and wait for the lights to go out. Then she'll be mine.

Her pink lips part like she's finally realized she's my prey. She slowly spins from me on pointed tennis shoes as if the runaway bride thinks she can flee from her own challenge. I lunge for her arm and pull her close.

"No, sweet bride, you started this."

She smirks and lifts her leg up to whirl away, but I catch her calf and hitch it around my waist. I bend her backward, forcing her to hook her leg around me or fall. Splaying one hand across her back, I use the other to grasp her neck and make her look at me.

"Do you think the devil would let his bride run from him?"

"Who says I want to?" She tugs my hips forward, pressing my cock into her center. Her long lashes fan over narrowed eyes, throwing down the gauntlet.

She wants this.

The thrill that runs through me nearly stops me in my tracks. A sinful grin spreads across my lips and I grind against her core before straightening us back up. I let her leg drop, but I tighten my grip on her neck and use my other hand on the small of her back to keep her flush to me.

We do a modified tango toward the throne before I lift her leg into a split and rest her ankle on my shoulder. I grind against her core and she clings to me, holding on to my neck and locking eyes with me as I sit on the throne with her straddling me this time.

She shifts in my arms to grab the back of the chair and sits up on her knees. I grip her bare arse underneath the tulle and lift her thighs on top of my shoulders to shove my face into her lace-covered pussy. Before I can make delicious contact, she digs her heels into my shoulder blades and leans back, unfurling her body into the air.

I can't see what she's doing with my head covered in tulle, but by the way her muscles move underneath my fingers, I can tell she's using every one of them to undulate against gravity. Gripping her arse harder, I press my face farther into her heat but stop short of touching her, giving her the sensation of my warm breath against her sweet pussy. I want her dripping and keening for me before I take her backstage.

My cock throbs against my waistband and I'm not sure how much more I can take. I lightly nip at her inner thigh, making her jolt in my palms before she bends backward toward the floor. Her spine folds against my fingers, and I pull away to see her arched in a bridge until she kicks off the top of the throne into another back walkover.

I jump up from the seat and lunge to stand behind her before she fully straightens. Once she's in my arms, my hands glide up her corset to cup her breasts and I turn us away from the crowd to keep them from seeing me span a hand over her chest. Even though I know I shouldn't, my fingers have a mind of their own as they massage over the soft mound of her breast and dip underneath the tight fabric, just grazing her nipple. Her moan vibrates against my palm as I whisper in her ear.

"Do you know what you're getting yourself into?"

"Surprise me."

She shivers as I grip her neck and cup her pussy through the tulle. Her gasp pushes her chest into my forearm and I shove my hard-on against her round arse. I expect her to try to run, but she leans into me, arches back, and wraps her arms around my neck, keeping up the illusion of our performance.

Or maybe that's all this is for her?

She's putty in my arms as my lips brush the shell of her ear to ask the question that's really on my mind.

"Do you know who I am?"

Her fingernails dig sharp cuts into my neck, and I hiss at the delicious pain as she leans back to meet my eyes.

"I don't know who you are... but we don't need to know each other to have fun, do we?"

My jaw drops at her casual delivery, but she laughs and breaks free from my hold to spin around and scratch my chest. Her claws end at my waistband as she crouches down on the ground.

It shouldn't matter that she doesn't give a feck who I am. That was the whole point of the plan to lure her into a false sense of security. But the reality knifes through me more painfully than the wounds on my neck. Much deeper than I ever thought *anyone* could hurt me, let alone Lacey O'Shea.

Before she can unsnap my pants in front of the crowd, I decide to end it. If Lacey thinks that I'm worthless, that all I'm good for is a good fuck, maybe I'll go along with my father's original plan after all.

Or maybe I'll show her just how wrong she is.

I snatch her forearm and lift her up off her knees. She rises on her tiptoes and spins away before suddenly stopping. Her body moves like water, fluid with the music right before she falls away from me. The crowd shouts, reminding me that we do, in fact, have an audience, one that thinks I'm going to let her fall.

Despite the inexplicable hurt in my chest, I don't even entertain the thought of letting her fall. Not bothering to keep up the pretenses of this infuriating dance I've trapped us in, I lunge toward her and scoop her up in the nick of time, catching her with my arms underneath her back and knees.

She smiles up at me like she knew all along that I would catch her. There isn't an ounce of doubt in her face, and for some reason, that soothes me despite the pang of guilt pricking my chest.

My mother used to say dancing is like love, it's not for the weak or heartless. But I had no idea I could feel anything like this. I'm trying my best to keep my walls up, but this set alone has made me entirely too vulnerable. That can't happen, especially not with the Keeper's daughter.

"This ends now," I growl.

"And how does it end, Devil?" she asks breathlessly, wicked temptation in her eyes as she wraps her arms around my neck, deciding her fate for me.

"With the devil fucking his bride."

Scene 5

IF LOVE BE ROUGH

I don't give Lacey time to reconsider. Whisking my wee runaway bride backstage just like I've been dying to, I ignore the confused protests from the audience. Hopefully none of those objections are coming from Monroe's sister and she's still passed out, but in any case, Merek will do his job and make sure that she and Roxy are taken care of.

As soon as I break through the curtain, I see Tolie pause midsentence with another dancer.

"What're you—"

"Show's over."

"But you still have... fuck—" He turns on his heel, knowing not to argue with me and breaks through the curtain to make his announcement.

"I guess the devil couldn't wait another second to have his bride..."

I tune him out and speed into the depths of Rouge toward his dressing room, leaving the stage behind. We may have just finished our act outside, but my night is just beginning.

With only the red LED lights on the ceiling to guide me, the halls are dim but full of people milling about. They're too busy assembling the next set, not paying attention to me in the slightest during their practiced, frenetic work.

The show is meant to be a burlesque combined with a male revue, but the O'Sheas have made it possible for the dancers to "schmooze" future clients in the privacy of their own dressing rooms. We McKennons are more casino people, but no matter what the method or the vice, backroom deals are a dime a dozen in the Garde. Tonight will be no different.

Lacey's arms are still wrapped around my neck. Once I'm inside Tolie's dressing room, I kick the door shut, muffling the thudding bass beat blaring from the stage. She tightens her hold on me as I shift my forearm under her thighs so that I can lock the door and tug off the bed's quilt. When the sheets are revealed, I set her on top much more gently than I thought I was capable of with the adrenaline pumping through my system.

After a year of obsessing over her, I want to take my time, but Lacey's having none of that. She trails her nails over my tattoos until I catch her wrists. Red peeps through the outline of the door and I lift her chin toward the light to meet her hungry gaze as I make my promise.

"If you mark me again, bride, you'll be marking me forever, and I'll have to do the same."

Her strawberry-blonde brows furrow as if she's just as confused as I am by the emotions swirling between us. A fleeting look of uncertainty passes over her face, but a smirk lifts her lips and I can tell she's decided not to believe me. She scratches my chest hard, all the way down to my waistband.

Your mistake, Lace.

The new indentations burn along the trail she leaves behind, but my cock jumps in my pants right underneath where her perusal ends. Her eyes widen with anticipation. She may have perfected the whole innocent act she performs for the world, but with me, she's being a fecking temptress and I plan to corrupt her more tonight.

I lean in closer, inches away from her gorgeous wet pink lips.

I'm still wearing the red devil mask that covers the upper half of my face, but I won't remove it yet. When I asked her on stage if she knew who I was, she claimed she didn't *need* to know. I'm just a fuck to her, so that's what I'll be until I need to reveal myself.

Her floral scent envelops me as I cage her in with my hands propped on the mattress. Hers hook into my breakaway pants and a *snap* on one of the sides makes her eyes jump to where she's gripping the fabric tight.

"Take them off, *tine*. You know you want to."

Her eyes narrow. "Tin-eh? What does that mean?"

My heart races at the slip, but I grip her wrists and use her hands to yank off my pants as a distraction. They rip up the sides like they're designed to do and fall to the ground easily, taking with them the small scrap of fabric that covered my cock. The move pulls me toward her, so close our lips almost brush.

In that moment, everything else fades as our breaths pump back and forth between us, making my chest touch her diamond-clad breasts. Without the spotlight and our pasts, our feuding families, my orders, nothing else matters. It's just us in the dark.

While wrapping my arm around her waist, I caress her cheek with my other hand and let all the desire I feel flare in my eyes as I stare into her baby blues.

"You're mine tonight, bride."

My voice is deeper and lower than I've ever heard it. It's a declaration, not a question. I'm not even giving her the illusion of a choice.

"Make me believe that's true... please."

Her voice breaks off at the end, and her plea carves deep into my chest. She's begging me, but why? From the outside, she's got everything she could want, so why would she want to feck all that up with a stranger in a mask? Is she in trouble?

If she needs comfort, though, I'm not the one to give it to her. If I execute the idea that's been burning in my mind all day, she won't want it from me anyway. Whatever I decide, everything changes for her tonight, and I won't lure her into thinking I'm some soft prince. I dressed as the devil for a reason.

She doesn't seem to need my reply, though, and her gaze drifts from mine to roam my upper body. Before she can take all of me in, I move her farther up the bed. She instantly clings to me, pressing her warmth into my abs, making my painfully hard cock tease her clothed entrance as I carry her.

When I lay her on the sheets beneath me, I begin to move down to the apex of her thighs. She licks her lips while she watches until the warm metal at the head of my cock brushes against her thigh.

That intense blue gaze narrows with interest, but I massage her toned thighs to distract her and her eyes roll back in her head. Her moan goes straight to my cock, making it pulse with need. I massage all the way under the tulle of her skirt and tuck my finger-tips into the thin waistband of her crimson lace thong. She writhes underneath my touch as I slide it down.

Our sensual dance made her pussy so wet that she's drenched the fabric, and my mouth waters at the sight. I toss the thong onto the bedside table beside the kit I hope I don't have to use later.

My veins pump with excitement at the thought of finally getting to live my fantasy. Propped up on my elbows between her thighs, I lift her legs over my shoulders, ready to dive in.

"Wait."

My heart stutters in my chest at the sight of her raised hand and her breasts nearly spilling from her corset thanks to her rapid breathing.

Did she change her mind? With everything her family has done to mine, my vengeful side almost wants her to try and stop me. How far will I go if she resists? I've done a lot of shite, most of which could have me locked up forever. But I've never hurt a woman. Do I hate Lacey enough for her to be the first?

Do I hate her at all?

With her satin-soft skin brushing against either side of my head, my hands cupping her thighs, her hot skin radiating against my cheeks... it all reminds me that I'm a breath away from every-thing I've dreamed of. If she says no...

I meet her eyes but keep my mouth shut, unable to say anything and afraid I'll feck things up if I do. Her teeth worry over her bottom lip as I lie stock-still, watching her through my devil mask and over the aggravating tulle that's the only barrier between us right now.

"I... I don't know your name."

Relief makes me light-headed and my chest flutters at the thought of her calling out my real name. It's on the tip of my tongue to confide in her, but I don't. O'Sheas can't be trusted and giving in after all this time will only ruin my plan.

Her fingers fiddle with her dress and the red light from the hallway glints against Monroe's godforsaken diamond. Keeping her legs over my shoulders, I lift my upper body up just enough to take her left hand in mine. Her brow furrows, but she doesn't stop me as I pull the engagement ring off. It slides easily, as if her finger hasn't gotten used to wearing it yet. Understanding softens her freckled features, and she doesn't even object when I toss it onto the bedside table, sending smug pride surging through me.

"When you scream for me, call me Key."

I have to bite my tongue to prevent myself from saying some-thing stupid, like her name that I'm not supposed to know yet, or promises I can't keep unless I go against my father's orders. I'll blow everything if I don't keep it together now.

"Key," she whispers between those two plump lips as if she's tasting it on her tongue for the first time. Her breaths slow and a sweet smile brightens her face in the red light.

"Perfect," I whisper back and break away from her gaze.

Pushing the tulle up her waist again to reveal her pretty, bare pussy in full view, I spread her thighs farther with my broad shoulders before diving in to finally taste her.

On the first long stroke of my tongue against her soft skin, her hands immediately thread into my hair and pull like reins. She's ambrosia on my taste buds, and her cries of pleasure are just as delicious.

When she tugs hard at my scalp, I moan into her entrance and swipe up her silky, smooth center, ending with a dance around the small bundle of nerves at the top. Her tennis shoes dig into my bare upper back, reminding me that I haven't even undressed her. I can't stop myself now, though. My hips grind into the bed, aching for relief, but I focus all my attention on her and shift so that my fingers can join my tongue.

I swirl my index finger through her arousal and continue to lave at her clit before pushing inside her warm channel. She hisses above me, but I massage her inner muscles until her thighs relax around me.

"Goddamn, you're tight."

That crazy Garde double standard flashes in my mind again. Has she really never been with anyone else? The thought makes me both possessive and murderous at the same time. A primal urge wants to be the only one who's gotten to touch her like this. But the fact that our society has had that much control over her makes me hate the Garde even more.

Experiencing her passion tonight and now having her in my arms, she feels like the woman in the background that I've obsessed over, not the vapid Garde "good girl" she makes herself out to be when she knows people are watching. My decision to go against my father's orders is almost made, but while my heart is all for it, my mind still bucks at the lingering fear that she's just another society clone in our fecked-up world.

Her moan snaps me out of my racing thoughts, and the demanding yank on my hair spurs me to keep going. I tongue her clit in a circular motion while feathering against her G-spot until she cries out my name again. Her channel grips my finger like a vise, but when she comes with me for the first time, I want to feel her let go around my cock. When her thigh muscles clamp against my ears and her shoes rub into my shoulder blades in an impossibly hard massage, I withdraw altogether.

"What? No. What're you doing?" The frustration tingeing her question makes me chuckle.

"Don't worry, bride. It's our final act."

I push up off the bed and sit on my calves. My cock bobs up, soaked at the tip, and Lacey's eyes widen at the metal bar of my apadravya piercing positioned diagonally through the head.

"You *are* pierced."

"You'll like it, *tine*. It hits right where you need it."

I grin wickedly as I loop her legs around me. Her hands grip my biceps, but she doesn't stop me as I wet my cock along her drenched cunt. When my shaft is just as soaked with her arousal as she is, I line up the head and watch our connection breach her tight opening. Her nails cut into my arms, flooding apprehension through my veins, but she sucks me in immediately and I moan, tipping my head back.

"I don't want this to hurt you. But, goddamn Lac—"

"Why would it... oh, *Key*—"

At the sound of her already crying out my nickname, I can't help it anymore and my hips drive forward. I couldn't stop even if I wanted to as I fill her in one thrust. One swift, brutally tight thrust.

I gather her in my arms before the instinct to keep my distance kicks in. Incredibly, even after I've caused her pain, she hugs me back, shaking in my embrace.

"Did I hurt you?"

Guilt seeps in until it registers that Lacey's shudders aren't from pain at all. I shift to release one of my arms from behind her back. When it's free, I push her soft hair off her forehead to meet her eyes. They're full of laughter that bubbles up her chest. A sweet, tinkling sound I've never heard from her before that makes my chest ache.

"Hurt me? No. I mean, it *has* been a while, but—"

"A while?" My pulse triples in time. "You've had sex before?"

Her eyebrow cocks high. "Of course I have. It's the twenty-first century, Key. You're far from the first guy I've slept with."

That anxiety I felt when she first cried out melts away, replaced by a confusing mixture of relief, jealousy, and certainty.

Everything locks into place while I watch her giggle underneath me as if following the Garde's archaic laws is completely ludicrous. That beautiful melody confirms the suspicions I've developed after studying her for the past year.

What she shows everyone else is a smoke and mirrors act, but this Lacey I have underneath me? She's real. All she needs is the freedom to ignite and I'm the match to her flame.

"I'm not the first guy you've slept with," I whisper and smile into her neck as I begin to slowly move inside her.

I'm the last.

Scene 6

BE ROUGH WITH LOVE

God, Key feels so good, and that barbell at the end?
Magic on the inside. But God, he's big and I wasn't
kidding when I said it'd been a while. Even though I
was more than ready, that first thrust stung enough to shock me.

I've already reassured him, but his movements are still slow,
almost as if he's afraid I'll break if he goes too quickly. I'm grateful
at the moment, though, because these smooth motions are getting
me used to his size. His hard, muscular arms encircle me, soothing
me as his cock pulses inside my already sore pussy.

He curses under his breath and his hips begin to grind into
me, pushing one of the metal balls of his piercing against my G-
spot.

"Oh my... Key... yes. Just like that."

"I don't know how much longer I can go slow, *tine*," his
growl rumbles through gritted teeth.

There's that word again, but this time an accent slips into his
gruff tone. His velvet voice, combined with the emotion he uses
behind the word, gives me butterflies I'm not ready to think
about. Something about him seems familiar, but he hasn't taken
off his mask, so it's hard to place who he reminds me of.

"I don't want slow," I whisper.

Everywhere our skin touches tingles, and when he shifts above me, allowing the chilly air between us, I almost regret telling him to go faster. What we're doing right now, though, feels way too intimate, and I can't let myself feel anything but pleasure or I'll crack.

Those intensely methodical strokes pump more quickly, rippling ecstasy throughout my body and making me forget my emotions altogether.

"Tell me if you want me to stop or if it hurts."

"For the love of God, please don't stop."

"Good, because I don't know if I could. You're hard to resist."

My heart skips at the sentiment and that sliver of anxiety returns. I wrap my legs around his hips and move with him until his pounding thrusts shove all other objections and apprehension away. His hips drive into me at the perfect cadence while still managing to get deep, making my pussy flutter around him and my muscles tighten.

"Oh, Key... Oh my god. This feels so good."

He gazes down at me through his devil mask and I suddenly want him to kiss me so badly I can't stand it. Making out has never been on my one-night stand agenda before, but I've also never felt like *this* before.

As my orgasm builds, so does the need to feel his lips on mine. On his next thrust, I press my mouth to his.

The way his body suddenly freezes above me is almost enough to make me stop, but I'm a girl who gets what she wants and I want him to kiss me back. I dip my tongue into his mouth with as much force as he's been using, trying to get him to thrust again. The second swipe makes him moan, and his strong body melts against me. His hand threads into my hair as he resumes his speed and he takes over the kiss with delicious force, devouring me with as much fervor and need as he did my pussy.

Everything about this man is hard, but I'm languid and soft as I move with him. The more powerfully he plunges into me, the more my muscles tense with building anticipation. His other arm bands around my ass while he pumps and his grip on the back of my neck squeezes almost to the point of pain. He holds me protectively, but he fucks me like he owns me. I've given in to him completely.

And I *love* it.

This may be my last night to be *me*. Lacey. Not the only daughter of the Keeper. A criminal's child. The Baron's future wife. The Red Camellia, a caged flower. Any man's thing to be traded for the good of the Garde. Tonight I get to pretend like my life is my own. I'm with someone I chose and even though he's a stranger, he doesn't touch me like one.

He growls into my mouth and my pussy flutters with the need to come. His pelvis grinds against my clit, stimulating me outside and in. Every time his pierced head grazes one certain spot, I coil and relax simultaneously until my muscles tense and don't release again.

I break away from the kiss and whisper against his lips, "I'm going to come."

"Come for your devil, *tine*."

As if he summons it himself, sensation explodes from deep inside my core, fluttering out in spirals all over my body like a twirling dress. His own orgasm drives his erratic thrusts and I tilt my head back so I can see him come with me.

His eyes are closed and ecstasy has him biting his lip. I push my fingers underneath his mask so I can see his face, but he thrusts harder and faster, sending pleasure cascading through my veins.

"Key!" I scream.

As my voice falters, I swear I hear the devil moan my name, but he nips me hard on my neck, making me cry out and lose my focus. I'm so lost in my orgasm that I can't think until my body is nothing but leftover jolts and ripples. His cock pulses inside me as we pant against one another.

Every inhale envelops me in his scent, like the faint smoke of sweet cigars mixed with amber. The rich smell is overwhelming, making me desperately wish I could stay here forever and get lost in him.

"I don't believe in love," I whisper, not letting myself second-guess the moment this time. "But I think—in another life, I think I could have fallen for a guy like you."

His biceps soften even as he wraps his arms around me tighter. He clears his throat, and I feel him getting ready to say something, but it's in that brief, quiet lull amid the slow rhythm of our sated breaths that it hits me.

My body might be my own. But it's only for the night.

"It doesn't have to be another—"

I just cheated on my fiancé... the future leader of the Garde and the only man who can save my father.

"Shit!"

Key's words cut off and his body stiffens above me. The freedom I just felt in his embrace begins to feel more like a cage. My heart races like a step dance and I can't fucking believe I just potentially destroyed everything and everyone I love for one single moment of freedom.

"I just cheated on my fiancé," I choke out, unable to keep the revelation inside any longer.

"No, you didn't," he growls against my neck.

"Yes, I did. Oh my god, yes I did. *Dammit.*" My chest constricts, forcing me to gasp for air underneath his heavy weight and the gravity of what I've done. "My friends are out there. They're going to wonder where I am. I need to go." I try to push him off, but he's latched on to me, making it impossible to get away. "Key, please. I need to leave. I can't be here. My friends might suspect something and tell my fiancé. If he finds out—"

"Fuck your fiancé."

The anger in his voice surprises me. "But Key—"

He finally shifts on top of me but doesn't give me enough room to move as he flicks on the lamp beside the bed and reaches for something on the nightstand.

The nightstand. Oh, shit, we didn't use a—

"Fuck your fiancé. Fuck your so-called 'friends.' I'll make sure that they get home safely."

"Wait, no. You don't understand the situation. I mean, I'm glad they'll be safe, but one of them is my fiancé's sister. She'll tell him everything."

"No, she won't."

I huff into his chest, getting frustrated now that he's not letting me up. "How the hell do you know that? You don't know her. You don't even know me, for that matter. I'm certainly not 'tin-eh' or whatever you've been calling me. And I'm definitely not 'your bride.'"

"We'll see about that..."

"What the—Key! I'm serious—"

"Listen, I made sure from the beginning that your nun friend couldn't video us. Besides, she slept the entire time we performed. The other one will be loyal. She wasn't too wasted and I've got someone out there that will make sure they get home."

I snort. "Seriously? I love the girl, but Roxy hasn't been loyal a day in her life."

"Maybe not to you."

The air in my chest caves in like I've been punched. It's a truth I've had to come to grips with over the years, but I shake my head free of it now. There's no point in letting reality hurt my feelings.

"Where I come from, family, friend, or enemy, anyone can turn on you if you play your cards wrong. Roxy won't be able to keep her mouth shut about this. It's too juicy a scandal not to use."

"That... makes me sad for you." He pauses in whatever he's doing, but his damp, sexy chest is all that's in front of me, so I can't see his expression. "You don't have to worry about that anymore. I'll make sure Roxana stays quiet."

"*Roxana?*"

I rear back and try to look at him, but I barely have an inch of space as he keeps sifting through a box on the nightstand. My heart starts to race as I try to push him off again.

"Key, answer me. Do you know Roxy?"

"Just trust me. No one will find out you're here."

A rustle beside my head has me trying to crane my neck.

"Key... wh-what's going on?" My heart stutters and every stupid decision that I've made in the past hour fly through my mind.

I've never needed bodyguards in Vegas. My dad practically owns the place, so I walk around town feeling untouchable. But right now, I'm slightly buzzed and in bed with a complete stranger. No one knows where I am and my captor has just promised me that no one will.

"Let me go! What're you doing?"

"What I should've done from the beginning."

"What does—"

Key bands his other forearm over my chest to pin me down. My yelp for help cuts off abruptly as a sharp sting in my upper bicep makes me hiss in pain. It takes bending my neck at an odd angle to see this devil depressing the plunger of a syringe into the muscle. I open my mouth to scream, but he moves from my chest to swiftly clamp his rough hand over my mouth so hard it pushes my head down into the pillow.

"Stop moving or you'll hurt yourself." He removes the syringe and tosses it to the nightstand, giving me just enough mobility to claw at him. "I didn't want to have to do it this way, but you've left me with no choice."

I'm desperate to get free, but I only manage to knock off his mask. His knees crawl to completely cover my body, stopping me from attacking him and I come face-to-face with my captor as he presses his index finger over his lips.

"Shh... shh, shh. Quiet, Lacey. You've got to trust me, *tine*."

My eyes widen as I finally get to see who I just slept with. His face is familiar, one I've seen in celebrity news headlines and on social media. But underneath his strong, auburn brow, his hazel eyes don't just feel familiar. I *know* them. I saw the same gold flecks in a lovely woman's gaze five years ago. The memory feels like it's from another life, one before everything imploded for my family.

Key... Kian.

No. No. No!

Whatever drug he just gave me surges through my body, exhausting me limb by limb. The haze on the edge of my vision takes over, and everything around me falls away, everything except for a smug smile on Kian McKennon's handsome face.

He flashes my engagement ring just as my consciousness fades entirely.

"You won't be needing this anymore."

Scene 7

WELCOME HOME

S oft satin hugs me and I stretch out with a light, content moan. The low noise scratches painfully at the back of my throat. I try to swallow to wet my dry mouth, but I end up wincing at the movement. The discomfort barrels reality back to me and I groan.

Today is my birthday and also the day I'm signing a marriage license with the one and only man who has the information to save my father.

But last night? Last night I imagined that I let my inhibitions go for once. I got to perform a show that ended all shows and had a one-night stand with a Las Vegas dancer. What happened after that is a hazy cherry on top of one of the wildest dreams I've ever had.

I'm not gonna lie, though, I'm disappointed it wasn't real. Ending up with a guy as free and exciting as Key would be a million times better than the truth. And if our first time together was that hot, we'd never leave the bed. Especially if it's this soft.

I stretch out into the sheets and grab on to the squishy memory foam pillow.

Wait...

I don't have a memory foam pillow.

The realization has me jackknifing into an upright position, sending blinding pain through my head. The first thing I see is the bedside table with a glass of water and a bottle of ibuprofen next to it. I'm disoriented and starting to freak out, but the ache is killing me so I take the pills and down the full glass, letting the cool water soak my parched throat.

When I finish, I glance around at the room's sleek, modern, black-and-silver aesthetic. It's all sharp lines, very masculine, and very unlike my pretty pastel bedroom or any hotel room I've been in.

"Where the hell am I?"

The silver pillow next to me still has a head-shaped depression, but the person is nowhere to be seen.

Who's home am I in? What happened last night?

I think so hard my brain begins to spin.

I got ready with Roxy, followed by the limo ride with Roxy and Maeve. Rouge. Then... it gets fuzzy as if I'm remembering something I imagined rather than experienced. I know I danced onstage with the hot devil named Key, but after... that was a dream, right? It had to be. There's no way I accidentally had sex with—

Nope. Nope. Nope.

I don't *feel* different. Shouldn't I feel different if I slept with my family's enemy?

Doubt floods my mind, accompanied by scenes I refuse to believe are memories.

But if it's true...

Dammit, what if last night wasn't a dream at all?

The shower suddenly turns on in the en suite bathroom and I realize I have no time to waste if I want to get out of here unnoticed. Thankfully, I'm still wearing my runaway bride wedding dress which means I have my phone in my pocket.

In no time, I'm scrolling through a bazillion missed calls and texts. There are several from Roxy who reported that she was—surprisingly—responsible enough to return a passed-out Maeve back to her hotel. Roxy also hoped I used my "Wish You Were Still Single" card to the best of my ability and swore she wouldn't tell a soul until I was ready to reveal the details—whatever that means. My heart stutters at the thought of her even mentioning any of it to *me*, let alone bringing it up to anyone else.

Roxy is hit or miss at keeping my secrets and I've had to learn the hard way that she isn't someone I can always confide in. No one in the Garde is. They're all out for blood, power, and status, willing to turn on people in a heartbeat. Roxy wouldn't betray me for any of those things, but she wouldn't be able to help herself from gossiping, either, especially considering this is one of the biggest life-ruining secrets I've ever had.

When I get to the message from my mom, my heart stops completely.

> **MOM**
>
> Where are you? I'm at the courthouse to witness you signing the papers. The Baron will be here any second.

"Oh, shit, shit, shit."

I stuff my phone back into my pocket before unraveling from the silver satin sheets and hopping out of bed. Cool air wafts over my naked butt, sending yet another shock of fear down my spine. With every passing breath, my insistence that the craziest parts of last night were only a dream gets weaker and weaker.

As I straighten the wild tulle of my dress over my bare ass, I search for my shoes and socks with no luck. Deciding to do the humiliating walk of shame barefoot, I tiptoe toward the bedroom's only exit, resisting the urge to snoop through the dark, open closet on the way. Once I sneak out of the room, I close the door behind me quietly and glance around for my escape route.

But I stop in my tracks at the sight in front of me.

It's a huge living room space and the window that takes up the entire back wall has me gravitating toward it. The valley stretches before me before giving rise to the beautiful peaks that surround the city.

New Orleans was an adventure, but it's good to be back in the Valley, even if it's only for a little while. After I get married this weekend, I'll have to live with Monroe in New York and I'll no doubt miss the chaotic party that is my hometown.

Even though daylight dims the bright lights, the iconic Las Vegas Strip is just as electric. The Eiffel Tower piercing the blue sky was always my favorite, night or day, and who doesn't love the water show at the Bellagio fountain? It's off now, turning the man-made lake in front of me into a mirror...

My pulse thuds as I scan my surroundings until each landmark pieces together into a map. My chest constricts as I slowly realize I am *inside* one of the few buildings in this city that isn't completely safe for me.

The McKennon Hotel.

The waterfall in the shower stops, snapping me into motion. I jerk away from the window to search for the door in this penthouse suite and pass what has to be thousands of dollars' worth of art and leather furniture. They're gorgeous pieces, but the decor is too bespoke for a normal presidential suite. Which means whoever stays here is a resident.

In the *McKennon* Hotel.

Not looking good on the whole "last night was a dream" front.

When I finally see the door, I rush past the artwork and grab the handle—

It doesn't move.

Frowning, I tug at it with all my might, but again, it doesn't budge.

"What are you doing?"

The smooth, deep voice shocks me into stillness. It has the barest hint of an Irish accent and I *know* if I'd heard it last night, it would've either tipped off his identity or gotten me off faster. Did he purposely hide it just to trick me?

I slowly turn on one heel to see Kian McKennon staring back at me, a dark-auburn eyebrow raised in question.

His lightly tanned, tattooed skin is damp from the shower, and droplets roll down his chest, dripping in every crevice of his sculpted body. One bead of water, in particular, momentarily banishes my panic. Lust takes its place while I watch the bead disappear along his Adonis belt into his white towel. The hastily wrapped cloth is the only thing he's wearing as if he realized I was trying to escape and rushed out to stop me.

"It really was you. I thought it was a dream," I whisper.

A smile quirks up his lips and I'm suddenly acutely aware I'm not wearing panties.

"Sex with me is so good it feels like a dream, huh? I guess you have that to look forward to for the rest of our lives."

"For the rest of our..." My voice breaks and I shake my head free of the *very* good memory trying to interrupt my train of thought.

When I focus back on him, Kian's frowning at me.

"Your throat hurts."

"No it doesn't," I lie, swallowing to get it to stop sounding like I'm speaking through gravel.

"It does. I can tell. Did you take the ibuprofen I left out for you?"

He steps toward me, sending me catapulting backward into the door and I jab my finger in the air.

"Don't worry about my throat. What's important is that I don't remember how I got here. Did you drug me last night?"

"I only did what I had to do. You left me no choice. Believe me, it could've been worse."

He raises his hand like I'm a wild animal he needs to calm down, and it irritates me that his gentle tone actually works.

But then his words register.

"Wait, what you *had* to do? Listen, you're crazy and I *have* to leave. I'm really late for an appointment—"

"—to sign a marriage license? Yeah, you mentioned that last night. Don't worry, I took care of it."

My heart trips in my chest. The man is talking in riddles and I'm too hungover to figure them out.

"I'm getting married this weekend and today is the only day the Baron's schedule is open enough to sign our marriage license together. My mom is a witness, and she's expecting me."

"Fecking hell." Key—*Kian* scrubs his way-past-five-o'clock shadow. "You know, it's Halloween, but you insisting on marrying Monroe Baron might be the scariest shite I'll hear all day."

I snort. I can't help it and the quick laugh eases some of the anxiety in my chest. But I'm still so fucking nervous. Kian seems charming enough, but the fact that I might've ruined my father's life pounds in my brain like a migraine. My whole family is counting on me marrying the Baron. What if I destroyed it all on a night out in Vegas with liquor, a male revue, and a one-night stand?

How cliché can I be?

"I need to go, Kian," I finally say out loud.

A scowl crosses his face and he sucks in a quick breath before letting it out harshly.

"Sorry, Lace. I can't let you do that."

Lace? He doesn't get to call me a nickname. Aside from the hate between our families, we don't know each other at all. I should've reached out to him when our arranged marriage agreement ended, but I was young and busy rebelling in New Orleans. Then when he broke off the engagement, I blocked him on all social media because I couldn't stand to see him partying it up while I was devastated over being discarded.

Anger heats my face and I catch myself pursing my lips when I notice what's in his hand.

He's holding up a ring. The Baron's *engagement* ring. I look down to see my left ring finger has a new, pretty, simple silver band on it instead.

What the fuck?

"This is a joke, right? Okay, ha ha, you got me. Very funny prank." I glare at him and hold out my palm. "Now give me the ring. I need it."

"Nah, you don't need this anymore." He tosses it up like a coin, making my heart plummet to my stomach until he catches it.

"Seriously, Kian? You're stealing the Baron's diamond ring? Aren't the McKennons billionaires?"

He barks out a laugh. "I stole my queen of diamonds last night. I couldn't care less about Monroe's fecking ring."

Sweat pricks my forehead and the simple ring on my left hand burns.

No.

In the Garde, I was a commodity to be bought, sold, and traded, but Kian McKennon stole me instead. And I have no memory of it.

He tosses the engagement ring behind him and my nerves shatter as it hits the ground. When he swaggers toward me, the heat in his eyes makes my lower belly flip and my pussy clench, forgetting all about the trouble the horny bitch got us into. I hate the way my body responds to him with one look like last night wasn't the biggest mistake of my life, and I'm down to make another.

"Call your mother, Lace. You're not going to make it to your wedding."

"W-why not? Just let me go, Kian. If the Baron finds out—" I shake my head. "I need to sign that license."

"You can't." He stops feet away from me to snag a stack of papers from the entry table. He flicks through them before finding the one he wants and holds it up for me to see.

At the bottom, there are several signatures: two witnesses, a judge, Kian's... and mine. It's a little wobbly, but it's there all the same.

A vision from my dream flashes over my mind. It's a scene of us in a midnight chapel in front of a priest and a judge, with a couple of random elderly women smiling behind us.

"No," I whisper and step back.

"I've got video if you don't believe me." He retrieves his phone from the entry table's catchall bowl and scrolls until he finds the video.

I inch forward, just close enough to see but not close enough to be drawn into the wild, magnetic energy between us.

There on the screen is me in my runaway bride costume and Kian in a handsome black designer suit. When it gets to the important part, I'm all smiles while I enthusiastically say Kian's real name and repeat my vows. Even I can't tell that I've been drugged.

The priest then shifts to Kian and my heart pounds. I squint to see his face, but the angle makes it impossible.

"I, Kian, take you, Lace—"

Kian shuts off the screen and plops the phone back in the bowl. "See? You can't get married to two people."

"I need to see the rest, Kian!"

"Oh... did you want to see me profess my undying *love* to you?" My breath lodges in my lungs, waiting for his answer, but he tsks and shakes his head. "Not with your attitude."

The trapped air releases, leaving an inexplicable twinge in my chest. I cross my arms, embarrassed that I feel anything at all for this infuriating man.

Why the hell do I care?

I don't. I can't. Not if I'm going to save my father.

"All I want to know is whether that video is legit," I insist through gritted teeth, trying my best to put up a confident front. "You drugged me. This can't be valid."

My voice doesn't have the fight it needs to be convincing. Everything I'm saying might be true, but no one would be able to tell that on the video or in my signature.

"You don't *seem* drugged in that video," he argues, reading my mind.

My *husband* is the picture of triumph as he taunts me, "I warned you that my bride couldn't run away from me."

Even though his smile is smug and sexy, there's something else I can't place. Before I can analyze it, he turns to wave his hand at the room behind him.

"Welcome home, Lacey McKennon."

Act 2

Scene 8

MURDER OR MARRIAGE

Seeing Lacey freak out about the fact that we're now married is both satisfying and disappointing at the same time. When I thought about breaking the news, I assumed I would only feel triumphant. But there's something in her expression right now that's making me second-guess everything.

"Welcome... home?" she asks, slowly shaking her head. "No, Kian. No. This can't happen. I need to go home. Like *home* home. Not here. I need to sign that marriage license. You don't understand—"

"What do you mean you *need* to?" I ask, stepping forward. She stutters back at the same time and I stop in my tracks. "Are you afraid of me?"

"No. Of course not. I just... you know, have to sign the license and I want to leave."

I study her face, taking in her flushed cheeks and the way she keeps glancing down at my damp chest. A smile crests my lips. She's not afraid of me. She's afraid to get *close* to me. I want to call her out on it, but the second half of her answer irritates me more.

"Vague answers aren't going to get us anywhere, Lacey."

"Okay, then. How about he's my *fiancé*—"

"No, you're married to me," I say slowly. Her eyes keep

flicking to my towel, so I rest my hand on the doorframe just above her head and wait with pleasure as her gorgeous blue eyes snap up to meet mine. "Monroe means nothing to you now."

I didn't mean for that to come out as a growl, but the way she shivers at my tone makes me think it didn't scare her. Quite the opposite if her thighs squeezing together under that sinfully short dress is any indication.

But my wee *tine* doesn't want to admit defeat. Her willingness to fight for what she wants is so refreshingly "un-Garde." She straightens her back and glares up at me defiantly. This close, I can see the light dusting of freckles that pepper her nose and the apples of her flushed cheeks. I get the nearly irresistible need to strip her down so I can kiss each and every one that covers her body.

"I am *not* married to you and I'm not marry*ing* you. According to the Garde, I can't get married until my birthday—"

"Which started—" I look at my bare wrist as if I'm wearing my watch. "Nine hours ago."

"How do you know my birthday?"

"Simple. It was *our* wedding date."

She narrows her eyes. "Well, this is against the Garde contract my father brokered—"

"*We* were the original contract that your father *broke*. I'm doing him a favor by keeping him honest."

"My father is honest! *Your* family is the one that broke the contract, not mine."

That stops me. I cock my head to the side, but before I can demand she explain, she shakes her head.

"Look, I have to go. Let me just leave, okay?"

She turns within the minuscule amount of space I've given her, and her strawberry-blonde hair wafts her sweet floral scent up to me.

She rattles the handle and growls when it doesn't budge. Her frustration is adorable.

"Open... dammit!"

"It won't. It's magnetized closed. It only works with a specially made key—"

"Give me the key then—"

"—And a code." If she's really fecking lucky, she might guess it. But that would mean she'd know my obsession truly started the moment she was promised to be mine.

She sneers at me over her shoulder. "A key *and* a code? Little much, don't you think? What? Do you have enemies or something?"

"Yeah, your family."

She rolls her eyes. "It was a rhetorical question. We're Garde. We all have enemies."

Her matter-of-fact delivery shocks me. My frustration leaks out, thickening my accent. "And you're just okay with that? You don't want to change it? Your father—"

"How about you just do yourself a favor and never talk about my father again, got it?"

I chuckle. "Oh, if you think this wee spicy attitude of yours will push me away, you're dead wrong, *tine*."

"God, stop *calling* me that! Also, why did you hide your accent last night? Why were you at my family's business in the first place? That was supposed to be my night. Tolie and Roxy—"

Her eyes widen and the fight leaks out of her as she slouches with her back against the door.

"Were Tolie and Roxy in on it?"

Her defeated, monotone question almost makes me want to lie to her, but I won't do her the disservice.

"Tolie's one of my men. He's on my family's side."

"But how? Why? I mean, he works for my father's entertainment company. Does that mean nothing anymore? My mom's been taking over the businesses. How did my mother not know?"

"Your mother has done a great job after your father fecked everything up for your family. But she can't know everyone's alliances all the time."

"Alliances? What alliances? Tolie's not even Garde!"

"He's my friend. Outside the Garde, that comes first."

"And inside the Garde?" Tears of anger well in her eyes. "What about Roxy?"

I drop my arm and back away a step. The move gives her space, but not so much that she can get around me. My fingers twitch to caress her cheek, but I resist the urge as I break down the role her friend played in all of this.

"Roxana's father is a McKennon man. Your father lost the Muñoz after his first arrest."

"That was... that was three years ago," she whispers softly.

After a moment, she gives the information a slight nod. Her lower lip wobbles just once. But then she stiffens all over and her face completely blanks. It's incredible to watch her swallow back her emotions better than any poker player I've ever seen. Incredible and devastating. Just like at a card table, I've already learned my opponent's wee tells, but right now, she's almost unreadable.

"Did she know..." She flings her arm out to the papers I set aside. "Did she know you were going to kidnap me and force me to marry you?"

"I didn't *force* you to do anything."

"You drugged me, Kian. I hardly remember the rest of the night after we slept together."

"I think the combination with alcohol—which I didn't realize you'd had so much of until Roxana informed me afterward—might be what's affecting your memory the most. The drug I used is an under-the-radar concoction that is specifically created to only act as a mild sedative and a truth serum. At harmful doses, the sedative can be too much and cause death, but—"

"Death?!"

"—but at the dosage I gave you, all it did was keep you relaxed and truthful."

"Truthful my ass. I would've never married you last night if I wasn't under the influence of something. Now answer me. What did Roxy know?"

Feck, I love this fire in her, but she's raging with me right now and I won't be able to reason with her soon if she keeps getting angrier. A few unbidden ideas come to mind—ways I could calm her down–but I'll wait and try those if my words fail.

"All Roxana knew was that I needed you at Rouge without bodyguards so I could meet you before you got married and it was too late. She didn't know the extent of my plan. Hell, I didn't even know which way things would go until we started dancing."

"How did you not know? Wasn't this all your idea?"

"The job wasn't just my idea. But how I executed it was all me."

"And why on earth would you go about it like *that*? You could've stolen me off the street if you'd wanted."

"Actually—" I cross my arms and lean against the wall. She follows the movement with a flush in her cheeks, tinting color to the blank mask she's trying so hard to wear. "—you're harder to get alone than you think. Before Vegas, your bodyguards were everywhere. Here, Monroe's bodyguards have been your shadow. Rouge was the first place I could get you alone. My mother made sure I learned ballroom dancing and I'm trained in mixed martial arts, so the simple routine Tolie choreographed for me wasn't hard to pick up. No one would've ever expected a McKennon to be on that stage. What happened after we started dancing was... improvised."

"What was supposed to happen, then?" Her brow furrows, but I can see the gears turning in her head. "You were... you were supposed to kill me. Weren't you?" She huffs a laugh and shakes her head. "Wow. You weren't kidding when you said things could've been worse."

"I made some executive decisions to avoid it."

"So... it was either murder or marriage, huh? No in-between?"

"There were a few options somewhere in the middle that I could've chosen from. But I picked my favorite."

"How does your dad feel about your decision? I'm assuming the McKennon put out the hit."

She's so nonchalant about it she could be casually asking how my father feels about the weather. I didn't want to tell her this part of our twisted love story, but as the Keeper's daughter, she was bound to figure it out.

"Killing the O'Shea's only possible chance to produce a male heir would've hurt the Keeper and the O'Shea name the most."

"So it's only natural that the order would be given from the head of the family that hates us the most."

"Naturally." I shrug. I'm trying to match her complacency, but I'm pissed. There's so much about this organization that I want to change, but she seems to accept their faults as immovable truths.

"So what about the priest and judge? Were they just up at that hour out of the goodness of their hearts?"

"That, and they're McKennon men."

"You guys have just converted everyone, haven't you? And the witnesses? Are they McKennon men, too?"

I can't help my chuckle. "You'd be surprised how many old women just hang out at midnight chapels so they can witness true love in the flesh."

"True *love*?"

"There are crazier love stories," I tease, enjoying her scowl. I push off the wall to rest my forearm on the doorframe right beside her head again, caging her in. "You know, the rest of our lives are going to be pretty entertaining if you're this easy to wind up."

The glint in her eyes tells me she lets herself imagine that life for a split second, but then she crosses her arms like a barrier against me and rolls her eyes instead.

"Great, just great. I'm not only allegedly married to a lunatic, he's a *romantic* lunatic."

"Settle down, *tine*. It's not that bad. We were supposed to get married anyway. Just switch the groom. What's the harm?"

"What's the harm?! Oh, right. You don't know because you know *nothing* about me. What everyone else sees isn't the real me—"

"I know. The woman you are when no one is watching is exactly why I chose marrying you instead of killing you."

Her eyes flare with curiosity before narrowing again.

"Well, whatever you *think* you know, you're wrong. Just like you're wrong about whatever you *think* happened last night. I'm marrying the Baron and he's made it very clear that it has to happen today or not at all."

"What a lucky woman you are that your *fiancé* could find time in his busy schedule to marry you. You know most people plan *around* a wedding, not vice versa. You should marry the man who makes every effort to be with you rather than treat you like an appointment."

"Like trick me, kidnap me, and force me to marry him instead?"

"Better to be obsessed over than ignored," the admission that I'm obsessed with her is a wee bit more than I wanted to confess, and it's made worse by the possession dripping in my voice.

Her pretty pink lips part and frustration makes her breaths come in pants, nearly spilling her breasts from her corset. The view makes my cock ache. I finally give in and brush my fingers down her cheek as I murmur the question that's been on my mind since I heard her say, "I do." She leans into my palm by a fraction, giving me hope.

"Last night, you said you could love a man like me. What's stopping you now that you know who I am?"

Her voice is just a whisper when she answers me. "I also said I don't believe in love. Loving someone doesn't mean you should get married. In the Garde, marriages... they're just transactions."

"Grand. Consider this one transaction in exchange for another."

She groans. "God, I wish it were that easy."

"It can be, if you let it."

"Going along with this will be dangerous."

"I'll be able to keep you safe, Lacey."

Worry pinches between her eyes as she shakes her head. "My safety isn't the only thing that matters."

"It is to me."

There's a silence like I caught her by surprise. Her face softens as she steps into me and I think I've possibly changed her mind.

"Then let me go, Kian. That's the only way to keep me safe in this situation."

What the hell?

My jaw clenches and I drop my hand. She's obviously trying to manipulate me by putting on this saccharine-sweet act, but why?

"Look, if you're really concerned about what will happen if Monroe finds out, I *can* protect you."

"Protect me? How?" She falls back and scoffs. "Other than the Muñozes, you have no support from the Garde. No inheritance. If you *have* nothing, you *are* nothing."

Anger wells up in my chest. "So you've bought into the Garde's measure of worth, hmm? That's disappointing. Maybe I'll just say feck it all, then, and send Monroe our wedding video—"

"No, you can't!" She grabs my forearm and her nails dig into my skin. "Kian, please, you can't tell him, at least not yet."

That confirms it. She may have been furious with me before, but at my threat, Lacey's wide eyes shine with tears, the rosy complexion in her cheeks has paled, and she's clinging to me like a lifeline. It makes me want to gather her up and tuck her back into our bed so I can utterly destroy anyone who has instilled even an ounce of this fear in her.

"Lacey... I know there's more to this than you're telling me, so I'm going to ask again. Why do you *have* to sign that contract? Your father's impending trial aside, he's still the Keeper, and you're the Garde's rare flower, effectively our princess. Make your own damn rules. Feck knows I did last night."

I try to soften my frustrated delivery with a smirk, but she looks more defeated than before and slumps against the door.

With my arms caging her in like this, the position makes me feel oppressive. I like to be in charge, but I don't have to swing my dick around to prove it.

Stepping back once more, I don't give a feck that she can see my towel tenting around my thickening cock. Even though my chest aches at seeing her distressed, I can't help the effect her body has on the rest of me.

Her pale cheeks pinken as her eyes dart down.

"Jesus," she mutters and her eyes snap back up to mine. "The rules aren't for me to change, alright? Only a man on the outs with the Garde would think I have a say in anything. I have to marry the Baron and I don't want to start off by disappointing him—"

I snort. "He's a Garde nobody who's trying to achieve his political aspirations by marrying our society's highest-ranking daughter—who's gorgeous, witty, and nearly two decades his junior, I'll add. How the feck could he be disappointed? And why would you care? Do you love him or something?"

"Of course not. We can't stand each other. I've heard the stories. The Baron is a man who will discard me for a better model once he's used me up, if not before that."

The disgust on her face pleases me to no end, but her words make me furious. If she knows what Monroe's capable of and how he treats women, why would she agree to marry him? Even now, after I've saved her from a life with him, she's still pushing back.

"Then is it a silly engagement ring that you want?" I ask, already knowing that can't be the reason, but hoping it riles her up enough to answer. "If so, I can buy you another, easy."

"Silly jewelry? It's a seven-million-dollar ring!"

"Exactly. Did he really have to try that hard to get you to marry him? All I had to do was dance." The smirk I've been trying to contain pushes its way back onto my face before I can quash it again.

She scoffs. "You don't know what you're talking about."

"No? Let's recap, then, shall we?" I go through my assessment, ticking each point off with my fingers. "You can't stand him. You don't want his money. You know he's only using you. So what is it that Monroe has over you, then?" Fear flickers over her face again and I know I've hit the nail on the head. "What *transaction* can be so important that you're willing to marry a man who would kill you just as soon as he would fuck you?"

"Isn't that the kind of man you are?"

I hold back a grimace and try to adopt a nonchalant expression.

"Maybe, but I've made my choice. Don't make me regret it." If threatening her is the only way to get the truth, I'll try anything right now.

Her scowl drops from her face and despite the fact that I intended to throw her off balance, her first hint of uncertainty toward *me* makes my heart seize.

"Well, at least you had a choice," she finally grumbles.

Those few words nearly knock me off my feet. I try to recall the cards she's played so far during our argument and try to guess which ones she still holds close to her chest. I know the Garde can be overbearing with its women, but wouldn't she at least have a say in something as important as who she gets to marry? Or has she only been working with the hand she's been dealt?

"When your father discussed you marrying Monroe, what did you say?"

Her face screws up. "What do you mean?

"When your father asked you if you wanted to marry Monroe... what was your answer?"

She crosses her arms and avoids looking me in the eyes. "I was never asked, okay? I was told and that was that. There was never a discussion."

Anger rises in my chest just as anxiety filters through my mind. "And what about me? Were you able to choose me?"

Her brow furrows. "What does that matter?"

"Everything you say matters. Tell me, Lacey." Her breath

hitches as I tip her chin up, forcing her to meet my eyes. "Were you able to choose me?"

"Yes." Her whispered answer warms the worry freezing my veins and air finally enters my lungs again. "My dad told me you were a candidate. Then I got to meet your mother, who was... God, she was amazing. I loved meeting her. So with you, I was given a choice and I said yes. But with the Baron? I-I was told."

Emotions swirl inside me and I'm not sure which one to hang on to.

I've learned more about Lacey in the last fifteen minutes than a year of obsessing over her as my mark. I thought she played a part in choosing Monroe as her husband, but I was wrong. She's always been under lock and key, and apparently, she's spent her whole life committing minor infractions almost like it's a game, pulling at her leash until she's threatened with a cage.

Last night was her final act of rebellion before she was trapped forever, and I stole that from her. I don't want to trap her, but if I'm going to keep her safe, I have to play the game she's been taught and call her bluffs to help us both win the hand.

"Why were you supposed to marry Monroe and not me, then? What hold does he have over you? Tell me so I can help you."

She shakes her head slowly. "It's more than just a mere business deal. He's... he's supposed to do something and I... I don't want to interfere."

"Stop being so vague and talk to me. I'll keep your secrets, *tine*, I swear."

She opens her mouth to answer, but it clamps closed, and that anger heats her eyes again. Something I said has set her off again, but I'm not sure what.

"No, you don't get to kidnap me, force me to marry you, *and* steal my secrets too. If you were looking for a pliant wife in me, you were sorely mistaken."

"Interesting, so you were willing to be a pliant wife for Monroe, then? Because I can assure you, *I* was never looking for a cardboard cutout of a Garde wife. I don't want to tame you, I want to free you."

The buzz of a mobile interrupts us. She digs into her pocket like the device will explode if she doesn't answer in time. When she reads the caller ID, she takes a deep breath of relief.

Who the feck is she that relieved to talk to? Is it the bastard her family chose over mine?

Before she answers, jealousy takes over, and I snatch the mobile from her grasp to answer it.

"Kian, no!" She lunges from the door, but I grasp her neck with my free hand and squeeze. She immediately relaxes underneath my hold and doesn't try to fight me off. A small moan escapes her with a delicious gasp that vibrates underneath my palm.

Interesting.

My thumb releases from the side of her neck and I graze the smooth skin as I look at the caller ID.

Mom.

Well, that's anticlimactic.

"I'll let you answer this," I loosen the rest of my fingers just enough for her to speak. "But only to tell her that congratulations are in order."

"Kian, I can't do that. I'm supposed to meet her at the courthouse."

"Well, then, tell her you're all out of fresh marriage licenses." The corner of my mouth ticks upward as a grin tries to break free.

"If I tell her I'm married to anyone but the Baron, my entire family is ruined!"

I want to shout that her father already tried to ruin *my* family and we've been clawing our way back up ever since. But tears brim her eyes, making them sparkle like gemstones and I can't bear to see my strong queen of diamonds cry, no matter the reason.

"If marrying a McKennon is as ruinous as you believe, go ahead. Answer." The caustic words hiss out of me as I hand her mobile back. "I'd love to see what lie you come up with to tell my new mother-in-law. Don't forget to set up a brunch date."

I release her and step back to lean against the couch, propping my hands on its leather arm.

She eyes me warily with a hint of confusion. At what, I don't know, but I stop overanalyzing entirely when she answers and Moira O'Shea shrieks like a banshee into the receiver.

Scene 9

HIGH STAKES

"*acey!* Lacey, are you okay?"

My mom's scream shocks me like a penny in a light socket.

"Mom! Mom! Are you alright? What's going on?!"

"Lacey! You're okay. Thank God. You didn't answer this morning, and I was afraid that poor girl was you!"

Kian feigns boredom as he lounges against the couch, his defined washboard abs now dry and casually engaged. But his dark-auburn eyebrow lifts slightly with interest.

"Mom, calm down. I can't understand you. You thought *who* was me?"

She gulps so hard my own throat aches despite the ibuprofen from earlier. My hand drifts to my neck where Kian's fingers were. Out of the corner of my eye, a small, infuriating smirk lifts his lips. I scowl at him in return.

"A woman was found dead this morning in one of the Rouge dressing rooms! Her face was beaten beyond recognition, but she was wearing a white bride costume and her hair was the same color as yours. I was so scared, Lacey."

"A-a woman was murdered last night at Rouge?" My eyes widen.

Kian's cocky expression disappears and he pushes off the couch to step closer. His thickly corded arms end in fists and I can see his heartbeat pulse in his veins. But when he stops a breath away from me, so close the heat radiating from his skin warms mine, I don't feel afraid.

I feel protected.

Dangerous.

"Yes! At our own business! The manager informed me while I was waiting for you at the courthouse. Your father doesn't call until the guards go on break later today, so I couldn't talk to him. And when I couldn't get in touch with you, either, I thought the worst!"

"Mom, I'm so sorry, but I'm okay." My eyes meet Kian's and the irony isn't lost on me at what I say next. "I'm safe."

"Where are you? Roxana insisted you were in your suite, but one of our bodyguards said you were gone, and Maeve claims you left them at the club."

My heartbeat races. Fuck, Maeve might not remember much, but she remembers one of the most damning pieces of evidence against me.

Kian shakes his head and whispers, "She was too wrecked to remember."

I nod at him and use his lie. "She's covering for the fact that she got too wasted last night to remember beyond the limo. Don't worry about me, though, I'm fine. What's happening at Rouge now? Are the police there?"

"The poor girl is being analyzed by the crime scene investigators and coroner. The police have requested that I go to the club since I'm the effective owner in charge. I'm leaving the courthouse now so I can answer any questions they may have."

"Do they know who could've done it?"

"They don't even know the victim's name, Lacey!"

"Okay, I'm sorry. I'm worried, too, and I'm just trying to wrap my mind around all this."

Kian's strong hand grips my nape and as much as I don't want to, I let myself find comfort in him as he massages the back of my neck.

"What's most important is that we won't be found liable. The lead detective is one of ours so we at least have that on our side if it turns out a deal went sour."

My lips roll between my teeth to keep from speaking my mind against an elder.

"Yup," I mutter, knowing she won't catch my sarcasm. "That's what's most important."

If someone innocent is dead, it shouldn't matter who's on whose side. The murderer should be dealt with accordingly, either in-house or by the government. But if the hit was done by a high-ranking member, neither will happen.

That's the way of it in the Garde. My family thrives in a society of handshakes and turned heads. Clay poker chips are as good as money and loyalty is only as good as the blackmail that secured it.

"Thank goodness Monroe hadn't arrived at the courthouse yet."

I frown. "He wasn't there?"

"No. I called to let him know about Rouge. I'd even hoped you were with him, despite the scandal it would've caused."

"What did he say when you called? Was he worried?"

There's a pause before she answers my question. "He, um, hasn't called back. One of his bodyguards promised to relay the message, but the Baron was preoccupied with business he had to take care of on the Strip. You know how Garde men are. Always so busy."

Yeah, busy gambling away his fortune.

"My fiancé was *so* busy he couldn't make sure I was *alive*?"

It should hurt that the man I was supposed to marry only cares about me when I'm worth something to him, but my disappointment lies with my mother. She wanted this arrangement about as much as I did, so the way she always sticks up for him stings.

But for some reason, Kian's protective scowl feels like a salve on the burn. I've never had someone care this much about me. Why does it have to be a man my family hates?

"It's best not to look at it that way, dear. Your father and I weren't a love match at first, either. I know you had high hopes for your first arrangement, but I wasn't your father's first choice either and we grew to love one another over time. I'm... I'm sure you and Monroe will become fond of each other, too."

"If he can spare a moment of his time to be in the same room with me."

I block out Kian's intense stare and shrug his hand from my shoulder. If I could flee from him and this vulnerable moment, I would. I jiggle the handle of the door halfheartedly just to make myself feel like I'm doing something.

"Speaking of sparing a moment, you couldn't spare one to get married this morning? Where on earth *were* you? The location on your phone is off. We talked about how dangerous that could be. How could you be so reckless?"

"I didn't—" A quick glance at Kian shows me the smug smile that seems permanently etched into his face.

"You?" I mouth.

He shrugs as if to say "guilty."

Of course he did. This psychopath has obviously thought of everything in his plot for what? Revenge? But people don't get married for revenge and the Garde uses overdoses and fake suicides to extinguish family lines. It can't be about money because the McKennons are billionaires—

But Kian doesn't see a cent unless he has an heir.

Without a Garde-approved marriage—which my father will *never* grant after Kian cast me aside—his inheritance will go to the Garde's coffers once Finneas McKennon passes away. Status and family get you in the Garde. Power and succession keep you in.

And it seems Kian just made the biggest power play of them all.

"Lacey!"

My mother snaps me back into the conversation. "Sorry, Mom. I thought keeping my location on only applied while I was in New Orleans," I lie. "You know, since the ruling family there refuses to join the Garde."

"Of course it's not just New Orleans. They honored their promise to leave you unharmed, but you need to be vigilant anywhere our enemies are. And if this was a warning, then our enemies are even in our own backyard."

"It could've had nothing to do with us," I counter, wishing it was true.

"Don't be naive. People will likely come out of the woodwork to stop your wedding with the Baron, especially if they know he's going to testi—"

"Okay! Okay, I'll turn my location on. I'm sorry." I hope like hell I've stopped Kian from hearing that Monroe is going to testify on my father's behalf. With the way Kian was interrogating me minutes ago, I don't think he knows. When he finds out, though, he'll have even more reason to prevent me from doing what I have to for my family.

"Good. Where are you now? I'll send a bodyguard—"

"—I'm hungover and getting a coffee near the Bellagio," I blurt out, instantly confused with myself that I didn't just tell the truth so a bodyguard could come save me.

"Lacey O'Shea, have you lost your head? First turning off your location, then getting so drunk you get hungover, and *now* you're getting coffee across the street from the McKennon Hotel? What if one of them—or God forbid *Kian*—sees you the day you're supposed to get married?"

Kian snorts. I cover the receiver quickly and turn away from his prying attention before responding.

"They can't hurt me in broad daylight. Besides, I'm leaving now."

"When you do, turn your location back on and call Monroe. Beg him for another chance."

"*Beg* him?" I grimace and look around to see if Kian heard

that, but he's gone. I'm alone. My mind races at what I should do, but my mother keeps talking, distracting me.

"Women of the Garde do what we have to in order to advance the elite of the elite. The men may rule this country, but the women rule the men."

"Unless the men kill us first," I mutter.

"Only if we give them a reason," she argues, as if that makes our reality better. "You know what's at stake. Your father needs you. What if the Baron decides not to testify because you've acted foolishly?"

My breath catches in my chest. "C-can he even do that? He wouldn't, right?"

"Why wouldn't he? If he refuses to marry you right away to punish us, how long will the Garde tolerate an inmate as Keeper? If they depose your father, what will keep the Baron interested since he would no longer be next in line to lead? He's already done us a favor by offering to marry you when no one else would. If the Baron doesn't want you and your father is usurped, we'll be extinguished."

My heart races as she speaks. For the first time, I'm actually grateful for Kian's promise to protect me. Even though the Baron has said he'll testify to free my father, Monroe has never promised me protection if our marriage falls through. If I do whatever it takes to save my father, will Kian still save me?

"It seems I've finally made you think of someone besides yourself. I know you'll do the right thing. I've just arrived at Rouge, and I have to go. Your father and I are counting on you."

With that, she hangs up. I lower the phone, warm in my hand —almost as hot as my cheeks over the revelations my mother just dropped.

What the hell am I going to do?

The sound of dress shoes on marble echoes louder in the living room until Kian is just feet away from me. I follow the black Ferragamo loafers all the way up his tall form to take in his sharp charcoal-gray business suit. It accentuates his broad shoulders, making him look bigger than he already is. His dark-red tie has fine silver threading that brings out the shine in the gold flecks in his hazel eyes. His gaze keeps mine as he casually flips a silver poker chip in the air and pockets it. He's so fucking intense that my lower belly flares with need. But that fire quickly blazes to anger once he opens his overbearing mouth.

"Did I hear you say the word 'beg'? What's so at stake that the great Lacey O'Shea has to beg for the old Baron to marry her?" there's a tinge of barely controlled rage in his voice that brings out his light accent. It dances under my skin in a shiver, but his mocking question grates on my nerves.

"None of your business," I mutter. "All you need to know is that whatever we did last night has to be undone. We can get an annulment—"

"The fuck we will." He pulls me so hard against his chest my breasts nearly spill from my corset. His intoxicating smoky amber scent overwhelms me and I nearly miss that he's still talking. "Everything you do is my business now. Especially if there were parts of last night that *can't* be undone."

Dread creeps over me like ice. "W-what do you mean? What did we do that can't be undone?"

He looks down at my rapidly breathing chest with appreciation before bending to whisper in my ear. His short, coarse facial hair gently tickles my cheek.

"We were skin to skin, *tine*. There was nothing between us last night, and there never will be."

"Nothing between us..." My heart stalls out. I remember thinking that we missed a step, but I was so caught up in the heat of the moment... "Oh my god. We didn't use a condom. Kian, I'm not on the pill!"

He shrugs like the smug bastard he is. "I raised the stakes, hoping it'd pay off. Looks like I won this hand. You may hate me for it, but I don't regret a single thing—"

The sting in my fingers tingles before I even register that I've slapped him.

Scene 10

A ROYAL FLUSH

Kian's hand is on my throat.

I've never seen someone move so fast. The scent and smooth texture of leather hit me before I realize I'm face-first in a couch cushion. Kian's hard thighs are stone underneath me, my breasts are shoved up to my chin thanks to my stupid corset, and my tulled ass waves like a white flag of surrender in the air.

His large hand yanks my dress up and I gasp at the cold air wafting over my naked backside. The chill is short-lived though, as his palm grabs a fistful of my right butt cheek.

"Kian," I huff. "What're you—"

Before I can fight him, his hand moves in my periphery and a sharp crack rings in the air. The slap on my ass is nowhere near as hard as I hit him, but I still yelp at the sting.

"Kian!"

"Never..." He smacks me again, making me howl. "Hit..."

Smack!

"Me..."

Smack!

"Again, wife."

Smack!

It's only five spankings, one after the other, delivered almost too swiftly for my body to comprehend. But my mind knows full well what's happening. A flood of shame rushes through my veins and emerges as white-hot tears that warp my vision. I refuse to let them spill down my cheeks, even as my bottom lip trembles. I clench my teeth to keep from crying out and ball my fists against the couch cushion, vibrating with rage.

This is fucking humiliating.

My so-called husband is *spanking* me.

As great as the Garde is at secrets, the worst-kept one is how the men treat their wives. They don't hold back when it comes to physically punishing their women. If the abuse ever gets out of hand, the Garde just covers it up. My father was an anomaly. He would yell, but I never saw him raise a fist toward my mom. The Baron, though, has promised to rule me with a firm hand.

I guess Kian is just like all the other Garde men.

I don't know why that realization hurts the most. The thought makes me sniffle and my body overheats with embarrassment until... until I realize the warmth has become something... else.

His palm caresses where it dealt the stinging blows. Strong fingers knead gently over the sensitive skin, heightened from his confusing torment. When I try to get up on my knees, he firmly pushes me back down with his hand on the back of my neck. I'm baffled by my body when it listens and silently lies across his thighs again. He squeezes my nape in approval and the sensual pressure both there and my glutes elicits a mortifying whimper from my lips.

"It feels good, doesn't it? This is what punishment should feel like between a man and his wife."

God, if this is how he's going to "punish" me, I can't wait to be bad again.

Using a gentle push with his fingers on my nape, he signals me to turn my head toward him until I can see his face despite the awkward angle. His hard jaw is set and there's a hint of sweat over his furrowed dark-auburn brows as if he's trying to maintain his control. Those hazel eyes tell everything, though. They're molten hot with need, and I bite my tongue to keep from begging him to fuck me again.

"Never strike me in anger, Lacey. Although the Garde may encourage abusive behavior, you'll find I don't give a feck what the Garde thinks. I don't want to tame that fire in you, but I won't let it rage out of control, either."

"Oh, but you get to hit me in anger?" I spit.

He shakes his head and kneads one of my cheeks even harder, traveling dangerously close to my aching center. My pussy throbs and twisted desire surges arousal to my core. My body has a mind of its own as my ass lifts slightly, begging for him to go lower. A hard thickness pokes my hip, and it takes my lust-addled mind entirely too long to realize he's enjoying this, too.

"Does it feel like I'm angry, *tine*?"

He thrusts against me slightly, making me hold on to his thighs for purchase. My legs fall open and his adept fingers finally find my core.

"Mmm, no. No i-it doesn't."

His fingers lazily play in my soaked entrance before one swirls and pulses against my clit in a quick tempo. A moan escapes me and I turn my head away from him. His fingers tighten on my nape until my chin rests on the leather as if he is afraid I'd try to flee. When I settle back down, his low rumble of encouragement makes my lower belly flip and his grip on my nape lightens in response.

"The way I see it, I'll never do anything that truly warrants you hitting me. I promise I'll never need your brand of punishment, but what about you? What do you think of my brand of punishment, wife?" The title hisses out of him, thick with possession.

"I'm not your wife," I meant for it to be a reprimand, but God help me, it comes out as a moan instead.

Suddenly, my clit is bereft of his touch and my left butt cheek is on fire from another spanking.

"Kian!" I squirm until his fingers promptly return to massage my clit.

"You're my wife, Lacey. You saw the papers, the video, and you have my ring. You may not remember our midnight wedding, but I'll never let you forget who you are married to. Me. Not Monroe fecking Baron. Understood?"

"Kian, I'm not—"

Smack.

"Son of a—fine, alright!" My release is so tantalizingly close I'll admit to anything. "I'm your wife, okay?"

"That's what I like to hear, *tine*." Kian murmurs assurances under his breath, making me shiver. "But one day I'm going to make you believe it."

His hand leaves my neck while his other keeps teasing my throbbing clit. Nothing is holding me down now but his stroking fingertips, and it takes me a second to realize that we both know he's got me right where he wants me. I'm not going anywhere.

I writhe against his fingers, searching for release, and my body grows feverish with need. He's bringing me right to the brink of an orgasm, but my empty pussy aches and I can't quite get there.

"Kian," I whine.

"Listen to you cry for me. I sated you last night and already you're wishing I'd fuck you again. You want me to fill you with my cock, don't you? Spill my cum inside you until it leaks from this sweet pussy?"

My cheeks burn at his dirty words, but I agree breathlessly. "Y-yes."

"I loved the way your tight cunt sucked me, fucking greedy for my cum." He leans forward until his hot breath tickles my ear. "I didn't want to leave your warm pussy, *tine*. I wanted to stay buried inside you for the rest of my life. And now I can make you feel this good anytime you want. Wouldn't you like that, wife? If I fucked you so good, you'd never want to run away?"

His words have me hot and aching and I can't answer him for the life of me. All that matters is coming.

He sits up, leaving my face cool without his warm breath. His fingers rub my clit furiously and the sensation has me spinning until finally...

Finally...

He leaves my core and slaps my ass cheek hard, jarring me from my sensual haze.

"Kian!"

He moves quickly out from underneath me and before I know it, I'm face-planting into the couch again while Kian stands. I scramble to sit up and smooth my ruffled skirt, using the simple movement to try to get my bearings.

When I finally look up again, ticked off and horny, Kian's hazel eyes glare down at me.

"I didn't... um..." I hedge, giving him the benefit of the doubt that this isn't a cruel joke. But his dark laugh says otherwise.

"You didn't come? Oh, I'm well aware of that, Lacey. I now know what it feels like to have you fall apart in my arms, and you were just on the brink of it, which is why I stopped."

"Kian," I scoff. "What the hell?"

"I felt your submission. Your real submission, not that pretend shite you pull to appease the Garde. But you need to know what it feels like to be properly dominated and to trust me when I do it."

"Dominated? What? And how can I trust you if you leave me hanging?!"

"You'll have to trust that I'll let you come when I return." His long fingers straighten his sleeves and fiddle with his silver, ruby, and diamond cuff links as if he's totally unfazed by what just happened. But the huge hard-on nearly bursting from his Armani slacks betrays him.

"Well, you didn't come either," I point out with a glare

toward his dick. I drag my eyes away quickly, though, once I realize I was trying to find his piercing beneath the fabric.

"Oh, don't worry about me, Lacey. This is Vegas. And seeing as how I'm an unmarried man, there will be plenty more opportunities to get my dick wet." He doesn't look at me as he says it, but his words knock me back all the same.

I'm shocked to taste the acidic tang of jealousy on my tongue. My hand rubs my chest as he finally looks up at me from his cuff links and sinks his hands into his pockets.

"I have business to attend to."

"Hold on. Where are you going?" I shift to get up, but my pussy flutters in protest and I think better about it. I also know for a fact I've left a damp spot on this leather couch that I desperately don't want him to see.

Although it'd serve the bastard right.

"Are you my wife?" he asks, throwing me off.

"No." The word rushes out of me on reflex and I immediately know it was a mistake.

He nods, scrubbing his coarse shadow of a beard before pointing at me with a wagging finger. "Then I don't see how where I'm going is any of your business."

My jaw drops at him using my own words against me. He ignores my shock to snatch my phone from the soft white rug where I must've dropped it and shoves it into his pocket.

"Kian—wait, that's mine!"

"You can get it back later."

"I need it now. What if someone calls?"

"Don't worry, I'll take a message."

My heart drops to my stomach. "But what if it's—"

"The Baron?" Kian's voice lilts up, mocking the title. "If it's your precious Monroe, I'll enjoy answering that call the most."

He turns around and adjusts himself on his way to the door, sending alarm bells clanging in my head as I finally realize he's not kidding.

"Wait, seriously, Kian. You can't leave me here! I need to go."

He grabs his phone from the entry table and faces me again with a sexy, teasing smirk that makes me want to leap over his lap again.

"This is your punishment for hitting me. You get to sit with your unsated lust and feel guilty about what you did to your poor, generous, dashingly handsome husband. Maybe next time you want to deny me respect, you'll remember what I can deny you."

I scoff, "So you've denied me, but you'll go get off at some club?"

"Does that bother you..." he pauses, that same damn grin flashing, "...*wife*?"

"No!" And it shouldn't bother me. All a Garde woman can ask of her husband is discretion, not faithfulness.

Not that Kian is my husband. And since he isn't, I can't even insist on discretion.

"Pity," he sighs as if he's the one disappointed in me. "Oh, before I go, I've made *several* copies of our marriage license, so destroy it if you want to, I don't care. But don't try to get yourself off while I'm gone. I'll know," he orders in an annoying singsongy voice as he turns and opens the door.

I jump up from the couch. "Kian, wait—"

"And try not to think of me too much when you disobey me anyway."

He winks at me while I lunge for the door, but he shuts it behind him before I can get there.

"Kian?" I bang on the door with the heel of my palm. "Kian!"

"You're in my suite in the McKennon Hotel." Kian's voice echoes at me, and I startle backward from the speaker I hadn't noticed beside the door. "The insulation and soundproofing is impeccable. I oversaw its installation myself. So scream all you want, Lacey McKennon. No one will hear you."

The truth of his words settles over me like a cold fog and I stare at the speaker for several long minutes. Once his threat stops ringing in my ears, I turn slowly on my heel toward the expensive furnishings in the living room with no way out.

Then it hits me.

He said he wanted to free me, but this is just another gilded cage. Only my husband has the key... and he has absolutely no desire to let me out.

I'm more trapped than ever.

Scene 11

ALL IN

"No phones," a deep voice emerges out of the loud commotion on the casino floor, and I lift my head away from my screen. The tall, black-haired bouncer's pale face blooms red, the color made even worse in the flashing lights of a nearby slot machine. "Shit, Mr. McKennon, I'm sorry. It's dark—"

"Don't let it happen again," I order before sliding my mobile in my pocket and exchanging it for my chip.

The rules in my family's casino obviously don't apply to me, but watching my wee wife on my security app is officially my new favorite obsession. Which means I need to put the distraction away and get my head in the game.

I don't recognize the high roller room's bouncer, but the fear in his eyes is familiar. The Garde has come a long way from its Mafia roots, but we're still not above the old ways. My own methods can scare the life out of even the most seasoned criminals.

"You're new." It's not a question, I already know the answer. "What's your name?"

"L-Lorenzo, sir. I'm sorry, Mr. McKennon. I didn't recognize you with your head down."

Scanning the casino, it doesn't take me long to find the issue.

A woman dances on the closest game table, but she's looking studiously away from us. The bouncer, however, glances guiltily at the woman before returning back to me.

I sidle up close to him, flipping my silver chip casually as I take up the space between us. My lips lift in a wry grin.

"Pretty, isn't she?" I tip my head toward the woman with her tits pushed up to her chin by a sparkly black bra and slip my chip back into a pocket in my suit jacket.

The bouncer relaxes a fraction and watches her like an eejit with a dopey smile on his face.

"Yeah, boss, she's a smokeshow—"

He grunts as the barrel of my gun pokes into his ribs. At the angle I've positioned myself, no one can see my weapon in the dark hallway. I clap my hand on his shoulder as his wide eyes snap to mine.

"Now imagine this is a knife. Imagine me running this blade between your ribs and into those precious lungs. I could carry you to one of the porter's cleaning rooms without anyone knowing you're drowning in your own blood until it's too late. Is staring at that pussy worth your life?"

"N-no."

"Smart man, because it's not worth mine either. You're here to keep McKennons—and anyone loyal to the name—safe."

I pull back and squeeze his shoulder hard enough to make him wince as I holster my weapon. A bead of sweat snakes its way down his temple and drips onto his suit jacket.

"McKennons aren't ones to give second chances, but you're new, so I'll let this be your warning. This is Vegas, Lorenzo. If you let something as common as pussy get in the way of your job, you'll be bobbing to the surface of Lake Mead next time there's a drought. Got it?"

He gives me an enthusiastic nod and I squeeze his shoulder once more for good measure, making him wince at my grip.

"Good luck with that wandering eye, soldier."

I step past him into the high roller room, where the atmosphere is instantly quieter and less smoky. The table games are more subdued since the stakes are higher and the players are more experienced than the average tourist. I stroll to the red curtain in the back of the room.

Merek meets me there with a scowl so fierce that it furrows from his brow all the way over his shiny brown scalp. His lips frown within his short, salt-and-pepper goatee and his huge arms are crossed, nearly bursting his all-black suit.

"You see that?" I know he did. Merek's going to light poor Lorenzo's arse up.

"Wish I hadn't."

"You've got to watch your men, mate. I don't want to have to sink my own soldiers."

"Oh, it won't happen again. I'll make sure of that myself." Before he pulls back the curtain, he nods toward the room and I bend slightly to hear his low whisper. "Got five of them in there with your father. Muñoz, Milton, Thomson, and that Italian, Luciano, with his capo from New York."

Aside from my father, I trust three of those men with my life. Another is loyal to McKennon wealth and power, and the last shouldn't even be in the bloody room, but his boss will keep him in line.

"The usual suspects then. Do they know?"

He nods. "No one's said anything yet, though. I think they're waiting for you to arrive to talk about the implications. Fair warning, the Luciano's second already had a couple drinks in him before he got here. I suspect he'll get rowdy."

"Perfect. I have some pent-up aggression I've been dying to get out."

Merek snorts. "Getting married is supposed to, uh, relieve that tension. It did for me, at least."

"Yeah, well, your wife likes you, mate. We can't all start off on the right foot."

"Try not kidnapping her next time. I hear that helps."

"Fecking arsehole," I mutter under my breath as Merek laughs quietly at my expense and pulls back the curtain enough for me to enter.

The Red Room is small, with only four tables for baccarat, blackjack, roulette, and poker. Cigar smoke fills the room, stinging my eyes despite the fact that I should be used to it by now. Only the poker table at the far right has any players, and their chatter is punctuated by the sounds of poker chips clacking together on the card table.

"My son! Saved you a seat, lad," Dad calls out with a long, Royal Courtesan cigar between his lips. Its gold wrapping and diamond-studded band glint in the light from the Tiffany stained glass overhead.

I pass the roulette table to sit in the empty seat beside my father and the Muñoz, already set up with seltzer and poker chips. There are six high-ball glasses at varying degrees of emptiness around the table, and the Muñoz's glass sweats into its teak McKennon Hotel and Casino coaster.

Focus.

After counting the chips in front of me, I slip my hand into my pocket and rub my thumb over the design on the chip I keep there. I sip the cool, sparkling water my father ordered for me and let it fizz in my mouth before swallowing. Taking a deep breath of the cigars' sweetness tingeing the air, I allow it to fill my nostrils, ridding the mouthwatering scent of my father's whiskey two feet away.

We both learned quickly what helps center me. Analyzing my surroundings, identifying the tiny tells everyone lets slip through, and remembering the people that matter to me most have been my three best techniques to stave off any cravings. Ignoring temptation is a lot easier than it was a year ago, before my mission with Lacey gave me purpose. I use those methods now, adding in the delicious vision of Lacey adorably pissed as feck at me upstairs. After my pulse relaxes again, I finally sit back to assess the other players and home in on the task at hand: a meeting of the families loyal to our name.

Merek informed me well about the attendees. There are no surprises so far other than the fact that each one smokes the same million-dollar cigar my father has.

"You broke out the Gurkhas, I see."

"Celebrations like this are perfect for them, don't you think? Here—" My father's worried glance is brief. No one else at the table would've seen it, and it disappears as he extracts a long cigar from the case at his right. He hands it to me along with a McKennon Hotel and Casino matchbook. "I already cut this one for you."

"Thanks, Dad."

I let go of the chip in my pocket and strike a match to toast the foot of the cigar. After letting it rest a moment, I place the cap in my mouth and draw in the smoky, rich chestnut, vanilla, and caramel flavors. The taste swirls over my tongue and I enjoy it before letting it escape slowly between my lips.

"Goddamn, that's good."

I don't allow myself many vices anymore, but bloody hell, a good cigar over a poker game is worth every breath.

Benecio Muñoz raises his to me and smiles kindly. "I hear congratulations are in order for our wild ace."

"Definitely fit the nickname with this latest stunt." Vinnie Flores, the Luciano's second, smirks with the kind of confidence only a man wearing a bad comb-over and a tracksuit can have. "It's been a while since you've graced us with your presence."

Everyone else is dressed to the nines in their suits and obviously still has their wits about them. But the pungent scent of booze wafts toward me with Vinnie's slurred words.

I can't stand the guy, but his drunken state not only helps me abstain, it'll also make it easier to beat him in this game. He's always had a chip on his shoulder with me for some reason, but he's loyal to the Luciano name and they are loyal to ours, so I'll bite my tongue about it until I have to address it accordingly.

Merek warned me that he's been behaving in bad form, so we'll see if tonight's the night.

"Marrying the Red Camellia. Bold move," the Milton points out as he leans forward around his heavy belly and tosses his chips into the pile to raise the bet. "One that was... authorized, I presume?"

"My choice was within the bounds of the order given by my father," I say without argument behind it. I knew my decision would be questioned as soon as I made it, but I don't fecking answer to them. "Once I'm given the card, it's mine to play as I please."

"What were the other 'choices'?" the Luciano asks. His family is part of an outfit in the Northeast. Historically, their ties still intersect with the Mafia, so they're ones to be wary of. But the Luciano has pledged his allegiance to our side, so we let him in. At least for now.

"I think it was defilement or overdose," the Thomson offers casually. The deep wrinkles in his dark-brown skin are mostly smile lines, but they're in a distinct frown right now. His loyalty is nearly as unquestionable as the Muñoz's and the Milton's, but his friendship with the Luciano is solid, which is probably why he fielded the stupid question before I had to.

We all knew the answer. I was supposed to either kill Lacey or "ruin" the Red Camellia by sending Monroe a video of a masked stranger deflowering his virgin bride. Monroe would've dropped her like a bad habit and it would've destroyed Lacey's "purity" for all other Garde marriages. The lack of suitors would, in effect, extinguish her family's line like they had tried to do to mine.

Vinnie snickers. "Guess Kian wanted to make a wedding video rather than a sex tape."

Ignoring the gobshite, I nod to the only woman in the room, waiting patiently with a deck of cards in her hand. "Deal me in."

She nods once and whips cards out to each of us in quick succession. As the new game starts I answer the question they're all dying to know.

"Killing the Red Camellia would extinguish her line, returning Garde money back to the pot. But grief is not nearly as satisfying as humiliation, and Charlie O'Shea deserves the latter."

"You didn't humiliate him, though. You married his daughter," the Luciano points out as he pushes his neat stack farther into the table with a steady hand.

"A third option we didn't foresee. I'll check this round," my father replies, holding his cards casually. It's his biggest tell. His grip always shakes when he's got a good hand, so he exaggerates a relaxed posture to lessen the tremor. "My son has proven himself to be disciplined and of sound judgment. If he chose to play the game this way, I trust him."

"So all that dancin' around like a whore last night was *sound judgment*?" Vinnie chortles, but the room turns chilly and his poised boss stiffens. "Did your boxing days back in Dublin help with your twinkle toes? You'll have to prove you can still throw a punch like a man before someone lets you back in the ring."

"Mind yourself," I warn calmly and puff my cigar. "I'd hate to have to call your bluff, Vinnie."

Out of the corner of my eye, I see him scowl and shift in his seat. His frown lifts up in the corner, though, and in my periphery, I catch him fidgeting under the table.

I don't care that the bastard is testing me right now. Of course there's pushback after being absent for so long. Figuring out how to get the Keeper's overprotected daughter alone was my main assignment, effectively putting me out of commission for most other jobs the past year. Coming back into the fold might take cracking a few skulls to remind everyone who the feck I am. If Vinnie wants to be the first casualty, so be it.

Jobs aside, it's also been a while since I've attended a game with so many Garde families as players. It's rare we're ever all in the same place. Garde tradition is that we only get together for charity benefits—which are sacred moments of good PR for the families—and highly secured meetings, such as this one, thanks to

Merek and his team. If we gathered too often, it would be easy for our enemies to take us all out in one hit.

It's why my father insisted I spend most of my life in Ireland and why the heirs to the two richest and most powerful names, the O'Sheas and McKennons, were never allowed in the same room. Our union was supposed to be a monumental effort to reunite the two dueling factions in the Garde. I thought the O'Shea was too greedy to let the deal go through, but Lacey's reaction has me wondering now.

I glance around the table, reevaluating our alliances and taking in their wee tells. Is there more at play here?

"As crass as my second may be..." The Luciano's annoyed eyes dart to Vinnie. At least the boss has good sense even if his capo doesn't. "You can't sidestep the question. Why did you marry her when that wasn't the plan?"

After drawing in more smoke from my cigar, I blow it out slowly through my lips, taking all the time I want before repeating myself for this motherfucker.

"I was within the bounds of my orders, I owe you no other explanation."

"That may be true. But if my family name is to back yours in any future Garde... repositioning, we need to know we're not dealing with a, well, with a wild card."

The players around the table shift in their seats as he continues, but my father and I keep playing the game, as if he's not challenging us in our own fecking casino.

"A lot has changed in the past few months while you were in deep with your assignment," he continues. "In New Orleans, the Bordeaux's twin extinguished the Chatelain line *and* killed Monroe's cousin, Jacques. The Baron will likely want payback at some point."

"The loss of the Chatelain wasn't a huge shake-up." Dad's face remains relaxed, but he stretches in his seat. The move makes him look bigger, and at nearly my height, he's already of formidable stature. "And the Baron's cousin was a snake in the grass, playing all sides. The Bordeauxs aren't Garde, but they have no intention of growing their territory into one of ours. If the Baron decides to retaliate, it'll be on his own dime."

The Luciano grunts and my father narrows his eyes at him. "Although, this might be of concern to you... the Bordeaux did warn me that the Chatelain had business with a syndicate up Northeast. With him and the Baron being interested in your neck of the woods, I'd caution you to be worried about your own territory rather than Louisiana."

"I know nothing of the dead Chatelain's dealings." The Luciano shrugs, his face blank. On anyone else, it'd look innocent or clueless, but the Italian is an emotional player. Being emotionless *is* his tell.

"Better find out then, lad, before it encroaches on yours," my father mutters, knowing as well as I do that the Italian is lying.

I have half a mind to throw both Lucianos out right now, but even enemies can be allies under the right circumstances. We just have to keep them right for the Luciano in case he tries to fold.

I study the queen of diamonds card in my hand, crisply new compared to the identical one I've carried in my pocket the past year. Pretending like I'm only interested in its artwork, I listen and watch my opponents over its corners. Our casino only uses the deck I designed, and for this queen card, the upright one at the top holds a red flower while the upside-down queen grips a sword. And out of the corner of my eye, Vinnie makes the same move under the table. I silently add this second infraction to my list of grievances against him before I speak again.

"To answer your question as to whether I'm a wild card." I clear my throat. "My reputation obviously precedes me, but I'm no loose cannon. Quite the opposite, I'm actually enforcing the Keeper's own edict."

"How so?" the Thomson asks. His wiry gray brows meet at the center as he casually places his bet.

"A Garde contract is law, and while the O'Shea believed he could break the initial marriage arrangement between our families, it's never been done before without reason, and he gave none. The Red Camellia was promised to me. We were meant to unite the Garde and end the divisiveness within. Monroe thinks he has clout, but his family is new Garde. He's only received half his inheritance because he doesn't have an heir yet, and he wants to be Keeper. He needs Lacey for both—"

"Isn't that why you wanted her?" Vinnie chuckles. "Squirt a McKennon kid in her so you can get those McKennon big bucks?"

I puff my million-dollar cigar, truly savoring the Royal Courtesan's flavor for the last time. Once I've had my fill, I lean around the Muñoz to blow a gray cloud at the man digging his own grave. As Vinnie swats away the smoke, I extinguish the rest of my gold cigar in the drunk Italian fecker's whiskey. It hisses as it hits the liquid and I leave it there, smiling at him as I settle back into my seat.

"I don't need O'Shea money, or my family's, for that matter. I was promised Lacey. The O'Shea stole her from me and tried to give her to another, but I stole her back. I don't like when people try to take what's mine, Vinnie. You'd do well to remember that in my own family's casino."

My eyes flick to his cards, letting him know I've seen him cheating—poorly—throughout the game.

Vinnie's face is fecking priceless. His normally ruddy pallor has whitened to a sickly pale and even though his eyes burn with hatred, his cigar wobbles in his teeth with fear.

The Luciano's olive cheeks have deepened to a rich, humiliated plum color and his dark eyes bore into his second.

Good. He should feel embarrassed that his own man is stealing in my establishment.

"It's nice to know there's honor among thieves, Luciano."

"Lucianos are no thieves," he counters.

Vinnie squirms beside him. Sweat prickles the eejit's forehead as if he's both angry and working hard to come up with a comeback at the same time.

"Aren't we all thieves?" my father jokes, trying to lighten the mood. "That's all the Garde is. A society of thieves with good PR."

"You even stole your own wife, Finneas. Like father, like son. It's funny how history repeats itself," the Muñoz chuckles along with the others while Luciano seems to relax. But I turn toward my father.

"What's the Muñoz going on about?"

"You didn't know?" the Milton asks and huffs a chuckle around his cigar. "It's why the O'Sheas hate your family in the first place. Your mother was promised to Charlie, but your father stole her away the night before her wedding. The only difference between you and your father is you likely saved your wife's life. The Baron's a monster with his women."

The truth in his last statement makes my blood boil, but I still can't get over the first half. "Dad, they're winding me up about you and Mam, right?"

My father's fair cheeks rosy up at the story. "It is the way they say. But your mother and I were in love first, and Charlie knew it. He wanted her for her family's power. I wanted her for her heart. Charlie may hate me for it, but I don't regret a single thing."

I said the same phrase to Lacey just this morning, and hearing my words from my father's mouth hits me in the chest. I knew my parents were in love, but I had no idea they nearly destroyed everything for each other.

The Luciano scoffs. "Love? What a ridiculous concept. You know what I think? Never fall in love with a woman, let alone a Garde woman. They only want to manipulate you for their own gain. Jesus, McKennon, you're a good man, but you're a romantic fool."

"Aye, perhaps. But us fools are the richest. Love makes a man strong. Greed makes him weak."

"No. Power and status make a man strong. Love makes him weak," the Luciano counters.

"Spoken like a man who's never felt it." My father gives him a pointed look and the Luciano glares a hole in his own cards.

"Maybe he's better off a cynic if falling in love makes him spout off sonnets like you, old friend." The Thomson's laugh lifts his wrinkles around his wide smile. "Your father's a real poet, Kian."

"Nah, if anything, I'm a philosopher. The poet was his mam. It just rubbed off on me."

"Either way, the world would be better if we could all lust for the women we marry instead of the women we fuck," the Milton chortles.

The room breaks out into laughter and my father raises his glass.

"May Kian be so lucky as to have found both in the same woman." The rest of us raise our glasses as he cheers, "*Sláinte is táinte*. To health and wealth, lads."

We all cheers and sip our drinks before returning to the game, but not before I catch that bastard Vinnie boldly making the same mistake he's made all night.

Son of a bitch.

"Now that the congratulations are out of the way," my father coughs and sits up. Feck. He's either got a bad hand, or he's about to piss me off. "I know it usually goes without saying, but keep this to ourselves for now. Other than a few loyal employees, you're the only ones who know this information. It won't be hard to figure out which one of you runs his mouth."

"Dad? Keep my marriage... quiet? Why the bloody feck would I do that?"

My father makes a big show of sorting his hand, uncomfortable with me questioning him in front of the group. But I don't care. This is shite.

"The original plan was to ruin the O'Sheas," he explains. "But we didn't care about the why of it all then, just revenge. Now you've aligned us with them and it's fallen on us to fix things. Thinking about this from all angles, it's as you said, laddie, the

Baron is new Garde. Why would the O'Sheas break our contract to betroth Lacey to *him*? Even if Charlie hates the McKennons for what I did to him decades ago, he's always looked out for the society. So why would he do something in direct opposition to what's best for everyone?"

"Because Charlie O'Shea would rather get shivved than let a McKennon be Keeper of the Garde?" The Muñoz jokes.

"Oh, the O'Shea is smarter than that," my father rumbles and shakes his head.

"I heard there was a murder at Rouge last night," the Thomson points out. "The girl had Lacey's fair skin, same hair color, costume, and everything."

Grimaces mar each face and curses float around the table. The Muñoz shakes his head.

"That has the Baron's stench all over it, Kian."

"Might be worth asking one of our friends on the force," my father proposes.

"Might be," I answer as air huffs out of my nose in frustration.

I had a feeling there was more to the Rouge murder. It's why I locked Lacey up in my suite to come to this meeting in the first place, to scope things out and keep her safe. But having the information said out loud by another Garde member and seconded by my dad confirms my fear that Monroe is playing dirty.

"Wasn't Monroe one of the financial managers in the O'Shea's businesses? Maybe he's got something to do with the O'Shea's arrest? Or trial, even?" the Luciano poses.

Alarm bells clang in my head, but I keep my face blank, not showing my hand. I don't want them coming to any conclusions that could be detrimental to Lacey. I need to find out what Monroe's got on the O'Shea myself.

I remain silent for a moment, organizing my own cards by value as I think everything over until I get the ace where I want it.

Keeping my marriage a secret is the last thing I want to do. I'd have that video of our midnight wedding playing on one of the many flashing billboards on the Strip if I could. But I can't shake the memory of Lacey's terrified sky-blue eyes when I threatened to send it to Monroe.

I nod to the dealer as I push my chips across the table. "I'm all in."

Out of the corner of my eye, I see my father's bushy brows rise. The slight movement makes me realize he's been watching me the whole time. By the way he regards me, I can tell he knows I'm already formulating a plan, but I don't want the rest of the room to hear it just yet.

"You're right, Dad. I'll figure out whatever Monroe and the O'Shea are up to. In the meantime, we need loyalty and silence. This society runs on secrets, I'm hoping I can count on you to keep mine as I've kept yours."

The families nod, but Vinnie's dark-brown eyes light up like he's finally figured out that comeback his two eejit brain cells came up with.

"The great wild ace doesn't want to show off? Nah, I don't buy it. What is it really, Kian?" His eyes suddenly widen in mock horror, putting on a show for everyone else as he asks, "Oh, shit. Maybe the virgin pussy wasn't all that good?"

I calmly leave my seat and hover near the roulette table until I find what I need. When I do, it's perfect timing with Vinnie shouting dramatically, focused on his audience.

"Wait? Was she *not* a virgin? Let's take bets, fellas. I've got a hundo on the Red Camellia being a whore—"

Crack.

His taunt is punctuated by his own bloodcurdling scream.

Scene 12

ROULETTE STAKES

Vinnie shrieks and clutches his wrist with his uninjured hand, eyes wide on my makeshift wooden stake pinning him to the table.

While Vinnie was insisting on making an enemy of me, I snatched the silver-painted wooden roulette rake, snapped it over my knee, and drove it through his hand into the surface of the poker table. Its green felt quickly blooms crimson as blood pours from the bastard's wound.

The family heads look on without pity. Instead, their expressions are filled with a mixture of contempt for Vinnie and a lust for bloodshed.

The rake's carved silver filigree glints in the overhead light as it sticks straight up to the ceiling. The sharp, broken end is embedded so deeply into the table that it doesn't move when I snatch Vinnie by his thinning black hair and hiss into his face.

"Try your pathetic sleight-of-hand tricks in my casino one more time and you'll be out of the Garde before you can collect your chips. Talk about my *wife* again, and even the fish won't feed off what's left of you. Got it?"

He nods frantically, "Y-yes, sir."

"Good. I knew we could come to an understanding. The Lucianos have always been a reasonable family."

"There are a few *idioti* every generation it seems," the Luciano mutters with a shake of his head at his cousin. "I apologize, McKennon friends. I'll deal with him in-house."

"See that you do."

I wrench the splintered end of the rake out of the back of Vinnie's hand with a twist, making him scream. Once it's out, he faints and his head thumps onto the table. His high-pitched shrieks cut off abruptly, creating the eerie sensation that they still echo faintly in the air. No longer able to hold a snakelike grip, his blood-soaked "personal deck" spills from his sleeve, fanning out underneath his injured hand. The metallic stench of blood is tart in my nostrils but tastes like sweet revenge. I don't revel in bloodshed, but I do enjoy a good comeuppance.

My father tsks. "The felt on these tables is impossible to really clean, you know."

"Consider it a business expense."

It'll be worth it if it reminds everyone of the cost of crossing a McKennon.

I select the ace from my own hand on the table and flick it against my fingers. The Luciano seems uneasy as his eyes dart from the card to his cousin.

His voice is low when he speaks, "Kian... I'll handle it. In-house."

I assess the anger furrowing his brow and his tense fingers steepled on the poker table before granting him a slight nod. The Luciano's shoulders relax a fraction, but it's the only true sign of emotion he shows as I point the ace at the rest of the seated table.

"Gentlemen. Can I count on you to keep this meeting discreet until I've figured out O'Shea's angle with Monroe?"

The chorus of agreement is all I need and I nod, taking that as my cue to go. Before I do, I place the ace back with the rest and flip my cards over to display the royal flush of diamonds. It's an unbeatable hand, but I leave the pot, only taking two ten thousand dollar chips from it. They have the least amount of blood splatter, but I still wipe them on Vinnie's god-awful tracksuit for good measure.

"Oh, and if your cousin comes back with you, Luciano, he wears a goddamn suit. This isn't the fecking Sopranos."

The Luciano crosses his arms and shakes his head at his unconscious capo. "He won't be coming back. A cheat is no cousin of mine. But your secret is safe with us, I assure you."

"Fair enough." I straighten my charcoal-gray lapels and crimson tie before flipping one of the poker chips to the dealer.

She catches it easily and pockets it without any emotion. Red Room employees have already proven their loyalty to the McKennon name time and time again. I know she'll keep quiet. Hell, I'm sure this isn't even the worst secret she's had to keep working as a McKennon loyal.

I give the men a mock two-finger salute off my forehead. "Until next time, gentlemen, I think I'll bid you *adieu*. Keep my chips as an apology for ruining your game."

I don't need to remind them again to keep their mouths shut. They know McKennon loyalty only goes as far as theirs, and they fecking need us if anarchy ensues.

"Talk soon, son," my father calls at my back as I turn. The others may not be able to hear it, but the pride and humor lifting his voice make me grin. "What can I say, gentlemen? The house always wins," I hear him chuckle as I exit through the curtains.

Merek greets me with a wide smile. "Sounds like it was an eventful game."

"You don't know the half of it." I glance around to see if anyone else could've heard Vinnie's screams, but the high roller room is empty.

"Cleared everyone out as soon as I heard Vinnie talking shit."

"Good man." I pat him on the back and walk on, pulling my mobile out before I call over my shoulder. "Keep your mobile on, mate. Let me know if you hear any rumblings of begrudgery from a certain Italian."

"Sure thing. Oh, and Key?"

"Yeah?" I lift my head up from my screen and turn to see mirth in my mate's smug face.

"If you want to get a woman to like you, you have to be likable first."

"Feck right off, arsehole." I roll my eyes and grin before turning back around.

"Sorry, Key. I don't know Irish," Merek laughs. "Sometimes you say 'fuck,' but sometimes you say this 'feck' word. How am I supposed to know what you mean?"

"Alright, then, *fuck* right off, *asshole*." I flip him the bird and he chuckles at my back as I exit the high roller room.

The music fills the space again, reassuring me even more that Vinnie's cries of pain were muffled by the blaring songs, the whirling notes of slot machines, and the Red Room's thick, noise-dampening curtains.

Lorenzo, the bouncer with the wandering eye, watches a porter like a hawk as the unassuming man mops the floor ten feet away from him. The casino janitor is one I recognize and has been with my family for decades. As I pass Lorenzo, I jut my chin toward the man working hard to keep my casino presentable.

"He's good."

"Yes, sir," Lorenzo replies to my back while I approach the porter.

"Mr. Logan, a word?"

"Oh, Mr. McKennon." He stops mopping and stands aside to let me by. "Careful, it's slippery."

"Actually, you're just the man I want to see. Are you in the Red Room today, Hugo?"

"Yes, sir."

"Perfect." I toss him the extra chip I took from the table as payment. "I seem to have made a bit of a mess. Would you take care of it for me?"

"Of course, sir, I've seen my fair share of messes in the Red

Room. I—" He blinks at the chip and his eyes widen. "Sir, this... this is ten thous—"

"A thank-you for all your years of hard work, loyalty, and *discretion.*"

I spin around and head through the convoluted maze of slot machines and tables before Hugo tries to insist the chip is too much money. He does it every time I tip him, regardless of the amount, but he deserves all that and more for cleaning up a crime scene. Like he said, it's not the first time he's done it, but it won't be the last either. I need to make sure my employees can endure the shite I pull every now and then.

As I navigate the casino toward the elevator, I finally get to pull up my security app to check on my wee captive bride. Last time I saw her, she was pacing and talking to herself. She never stops moving, that one, and I love watching her like this, with no one else's expectations curbing her energy. Being around her is the spark of fire I've craved in my life and I hope it never goes out.

Once the screen pulls up and the sight of my living room comes into full focus, my eyes narrow to see it better. When I take it all in, a mixture of shock, irritation, and pride springs up from my chest and escapes in a laugh.

"Jesus, Mary, and Joseph, *tine*, what am I going to do with you?"

I press the button for the suite's speakers at the bottom of the screen. As I lift the receiver to my lips, I adopt the low growl that seems to both set my wife off and turn her on.

"What the feck do you think you're doing, Lacey McKennon?"

Scene 13

SOLO TANTRUM

ccording to the microwave, it's been twenty-seven minutes and I still don't have my shit together.

The first eight consisted of me raging against the locked door and trying to find a key. The next nineteen were spent wallowing in self-pity.

During the pity phase, I began to feel ashamed that I'd wallowed longer than I'd raged. Then I realized I'd been whining over being locked up in a penthouse prison when my own father is in *actual* jail. But that got me worrying about what will happen once the Baron finds out I'm already married. On top of all that, visions of a dead woman I've never met flashed through my brain on repeat, making me feel guiltier than ever because I can't stop wondering if the murder at Rouge has something to do with me. Then I berated myself for being arrogant enough to think everything is about me.

And while I paced, stretched, and fidgeted about the suite, ruminating and trying to calm myself down, I caught my reflection in a mirror—still in my ridiculous tulle Halloween costume —and I got pissed all over again.

I made the stupid decision to sleep with a total stranger, but it was supposed to be my last night of fun. Now I've got a marriage and a potential mini-McKennon to worry about.

Oh God.

That last reminder makes me queasy, which makes me spiral into how insufferable I'd be if I ever got morning sickness.

It'd serve him right having to take care of me puking my brains out.

I pause at the thought.

No other Garde man I know has ever stepped foot near his pregnant wife, let alone helped her when she had morning sickness. So why would I expect Kian to be the exception?

Because he is.

"Okay, brain, you're going to have to stop having a full-on conversation with me right now. It's getting weird."

Anything is better than romanticizing the man who kidnapped me, so I shake my head to clear my mind and go back to wallowing.

I was a "Garde good girl," as Roxy put it. Or at least I was so good at pretending, people didn't notice the difference. I know my role. I never embarrass my family or ruin alliances. I even tricked myself into thinking I was the one who was choosing to marry the Baron.

And now that carefully curated facade of a life is being challenged by my family's enemy because of *one* unforgivably stupid decision.

Fucking Kian McKennon.

I was willing to go quietly down the aisle with the Baron smirking behind his fading, dirty-blond goatee. But now that Kian has stolen all of my so-called "options," the frustration, desperation, and hopelessness of the last few years boil over and spill out as rage.

"Fuck you, Kian McKennon!"

I scream the words over and over again at the top of my lungs until my aching throat rebels and grows hoarse at the end. A frustrated groan rumbles from my chest and I collapse onto the leather couch dramatically. The flair actually helps me not feel so sorry for myself, but it does nothing for that *other* frustration still burning in my core.

Screw Kian for denying me an orgasm. Yeah, sure, I shouldn't have slapped him, but he *spanked* me!

And I liked it.

"Nope. Nope. No, I didn't. And even if I did, I'm not thinking about it."

Propping myself up on my elbows, I stare at the door, wondering where the hell Kian went off to. Probably a strip club if his hard-on and innuendo were any indications.

I rub the wisp of pain floating in my chest.

No! No. No. No. I will not feel jealousy over that man. I lie back down and stretch my legs on the couch while I attempt to channel my thoughts into something worthwhile.

When I dance, it helps to visualize my body moving and flowing into each position. Coming up with strategies to navigate life in the Garde is like coming up with my own choreography. It's usually easy to figure out my next steps. But Kian has thrown off my routine and I'm at a loss for what to do.

At least my head doesn't hurt anymore, although the screaming hasn't done my throat any favors. My body and mind are nowhere near peak shape thanks to the alcohol, bad decisions, and whatever drug Kian injected in me.

Prick.

"You're a prick! You hear me, Kian? You are a PRICK!"

I huff and roll off the couch—just as theatrically as I landed on it—and trudge to the kitchen. For the thousandth time in thirty-something minutes, I'm busy talking to myself and wishing he could hear me... when my eyes spot the speaker by the door.

The one he taunted me through.

Can he hear me even if I don't engage the speaker? And if he can...

"Can you see me, too?" I whisper and begin to tiptoe around the room, my head on a swivel. I don't know what I'm searching for, exactly, until I find them.

Nestled in the ceiling corners are small, round domes the size of golf balls and the same crisp white color as the walls. They're just like the ones that hid security cameras in my house growing up. Does Kian's bodyguard have a security app on his phone?

No. There's no way Kian would've wanted someone else seeing me get "punished" earlier.

But *Kian* would definitely have the app on his phone. Hell, he's probably watching me lose my mind right now.

Only one way to find out.

I carefully school my face as I enter the kitchen and nonchalantly use the hair tie on my arm to tame my tangled tresses into a practical high pony. If I'm going to fucking war, I'm not going to let bed head stop me.

There's no alcohol in the kitchen—or anywhere in the suite, for that matter. I checked during the wallowing phase. If there had been any, I'd have already drowned my sorrows in the bottom of a bottle.

I settle for a glass of cool water from the refrigerator and lean back against the counter to sip it. I'm in the perfect spot to see through the kitchen's open door into the living room and its priceless decor.

The room is displayed like a museum, reminding me of an article I read in a modern architecture and interior design magazine. The featured owner was a single bachelor who hardly ever spent any time enjoying his home because he traveled for work. Even though the magazine tried to glamorize the enviable style of the rich and famous, in real life, it always looks so... *lonely.*

If Kian wants me to have his children—not that I ever would —but hypothetically, if he wants me to, they're not going to live in a place like this. *I* grew up in a place like this, one where children are seen but not heard, and even with parents that loved me, I hated it.

Most Garde children are just a means to an end, a way for parents to ensure the family inheritance stays within their lineage. The height of the family tree is more important than the living branches within. All one needs to secure the windfall is a single heir. That's the only goal the Garde's greedy, loveless marriages ever shoot for.

In the society's early days, infighting among siblings was a huge problem. There are plenty of stories about one child destroying, ruining, or even murdering their own kin just for money. Sometimes the parents even got involved, choosing sides and favorites and covering up the crimes. It was sick.

Would Kian be like that as a father? Does he only want an heir so the pretty things in his living room stay in the McKennon name?

What would he do if all his pretty things just suddenly... broke?

As I meander through the kitchen, sipping my water, I casually try to open drawers, looking for forks, knives, or any sharp objects that'd be a good weapon or tool for destruction. But in this suite that's totally unsuitable for kids, Kian has childproofed everything. I'm annoyed if he actually thinks that could stop me... but then I get even *more* irritated when I can't for the life of me figure out how to get past the damn things.

When I finally give up, I finish the last half of my water all in one gulp and set the glass on the countertop with a little too much force. The clinking sound makes me wince.

"Shit." I snatch it off the marble to make sure I didn't... chip... the...

Crystal.

A wicked smile curves my lips.

Perfect.

I raise my arm high and slam the glass against the black-and-white checkered marble flooring. The thousand-dollar glass shatters into just as many pieces.

"Oh look at that, Kian. A dollar for every shard." A manic

laugh bubbles out of me and I point to the security camera in the corner of the room. "You're going to regret making me your wife, *husband*."

I ransack each cabinet until I find every porcelain plate, crystal glass, and dinnerware piece that Kian owns. Each one meets a shattering end as I pitch them at the closest hard surface and revel in the cacophony of chaos. When I'm out of breakable tableware, I search through the glittering debris for a piece that's long enough to use. But as I'm sifting, a particularly sharp shard embeds itself into my bare foot.

"*Ow*, ow, ow, ow, *oww*-ah, *Jesus*."

Watching my step, I hobble up onto a clean countertop and gingerly pull the fragment out before dumping it in the trash can stowed inside a cabinet beneath the counter. I unfold one of the thick paper napkins beside the sink next to me and press it to the cut to staunch the bleeding. After a minute or so, I pull it away to analyze the damage.

Only a sliver of skin has been sliced open and it shouldn't require stitches to heal. Blood has thoroughly soaked the *M* monogram on the napkin, though, so I grab another to wrap around my heel, and hold it until the bleeding mostly stops before tossing both napkins into the trash.

Undeterred from my mission, I check the marble tile before I carefully slide off the counter and use the balls of my feet to awkwardly march into the living room to do some real damage.

My first casualty is a gorgeous Versace pillow and I turn to one of the cameras and smile sweetly as I unzip the closure. My evil plan would be much more satisfying with a knife, but I don't want to chance getting cut by glass again, so I can make do with moderate mayhem rather than total destruction for now.

Tiny feathers burst out of the pillow and fly away, and I move on to the next, and the next, and the next after that, without stopping. My pace grows feverish until feathers drift around me and rest at my feet like soft confetti.

"You have more decorative pillows than my mom, you know!" I yell. "Well, you used to."

When I don't get a response, I keep going, grabbing the leather cushions off the couch and tossing them at anything fragile I can see.

"What's the point of a fluffy... feather... pillow... if the fabric case is hard as hell? Huh?" I shout into the empty space.

I'm beginning to feel silly that I keep putting on a show without knowing if there's an audience. But I'm on a roll now, riding the anger that's been nagging me for years.

If it's fragile, I break it. If it has threads, I unravel it. And if it's light enough, I throw it. Nothing's safe in my path and I'm a whirlwind until I'm out of shit to ruin and the entire room is in disarray.

When the air-conditioning hits the feathers just right, they catch the breeze and spin away. Deconstructed blankets are strewn about in tangled threads, and cushion cases lie haphazardly around the room. Steel and glass art jut up from the floor like debris after a storm.

I take a deep breath and settle my hands on my hips, basking in the first completely unhinged moment I've ever let myself have.

But the triumph I expect never comes. Instead, disappointment seeps in, clearing the red haze from my vision.

I glance up at the emotionless cameras and plop onto the soft white rug in front of the faux fireplace. A cloud of feathers poofs up and drifts back down around me. My fingers fidget with one of the wool strands left over from a cashmere blanket I massacred.

"Where the hell are you?" I mutter, hating that I care so much about the answer.

"What the feck do you think you're doing, Lacey McKennon?"

And... just like that, I'm pissed all over again.

"Lacey O'Shea!" I yell at the speaker near the door. "Fake marriage or not, I still haven't changed my name!"

"An oversight I'll remedy immediately, I can fecking assure you. What the bloody hell are you doing to my suite?" The emotion behind his Irish lilt gives me the reaction I've been dying for since I threw the first crystal glass.

"*Your* suite?" I ask, a coy smile forming on my lips now that I know he can see me. "But we're *married*, baby. What's yours is mine, right?"

A growl echoes over the speakers and slams into my core. My pent-up orgasm from earlier floods to life again, and another idea filters through my mind. I'm kind of mad I didn't think of it before. It would've been a hell of a stress reliever.

"What's mine is yours alright and your arse is mine in less than ten minutes."

Promise?

I bite my tongue to keep from saying it out loud.

"About that..." I arch backward to slowly lie down on the bed of feathers, cashmere, and cotton I've made for myself. "I didn't like the way you treated *my ass* this morning."

"Don't lie to me, Lace. I felt how wet you were. You were putty in my hands. I could've slipped inside you and made you come in one thrust."

A delicious shiver erupts goose bumps in a wave across my skin. His dark chuckle rumbles over the speakers, but I keep my wits about me this time.

"Yeah, well you didn't... so I guess that leaves matters in my own hands. Now how on earth should I go about doing that, hmm?"

Determined to go through with my threat, I position myself so that one of the cameras can see my bare pussy underneath my tulle skirt. I spread my legs wide before snaking my fingers down to dip into my core.

"Lacey..." He swallows after saying my name. The warning in his deep voice makes my clit pulse and I immediately start swirling my fingers around it. "That cunt is mine. Your orgasms are mine. You... are *mine*. If you make yourself come before I get there—"

"Yeah, yeah, yeah…" I huff breathily as I slip two fingers into my already slick pussy. I push off my heels to get a better angle, but the pressure on my injured foot makes me hiss.

"What's wrong, *tine*?" Kian's voice is dark and delicious, promising the sweetest of sins. "Is your swollen, needy pussy sore from my cock? Or is your arse aching from my hand?"

"No," I grumble and shift my weight off my injured foot.

He's not wrong, though. My pussy *is* sore thanks to his size and I can almost feel his large hand still spanking my sensitive ass cheek. But I'd sooner become a nun than admit that to my fake husband.

"If you wait for me, *tine*, I'll be gentle," he croons as my fingers stroke against my G-spot and the heel of my palm massages my clit. "I'll dine on that sweet pussy, making sure you're ready for me. Then I'll thrust into you deep and slow until your cunt squeezes the life out of my cock as you come."

"Why should I—" I moan loudly, partly to rile him further but mostly because I'm quickly approaching the brink. My other hand tugs my corset down and plays with my peaked nipple. I badly want his tongue there instead, but I don't want to stop now. "Why should I w-wait for you when you've been out getting off without me? Was she… was she pretty at least?"

Wait, why the hell did I ask that?

There's a pause and I don't realize I've stopped breathing until he answers.

"There's no one but you, *tine*. There hasn't been for a while."

My fingers still completely. Hadn't he said he was going to a strip club? Did he say those words exactly? Or did I infer it? I'm about to ask when an elevator ding sounds from the speaker.

For the first time, it occurs to me that he could be saying these things with an audience. A confusing mixture of humiliation, shame, hurt, and desire swirl through me at the thought.

"Where are you?"

"Somewhere secluded enough that no one will hear me seduce my wife or hear her sweet moans."

A frisson of pleasure builds inside my core—but *not* because of the rumbling voice coming through the speakers all around me. I only saw the one beside the door, but Kian must've changed where it outputs because his sexy accent now plays throughout the suite in surround sound.

"I-I don't need your seduction, Kian. I can come—" I draw out a long moan, and I slip my fingers out from my core to focus on my clit and chase my orgasm again. "I can come all on my own."

"I'm also close enough that if you come before I get there, I swear I'll make you regret it, Lace."

"I said I don't need you! I don't need anyone! You men are the useless ones, not women."

There's silence on the other end, so I perfect the pressure on my clit. My lower belly tightens, bracing my muscles to feel the rush that's on the verge of rippling through me. Another moan slips out and I cup my whole breast and massage it hard.

"The things I can do to you and the way I can make you feel make me far from useless, wife."

"It feels so good without you, though."

His growl nearly pushes me over the edge, "For feck's sake, Lacey. This is your last warning. If you come without me—"

I cry out as my fingertips finally find that perfect rhythm and a gentle wave of pleasure flows over me. It's nice and somewhat satisfying, but from the way I'm carrying on, you'd think it was the best orgasm of my life—

The door crashes open and slams shut. I sit up to see the molten gold flecks in Kian's hazel eyes shining and his dark-auburn hair askew like he's been ripping through it all the way here. With every breath, his strong chest nearly bursts from his dress shirt underneath his suit jacket, and his cock is so painfully strained against his slacks that I can see the piercing's imprint in the fabric.

Good. I hope his dick suffered having to watch me come without him.

"See? I didn't need you at all."

He shrugs out of his jacket and tosses it to the floor as he prowls toward me. A hungry, crazed smile slowly forms on his face.

"Oh, you're going to wish you'd waited for me, *tine*."

Scene 14

VIOLENT DELIGHT

I have the distinct feeling I might've made a mistake.

Kian somehow toes off his shoes without even stopping as he stalks closer. I scoot back and a nervous laugh escapes me, but I play it off with a smug smile.

"Why wait when I can do it all on my own? You already denied me once—"

He lunges for me and I scramble away, but he catches my ankles and yanks me to him. The move drags my dress up to my hips, leaving me naked from the waist down, and he kneels between my open thighs.

"Kian! What're you—"

"Your safe word is '*is tú mo rogha.*' Use it when you really want me to stop. I won't until you use it, am I clear?"

"A '*safe word?*' Really? I thought it was supposed to be *one* word, not a whole damn sentence. And why can't it be something easy like 'pineapple?!'"

I've obviously heard of safe words before, but only in the context of sex clubs and movies. I didn't think people used them in the real world, or at least not in *my* real world. Garde men don't stop if they want something. They just take.

He stops suddenly to take my hands in his calloused palms

and leans over me to fill my vision. The rich smoky scent of cigars and amber fills my nostrils. His hazel eyes are intense as he looks in mine.

"This is important, Lacey. *Is... tú... mo... rogha.*"

I narrow my eyes, watching his sensual lips form around each word before I try my best to repeat him.

"Iss... too... mu... row-ah."

A spark glints in his eyes and he nods. "*Is tú mo rogha.*"

"Iss too mu row-ah."

The air is thick and heavy around us. I don't know what I just said, but it definitely means more to him than "pineapple." My heart thunders in my chest and I want to ask, but I'm afraid I'll like the answer... and I'm not ready for that.

"Yes, *tine. Is tú mo rogha.*"

He's brimming with energy and my body aches to connect with his, even after already coming once.

"Iss too mu row-ah is my safe word," I agree. "I'll use it when I need to."

"Feck, you're perfect," he mutters before he dives between my legs, sucking on my clit and easily sinking two fingers into my wet pussy.

"Holy shit—*Kian*! You're just going to—*oh my God.*" I seize his hair with one hand and a fistful of cashmere and feathers in the other while I try to find purchase.

I'm already primed and ready, thanks to my own fingers, and Kian wastes no time curving his up and stroking me inside while his tongue dances with my clit on the outside. As I climb to the peak I didn't have time to fully descend, I brace myself for him stopping and denying me again.

My eyes slam shut as I concentrate on hiding my reactions so he won't use an impending orgasm against me. But despite my best efforts, my body tenses and my breath comes in ragged pants. I tug his hair hard to direct his tongue where I need him, praying he won't stop as I finally reach that precipice...

"*Kian!*"

I tumble down, down, down. My pussy pulses against his fingers as my body contracts and jolts with my orgasm. It's intense, much better than anything I've ever achieved on my own, and I cling to his hair, crying out at the rush of bliss thrumming through my veins.

"Kian, oh my god. I was afraid you were going to stop again." A light laugh rolls from me until I look down and see Kian's eyes.

Dark need hardens his jaw and sharpens his cheeks above his scruffy five-o'clock shadow. He withdraws his fingers and crawls over me before attacking me with a kiss.

The heady taste of my arousal overwhelms me. Against my better judgment, I melt into him and wrap my arms around his neck. His tongue invades my mouth and I accept him fully, moaning into his.

We dance with tongues, bites, and nips and his hands roam over my body, softly caressing, massaging, and kneading. His long fingers untie the small bow at the top of my front-lace corset. Just that simple release pops it ajar, and he yanks both sides of the sweetheart neckline apart, spilling my breasts out of the enclosure they'd been stuffed in.

"Mm, that *alone* feels orgasmic."

His low chuckle makes my pussy spasm. "I promise I'll do better than a corset, *tine*."

Once the corset is unraveled, the rest of the dress falls apart, and Kian makes quick work tugging it down my body.

The cashmere is gentle on my skin, but gentle isn't what I need right now. I'm angry, confused, and so fucking turned on. I want Kian's heat and the fury I caused to join with the inferno already raging in me.

"Need to feel you..." I mumble against his lips and tug his tie, loosening it. He flicks his wrist, removing it deftly, and the rest of the crimson silk drifts to the ground.

As soon as it's gone, I attack his shirt, unbuttoning it until he rips it apart himself, popping buttons onto the ground. Once he shrugs out of it, he wraps his hand around my neck to guide me back onto the rug, where he gives me another scorching kiss.

His abdominal muscles contract and relax underneath my fingertips as he caresses down my arms. The featherlight touch is sensual and careful, but it's still almost too much after two orgasms.

When his trail reaches my palms, he intertwines our fingers to hold my hands and my heart skips at the intimacy. When he stretches them over my head and settles his weight between my legs, his searing hot chest makes my aching nipples tingle and I arch up from the floor with a moan. He dives his tongue into my mouth, distracting me from the new pressure tightening around my wrists. I bite his lip and he growls before pulling away from our kiss. A giggle escapes me and I try to sit up with him, but something tugs me back.

My brow furrows and I look up to find his tie hooked on one of the coffee table legs and knotted around my wrists.

"Kian, what the—"

I stop midsentence and really study his expression for the first time.

While desire and a whole slew of confusing emotions drive me, it's clear from the intense way Kian's hungry eyes are eating up every bare inch of me that something much more primal fuels him. His gaze never leaves my body as he unzips his pants and springs free. The silver piercing at the end of his long thick cock glints in my periphery, but I'm so enraptured by his stare that I don't look down to fully enjoy the view.

"Kian?" I hedge quietly.

It's enough to bring him out of whatever trance has taken over him. An evil smile carves across his face as he wraps my legs around him and positions himself at my entrance. My heartbeat races when he bends down to whisper against my lips.

"You thought denial was bad, *tine*? Let's try overstimulation."

My brow tugs at the center. "Over...what—"

Kian impales me before I can finish my question and doesn't

give me any time to adjust. He pounds into me hard, in and out at a punishing speed.

"Kian!"

He sits back on his heels again and yanks me up his thighs, forcing my lower half into an angle that makes the ball of his piercing drag mercilessly across my G-spot. I moan and squirm on his brutally thick shaft until his fingers dig into my upper thighs, holding me steady as he moves.

"Kian, wait! It's too much—"

"No, I gave you the option, Lacey," he growls. "You could've had sweet, soft, and slow. You could've been rewarded for trusting me today. I wanted that."

He wanted sweet?

"But your only job was to leave this pussy"—he slaps my clit and I cry out—"*alone.* Not only did you disobey me, you fecking flaunted your disobedience in my face. I nearly came in my pants at the sight of you stroking your glistening cunt. After that? Game fecking over. You could've had sweet, *wife,* but you chose rough when you didn't choose me."

He scoops his hips and the pierced tip of his cock hits a deep spot that immediately sends shivers of pleasure rushing through me.

"Oh my god!"

He switches to shallow pumps and stares at our connection with awe. "Look at us, *tine,* the way your cunt sucks me in. Your pretty pink pussy is red and swollen, but she's still a greedy little slut trying to swallow my cock."

I wish I could touch him, but his tie has no give to it, so I settle for driving my hips to meet his. When yet another orgasm comes out of nowhere, I chase the high until my muscles weaken from pleasure.

"Goddamn, Lacey," Kian leans over me and lifts my ass as he keeps pumping. "I can feel you come on my cock. Did you know that?"

He slows his thrusts and bites my ear, sending a shock of pain shooting down my spine and goose bumps erupting on my skin. Despite the sensory overload, my pussy is so desperate to please him it tries to flutter again, but I'm totally spent.

Or at least... I *thought* I was.

He drives into my overworked inner muscles in long, deep strokes until another tingle of pleasure ignites. I've never come more than once, let alone twice. And now, *four* times? This is insanity.

"There it is, *tine*. Let me feel you come again."

"No... Kian, I don't think I can." Even now, the flame flickers, but it's weaker than the rest, like those muscles are too tired to keep up the race.

"You will." He shifts and massages my clit with his thumb, drawing a moan from me as he slams into me again. "Today, you stole an orgasm that was meant for me. Give me one more and we'll call it even."

I try to shake my head, but his finger adds more pressure and he pumps into my exhausted core with long, deep strokes.

"You may be disobedient, wife, but your body answers to me." *Thrust.* "My fingers, my tongue, my cock." He punctuates each word with another plunging stroke. "You're all mine, Lacey. *Only* mine. I made sure of that."

He bites my throat and sucks so hard that the building flame explodes into a bonfire. My legs tighten involuntarily around his waist and I meet him with every pounding beat. We're fused together in a punishing dance. My mind and heart aren't sure how much more we can take, but my body is ready for whatever our new master thinks we can handle.

His fingers bruise my thighs and my inner muscles strain to grip him until he furiously increases his pace and I can no longer keep up. My pulse thumps in my ears and I cry out as another relentless, slow-moving wave of euphoria pours over me.

"Kian! Please!"

I don't know what I'm begging for, but this new tsunami of pleasure is unlike anything I've felt before. More like a constant state of hyperarousal right on the edge of pain than an erotic dance with a beginning, middle, and end.

"Kian, please! I can't anymore. Please!"

His thrusts slow, giving us both room to breathe. At this speed, I can feel his cock's sleek barbell again as it grazes over my G-spot. His tan skin glistens with sweat and his chest rises and falls with his panting breaths. But he never stops. He maintains the new pace and wraps his hand around my neck while using the other to gently massage my breast. His velvet tongue brushes against the shell of my ear, giving me a full-body shiver.

"One more, *tine*. Just one more."

I shake my head. "No, Kian. Please. I need... I need a break."

He growls against my neck above where his fingers begin to squeeze, and I moan at the vibration against my skin.

"You know what to say if you really want me to stop."

Is tú mo rogha.

It's on the tip of my tongue, but I bite my swollen lip. Excitement and pride light up his face and my heart soars.

"There's my *tine*. Give me one last one."

"Please, Kian. I really... I really don't think I can." My eyelids flutter closed, even their weight too heavy to hold up.

He suddenly shifts me in his arms and captures my breast, sucking nearly half of it into his mouth and making my eyes snap open. Not neglecting the other one, he pinches and tweaks my nipple between his thumb and forefinger. My sensitive peaks are on fire with sensation as his tongue and fingers flick over them, sending light stinging zings straight to my clit. His thrusts grow stronger, his piercing an added pleasure along my channel. When he ruthlessly bites my breast, I cry out, only to get cut off as he wraps his hand around my throat.

He loosens his grip for just a split second, prompting me to take a huge breath before he tightens again. As my heartbeat thumps strong underneath his fingers, my skin, muscles, core—everything—begins to pulse with it, building into blinding ecstasy. I lose my mind to the heightened awareness and my vision fades at the edges. My body bursts into flames as the fire within takes over in a conflagration of delicious euphoria and sensation.

My small moan vibrates against his fingers and Kian groans.

"Feck, Lacey. I knew you had another one in you. Come with me, my gorgeous wife. I'm almost there."

He sits up and leans over me, his hand still wrapped tightly around my neck. It isn't until the pressure on my hands releases that I realize he removed my binding. My arms feel like they're floating as I try to bring them back down, and the rest of me drifts with them.

Everything dims in and out as Kian grips my hip. His eyes rove over me like a victorious warrior who's just conquered his enemy. And he sort of has.

Pleasure rises to the surface of my skin, bubbling just underneath as if it's ready to boil over at any moment and my face swells and pulses from his grip on my neck. He swears as he moves from my hip to massage my clit with his thumb. My eyes drift closed again and my nails dig into his forearm as my legs tremble for release.

I'm almost dreading the inevitable, like I'm about to leap from a twirling pirouette without knowing if there will be a floor to catch me.

"Fuck, this is it, baby. Come with me. One more time for your husband."

At his command, my eyes open to witness him come. Last night, his face was dark in the dressing room. But here, in the light of day, his ecstasy is plain on his face.

His neck strains with the force of holding back and his hazel eyes burn into mine as he grits his teeth. Veins on his temples pulse with his thrusts.

But when his thumb swirls faster on my clit again, I lose all focus.

"I said, come with me, wife."

One long, deliberate stroke ends with his piercing hitting the perfect deep spot in my channel. His hand on my throat finally lets go and I gasp to breathe.

My body detonates, racking me with waves and waves of delirious rapture. It flows through me and Kian cries out as his thrusts grow wild.

His stern features crumple as he comes. My vision blurs and all I can see is Kian's ecstasy while I battle my own. It's taken me prisoner, holding me captive as I fully submit until I can't take it anymore.

"Iss too mu row-ah! Iss too mu row-ah! Please... please..." I scream out, on the verge of tears as Kian finishes his final stroke inside me, securing himself between my thighs.

Exhaustion slams into me and I can no longer hold my legs up, but he catches them and wraps me in his arms as he sits up, holding me tight against his heaving pecs. The crashing waves recede, returning my vision and hearing back to me slowly, making me realize I'm still chanting my safe word. When Kian shifts underneath me, I dig my nails into his back.

"No, iss too mu row-ah, Kian... please. No more."

"Shh, shh, *tine*. You did so good for me, baby. I've got you. It's over." He strokes my back in smooth circles and rocks me gently as he whispers, "*Is tú mo rogha*, Lacey."

Scene 15

GENTLE TRUTHS

K ian curses as his cock slips out of me and I gasp at the sudden emptiness. The loss slams into my chest and my eyes burn with tears.

What the hell?

Little rivulets run silently down my cheeks as he gathers me in his arms and picks me up bridal style. I cling to him like a lifeline, but I know he won't let me fall.

That thought reminds me of last night when I just *knew*, without a shadow of a doubt, that he would catch me during our sensual dance. Why did trust come so naturally with him then?

Why does it now?

I try to push the question away, but I don't know how much longer that will keep working before I have to confront how he makes me feel. The thought makes me shiver in his arms.

"I've got you. You'll feel better in just a second. I'll take care of you," he reassures me and I snuggle against his warm chest.

I feel heavy in my body and I'm not even the one having to carry me around. His hand presses into my back, caressing my spine, while the other supports my ass as my languid body threatens to fall. He walks us through the suite until we reach the en suite bathroom.

"Can you stand?" he asks.

When I grunt my response, he chuckles. "I'll set you here then."

He places me on the edge of the tub and does a double take at the tears on my face.

"Oh, sweet *tine*. I'm going to take good care of you, baby." He wipes my damp cheeks before kissing my forehead.

"Why am I crying?" I whisper quietly and swipe angrily at my weeping eyes, embarrassed.

But Kian is gracious and gentle with his answer as he fills a tub the size of a Jacuzzi with water.

"It's the endorphins. Your body doesn't know what to do with so much pleasure forced on it all at once. That many orgasms have sated you to exhaustion, while your mind is confused and overwhelmed. Don't worry, I know how to help."

He pours some salts into the rising water and a sweet vanilla-and-orchid scent wafts into the air.

"A bath? That'll fix everything?"

"Trust me, Lacey." His voice is playful as he goes about making the perfect bath, naked and unaffected by my skepticism.

I scowl and lean back against the wall to watch him work.

The edge of the tub is cool beneath me and the cold wall almost hurts my overly sensitive skin. But the steam from the bath and the soothing aroma seep into me, making me relax further and I close my eyes.

"*Tine*, stand for me." My eyelids drift open again to see the tub is nearly full and Kian's hand is out for me to hold. "I want to get you into the tub safely."

I nod and let him guide me into the nearly scalding water. It feels amazing on my skin as I dip my toes and climb in. I stand in the center, not ready to dunk just yet, and I'm soaking in the warmth that reaches my knees when I feel an unfamiliar sensation between my legs. I look down to see Kian's cum dripping down my inner thighs and I gasp.

Shit.

I've *never* not used a condom, and here I've gone and done it twice with a madman.

What the hell is wrong with me?

Anxiety floods my veins and I grab the closest hand towel to clean it up, but Kian reaches over the edge of the tub and snatches my wrist.

"Don't."

"But, Kian—"

His stare is pure possession and I'm caught in the intensity of it as he gently pulls me toward him.

"Open," he commands and I step wider without thinking. His hazel gaze leaves mine as he scoops the cum leaking from me and dips his finger back into my core to coat my channel with his essence. The motion makes me wince and moan at the same time, my body confused as to whether this is pain or pleasure.

"Now close."

My legs obey instantly, slamming my thighs together as soon as he leaves my entrance.

"When you sit in the bath, keep them together until I say open."

I shake my head. "Why?"

"Do it, or we'll go for five more."

My eyes flare wide. I back away and try to maneuver into the water with my legs tight together like a vise. It's much deeper than I anticipated, rising just above my breasts as I sink in.

"Mm, this feels good."

The heat soothes the muscles I didn't realize were aching. I close my eyes and begin to lie back, but a splash catches my attention. I turn around to see Kian's huge dick swinging just above me at half-mast.

"Um... what're you doing?"

"Getting in."

I scoff and move to climb out, but Kian is too fast. He hooks his arm around my waist and nestles behind me before I even realize what's happening. When I try to wriggle away again, he tugs me back to him easily, sloshing water up the sides.

"You're always trying to run away from me, *tine*. Just stop and soak this in for a moment, yeah?"

My scowl scrunches my forehead and I glare at his toes underneath the water on the other side of the tub as if they're at fault.

Even if Kian could see my annoyance, I don't think he'd care. It's probably for the best because my irritation quickly subsides as he holds me close. Despite his rock-hard thighs, he's surprisingly comfortable. I settle against him and bask in his warmth and strength. I've never felt so protected and needy at the same time. It's... confusing.

But when his length grows harder against my lower back, I tense. The corded muscles in his arms stiffen around me like I'll try to flee again and he chuckles into my hair just above my ear.

"It's not my fault you're waking him back up. You keep moving."

My heartbeat races at the prospect of teasing him more, but my pussy aches, reminding me that I desperately need a break. I try my best to relax and sit still for once in my life. After a few moments, Kian rewards me by carefully tugging my hair free from my ponytail. My scalp relaxes as my strawberry-blonde hair falls in a curtain. The ends float in the water, turning ruby red around me and I watch them drift about.

With Kian out of my direct vision, I finally have the courage to ask the question I was too afraid to ask earlier when he was staring so intensely above me.

"Kian?"

"Yeah?"

"What did my, um, safe word mean? Iss too mu row-ah."

There's a breath of a pause before he grumbles against my neck and pours soap into a washcloth.

"It means 'pain in my arse.' Now stop moving, or I won't be able to wash you before I fuck you again and none of this will work."

"Oh, nice one. I wish I'd known I was yelling that you were a pain in my ass over and over again." I huff and roll my eyes until the rest of what he said registers. "Wait... what won't work?"

"This," he grumbles and swipes the soapy washcloth up my arm. His tone is frustrated, but his touch is reverent and makes me shiver as goose bumps follow the path of the washcloth. "I've never done this part before."

"Sex?!" My eyes pop out of my head and I try to turn, but he bands his arm over my breasts.

"No." He laughs. "*That* I'm well versed in."

I grimace at the thought, but there's almost a vulnerable edge when he murmurs, "It's the aftercare that I'm new to."

My lips part on a silent gasp.

"You... You've never done this with anyone else?"

Oh my god, this is so not my business.

He wets the washcloth under the faucet and squeezes it out before he answers.

"I haven't. I didn't care about it before, but now I do."

"So, um, what changed?"

"No one else was my wife."

My thoughts race a mile a minute at the implication of his confession, but Kian seems like he's in a trance as he drags the washcloth thoroughly up and down both my arms and over my chest. I tense, expecting him to tease my battered nipples, but the cloth just dips into the water and gently rubs over my skin.

When he moves on to wash my upper chest, he pulls my hair to the side and makes a hum of appreciation before caressing my neck.

"Mmm, these marks are going to bruise nicely."

I shiver at the light touches on my abused skin and my lower belly flutters.

"Is that what you meant when you said if I mark you, you'll mark me forever?"

He chuckles. "No. I marked you as mine when we got married."

He lifts my left hand and twirls the simple band on my ring finger. The light catches the silver and my brow furrows.

The Baron's ring annoyed the ever-loving shit out of me day in and day out, so I only ever wore it when I was in public. But Kian's ring already feels so normal that I'd forgotten it was even there.

As I'm marveling at that revelation, his voice grows thick and possessive while he strokes my neck.

"These marks will fade, but I'm a part of you now. Whether it's my fingerprints... my ring..." He reaches between my legs and I bite my lip as he runs a finger along my entrance. "My cum..." His other hand spans my lower belly and he growls low into my ear. "Or my child... you will always have me with you."

His words should scare me, but I swear his touch has already trained my body to either come or calm for him. My breaths come in impatient pants while his fingers dance around my clit. Even though I'm sore, when both his hands disappear, my pussy twinges in protest.

"I took you hard today. Denied you earlier, then forced pleasure onto you. The heat, Epsom salt, and touch are supposed to make you feel better. Even more sated than before."

The washcloth continues its journey over my curves and I moan as my head falls back against his shoulder. My eyes keep wanting to drift closed and my heartbeat slows as I revel in the attention.

He leans around me to grab my knee and continue his ministrations. I stretch my leg high over my shoulder so he can get my feet. His laugh rumbles against my back as he reaches.

"So fecking flexible. I can't wait to see how far you'll go for me."

His words warm my core. I shouldn't care that he says nice things. I shouldn't care that he's treating me like I'm precious to him right now. But I really, *really* do and I don't know what to make of that.

"Don't strain yourself, though, Lace. This is supposed to be relaxing."

"Stretching *is* relaxing." I smile. I'm not lying, but when he gets to my heel, I hiss in pain.

"What is it?" his voice deepens with concern and he bends my leg so he can see my injured foot. "What happened here?"

"It's nothing—"

"It's not fecking 'nothing,' Lacey. How'd you get this cut?"

"From, um, destroying all your glasses." I wince. I was so pissed at him before, but several orgasms and a warm bath later and I'm not feeling nearly as destructive.

He huffs. "I'll make sure to have that cleaned up so you don't fecking hurt yourself again."

"I'm seriously okay. I did way worse to my feet when I practiced pointe."

"Hmm." He turns it slightly to examine it before releasing my foot back into the water. "It does look like just a wee cut. But you're lucky that's all it was."

When he continues with the cloth along my skin like we never spoke about me trashing his suite, my jaw drops.

"That's it? You're not mad?"

"At you hurting yourself? Furious. But I've punished you enough for one day."

"No, I mean about ruining your home."

I feel him shrug. "They're just things, *tine*. Things don't make a home. Although, it was a hell of a way to tell me you hated my suite. You can pick out the next decorator to design our living room the way you like it."

"But you were so mad when you came home—"

"I thought your tantrum was adorable at first. It was you making yourself come without my permission that brought about your punishment."

"Jesus, noted. Next time I want to get bathed and pampered, all I have to do is get myself off without you."

I bite back a smile as I wait for his response. He doesn't disappoint as my name comes out in a low growl.

"Lacey..."

"I'm kidding. I'm kidding." I giggle. "You know, you said I was fun to tease, but you're pretty fun to rile up yourself."

He huffs a chuckle but returns to washing me. "Open for me."

A warm shiver of delight rolls through me and I bite back a smile while I spread my legs for him. I brace myself as he dunks the washcloth between my thighs. Even though he gently tends to my swollen center, I hiss at how sensitive I am.

He doesn't try anything further, only paying strict attention to being methodically thorough. It isn't until his length hardens against my lower spine that I realize he's affected too and a smug smile curves my lips.

As he finishes cleaning up the remnants of him from between my legs, a thought buzzes through my brain like an electric shock. I was too thoroughly fucked moments ago to bring it up, but my mind is finally clearing now.

"Kian, we need to talk. You didn't use a condom again. It's been months for me and I've been tested, but, um... what about you?"

"Same. And I haven't been with anyone since the night my father told me you were my next mark."

"Your next *mark*?"

"You know about my orders. I became obsessed with my new assignment, but even then, I wasn't sure how I wanted to accomplish it. I guess a part of me always hoped it'd end like this."

My chest pounds, but I try to focus. "Kian... this isn't an end. This isn't even a beginning. I have obligations, responsibilities to my family and the Garde. And what about babies? I told you I'm not on birth control."

The washcloth stops, and he sets it to the side before wrapping his arms around me. It's comforting, but I quickly realize his soothing embrace is just as binding when he doesn't give me an inch to move.

"It'll be fine, *tine*."

"It'll be *fine*? How do you know it'll be *fine*? Do you have an in with God and know the future or something? Maybe we can go to Mass together this Sunday and you can introduce me."

"Lacey—"

"You came inside me, Kian. *Twice*. What if I get pregnant?"

"You're my wife." His nonchalant shrug splashes the water.

"Kian..." I groan. "I'm not your wife."

"You are, and we just consummated our marriage. Congratulations, Lacey McKennon, there's no going back now. I'm not letting you go without a fight."

No going back now.

I go limp in his arms.

"*Tine*, listen..." He strokes my arms softly underneath the water as he talks. "I want kids. You want kids—"

"How do you know I want kids?"

"Because when you took your gap year after your dad was arrested, everywhere you traveled, you visited a local orphanage. It's an educated guess after that."

My cheeks burn. "You know about my gap year?"

When my father was arrested the first time, I couldn't deal. I took a year off school and went anywhere but home. If I'd known then that a judge would confine him in jail before his trial, I would've spent that time with him. But I didn't, and instead, I had a fabulous, extravagant time for social media and put on a front that the O'Sheas were still invincible.

It was in the downtime I had by myself that I actually enjoyed my trip. I loved to buy toys, visit the local orphanage or shelters, and watch the kids play with them. That time made me fall in love with the idea of a true family, not just one that thrives on political gain.

But how does he know that? I've never told anyone.

"I've kept tabs on you ever since you were promised to me, even when the contract was broken. So am I wrong?"

I shake my head. "No, I do want a family. I just... never thought it'd happen the way I wanted."

Kian sighs. "Honestly, it still might not, but as long as I have a home with love in it, I'm fine with whatever happens. The Garde has a history of infertility—"

I scoff and words spit out of me before I can stop them.

"Greed and infertility are *not* the same things. Parents don't want to chance their kids killing each other and losing the family's inheritance. Greed is the only thing that's hereditary in the Garde."

"Not all families," Kian responds quietly. After a beat, he takes a breath and speaks low as a whisper. "My mom had a few miscarriages before me. I should have an older brother, but when she lost him, my father almost lost her. Dad refused to have more after that, afraid he'd lose her—"

"Really?" I can't help the shock in my voice. To most families, heirs are born at any cost. The future head of a family name wanting to give all that up for his wife is unheard of.

Kian nods. "She'd always wanted to be a mom, though, and she begged him. He was never very good at saying no to her. They tried one more time and then came me. I was a difficult delivery and my father really put his foot down after that. But that's why my parents stopped. Not greed. Love."

"So... you believe in love? Like truly?"

He nods against my head, and I feel his warm breath on my scalp. "Without a doubt."

"But love is practically old-fashioned in our world."

"Not in mine."

The words stun me into silence and the only thing that can be heard is the soft lapping of the bathwater against the sides of the tub. My reaction isn't just to the story, though, but to the vulnerability within the confession. And the secrets.

The Keeper of the secrets, not the money, is who is truly in charge in the Garde. The head of the society is a kingmaker and a king slayer, depending on the wielder. As our Keeper, my father has kept peace among the members mostly because he's been fair and kept the trust of each family, rarely using their secrets as a sword.

But rumors have circulated for years that the McKennons' reputation had been slain. I thought it was because Kian broke our marriage contract and went on a two-year-long bender three years ago, but did my father use a secret against them? If he did, it was only in retaliation because Kian refused me... right?

And yet...

Kian stole me, tricked me into marriage, and he wants me to have his children. Why would he do all that after refusing to marry me?

I'd think it was an elaborate ruse, but now he's trusting me with family secrets, ones I'm sure my father doesn't know. If he had known them before Kian was born, what lengths would he have gone to ensure a McKennon heir never existed? That his biggest rival could never rise up against him? The McKennons are billionaires. That's a lot of money that would go to the Garde's pocket should the McKennon die without an heir. It would've been chaos.

"Why are you telling me this?" I whisper my thought out loud.

"A secret for a secret," Kian murmurs and unplugs the tub. The water drains slowly, leaving cool air on my skin in its wake. "You have answers I need."

Goose bumps erupt on my arms, but with Kian's warm body still flush with mine, I'm anything but cold.

Is this why he's done all this? At one point, I thought it was to get his inheritance, but is it only for my secrets? What on earth do I know that Kian doesn't?

My chest tightens.

If it has anything to do with my dad or his case...

"What do you want to know?" My voice is small, unrecognizable, and Kian slowly tightens his arms around me.

"Why were you engaged to Monroe?"

Scene 16

BITING BACK

My pretty wife stills in my arms, but I'm prepared when she shoots up, trying to escape me. I knew before I asked my question that she might figuratively *and* literally try to buck against it. There's a secret in her that she'll die to protect, but she'll have to get through me first.

She thrashes about and I tighten my hold, wrapping one arm around her waist and the other across her chest. Even as I try to wrangle her, she lashes out like a caged animal and bites my forearm. Fire blazes beneath her teeth and I know she's tasting blood.

I lean forward and plunge her under without thinking. She unlatches to scream and it warbles through the water as she scratches me. My rapid heartbeat thunders in my chest, anger and worry dueling with reason.

As soon as she stops mauling me, I yank her up by the back of her neck as fast as I can. When she breaks the surface, she's coughing and choking too much to try to get away from me again.

"Wh-what the *fuck*, Kian?!" she sputters and glares daggers at me. Blood-red droplets tinge her pink lips and the garnet swirls seeping from my forearm prove she got me good.

"You're fine," I swallow thickly, telling myself more than her

"I'm *fine*?! Stop saying that word! Fine, fine, fine! I'm not fucking fine!"

"You were under for barely ten seconds. If you'd stopped fighting me sooner, it would've been fewer. You're lucky that's all I did after you fecking bit me like a goddamn wild animal!"

Even as I yell at her, I check her pulse with my fingers. It's rapid but hearty, and although her chest is strawberry red from exertion, she's breathing enough to practically have steam coming out of her nose. She swats my hand away before I can assess her further, but her fiery temper and angry eyes tell me more than anything else that she's okay.

"You tried to drown me!" As she shrieks at me, I wrap a long hand towel around my forearm to stanch the bleeding.

"I didn't and you bloody well know it. You only get"—I pull the knot with one hand—"as good as you give"—and tighten it with my teeth before I meet her angry glare with a pointed look—"*wife*. Remember that in our marriage. Maybe you'll survive it. I swear to Christ, though, keep acting like a feral cat and you won't."

Her eyes widen as she tries to read me, obviously wondering if I'm full of shite. I want to be, but if she pulls a stunt like that again, I'll have no choice but to actually punish her. If I were any other Garde member, she would've never come up for air.

My jaw clenches to the point of pain as I wait impatiently for her to stop studying me. Three droplets trail down her pouting face before she finally replies.

"I can't decide whether you're my savior or my worst nightmare."

"Best think of me as both then, it's safer that way."

Without waiting for her response, I stand and let the water sluice down my frame. Her eyes follow the defined hills and valleys of my muscles better than any of the beads of water. Resisting the urge to smirk, I climb out and dry off with a towel before wrapping it around my waist. She's still appreciating the view when I hold up another fluffy white towel for her to step into.

"Up."

Her brow scrunches. My fiery wife has a shite poker face with me, but knowing she's dropping her defenses pleases me to no end.

"What're you doing?" She rises slowly and crosses her arms, inadvertently pushing up her glistening breasts, prompting my cock to twitch behind the cotton.

Fecking hell, I can't get enough of this girl.

"You're wet, Lacey, and not for the fun reasons. I'll be forced to remedy that if you don't dry off and put some damn clothes on."

As if a switch has flipped, she snatches the towel from me and wraps it around herself.

I suck my teeth and sigh. "Shame. Torturing a few more orgasms from you would've been fun."

Her narrowed eyes look all the angrier thanks to the spiked wet lashes framing them. Despite her reservations, she still lets me help her out of the tub and lead her into the bedroom.

Once we enter the spacious room, her eyes dart to the exit.

"Thinking of running?"

"I wish, but I'm obviously not good at locks," she grumbles. "I'm thinking I could really use a fucking drink and a change of clothes. I don't think I've ever survived this much chaos for this long without alcohol and a wardrobe change."

"Out of luck on alcohol, I'm afraid. I'd get you water, but I hear I'm fresh out of glasses." My brow rises.

"Ugh, *fine*. What about clothes? I don't want to put that dress back on."

"No need to worry about that. You've got plenty of clothes to choose from here."

Her eyes roll so hard I think they'll fall out. "Let me guess, you want to pick everything your *wee* wife wears?"

"I'd rather you be naked, but in the alternative..." I flick on the light inside the closet's open door and give her side of the small room a dramatic flourish. "I had these delivered while you were—"

"Drugged?"

"*Asleep.* More will come, but this was all I could get on short notice."

She walks through the closet, gliding her fingers over the different garments. I think I've finally tipped the odds in my favor, but when she replies, her voice drips with contempt.

"Did you have a pretty assistant go get them?"

"Jealous, *tine*?" I snort. "Tolie's not really my style, but I'm sure he'd love to know you called him pretty."

"*Tolie* found these?" Her face lights up as she searches through the closet with new fervor.

"The one and only. He also brought makeup and apparently a magic hair dryer? I don't know what the feck that is, but it's all in the bathroom."

Our mutual friend is nocturnal and as soon as the show ended at Rouge, he answered my call and jumped at the opportunity. He loves to do this shite and already knows Lacey's style. Not to mention the fact that the second she name-drops him in a post, his mobile will blow up with celebrities and A-listers wanting him to fill their closets.

While she browses, I check underneath the fabric covering my wound. Her marks are raw and pink where she tore into me, but there's no new blood, so I untie it. I wait to confirm the bleeding has stopped before tossing the towel into the trash bin. Unfortunately, I've found that no matter how many times I wash it, blood doesn't come out of the crisp white cotton.

"Wow, Kian. He did an excellent job. I had no idea he was into fashion. Why didn't he tell me?"

I shrug. "He's shy sometimes."

Tolie might not be Garde, but his secrets are safe with me. I won't tell her that my best friend hasn't yet figured out that he's trapped in the same destructive loop that held me captive for so long. It was much easier to haul myself out of the Las Vegas underworld once I found my purpose. Hopefully when he finds his, it'll help set him on the right path, like it did me.

"Well, you better have paid him. And the shop owners. It had to be a pain in the ass to be woken in the middle of the night like that."

"Of course I paid everyone, plus extra for their discretion." I scoff and tug the drying strands of my hair in frustration. "Do you really think so little of me?"

"Do you really think so little of *me* that you'd believe I would be thankful for *anything* you do after the shit you've put me through?"

"Goddammit, Lacey. You're hard to please, you know that? Most women would kill to have a closet filled with designer clothes. Most Garde women would be kneeling at my cock in thanks right now."

Jealousy flashes over her face, but it disappears when she snorts.

"You obviously don't know 'most women' then. *Most* women wouldn't be grateful if their kidnapper filled their cage with shiny objects to distract them. I'm not a fucking bird." She pauses in front of a white dress and holds up one of its sparkling, sheer sleeves with interest before she remembers herself and glares at me again. "Am I supposed to be impressed by this? I couldn't care less. You have more money than God. A little Alexander McQueen and Chanel are a drop in the bucket."

Her scorn stings more than I'd like to admit.

"Alright then, what kind of gifts do you like, my wee Garde princess? A pound of flesh for the Red Camellia perhaps?" I cross my arms, letting her see the punctures her angry teeth dug into my forearm. I'm quite proud of the mark my *tine* gave me, but she winces as her eyes flicker across it. Though they linger on my biceps and chest, she snaps out of it before I can tease her.

When she meets my gaze, mischief glints in her eyes and my pulse skips.

"Well, the *last* gift I got was a coupon book to hang out anytime I want."

The burst of laughter from my chest makes her jump. "What, did you get that from a five-year-old? Was it in crayon on construction paper too?"

"No." Her jaw sets and she juts her chin at me. "It was from someone special."

"Who?" My voice is sharper than I intended. Heat flares along my neck and cheeks.

She shivers and pulls the towel around her breasts tighter before crossing her arms over her chest, no doubt to cover where her nipples have begun to poke through the cloth.

"I'm not telling you. Wouldn't want you to swing around that big dick energy that you're so proud of and smack them with it."

"Whether you tell me or not, I'll figure it out. But right now, as much as I love verbally sparring with my new wife, we need to talk. Sit on the bed. You don't mind if I pick out your clothes for you since you're *so* unimpressed by them anyway, right?"

"Go ahead. It'll help me learn what kind of over-the-top billionaire playboy you are. Would you want your wife to dress like a nun or show off my *ass*ets? There's no in-between for guys like you."

My brow rises.

"Jesus, Mary, and Joseph, you know me so well, do you? How about you sit and quit fighting me for a moment and we can actually get to know one another. It's either that or I throw all the clothes that you allegedly couldn't give a rat's arse about into the Bellagio fountain and have you walk around here naked for the rest of our days."

She harrumphs but stomps to the bed and sits. No one ever fecking challenges me like this and I love that she's feisty enough to play with me. But the day is getting long, I'm no closer to answers than I was this morning, and I've fallen into more questions.

"Grand, now tell me. Why was it so important for you to marry Monroe?"

Her shoulders tense, but she's not fighting me yet, so it's progress.

I risk going inside the walk-in closet to get dressed and pray that I can trust my wife not to have devised a plan to murder me by the time I come back out. Tossing my towel into the laundry basket for my housekeeper, I make a mental note to call for a cleanup crew. I'll have to pay them triple, plus hush money, to have them tidy the mess in the living room. I can't have the whole hotel knowing my brand-new wife threw a tantrum.

I can't have the whole hotel knowing about her at all...

My father wants us to keep our marriage quiet for the time being, but the mere thought makes my chest ache. I don't want to go along with that plan, but depending on how much Lacey is willing to divulge, he might have the right idea. If I have to pretend like we're not married, though, then the least I can do is make sure she's wearing white.

I find the dress she lingered on earlier. She may insist on being stubborn, but I could tell she loves it, so I set that outfit aside and push those other thoughts out of my mind..

With her taken care of, I put on a pair of boxer briefs, black slacks, and a black dress shirt with the sleeves rolled up to show off Lacey's teeth marks. I forgo buttoning it, though. My wife has a thing for my tattooed pecs and abs and I get a thrill whenever I see that hunger in her gaze.

"I don't hear any answers!" Her defeated sigh outside the open door is barely audible with all the fabric around me muffling it. "Tell me the real reason why you were engaged to Monroe."

When I emerge with a white bra, heels, and the Alexander McQueen dress she taunted me about, she's miraculously still sitting on the bed. Resolve has thinned her lips into a determined line and she nods once before meeting my gaze.

"When your family broke the engagement after my father was

arrested, Monroe was the only one to step up and say he wanted to marry me."

My head spins at the accusation. "That's a load of shite."

She scoffs. "Which part? The 'your family thinks mine is scum because my dad was falsely accused' part? Or the 'no one wanted me' part?"

"Both actually. Whoever told you no one wanted you was a fool. And the first part is also a lie. The McKennons didn't break off the engagement."

"Kian, what's the point of lying? I *know*, okay. My dad told me. You, or your family, backed out when we needed you most because you didn't want to associate with a criminal—"

A laugh bursts from my chest and her round cheeks pinken with anger. "Don't laugh at me!"

"I'm not laughing at *you*, but don't you hear how fecking ridiculous that sounds? *Everyone* in the Garde is a criminal. Some of us more than most, but your dad got popped for doing the exact same shite the rest of us have done. Hell, if the rumors are true, O'Shea might not have even done it."

Her eyes brighten. "Do you think he was framed, too?"

"I don't know whether he's been framed or not, but what I do know?" I lay the clothes on the bed beside her before locking my gaze with hers. "My family didn't break off the engagement, *tine*. Yours did."

Scene 17

YOU WEAR WHITE

N o. No. No.

I shake my head slowly.

"Why... why would my father do that?"

"I don't know. The O'Shea never gave us a reason. One day he notified my father that he was breaking the marriage contract and never gave cause. It's the first time that's *ever* happened in Garde history. The McKennons have lost business deals and friends because the society thinks the Keeper must've found out a terrible secret about my family. They assume there's something horribly wrong with us—with *me*—because why else would he have broken our deal? Your father reinforced those beliefs when he chose Monroe fecking Baron as your husband, a man whose family only just got accepted into the Garde and one who very likely killed his own father to gain half his inheritance. So you tell me. Why the feck did Charlie O'Shea try to destroy my family and put his only daughter in danger?"

Stress rolls in my stomach and bile bubbles up my throat.

This can't be true.

It can't be. Because if it is, then my father has been lying to me for years.

Kian releases his crushing hold on his dark-auburn hair. It

looks brown when it's damp and apparently like he's been electrocuted when he's frustrated. Concern furrows his brow and his calloused hands grip my shoulders gently as he tries to get me to spill my secrets.

"You can tell me, *tine*."

My own soaking wet hair drips on my shoulders, making me shiver, and I lean into him, even though I know I should be running the hell away.

"I'll tell you my secrets if you tell me yours, Kian McKennon."

His jaw tics. "What do you want to know?"

My breath catches at the opportunity, but it doesn't stop me from asking the question that's been burning in my mind.

"Why did you marry me? The *real* reason. What's in it for you?"

He shakes his head slowly. "I won't tell you that. Not yet."

"And why not?"

"You haven't earned it."

I scoff. "That's rich. Just like a Garde man. Thinking he can take while refusing to give. You deserve everything and I deserve what you deign to give me, is that right? Is that how it's going to be?"

"Of course not—"

"Then stop asking for answers I can't give! Your reasons for holding your cards close to the vest are just as valid as mine, I can assure you."

Honestly, I wish I could confide in him. I want to talk to *someone* about the fact that my father has been lying to me and that he sabotaged my marriage arrangement with Kian to...

To what? Secure the Baron's testimony? I'd thought Monroe had stepped up to the plate to marry me when no one else wanted to and that, as my father's financial manager, he was able to testify on my dad's behalf. In my naive mind, one didn't mean the other and that's what my father had me believing, too.

But what if the Baron is only testifying *if* I marry him? If that's the case, there has to be an explanation for why my father lied to me. He wouldn't do that for no reason.

And Kian wants my dad to go to prison, right? If I told *any* of those secrets to Kian, he could sabotage my dad's trial. The risks are too high.

He ruffles his hair and paces until he halts midstep. His eyes narrow on me like he can read my mind if he looks hard enough.

"Does it have to do with your father's case? Maybe I can help."

"He... I..." Kian's chest stills as he holds his breath, but uncertainty gets the best of me. "I can't say. I want to, but I can't."

Disappointment slouches Kian's shoulders and my chest caves in with guilt.

"You don't trust me."

I *want* to trust him, and in some ways, I do. I don't know when that began exactly, but even though I may trust him with my own secrets, I can't trust him with my father's.

"I'm sorry. I'd trust you if it was just about me, but it's not my secret to tell. Whatever I say could hurt my family, and I'll do anything to prevent that."

Kian's head tilts and my heartbeat skips as my mind mulls over that last sentence. Even with so few words, I've still said too much. Hopefully he doesn't make me regret it.

"I admire your loyalty to your family, but—"

Something buzzes in the other room and I sit up to hear it better.

"Is that my phone?"

I'm about to go look, but Kian leaves the bedroom and comes back with his discarded slacks. He pulls the device from a pocket, and at first, his lip curls as he analyzes the screen, then a smug smile replaces the scorn.

There's something like pride brightening his face as he hands me the phone.

"'The Baron,' huh? Not his name, no picture. Quite the

personal touch you've got there for the man who was supposed to be your fiancé."

I roll my eyes as I take the phone from him, but what can I say? He's right. Even in my contacts list, it's obvious I want nothing to do with the man. Kian chuckles as he plucks a silver poker chip from his pocket and flips it in the air.

Trying to ignore the anxiety constricting my chest better than any corset, I follow the chip's gleam going up and down... up and down. It's soothing, like a hypnotic meditation, and when I'm ready, I take a deep inhale and exhale at the same tempo to brace myself.

On what has to be the very last ring, I pull my towel farther up my chest like a shield and finally answer.

"Hello—"

"Lacey O'Shea, why the fuck isn't your location on?"

"Charming," Kian mutters as he catches the chip again. My eyes widen at him to get him to shut up and I speak in a rush, hoping the Baron didn't hear.

"I'm so sorry, I keep forgetting to turn it on—"

"My bodyguards have been looking for a whore in a runaway bride costume all morning!"

"There's your first fecking strike, arsehole," Kian growls.

"Lacey, who was that?"

I leap up from the bed and clap my hand over Kian's mouth so quickly I almost fall. He pockets the chip and grabs my waist to steady me, but he doesn't let go, and I... don't want him to. As nerve-racking as it is having to stop him from interrupting, it's nice to have someone who has my back during one of these calls.

"Who was what, Monroe?" I ask.

"Is there someone with you? Where are you?"

My mind races to think of a distraction, but all it can come up with is what's been bugging me since I talked to my mom earlier today.

"Where were you this morning? My mom said you weren't at the courthouse."

Monroe scoffs, but my diversion seems to do the trick, so I don't care if he gets angrier at me.

"Well, when they couldn't find you, obviously I didn't bother going to the courthouse. Why would I waste my time for a silly socialite who's too hungover to get married?"

Kian's hands tighten into fists, but Monroe just gave me an out and I flee to it.

"I know. I'm sorry. I just got... *so* so drunk last night. I've been recovering all day—"

"I don't give a fuck about your excuses. My lush of a sister couldn't give me any details about last night, and frankly, I don't want them, nor do I care. You will now be on your best behavior. Starting tonight at dinner. You'll meet me at Vincelli's at six."

I pull the phone away from my ear and my eyes widen at the time. "That's in... an hour? It takes me that long to get ready."

"Not my problem. We have things to discuss and I won't wait after you stood me up this morning."

"But tonight's Halloween. People will expect me to go out—"

"Oh, please. Don't give me that. You weren't going to go out tonight if we had signed our license this morning, anyway. Vincelli's at six. Be there, or you won't like my decision."

A decision? What decision...

My pulse quickens, but I don't dare ask what he means with Kian looking at me with so much curiosity.

Not that it matters since the prick hangs up anyway. I shake my head and Kian gently moves my hand from his mouth.

"Do you ever get to finish a sentence with that gobshite?" he asks and I sigh.

"That was one of our better calls, actually. I was expecting worse after this morning."

I turn away from him and pet the silvery organza sleeves of the gorgeous, simple white dress Kian picked out for me.

"You want me to wear white?"

"Well," I feel him come up behind me and I have to resist the urge to relax into him as his warm hands squeeze my bare shoulders. "It *is* your wedding day."

A laugh huffs out of me and I give in to lean back against him. "Allegedly."

Silence rests over us. Is his mind racing like mine is? Is he bracing himself for what I'm going to inevitably have to do? Will I have to face it alone, like everything else?

"I have to go to this dinner," I finally whisper.

"No, you fecking don't, and you're not going to."

"Yes I am." I turn around and let my worry show on my face. "You don't understand. There's more at stake here."

"Help me understand, then. Let me help you, Lacey."

My mouth opens, but my mind stops it just in time. They call Kian "wild ace" for many reasons, some more mercenary than others. Aside from it being his brutal calling card, he's unpredictable, and without knowing what the Baron is thinking, I can't place my father's life in Kian's hands.

"I can't tell you. Not yet."

He sighs and rests his hand around my neck. I should be scared after everything he's pulled, but my muscles relax under his touch.

"If you're not going to tell me what Monroe has over you, I will find answers on my own. And you can't be angry at the way I get them, either."

I open my mouth to argue with him, but I snap it shut.

Do I want him to know my family's secrets? If he learns them without my help, then it's not *my* fault if they get revealed...

Once again, Kian's giving me an out. First from marriage with the Baron, and now from being a snitch with family secrets that technically aren't mine to share.

I shrug a shoulder, trying to seem nonchalant while hope flutters in my chest.

"Do what you need to."

He scoffs. "I need my wife to stay at home with me and not go to dinner with another man."

"He has answers *I* need! I don't want to go any more than you want me there. Once I trick him into blabbing to me, I'll go home, alright, but that sure as hell isn't your penthouse."

"Still don't believe we're married, then?"

I snort. "Oh, I believe it. You're just the type of man to steal a wife."

He huffs and shakes his head. "You really don't get it, do you? I know you had no choice with Monroe, but didn't you ever wish you could marry for love?"

"What?" The question startles me so much my voice squeaks. But then I laugh. I can't help it. "Women in the Garde don't fall in love. We smile while the men make money and we make babies. And the last one is only if we're lucky. Where is this coming from?"

He groans. "Fecking forget it." He shakes his head and huffs as if he's made a decision. "Look, if you won't let me help you and you insist on going to this dinner tonight... we've got to bluff."

"What?" Shock and relief war through me. "How?"

When he speaks again, it seems like he's having to drag out every word. It makes my own throat dry up and I swallow.

"My father is concerned about us."

I blink. "The man who wanted to have me killed or ruined is concerned? For me?"

Kian nods and the veins around my bite mark on his forearm bulge as his fist tenses beside him. My god, he must really hate whatever he's proposing right now.

"Since we're married, our families are tied forever. My father and I want to make sure we know all the facts and circumstances that led to your father and Monroe's unlikely alliance. Our parents hate each other, but what happened after your father was arrested makes no sense. So until you tell me the truth or until I find answers on my own, we have to keep our marriage quiet during your dinner tonight."

A sudden jab in my chest makes me tense as he continues.

"The dinner is already quickly approaching, so you'll get

ready here, then you'll go to dinner to placate Monroe. After that, you'll come back home."

"Home... like the O'Shea hotel?"

He grunts. "Of course not. Your home is here now. With me."

My stomach flips at the sentiment, but I shake my head. "You know that won't work. We'll be found out in a second. I have to go back to my residence at the O'Shea. I'll be safe there."

His brow furrows as he shakes his head. "You'll stay here, Lacey. Hopefully dinner will give you some direction and we can discuss where we want our next steps to go."

My lips roll between my teeth as I think about his proposition. More than anything, I'm surprised that I wish I didn't have to leave. But I love that he's trusting me with my decision to keep my secrets and giving me the opportunity to find out more information from the Baron myself.

When I nod my acceptance, Kian mirrors the motion.

"Grand. And I'm putting one of my men on you for protection."

"No, the Baron will find out. He already has his bodyguards on me every second he can! It's a miracle they haven't found me yet."

"It's not a bloody miracle, it's the *McKennon* Hotel. Do you think we'd ever let Monroe or his men step foot above the casino floor? We only allow him there because he loses a shite-load of pride every time he gambles."

"But, Kian—"

"This is nonnegotiable." The hardness in his voice makes me swallow back the rest of my objections. "It'll either be me or someone I trust who will be watching you from the moment you leave, or the whole thing is called off and I play our fecking wedding video on the biggest billboard in Vegas."

My belly flutters at the thought, but then the reality of my situation hits me again and the breath in my lungs freezes.

"You wouldn't."

"Test me, and I'll have no problem showing it off. I could give feck all about any of these pretenses, but you and my father are of the same mind and I'm trying to put my trust in you both. I won't budge on your protection, though. There's still the matter of the woman who was murdered at Rouge. We haven't ruled out Monroe's involvement, but hopefully I can get answers on that soon enough."

Blood drains from my face and queasiness churns in my stomach. "Fine, okay. But what if he sees one of your men?"

"Then so be it. The man is a New Yorker, Lace. I don't care what power he's managed to swindle in the Northeast, this is Las Vegas. Your father might've tried to extinguish my family, but we've fought our way back to the top. My dad has found loyalty from families on the inside, and I've collected allies and businesses from Ireland to Vegas without the society's influence. Charlie O'Shea reigned over Vegas once upon a time, but now I rule its underworld. No one has the pull I have. Not Monroe, not your father, not even the Garde. No one can best me in *my* city."

Shock makes my jaw drop.

He doesn't need the Garde?

If that's true, Kian McKennon is one of the Garde's biggest threats.

Total control of assets is a tactic the society uses to maintain loyalty. We don't get a dime of our inheritances until our parents die. Most of the members rely on an allowance from their parents in the meantime and can't seem to—or don't try to—make a buck on their own. That's what Kian is supposed to be: powerless. At one point, I wondered if that's why he insisted on marrying me. But if he's amassed wealth, power, and loyalty outside of the Garde, he doesn't need me or our society. The Garde needs *him*, or he'll become a danger to its very existence.

"So we do this together, or we don't do it at all, alright, wife?"

I nod slowly, still too stunned to come up with an argument.

"I have a few more stipulations if you want to keep me from calling Monroe right fecking now and tell him to bloody apologize to you. I'm already counting in my head."

"Counting?" My brow lifts.

"My grievances with him."

"I don't know if I could do that." A laugh huffs from my chest. "There are too many to track."

"Don't worry, this will all be over before I have to count too high." A slow grin lifts his lips at the promise. His confidence gives me hope. Too much hope.

I find distraction in a silver button at the bottom of the dress's sleeve as I try to tamp down the foolish feelings lightening my chest. But Kian gathers my hands in his, prompting me to look up again. His gaze captures mine completely as he kisses the simple silver ring that already feels like a part of me.

"If we're to hide our marriage tonight, *this* never leaves you. Understood? I get not being able to wear it. But I want it on you at all times."

My lower belly flips and my heart tightens. "I... I can do that."

"I'll be there, so if you need me or if you ever feel unsafe, my number is in your mobile. I made you put it in last night."

I roll my eyes. "Of course you gave me your number. That's the least psychopathic thing you've done yet. Anything else?"

"He's not allowed to touch you."

I shrug. "Easy. The Garde won't allow it. Not intimately anyway."

Kian squeezes my hands and locks eyes with me.

"Lacey... *no one* touches you. At all."

"I don't want him to, but..." My lips tighten before I ask, "How do I make sure he doesn't? I can't very well tell him my husband will kill him if he does."

The dark laugh that escapes Kian makes my nipples peak.

"All you have to do is report it to me, *tine*. I'll take care of the rest."

Act 3

Scene 18

THE BARON'S DINNER

I thought waking up married to a stranger was nerve-racking, but it's got nothing on waiting for a fiancé who has no idea he's an ex.

The Italian restaurant is one of Vegas's see-or-be-seen restaurants. It occupies the top floor of the tallest high-rise on the Strip, and it's one of the few places in the city that's untouched by Halloween, maintaining the elegant atmosphere the rich and famous expect on a night out at Vincelli's. Politicians come here to break bread and make deals all the time, and it's right across from the Baron Hotel, so it's no wonder Monroe picked this place.

Floor-to-ceiling windows provide a three-sixty view of the vivid lights that whirl, flash, and strobe in the Valley. Dusk makes for a stunning backdrop at this height. Dark-purple mountains pierce the sky at the valley's edge, highlighting the vivid sunset's blues, pinks, and reds.

My eyes stay trained on the city below to keep from searching the restaurant. Thanks to my bouncing knee, I've had to tug down my white dress at least three times to stop it from inching farther up my thigh. When I'm not fixing that, I'm fiddling with the simple silver wedding ring in my dress's pocket.

I found the Baron's diamond ring on Kian's living room floor, but I couldn't bear to put it back on. It's in my clutch if I need it, although I hope Monroe won't notice its absence since my organza sleeves are long enough to cover my fingers.

While I would rather throw the Baron's ring into Lake Mead, it's hard to fight the urge to put on Kian's ring. I don't want to slip it onto my right hand and chance the Baron questioning where it came from. And I might be bold, but wearing it on my left hand would be fucking suicidal.

It's taken a lot of willpower to stop myself from glancing around the restaurant to look for Kian. Before I left, he kissed me goodbye like it was the most natural thing to do and promised that he'd be here watching me.

No. *Protecting* me.

Appreciation warms my skin and as I sip my wine, I give in to temptation and peek around the busy dining area.

I find him instantly, sitting at the bar in the center of the restaurant and nursing a water glass. A mirror stretches above the liquor display and our eyes lock in the reflection like two magnets drawn together. He won't be able to hear my conversation with the Baron that far away, but his presence alone helps me and a calm wave rolls over me, settling my bouncing knee.

The playful, mischievous smile that I've somehow already grown used to is gone now. But his hazel gaze is full of fire and promise as he peers over his glass up at me. He's wearing the black button-down he wore when he picked out the dress I'm wearing now, and his sleeves are still rolled up, almost like he's showing off the bite mark I gave him.

My phone buzzes in my lap and I peek at it—

MY HUSBAND

Shock zings down my spine and I slam the phone back onto my lap before I can read the message.

Thank God no one is paying any attention to me freaking out at how Kian entered his name into my contact list. I subtly glare at the handsome jerk who is now smirking at me from the bar.

Before I read any further, I change his name to "Roxxy." If the Baron somehow sees my phone, I can have plausible deniability that it's my friend and I won't be signing my own death warrant.

Crisis averted, I swipe through my apps to see what he said.

> ROXXY
>
> Seeing you in the dress I picked out makes me want to crawl under that table and feast on you instead of whatever the feck the chef brings.

Heat blooms in my cheeks and I know I'm the color of a freaking tomato, especially compared to my white dress. I roll my lips between my teeth and text back.

> Good thing Tolie brought me stage-worthy makeup or everyone in here would be able to see all the bruises your hungry mouth and little hand necklaces left.

He frowns at me in the reflection and my phone buzzes again.

> ROXXY
>
> You know my hands aren't little.

I snort while another message comes through.

> ROXXY
>
> And I like my marks on you.

My stomach flips before I flirt back.

> And I like mine on you...

I smile behind my glass and his lips quirk up. My pussy clenches, forcing me to cross my legs under the tablecloth.

"Lacey!"

I jump at the sound of Monroe's voice, the nasal tone more effective than any cold shower. My head swivels to find him following the hostess toward my table and I sneak my phone back onto my lap. I try to wave politely, but his eyes are on the tall, pretty blonde hostess's ass now.

At the edge of my vision, Kian's brow furrows with irritation. I avert my gaze to the wineglass I've been steadily nursing from the moment I sat down. I wish like hell that I could knock it back, call it a night, and leave with the man who makes me feel needed with one clandestine look. Instead, my fingers tremble while I sip and I gently place the glass back on the table.

Monroe smiles at the hostess, a charming expression if all the warmth hadn't been sucked out. By the time they reach my table and he sits, Monroe has already ordered a bottle of wine and no doubt wishes he could have her for the main course.

"Your waiter will be right back with your cabernet, sir." The hostess gives him a cursory smile and tries to go, but Monroe grabs her hand.

"*Monroe*," I hiss.

He glares at me, but it gives the hostess enough time to slip her hand out of his grip.

"Sir, um, can I help you?"

Monroe pouts at her. "You're not going to be our waitress?"

She blushes as she shakes her head and glances at me nervously. The poor thing is probably worried I'll care. I don't. If I ever did, it was the first time he acted this way, but that was so long ago I don't even remember it now.

As he leers and flirts, it gives me time to study him and figure out what face I'll need to wear for him tonight. His faded, dirty-blond hair is slicked back, and his already fair skin looks pale in the restaurant's mood lighting. Whenever he moves, his reeking cologne wafts toward me, making me want to gag. His blue suit and bright red, white, and blue tie is politics ready. No doubt he wants to make himself available to schmooze if someone important walks by our table.

The hostess is clearly uncomfortable with the amount of attention he's giving her, but I've tried to save women from moments like this in the past and it's only ended bitterly for the both of us. Luckily for her, a waiter motions her away and she gets to leave with a relieved smile.

My ex-fiancé ogles her ass again as she goes, but once he turns around, the veil of charisma vanishes at the sight of me. He's nearly two decades older, but the only time his age shows is when his frown lines carve deep grooves in his forehead as he scowls at me.

His cold disappointment is so different than Kian's heated passion. To the Baron, I'm a means to an end on his way to getting what he wants. But to Kian... I'm *all* he wants.

My chest flutters at the thought before I shove it away.

Jesus. Get a grip, O'Shea. It's showtime.

While Monroe checks his gold pocket watch, my mother's countless lessons kick in.

I plaster on the expression a good Garde girl wears. Bright big eyes. A polite smile. Hands nestled demurely in my lap. No bouncing knees. No playing with my ring. No fidgeting whatsoever. And finally, legs crossed at the ankles, so I'm slightly off balance, the way men like us to be.

By the time Monroe is tucking his watch back into his suit jacket, I'm in position, waiting to be spoken to. He soaks in every second of weighted silence as a meager power move before he finally speaks.

"You're on time at least, although if you'd been late, you could've put more effort into your hair and less on that gaudy makeup you insist on wearing. Caking it on makes you look like a whore. It's embarrassing."

My smile doesn't falter as I reply. "I'm sorry, Monroe. I tried to freshen up the best I could on such short notice."

His eyes narrow.

Oops, should've left that last part out...

"Well, I guess it could be worse, couldn't it? You could've

ended up like that dead girl found this morning. Tragic, but I warned you last night. That could've been you."

My heart stalls in my chest. Kian said he's looking into who murdered the woman at Rouge, but I dread the answer. Hopefully he'll have one soon.

Monroe twists in his seat.

"Where the fuck is our waiter?"

"Here I am. Sorry about that, sir."

The waiter appears out of thin air and dives into the description of the wine as he uncorks the bottle, switches glasses for me, and pours an ounce for each of us to try. But I'm too stunned to drink it because *Tolie* is our waiter.

He smiles at us in a black uniform while Monroe tastes his wine. Tolie's spiked purple hair has been tamed into a pompadour and his ear and eyebrow piercings have vanished. He looks every bit the part of a waiter in a high-class, uppity restaurant.

What the hell is he doing here? He works for Rouge, not Vincelli's...

My friend winks at me behind fake black-rimmed glasses, and my lips tick up. It's breaking character for both of us, but much too subtly for Monroe to notice. In fact, Monroe doesn't give either of us nearly the amount of attention he gave the pretty blonde that seated him.

"Oh, ma'am, I *love* your dress. Who are you wearing?"

"Why thank you." I can't hide my smile now. "It's Alexander McQueen and styled by Tolie Hendrix."

"Oh, I hear that Tolie has great taste—"

"Wine's good," Monroe interrupts while he shoots daggers at me with his eyes. "I'm ready to order."

Not missing a beat, Tolie ignores my ex-fiancé's rude behavior. "Very good, sir. What can I get for you two?"

As Tolie gives me a hearty holiday pour, like the good friend he is, Monroe orders steak for himself and a garden salad without dressing for me.

My friend frowns. "Would you like anything with the salad, ma'am?"

Baron shoots daggers at the side of his head. "She will have the salad. Just as her *fiancé* ordered. Now chop-chop. We don't have all night."

Like the entertainers we are, neither I nor Tolie let our vapid expressions change at his terse command.

"Certainly, sir. Enjoy your wine."

As Tolie walks away, I catch Kian's gaze in the mirror, hoping he sees the small appreciative smile I flash before I focus back on the threat in front of me.

I don't know how he did it, but I'm sure Tolie is working our table tonight because Kian arranged it. Tolie won't be able to help me navigate the minefield that every conversation with Monroe turns into, but knowing I'm not alone in this gives me courage that's normally nonexistent around the Baron. Rather than let my nerves take over or slide into meek Garde habits, I rack my brain to figure out how to get the information I need.

"I'm sorry about last night," my good sense claws the lie from my throat and it's then that I realize I'm *not* sorry for last night. At all. About any of it.

Good God, I can't let Kian know that. I can see his smug grin already.

Monroe narrows his eyes and shakes his head. "I don't believe you, but you better make the world believe it. The press has already made me out to be a fool."

He scrolls through his phone before turning it to face me.

My heart plunges into my stomach.

No one was supposed to be able to photograph or record inside Rouge. Not only is it club policy, Kian tried to make sure of it. But there we are on my ex-fiancé's phone, dancing together.

The photo captures the moment Kian caught me before I fell. Our chemistry is palpable, even through a screen. In another life, I'd frame it and put it on our dresser.

No... *my* dresser. *Mine.*

I ignore my little mental slip and try to see if I can tell it's Kian, but his mask might have saved us both. He gazes down at me from behind it as if I'm the one for him, and I cling to him like he's already mine. If a picture is worth a thousand words, ours tells the beginning of an epic love story. But in Monroe Baron's hand, it's a tragedy, a nail in my coffin. Especially when I see the headline.

"O'Shea Heiress Dances with the Devil," the Baron reads for me. "The subheading says, 'Does her fiancé have the heart of a saint? Or is he just a fool?'"

"Monroe, nothing happened," I mumble through numb lips.

"I hope not," he scoffs. "This picture? The dance? It's bad enough. If I'd had any idea you were going to pull a stunt like that, I would've locked you up and never let you out. I might still do that."

"It was just dancing—"

His phone buzzes in his hand and he holds up a finger to shush me. "One moment... Ah, right on time."

He answers his phone right there at the table with a smug smile on his face. "It's nice to hear from you again, Keeper. You O'Sheas are punctual today."

Scene 19

HER PUNISHMENT, HIS PARDON

My blood freezes.

"You're talking to my dad?"

Monroe glares at me. "Yes, I'm actually with your daughter right now, Mr. O'Shea. You can talk to her, of course. But there's a little matter we need to discuss first."

Ice-cold sweat pricks my forehead as he continues.

"Lacey went against my wishes last night and got drunk during her bachelorette party at your establishment. This morning, she didn't show up to sign the marriage license, hasn't had her location on all day long, *and* she's been dodgy with her answers to both me and her mother. God knows what she's been up to the past twenty-four hours. I'm afraid I'll have to start keeping better tabs on her like we've discussed."

My brow furrows as Monroe places the phone in the middle of the table and presses the speaker icon. I glance around, worried that people will eavesdrop, but when my father speaks I have to strain to hear him, thanks to his old phone.

"Monroe, I'm sorry. I had no idea she would behave so poorly." My heart aches as my father apologizes rather than defends me. "I... I think keeping better watch over her might be the remedy, at least until the wedding."

"Speaking of which. Due to your daughter's actions, I'm going to have to postpone."

My jaw drops as my father repeats the last and adds, "But... it's supposed to be this weekend. Then the prosecutor will go forward with the trial."

"Ah, yes, the trial... I've been thinking about it. Why would I testify without security that Lacey can even have a child? It isn't in my best interest. Perhaps your attorney can keep kicking the can down the road and put it off for another year or so until Lacey and I have married and she's had an heir. If not, I could always testify during appeals if I feel so inclined that is."

Blood drains from my face and I gulp.

What the fuck?

I knew I had to stay in line, or I'd risk upsetting my future husband, a man whose reputation for hurting women precedes him. But I'd always assumed if Monroe was subpoenaed, he'd *have* to testify.

"I didn't know you had a choice," I whisper.

"That's not the deal, Monroe," my father growls, giving some of the O'Shea edge he's known for and pumping hope into my veins. But both vanish as he continues in a more docile tone. "I'm sure anything you have in mind will keep Lacey in line. I'll talk to her."

"I'll have to tame your daughter, or I simply won't be able to marry her, and I won't testify at all. That *was* the deal. You broke off the engagement with the McKennon heir to obligate her to me, but if she doesn't get on board, then I don't have to fulfill my end of the contract."

So it's true.

The knife my father began sliding into my back three years ago has moved so slowly over time that I never felt the sting. He made me think he and Monroe were doing me a favor, that no one wanted me. But he's *using* me. That revelation lodges the blade inches from my heart and now there's no question of how expendable I am. Even to my own father.

"Monroe... she doesn't know the stakes. She thinks you're marrying her because no one else would, not that you'll only testify if she marries you."

"Well, she knows now." The Baron's pale, thin lips widen into an ugly smile. "You're on speaker, O'Shea. I suggest you inform her of the risks of her behavior, or *I* will. And neither of you will like my methods."

My father sucks in a breath and I wait for him to say something—*anything*—to fix this. But instead, he drives the dagger home.

"I'll make sure she understands."

My chest aches and I can't breathe. This betrayal might kill me.

"Good to hear it. And as for a wedding... I have no desire to get married legally or publicly during this scandal. I'll wait until it dies down to decide whether I want to marry her at all. Hopefully, it's before you're convicted. Exoneration in the appeals process is much harder to come by than acquittal in trial."

My skin grows hot and the mock neck on my dress chokes me. I pull at the edges to try to get some air and my knee begins to bounce again.

Monroe hands the phone to me like he's passing a loaf of bread and I smash my finger against the speaker icon. My father's deception has me on the verge of tears, but I blink them back and fake a brave voice.

"Dad?"

"My little camellia, are you okay?" The knife twists.

Do you care?

"I am... but I... I don't understand."

"I'm sorry you had to find out this way. When Monroe told me he could testify on my behalf if you married him instead, I did what I had to do—"

"For you," I finish.

Is it selfish of me to be mad at him for trying to save his own freedom? Maybe, but God, did it have to be at the expense of my own?

"I didn't do it just for me. I did it for everyone. If I go to prison, the Garde will strip me of my title. Anarchy will reign until a new Keeper fights his way to the role, and you'll be... extinguished. It's the way of the Garde. Nothing is ever freely given or gained. Not even innocence. My attorney says the testimony will be enough to get me acquitted, but Monroe won't divulge what it is to anyone else until the trial. He can set me free and..." My father's heavy sigh tugs at my heart, but what he's saying makes me want to rip the pain out of my chest. "He can set me free, and you have to do whatever it takes to please him to make that happen. I'm sorry, Lacey. I hate to hear my little flower be so upset, but as the Red Camellia, you must do your duty to the Garde. It's how it has to be."

Questions burn on my tongue, but I can't ask them with Monroe staring at me, swirling his cabernet. Besides, if Monroe is threatening to refuse to testify, then there's only one person who can help me now.

As if my thoughts have summoned him, I see Kian in my periphery, leaning over the bar to talk to Tolie, his phone in his hand. Tolie glances at me and nods before Kian puts the phone to his ear, hops off the stool, and walks out.

Fear knifes in my chest and my phone buzzes in my lap. I don't check it though. I'm sure it's Kian telling me Tolie and one of his hidden security guards are watching over me while he steps out for the call. It's not like Monroe can do anything in a crowded restaurant.

I swallow and try to focus on the call with my father.

"Okay, Dad... I understand."

"I knew you would, princess. I'll call you this week, but I have to go—"

"Dad, wait, um... what does 'tin-eh' mean?"

My dad's Irish roots have been all but Americanized, but I'm hoping he remembers some of the language his grandparents spoke.

"'*Tine?*' Ah, let's see. It's been decades since I've heard the Irish language. If I recall correctly, '*tine*' in Irish means 'fire.'"

Fire.

I've cursed Kian, fought him, destroyed his things, and even bit him, but from the moment I met him, he's called me his "fire." One he promises never to tame.

That numb feeling I've had slips away as certainty warms my chest, solidifying my decision. I desperately want to ask what "iss too mu row-ah" actually means, but Monroe is already frowning at my change in topic. I'm sure it isn't "pain in the ass" like Kian claimed, but I'm not so sure my safe word should be used in polite company anyway, let alone ask my father.

"What brought that question on, sweetheart?"

"Nothing. Just curious. I love you, Dad. And I miss you," I say on autopilot and I'm sure I mean it deep down, but right now, I don't feel it. "You said you'll call this week?"

"Yes, of course. I love—"

The Baron snatches the device before I hear my father finish.

"That's enough of that. People are staring."

It's on the tip of my tongue to point out that there are exactly zero people paying any attention to us, but I'm saved by Tolie.

"Ma'am, here's your salad. Chef *Key* made sure to add grilled chicken and dressing on the side in case you wanted something more filling than rabbit food."

I roll my lips inward and bite them to keep from smiling as Tolie winks at me. His face blanks to pure professionalism in an instant and he turns without missing a beat.

"And sir, here's your steak... is there anything else I can get for you?" Tolie lingers while he pours more wine. I take a sip as soon as he's finished, trying to calm my nerves.

"No," Monroe answers tersely and begins to cut his filet.

"Allllright then, I'll be back to check on you shortly."

Before Tolie gets even feet away from our table, Monroe

grunts, "The staff didn't use to be so unprofessional. I guess they'll hire anyone these days."

Tolie glares at the back of his head, but I don't dare react. Monroe notices none of it as he shovels a piece of meat in his mouth and points his knife at me.

"So, *fiancée*. How was your talk with your father? Enlightening?"

"Yes." My voice breaks at the simple word and I take a huge gulp of wine, hoping a buzz will mellow out the anxiety consuming me.

I'm stressed, but Monroe threatening not to testify isn't the power play he thinks it is. Now I know it's worth the risk to find allies. Thankfully, I happen to already be secretly married to a ruthless, obsessive bastard who's offered to help.

Once this dinner is over, all I need to do is convince Kian to hide our marriage a little bit longer. I have to find out what information the Baron knows that's so important it can guarantee my father's freedom.

"I hope you understand now that I can do anything I fucking well please. *I* hold your father's fate in my hands. I can let him live or let him rot. At this point, I refuse to testify until after we've married and you have my heir. If that isn't until his appeals process, then so be it. Granted, that's if he survives jail in the first place."

My heart lodges in my throat. "What?"

"You didn't hear? There've been fights in the jail recently. Scary things. Anyone can get shivved if they're in the wrong place at the wrong time."

"Is... is my father in danger?"

"Of course he's in danger. Don't be stupid. You didn't think jail was *safe*, did you? Just because your daddy smuggled a phone doesn't mean he's protected. It means when he's no longer useful to people in there, he's got a target on his back. Like you do out here, actually."

Anger heats my cheeks. "Is that a threat toward me, Monroe?"

"More of an... *observation*. Prisons have their own rules, and the Garde has ours. I suggest you get in line, dear fiancée. I refuse to have my reputation ruined by marrying a slutty socialite, and if I don't marry you, I don't testify, and if I don't testify, your father could rot in prison for the rest of his life, however short his fellow inmates decide it may be. But luckily for everyone, I've ensured none of that will happen."

"What do you mean?" I tug at my stifling neckline.

"You'll stay in my suite from now on." He nods his head out the window at the building across from us. "At the Baron Hotel."

"Your suite?" My eyes widen and my heart thunders in my chest as I try to come up with an excuse. "But the Garde doesn't allow us to live together before marriage."

He huffs and shakes his head. "One would think the Garde would have spurned at least *some* old-fashioned ways, but evidently a female's virtue is still prized above all. You won't live with me. My rooms comprise the entire top floor of the hotel, but you'll stay in the smallest one, the Elephant Suite, with body-guards outside your door at all times. It's both suitable for the society's sensibilities and ensures you never leave unless I'm with you."

My brain runs a mile a second and my heart is beating so hard that my chest hurts. As Monroe stabs pieces of steak to shovel in his mouth, I take another gulp of wine and glance around.

Kian hasn't come back yet, and I don't see Tolie. I sip more to try to calm myself down, but the buzz is dangerously careening into tipsy territory and there's still no end in sight for my heart palpitations.

"You can't just lock me up, Monroe. You said it yourself. I'm a socialite. People will know something's wrong if I don't go out."

His eyes bore down on me and I feel myself and my resolve getting smaller with every word between us.

"That's been taken care of. According to the statement I put out in your name, you're guilt-ridden. You *begged* me not to call off the wedding, but you understand I need time to heal. You've sworn off social media and you're requesting to be left alone while you work on yourself. To help you with that, my IT guy has ensured that my suite has minimal access to the outside world. You can text and call so people don't think you're dead, but you'll have no internet. You'll spend the next couple of weeks—or months—atoning for your sins. Going to Mass. Hopefully, I'll forgive you, but you've insisted on staying in my suite while I'm out of town to prove you're not the party princess everyone thinks you are." He scoffs and pokes my empty wineglass. "Even though your current state doesn't do you favors."

The walls of my reality are already closing in on me, trapping me, and I'm not even locked away yet. As much as I hate the stigma that comes with the word "socialite," I do love to be social. It gives me energy to meet new people, try new things. Even short periods of time without being able to dance, go outside, or see people drive me crazy. Adding in no social media or being able to contact anyone...

"Monroe, I can't. Please—"

"I couldn't give a fuck," Monroe hisses and leans over the table to grab my forearm *hard*.

His grip hurts, but I don't dare cry out. I don't want to see the satisfaction on the asshole's face.

"I don't think you understand the gravity of this situation, Lacey. Your father needs me, and yet you had the audacity to embarrass me. I should break it off now, but I have my eyes on the prize. I will receive my inheritance. I will rule the Garde. And you will be my wife." He grabs a fork, shoves the handle into my hand, and lets go of my forearm. "Now eat. You're causing a scene, and I swear to God, if you humiliate me again, you won't like what happens to your father. Behave, or this merger will never go through."

Merger... as if a marriage is just a business deal to be brokered.

Which, with the Garde, I guess it is. And I'm the commodity.

But I'm *more* than that, dammit. I've relied on the world assuming I'm a stupid socialite countless times. Why not use it to my advantage now? I've already decided I need to know what Monroe's testimony is going to be so I can get my dad out of jail myself. What if Monroe keeps files in his suites? The only way to find the answers is to play his game and if I play my cards right... maybe this could work.

"You said you're going out of town?" I ask, like prey keeping track of its predator.

"I'll be flying for business back and forth from New York. By leaving you behind, the world will see that I'm teaching you a lesson and I'm no spineless fool. We can discuss our wedding details after you've proven you can be a good politician's wife. For starters, eat your dinner. People are staring."

I glance at my untouched food, but my mouth is so dry I know I won't be able to choke anything down.

"I... don't want this."

I'm not sure whether I mean the food or life in general at this point. Probably both. But the Baron stabs another piece of meat, pops it between his lips, and jabs his knife in the air at me.

"This life was chosen for you and you've loved it until your responsibilities caught up with you. But now that you can't live like a spoiled princess anymore, you don't want to play the role. It's time to grow the fuck up and learn that no one in this world gives a fuck what you want, only what you can give them, Lacey O'Shea."

...*McKennon.*

The last name whispers across my mind. Under the table, I loop my finger into the simple ring and wait for the silver metal to match my warmth.

The Baron is right about a lot of what he said, but not everything. It's never been more clear that no one in this world gives a fuck what I want...

...except for Kian McKennon.

Scene 20

ACE-QUEEN OFFSUIT

Leaving Lacey behind at the restaurant made my fingers twitch with anxiety, but my father called with urgent details on the Rouge murder and demanded I meet him this instant. I would normally obey an order from my dad without question. But as soon as Tolie calls me to say he's bringing them the bill, I'm heading to Vincelli's to take Lacey home, whether my father is finished or not.

Thank Christ for Tolie, though. He's worked in this town long enough that he knows everyone. It was easy to convince the staff—many of whom were his friends—to let him take a table, especially after I promised to triple their tips for the night.

He helped me keep tabs on their conversation, but he also made Lacey less nervous. My poor *tine* was a bundle of pent-up energy sitting there by herself. Texting flirty banter seemed to help in the beginning, but once I saw her face turn sheet white at the sight of Monroe, I was thankful I already had Tolie in place. Now *my* nerves are running rampant and I won't be able to relax until my wife is back in our bed.

I flip my silver chip up and down to busy my fingers as I enter the Red Room. Thanks to the porter, Hugo, it looks spotless, although it still has the sweet, smoky scent from the cigars this morning. The only other person here is my father, who sits at the poker table with his spectacles on, texting on his mobile in front of a partially made grid of cards.

"Dad, you call me to haul my arse over here when I'm in the middle of something and you're playing poker patience? Not even playing, you're texting. I can tell you right now emojis aren't going to help you get any better at the game."

My father grunts and glances over the rim of his glasses at me. He watches as I toss my chip in the air. Usually it calms me, but it's not working right now.

"Anyone with you?" He bends to retrieve something from underneath his chair.

"Merek's working my casino on Fremont and Tolie's at Vincelli's... where *I* should be."

"Ah, with the O'Shea girl."

"The *McKennon* wife, you mean." I catch my chip and give him a pointed look before pocketing it.

"Of course," he mumbles.

He put on a good show this morning and I know he believes I did what I thought was right. But Finneas McKennon isn't one for loose ends and until we understand what ties Monroe to Charlie O'Shea, Lacey's unpredictable loyalties make her just that in his eyes.

"What've you got for me, Dad? Seriously, I need to get back."

"She's in fecking public, lad. Calm down. She'll be fine." As my father gripes, he slaps a manila folder onto the felt poker table and I snatch it up to open it.

"Is this it?"

He nods in my periphery while I sift through the papers, scanning over reports as he briefs me.

"This is all the investigators have so far. I called you straight away because my contact is eating at one of our restaurants on the casino floor during his break. While he's here, he's allowing us to study the preliminary file, but he's taking it with him before he leaves.

"Why wouldn't you simply take pictures of the thing, then?"

My father scowls at me. "I don't want this shite on my mobile. Our interest in a case that has nothing to do with us makes us look suspicious as it is. If we ever get subpoenaed and can't get out of it like what's been done to the Keeper, we don't want a mega-date trail, or whatever the feck it is you lads call it these days."

I huff and shake my head. "I can't be arsed about a *metadata* trail, Dad. Lacey's eating dinner with fecking Monroe—"

"Read the file quickly then and get on with it. It's not much, but it's enough that I knew you'd want to take a look at it yourself. We only have the coroner's notes since no autopsy has been done yet. For all intents and purposes, it looks like the victim was bludgeoned to death in one of Rouge's dressing rooms. No witnesses."

I stop mid-page flip at the first printed photo. My stomach knots at the brutal murder scene. The woman is sprawled out on the carpeted floor, her bride costume in disarray and her legs twisted at a painful angle. Every inch of her is bruised and blood-ied, to the point that her face is unrecognizable. Terror knifes down my spine at the sight of her long, strawberry-blonde hair until my mind registers that it's not my Lacey.

"Fecking hell. No wonder Moira O'Shea was in a state this morning."

"The investigator said the victim dyed her hair... but that color *is* unique."

"Makes you wonder if they got the wrong target." My eyes flick to my father's raised, bushy gray brows before I continue through the report. "Any idea who the murderer was?"

"The police are questioning her fiancé. The man has a crim-inal history of domestic violence and he didn't make it to his shift last night. From what my contact said, they're going to arrest the suspect after they finish interrogating him."

"And what do *you* think?"

He rubs his eyes underneath his glasses. "I don't know, son. There's history between the victim and the suspect, the experts think they've got their man, and it's also not a typical Garde murder. Too sloppy. All initial signs point to the Baron not being involved."

"Monroe isn't a typical Garde member. He's not accustomed to our ways yet."

My dad shrugs. "That's true. But coincidences happen."

I shake my head. "I don't buy it. Monroe all but admitted it earlier today on his call with Lacey. I think it's more than a coincidence."

"Maybe a warning then? To teach her that she can't defy him? Garde men have done much worse to willful wives."

"She's *not* his wife," I growl and my father holds up his hands.

"I know, son... but *he* doesn't."

The truth makes my lip curl and I yank at my hair. This plan chafes against everything I believe.

"Charlie told Lacey that *we* broke off the engagement and that Monroe was the only one who was willing to marry her."

"What a fecking gobshite O'Shea is," my father mutters. "Of course he'd lie to his own daughter."

"Yeah, but why?"

"Well, as a father myself, we never want our children to see our flaws. Maybe the truth would taint him in her eyes. But *we* know there would've been plenty of suitors, so why did he pick Monroe?"

"I think Monroe has something on the O'Shea. Lacey mentioned she would do anything to protect her family and it's not her secret to tell."

"That kind of loyalty may keep her alive... or not." My father grunts. "I've got to say, I didn't anticipate such a difficult hand when I gave you the queen card a year ago. We'll have to figure out her secrets on our own, then, won't we?"

"*Or*, I ask the Keeper of secrets himself."

My dad's lips purse and his eyes narrow. "You think the O'Shea will talk to you?"

"I'll make sure he knows his son-in-law won't take no for an answer. I should refresh my memory about his case before I go. Lacey thinks he's been framed."

"It wouldn't surprise me, although he's certainly no saint. We're all guilty of something. Being in the Garde gives certain freedoms, but I'm not keen on my son getting roped into this mess. Charlie might be our king, but we're all one bad police search away from getting caught for something ourselves."

"I want to find out from the source, Dad. It's only been hours and I'm already tired of hiding my marriage."

My father points to the teeth marks on my bare forearm and chuckles. "Clearly not hiding too hard. I see she's already taken a liking to you."

I smirk. "My wee wife bites back, that's for sure. You should see my suite. I'm going to need the cleaning crew to come before one of my cousins brings their wee ones over again."

"If she's as fiery as your mother, you'll have to woo her, you know. Not just steal her."

I huff. "I already bought her a whole bloody wardrobe and she wasn't pleased at all. And I don't know how much *wooing* I can do with our marriage under wraps."

"Women don't need much, son, and Garde women already have everything they want. But your mam taught me that thoughtfulness always wins. That's all she'll need."

"She *needs* to be safe with me," I growl. "And away from fecking Monroe."

Dad laughs and shakes his head. "Don't worry about the Baron, lad. No matter what influence he has on the O'Shea, he would've never been able to take Lacey on. Not without stomping her spirit."

"Now he won't get to do either."

A smile reaches my father's eyes as he removes an ace of hearts from the grid in front of him. He lays it closer to me and taps it.

"Who would've guessed the wild ace had a heart?"

His grin sparks my own and I pull another card from the grid to place the queen with the red camellia in her hand upright beside the ace.

"Only for his queen of diamonds. An ace-queen offsuit is a good starting hand, you know."

"True..." My father seems to weigh the statement. "But, still... difficult to play."

"Depends on the player. And I'm the best." I wink at him and he barks out a laugh before I return the manila folder to him. "It sounds like you lot are sure the police have got their man, but I want to be one-hundred-percent certain Monroe had *nothing* to do with it. I've got to go back to Vincelli's now, so keep me updated if there's anything new."

"Will do, son."

The moment I step outside the Red Room, Tolie calls and I answer it on the first ring.

"Update? I'm heading back now."

Tolie swears on the other end, "Fuck, Key, you're not gonna like it."

My anxiety spikes, made all the worse as I pass by a slot machine with a jarring jingle. I shove my hand into my pocket to smooth my fingers over my chip.

"Tell me."

Tolie sighs. "I rang up the check and was about to text you, but when I looked back, there was only cash on the table. He took her."

Adrenaline floods my veins and I pick up speed, navigating the flashy slot machines and the drunk patrons in their Halloween gear.

"What the feck are you going on about?"

"I mean, Monroe took Lacey. I followed the best I could. He took her to the Baron Suites—"

I hang up before he can finish and my fingers fly over my screen.

Are you okay?

Calling her could put her in danger, and I'm hoping that cheeky stunt I pulled when I entered my name as "My Husband" in her contacts doesn't feck everything up. I already risked texting her once when I messaged her on the way out of the restaurant to tell her I'd return.

She hasn't texted me back yet, but I message Merek to get a team on the Baron Suites. When I finish, I stare at my screen, no longer caring if I bump into anyone as I walk.

Sweat beads on my brow and my mouth goes dry, but I refuse to look to a bar for relief. My finger presses on my chip so hard that I begin to lose feeling in my thumb. The urges never truly go away. They lie dormant, like a snake in a hole, biding its time to strike, and stress has always made me the perfect prey.

Feck, if she doesn't message me back—

As soon as the text comes through, I'm reading and typing at the same time.

MY WIFE

> Miss me already?

I'm serious. Where are you? Where did he take you?

> How did you know?

Tolie told me. Now answer the question. I'm not fecking around with your safety.

My mobile vibrates as she calls me. The candid picture I took of Lacey's gorgeous sleeping form fills my screen before I answer.

"Talk to me, *tine*."

She sighs. "I can't for long. He said I wouldn't be able to have internet, so I'm glad I can get texts and calls at all. I haven't found cameras yet, but I'm thinking he might not have them because he's got bodyguards that are going to check in on me every hour. I was able to sneak off into the bathroom—"

"Who? *Who* has bodyguards on you?"

Even though I already know, my breath pauses with hers before she answers in a voice barely above a whisper.

"The Baron. Someone took a picture of us at Rouge. He didn't recognize you, but someone recognized me. It's in the press."

My pulse skyrockets. If I hadn't been so preoccupied all day, I would've caught the press coverage. I *should've* caught it, but finally having Lacey in my grasp has consumed my thoughts. I haven't been paying enough attention to my opponent's moves and the motherfucker just stole my queen.

"What did he say?"

"He's decided that I'm too much of a liability for his reputation, so he's putting me up in the Elephant Room, one of the suites on his floor."

"*Fuck.*" I tear at my hair and stagger to a wall to lean on it. "Is he staying there with you?"

"No, thank God. It's a nice-sized studio with a bed, bath, living space, and kitchenette, but it'd be way too small for the Baron's big head to stay here. Although I'm not sure what suite he entered after he locked me in this one. The Garde doesn't allow us to live together, so this was the closest thing he could think of to keep an eye on me."

"Jesus," I mutter. Intervening will cause a war, but I don't care. "Okay, I'll get you out of there—"

"No!"

My heart stops. "*No?* What do you mean, *no?* I'm coming to get you and that's that."

"Why? So you can lock me up instead? What's one gilded cage for another, right?"

My fingers squeeze and my mobile creaks in my hand as I growl into the receiver.

"You'd rather be tortured in *my* cage than Monroe Baron's, I promise you that."

"Did you find anything out about that woman at Rouge?"

Her sudden topic change gives me whiplash and I scoff.

"You can switch subjects for now, but we're getting back to this one before we finish talking. The authorities think the murderer was the victim's fiancé. My dad thinks they could be right. It was too... *messy* for the Garde to have been involved."

It's on the tip of my tongue to tell her my suspicions, but it does her no good if I'm just being paranoid.

She sighs on the other end. "Okay, okay, good. That makes me feel better then."

"You *feel* better? Great. I'll come fetch you and you can feel better in my arms at home—"

"Kian..." My name is a whispered plea on her lips and it makes me stop to actually listen. "I... I need to tell you something."

Her normally strong voice wavers at the end and I rub the ache in my chest. I hate that this secret hurts her, but worry and pride war inside me at the fact that she's finally confiding in me.

"What is it, *tine*?" I murmur.

She exhales. "I talked to my dad tonight. He admitted he broke the contract. The Baron made a deal with him three years ago that he would testify on my father's behalf to get him free, but only if I married him."

"Bloody fecking hell."

It makes so much sense, but any respect I ever had for Charlie O'Shea goes up in smoke.

"And I couldn't tell you this earlier, but with everything the Baron said tonight—"

"Tell me."

"He's *supposed* to testify on my father's behalf, but now he's holding it over my head, threatening to refuse or wait until after the trial when I've proven I can have his heir. Which means there's no guarantee he'll even honor the bargain if I marry him. I always thought he'd have to testify if he was subpoenaed."

"There's a lot normal people are required to do that the Garde finds ways around."

"So, that brings me to my decision." Her voice shakes and I know I'm not going to fecking like this one bit. "I need to keep up appearances. Play the Baron's game and keep our marriage quiet—"

"*Fuck* no," the objection snarls out of me.

"You said yourself that your father wants us to keep things low key until we learn what's going on between my dad and the Baron. Well this is it. My dad is innocent. I know it. I need to find out what the Baron's evidence is so I can figure out how to get it into the trial without him."

The meeting with my father and the heads of households comes to mind. I trust those men, not with my life, but with my secrets. And as much as I hate to admit it, we *all* need to know what Monroe is up to. If he has the kind of pull to decide whether to free or take down the Keeper of the Garde, what's to stop him from turning on any of us? He needs to be brought to heel. And the only way to do that is to trick him.

But I have to know Lacey is safe before I agree to anything.

"Has Monroe touched you?" I ask.

Her hesitation makes me growl, "Lacey—"

"Just my forearm. That's it."

Strike two.

"Which one?"

"What does that matter?"

"Which... one?"

"Um, okay, my left one, if it's that important."

I make a mental note and nod. "Thank you for telling me. And he isn't staying with you, right?"

"No, that's the good part about all of this. He says he'll come back from New York every now and then for photo ops and press junkets, but mostly he wants to teach me a lesson and isolate me—"

"—which you'll hate."

"Ugh, yes, but I'll put up with it until I have answers. Once I find out if he has cameras, I'm going to search for evidence here."

"And if he doesn't keep any there?"

"Well, um, then I will... uh..."

I don't let her stammer long, just enough for her to realize she needs me. When she stops talking altogether, I make my pitch.

"While you look for evidence where you can, I'll do what I can—"

"No. You don't have to get involved. All I ask is for you to be okay with keeping our marriage quiet. You don't have to—"

"I'm helping you. I don't want you to do this alone. And all *I* ask is that you call or text me every day. The day you don't will be the last you're out of my sight. Do you understand? In the meantime, I can find out shite a lot quicker than you can up in that tower, Rapunzel. I'll do whatever it takes to get you back into our bed."

There's another pause before she whispers, "Even if that means freeing my father?"

"I'm not doing this for your father. I'm doing this for you."

"Well, I know your family hates him and... and he's not perfect—"

A dark chuckle escapes me. "Believe me, *tine*, whatever your father's done? I've done worse. Stay safe and I'll take care of everything down here. But once all this is over and you're back in our bed, I'll get my hands on Monroe Baron and he'll find out exactly what I'm fecking capable of."

Scene 21

NO NEWS IS BAD NEWS

November 1

ROXXY

Any luck on finding bugs or cameras?

MY WIFE

Nope. Not yet. Do you think we were safe on the phone yesterday?

If we weren't it's too late now. Let's be more careful from here on. Don't say my name out loud and don't talk about anything important. If he doesn't have video, he still might have audio.

Good idea.

Call from Roxxy

...

Call from My Wife

...

MY WIFE

Off to bed. <3 Call tomorrow?

ROXXY

You have my word, tine.

November 2

MY WIFE

LOL on not getting married today. Been there. Done that.

ROXXY

I would've never let that happen.

YUP. My family's enemy liked it so he stole me and put a ring on it, haha.

Are you wearing it, like you promised?

Hey, now I didn't say I'd *wear* it. Just that I'd have it on me at all times. :P

So where is it now?

I don't know, maybe I lost it.

Lacey.

Jesus, fine, don't yell at me.

I'm playing ring toss with a baby elephant statue's trunk. It's harder than it looks.

Fecking hell, is the Elephant Room still elephants everywhere? The Baron Suites used to be a safari themed hotel of ours. The top floor had animal themed rooms and the decor was... something. Definitely over-the-top.

Um, yeah... OTT is one way of putting it. There's literally an elephant painting that takes up a whole wall. No scenery. Just a big-ass elephant. I haven't even been able to count them all yet.

I guess they didn't change much when the Baron won it from my dad. That's useful to know.

...

Call from My Wife

...

Call from Roxxy
Contact Name Changed

November 3

MY WIFE

You'd be happy to know I changed your name again.

MY HUSBAND

I didn't know you changed it the first time?

Yeah, you were Roxxy at the restaurant. But this morning I changed it. It's weird not being able to say your name out loud, tho.

I'd rather hear you scream it.

OMG. Yes the whole new name situation is definitely a good call if you're going to sext me.

So what's the new name? Who's sexting you now?

Not saying :)

Tease.

I'm the tease? Sir...

Oh, I like the sound of that. Maybe I should incorporate it into your next punishment.

We've got to get me out of here first. Any luck on your side?

I've got some irons in the fire. Best not to make it a habit of texting vital information here, in case he gets your mobile.

Um, hate to break it to you, but if he sees any of our text messages so far, we're hosed. How about we don't text incriminating messages, but I still delete the worst ones?

That will work. I have an appointment with someone who should help us, but I can't get in for almost two weeks.

2 weeks in here?? That sounds like torture. I'm already playing with the elephant figurines like Barbie dolls. Once one of us finds out the Baron's testimony, I'm sprinting out of here.

I can't wait to have you back with me.

I never thought I'd say this to someone who kidnapped me, but I can't wait to be back with you, too.

Talk tonight? I have an elephant family reunion to plan.

You have my word.

<3

...

Call from My Wife

November 4

MY HUSBAND

You wearing my ring, yet, tine?

MY WIFE

NOPE. I'm still protesting this stolen marriage :P

But the Baron's is still in the clutch I took to dinner on Halloween. That was a stellar outfit you picked for me, btw.

You looked fecking edible in it.

Has your ex-fiancé given you a wardrobe?

Not nearly as glamorous as yours. Let me put it this way, my dress has yellow ribbons on it. Kind of like what a little girl would wear. And it's one of the better ones. *BARF*.

That's disturbing.

Yeah, tell me about it.

At least I haven't found cameras. Maybe I can brave calling you outside of the bathroom. Hiding out in this shower is fun and all, but talking to you into the *wee* hours of the morning like we did last night can give a girl a crick in the neck.

Do you need me to massage it out for you, tine? You know how good I am with my hands.

Jesus, don't tempt me. I'm already wanting to quit. I thought dance disciplined me, but I guess not.

If you want to leave, that's bloody fine by me. Say the word.

Ugh, NO. You're supposed to help me not give up!

Speaking of which, I've only been casually searching so far for any paperwork or files in case there *are* cameras. Nothing yet. :(

Once I know I'm in the clear I'll go full tornado.

Whatever evidence he has likely won't be out in the open. Keep checking for surveillance. Under tables, ceiling corners, in light switches, lamps, doorknobs.

Would you be able to get into the other suites?

While he's gone. Stay away from that gobshite as much as possible when he's in town.

You've called him that before and idk what it means but I approve, lol.

It's a no on the other suites, I'm afraid. Mine's not connected with any of them.

Same suite names, same decor, same room setup. I'll have to see if my dad still has the blueprints.

It's hot when you go all James Bond. Like my very own Pierce Brosnan.

You like that? Well, abandon this mission and meet me in our bedroom in an hour so I can give you my secret package.

BAHAHA, OKAY BYE. Nice try, 007, but I'm on to you.

Call tonight?

You have my word, madam.

<3

...

Call from My Wife

November 5

MY WIFE

What are you looking at RIGHT NOW. GO.

MY HUSBAND

The Eiffel Tower. You?

Wow, weird. Same actually.

Did you know it took me until middle school to realize that the actual Eiffel Tower is in France? And that the fake one on the Las Vegas Strip is actually in *Paradise* Nevada, and not Las Vegas?

MIDDLE SCHOOL KIAN. MIDDLE SCHOOL.

That's a brutal look for your American education system. No wonder my dad had me brought up in Ireland. I thought it was so I could be close to my family, learn my language and culture, and be safe from the Garde. Now I know the real reason. Are you embarrassed?

Not as embarrassed as I am to be married to you. :P

Ouch.

Say you're sorry, tine.

Sorry. Kidding. Kind of.

Is it so bad?

Surprisingly, no.

I know I suggested last night on the phone that we text throughout the day and call at night, but can I call you right now? This might sound clingy but I need to hear your voice...

Call from My Husband

...

MY WIFE

Thank you for today... I needed it. Back to regularly scheduled texting program tomorrow?

MY HUSBAND

Whatever you need, tine. I'm yours.

<3

November 6

MY HUSBAND

Have you found any cameras?

MY WIFE

Nope, not yet. But I found the cleaning services' restock of booze above the refrigerator!! THANK GOD!!! There's got to be enough for a week. Maybe two. I'll have to ration it. Don't know how long I'll be stuck in this elephant hellhole.

Shouldn't be hard to abstain right? It's only noon.

Keeping myself occupied is harder than you'd think, I already choreographed that dance I told you about last night.

The one you imagined to "Hold Your Breath" by Asteria? I listened to the song. Great beat.

It's one of the few tracks I had downloaded onto my phone, but it's my fave. I'm going to practice my choreo until I have it perfect.

You'll be out of there before you actually perfect it. I'll make sure of that.

Yeah I've only broken the seal on one of the bottles so far. If I have to go through them all I'll crack, I swear, lol.

Strange use of "lol."

Hey some of us use text speech when we, you know, TEXT. I know that's a weird concept for some... LOOKING AT YOU KIAN... :P

Have you been able to talk to anyone else besides me?

Not really. I don't want to endanger anyone more than we already have, so I've only reached out to Roxy and my mom.

Roxy has been hard to get a hold of, but I know my bestie. She's probably feeling guilty about this whole situation. We're dancers but when it comes to our problems, we're natural-born runners. She'll turn up soon, I'm sure.

And my mom...

She doesn't think anything's wrong with what the Baron's doing and she has her head in the sand about my dad.

You talked to her about it?

As much as I could. Dad was supposed to call today and he never did. I'm worried about him, but she said worrying causes wrinkles and if I can't get Botox in the Elephant Room I need to stop thinking about things that cause frown lines.

I'm not sure I like your mother.

I'm not fond of her myself right now.

I want to practice my dance and the shower floor is cold on my butt. Talk tonight?

You have my word.

<3

...

Call from My Wife

November 7

MY HUSBAND

On my way to meet a tattoo artist friend of mine and it looks like the Bellagio Conservatory has a new exhibit. I haven't gone since your mother put on that camellia exhibit years ago.

...

MY HUSBAND

Lacey?

MY WIFE

Hey, sorry, working on my routine. I saw your message midpractice, thought about responding, and obviously didn't. Oops, lol.

My Wife: That exhibit was my favorite so far. I had no idea there were so many different shades! Why couldn't I be the pink "Ballerina Camellia," or the soft white "Seafoam Camellia?"

You wanted to be called the Seafoam Camellia?

Ugh, no. But after that, red seemed so blah. And I was thinking about it while I danced today...

The Keeper's daughter is a color of a "Camellia," right? So why am I red? It feels like they chose the bright red hair color at birth and ran with it.

They did. You didn't know?

SHUT UP NO THEY DIDN'T!

JK.

How's that for your "text speech".

Screw you, Kian McKennon.

I used to think my dad gave me the nickname. Once I found out the Garde did, the name soured for me. I didn't want to know anything about it after that. But now I'm curious... do you know why I'm called the "Red Camellia"?

It's the color your mother's family chose to represent their name when she married the future Keeper. The women that are born of, or marry into, the Keeper's family all get a color. It's a way to intertwine the family histories.

So guy's last name + girl's color = new Keeper line?

Right. If we have a son, his fiancée would be called her family's color and the line would carry on in our name. If we have a daughter, the Keeper position will stay your bloodline's color, but with her new last name.

Listen, *husband*, I haven't decided yet when I want kids AND I haven't even changed my last name. Cool your jets, mister.

In due time, wife.

We'll see about that :P

Regardless, you're my queen of diamonds.

Lol, and you're the Garde's wild ace?

An ace of hearts, to be exact.

That's cute. I would've never dreamed that my husband would be such a romantic. It's a sweet surprise.

I look forward to surprising you every day.

OMG, stop. You're being too sweet now.

Okay, I have to go or I'll cry in this shower for the second time today, lol. I'll call you tonight!

You have my word.

Wait, you cried today?

Is everything okay?

...

MY HUSBAND

Talk to me, tine.

...

Call from My Husband

November 8

MY HUSBAND

Are you feeling better today? I wanted to let you sleep in before I messaged since I kept you up all night.

MY WIFE

This mimosa helps :) All problems are solved by brunch food. Mimosas are my fave solution.

Mimosas aren't food. You've been eating actual meals, right? I know you said during our first phone call that his bodyguards are getting you takeaway.

Yeah, they bring me food. Except for this orange juice, it's mostly salad. I didn't even eat this well in my dancing prime.

Is it filling? My head of security, Merek, could infiltrate the bodyguards and get you some food at least.

NO! I keep telling you this. We have to find out what the Baron's evidence is. I'm not going through all this BS just to have my dad go to jail for the rest of his life. Yesterday I went nuts and I searched everywhere, cameras be damned, and I didn't find a fucking thing.

From our calls, I know you're working to help me. Consulting your police contacts, talking to the family names even tho they don't know anything, and you have that appointment with whoever the fuck next week, so thank you for everything you're doing...

but I can't talk to you if you keep suggesting ideas that could fuck this all up. If I have to be here, I need you on my side or I really will crack, Kian. I swear to god.

Missed call from My Husband
Missed call from My Husband

MY HUSBAND
Lacey, answer your mobile.

MY WIFE
I don't want to talk to you right now. Let me cool off.

There was a lot of emotion behind that text and I know it wasn't all directed at me. Call me, tine.

I'll call tonight. I can't right now.

...

MY HUSBAND
It's nearly midnight...

Missed call from My Husband

Call from My Wife

November 9

MY HUSBAND

Thank you for calling me back last night.

MY WIFE

No problem.

Besides, it's nothing a little tequila can't fix :P

You opened a new bottle?

Oh, honey, I have opened *quite* a few. But I decided to go with water this morning. After you called last night my elephant friends kept egging me on to do shots and I fell on my ass doing a simple grand plié. Embarrassinggg.

I like what you do to my ass way more ;)

Did you hurt yourself? What time did you go to sleep?

Nope. Just humiliated myself in front of my audience. My fans love me no matter what, tho.

I know I've asked during our calls, but has anyone missed me on the outside?

I'm sure they would be more vocal about it if it wasn't for that press statement Monroe made on your behalf. Most people have taken it as truth and they're trying to give you space.

I fecking hate it. I can't wait to set them right.

Aw my hero wanting to save the day.

I'm no fecking hero. But I'd do anything to keep you safe.

Such a softy.

Only with you.

Dad says the best way to a woman's heart is thoughtfulness.

Aw, no wonder your mom loved him.

She was one of the reasons why I was excited to marry you.

She loved you. She was always our champion.

I'm sorry she's gone.

Thank you. It'll never be easy. But it gets easier.

She said the way to a woman's heart is to twirl her around on the dance floor. It's only partially worked with you.

I need to step up my thoughtfulness if I'm to win your heart.

Help me free my father, and you'll have it.

You have my word.

<3

Call from My Husband

November 10

MY HUSBAND
I want to hold you.

MY WIFE
I want to bone u :P

That can be arranged, tine. You'll be back at our suite in a heartbeat.

YASS I want all the bonig!!!!

Are you okay?

Um, duh, obvi. Partying like a rockstar in the LV.

Okay.

We didn't talk much last night, I'm worried about you.

Listen, Keyster, Im having the time of my life. Me and my elephant fiends are chilling looking at the fake Eiffel Tower and pretending were in gay Pariee. Oui oui and enchante and all that shit.

Lacey, are you drunk?

Mayyyybeee.

It's not even noon and you're all alone, Lacey.

Noon-thirty-seven to be exact. And yeah, im all alone, dont you think I ducking know that?

Whatever you're drinking, stop right now, Lacey, or I swear to Christ I'll come get you myself.

Lacey, Lacey, Lacey. So many Laceys and no Laces or tines or wifes.

God, *fine*.

U know I could be doing shots and youd have no idea.

I think I'd have some idea.

Nope. I'm a mystery drinker. Full ove all the ducking mystery.

Yeah, keep saying shite like that and tell me you're not wasted.

It's up. Happy now, mom?

I won't be happy until you're safe under my roof.

Your roof. The Barons roof. So many roofs, but never mine. Who gives a duck about roofs? Just let me dad go and let us drink in peace.

lol "me dad".

I'm a pirate.

My meeting is next week. I tried, but he couldn't do an earlier appointment.

And you still wont' tell me who it is. Secrets dont make fiends Kian.

I think that's exactly what they make.

What?

Nothing. I'll tell you who I met with after my meeting, I swear. I just don't want you to get your hopes up.

FIne. I'm tried. Ill talk to you tonight.

Do I need to come up there?

JUST A NAP JESUS LEAVE ME ALONE

...

Missed call from My Husband

...

Call from My Husband

November 11

MY WIFE

Sorry about yesterday... I think being here finally got to me.

MY HUSBAND

I can come get you anytime you want. Say the word, tine and I'm there.

Until I know I can get my dad out, I'm staying here. You'll start a war if you come get me and then I'll lose everything. Please... if you don't have answers, stop giving me an out. This is hard enough as it is.

But this is tearing you up, Lace.

Have you been dancing? That seems to help.

You're right. I should do that. In fact, I'll go do that now. Talk tonight?

Sooner. I'm messaging you before our call to check in.

...

MY HUSBAND

How was dancing?

Lace?

...

Missed call from My Husband.

MY WIFE

I'm fine. Napping.

Missed call from My Husband.

November 12

Missed call from My Husband.

MY HUSBAND

Lacey if you don't fecking text me or call me right fecking now I'm coming up there I swear to fecking Christ.

MY WIFE

Ooo, look at you acting all scary.

My Wife: Come to think about it... I *should* be afraid of you.

Afraid of me? Why?

Spoiler alert, you kidnapped me and forced me into marriage. You're kind of terrifying.

And yet you've never been afraid in the slightest. I think you even like me.

Don't get cocky.

Bet I can prove both.

Alright, let's hear it.

What do I get if I win?

A big thumbs up.

Idk you decide.

How about I save it for a rainy day.

Sounds suspicious, but I'm feeling risky, lately. What do I get if I win?

You won't.

How does Monroe's suite look?

Mkay... and you always get onto *me* about topic changes, lol. I'll play along.

It's a nice size. Studio style + lots of furniture and hidey-holes, a dwindling liquor stash above the fridge, and a kitchenette. TV that only plays local channels. Super elephant-y. Lots of colors. Nothing soft. Hard queen-sized bed. Great view of everything I'm missing outside, tho. Super not making my FOMO worse at all.

So there's no mess?

other than my mind? No...

There's your proof right there. If you were ever afraid of me, you wouldn't have trashed my suite.

Hmm... okay. I see what you're saying. I'll admit I've never been afraid of you, but *liking* you? That's taking things too far, sir!

Call me sir again and I'll show you how far I can take you.

JEE-SUS.

Your wedding ring proves you like me.

...what about it?

You've kept it, even though you could've thrown it away. And yet you let me take Monroe's ring off you the night we met.

I never want to wear his again.

Maybe one day I'll put yours back on. You know, when I've decided not to be permanently mad at you anymore.

I care for you, Lace. I'm worried about you.

Please don't worry about me. Seriously, it's just a little alone time. Every girl needs it.

My wee tine needs room to be free, though.

I forgot to tell you. I found out what tine means.

And?

And... I like it.

And I like you, too.

Call tonight?

You have my word.

<3

...

Call from My Husband

November 13

MY WIFE

The Baron called. He said he's back Sunday. He wants to go to Mass to show off his converted whore.

MY HUSBAND

He said that to you? Those words?

Lol, why is it scarier that you don't use all caps when you're pissed?

Lacey.

Yeah, he used those words.

That's a third strike against him.

Are we doing baseball, here? Or bowling... I don't know the rules to sports with balls.

It's my own system. The rules are don't fecking piss me off and don't take what's mine.

Oh, are those part of the infamous "wild ace" rules? We love dark and mysterious Kian when he's not being dark and mysterious with us.

Us?

Me and my elephant friends. We're having tea together to celebrate the Baron telling us not one fucking thing that could help with my father, even though I used all my sweet talking to schmooze him.

And by tea I mean tea-quila.

Lacey, we talked about this.

Let me have fun, please? I need *something* right now.

What about dancing?

If you keep berating me about my coping mechanism I won't stop doing it, I'll just stop bringing it up. You know that, right?

Yeah, I do. More than you know. That's why I'm worried.

Okay Kryptic Kian.

I told you I'll tell you about it someday. In the meantime, please try to find different outlets.

Mkay

Will you be attending Mass at St. Patrick's?

Would a brown-nosing Garde member ever go anywhere else? The Baron's certainly not going so he can impress Jesus.

My meeting this Saturday will hopefully prevent you from having to go with him at all.

Yeah, I'm not doing the whole "hope" thing, anymore. Just living day by day.

Stay with me Lace. I know you're isolated right now, but you can't let it get to you.

I know.

Talk tonight?

You have my word.

<3

...

Call from My Husband

November 14

MY HUSBAND

You okay? You seemed distant last night.

...

MY HUSBAND

Lacey?

MY WIFE

Just tired. Lots of energy expended lying around all day hating your life, LOL.

Lacey, you can't just say "LOL" after a fecking statement like that.

Sheesh, sorry. "lol" then.

The caps don't matter. The sentiment matters. Hating your life isn't a joke, especially not when you're coping with alcohol. It's a downer. I know more than most what it does to people.

...

MY HUSBAND

Lacey?

MY WIFE

Okay.

Have you tried dancing today?

I'll do that. Got to go.

Call tonight?

Sure.

...

Missed call from My Husband

MY HUSBAND
Lacey?

...

MY HUSBAND
I care about you, tine.

November 15

MY HUSBAND
Say anything or I'm coming up there.

MY WIFE
Hey, sorry. I got my period yesterday. I'm just going to crash all day.

Shite, sorry you're not feeling well.

...

MY HUSBAND
Call tonight, then? My meeting is early tomorrow. Do you want me to text you before?

...

MY HUSBAND
Lacey?

...

MY HUSBAND

I'm calling tonight. If you don't answer, I'll text or call before my meeting.

...

Missed call from My Husband

November 16

Missed call from My Husband
Missed call from My Husband

Scene 22

POOR PRISONER

I had a feeling Lacey wouldn't answer this morning, but it doesn't make her silent treatment any easier. Even though I wasn't ecstatic to hear I won't be having any wee strawberry-blond McKennons running around anytime soon, I'd love for her period to be the only reason she's grown more distant the past few days. I'm worried her refusal to respond to my third call in a row has confirmed my fears.

Lacey's lost hope, which means I'm losing Lacey.

Guilt tinges my thoughts as I sit impatiently in the jail's parking lot. If it were up to me, I'd get her the hell out of Monroe's suite in a heartbeat. But she's right. If I stole her back, I'd be starting a war with Monroe, her family, and any member of the Garde loyal to either of them.

I'll admit that when I married her, I was acting partly on impulse. But the way I feel about Lacey has raised the stakes, especially with what I know now. I can't have my wife hating me for the rest of our lives because my actions sent her father to prison, and I'd never forgive myself if she got hurt in the fallout.

Even today, I didn't have the bollocks to disclose my plans because I didn't want to tell her why my meeting was delayed for nearly two weeks. The administrative assistant was vague on the details, but the little I do know would crush Lacey.

Life in the Garde means that prison is always a possibility, but we've all got something on someone, so the likelihood of that happening is slim to none. If I ever wind up in a cell, though, I'm taking out every motherfucker who put me in there before the bars slam shut.

As soon as the clock on my mobile rolls over to the next hour, I sigh and adjust my garnet silk tie in the rearview mirror, grab my leather briefcase prop, and step out of my Audi without waiting another minute. This time of year, the air is brisk and dry as always, but that unbearable heat of summer doesn't slam into you when you go outside. I expect the cooler air to greet me now, but my skin is flushed with apprehension.

The jail's tinted glass doors act as a mirror as I stride toward them. My back is straight, one hand in my pocket while the other holds my briefcase loosely at my side, and unlike usual, not an auburn hair is out of place. On the outside, I'm playing the part.

But on the inside, my heart thumps, my mind races, and my fingers grip the chip in my pocket tighter and tighter the closer I get to the doors. Walking *into* the prison, a place I've killed to stay out of, feels like a death sentence of its own, and my gait slows with every sluggish step.

A year ago, I was a captive to my vices and I still fight every day to stay free. Trapped in this hellhole—cramped rooms, never getting to smell the fresh air or have a moment of freedom— would be my worst nightmare. Is that how Lacey feels in her gilded cage?

I have to get her the feck out of there.

I try not to think about how naked I feel without a weapon as I empty my pockets into a tray, go through the metal detectors, and sign in. Once I've finished, I snatch my chip up and press it into my palm so hard I'm sure the number is indented into my skin.

The prison guard escorts me to a private room, just like I

requested when I made the appointment. It's a small, windowless space with painted cinder block walls that makes my skin crawl with claustrophobia. The only furniture to speak of is a metal table with a chair on each side.

As I pull out the chair facing the door, the legs scrape the concrete with an awfully harsh racket that claws my nerves. Doing my best to ignore the feeling, I plop into the seat, lay my briefcase beside me, and prop my feet on the table before I pretend to play a game on my mobile.

The squeak of metal on metal brings my attention to the door. I lean back and balance on two legs of my chair before lacing my fingers behind my head to further my devil-may-care charade. But once I see my "client," all pretenses slip away.

"*Charlie?*" My rough voice is nearly swallowed by the clamor my chair makes as it crashes to the ground and my eyes widen at the sight of the man filling the now-open door.

Our Keeper, Charlie O'Shea, is a shadow of the Garde king he once was, wearing a dingy gray hospital smock and baggy orange pants. A chain wraps around his waist, connected to cuffs on his feet and bandaged hands, making it hard for him to shuffle inside. But it's not the new outfit that has me so shocked.

One of Charlie's sharp dark-blue eyes narrows at me, while the other is swollen shut. His brown curly hair and thick beard have been shaved to the skin and his strong jaw is slightly crooked as if it's been broken. Pride hardens his perceptive scowl, even as he limps and his shackled hands tremble.

"You and your lawyer have thirty minutes," the guard shouts and slams the door behind him, making Charlie jolt where he stands.

I dip my hand into my pocket and rub my chip as soon as the door closes, trying to remind myself why I'm here and not to lose my shite. But at the stark reminder of who I could become one day, goddamn, it's sobering in the worst way.

Charlie gingerly sits in the hard metal seat across from me and

I try to play it cool with a smile I'm sure is barely more than a grimace.

"Jesus, Mary, and Joseph, you look a mess, Charlie. No wonder they said I couldn't see you for two weeks."

"I was in the infirmary. I've gotten caught in the middle of a couple fights." His voice is more gravelly than I remember, but he levels me with his signature glare. One I've now seen on his very own daughter. The thought makes me smirk and my body relaxes in the familiarity.

"I can show you an uppercut or two if you need."

He clears his throat, but the hoarse timbre doesn't change. "Are you the new associate?"

"What?" I ask, my brow furrowed.

"Since you're my *lawyer*... I've met all the associates at the firm. You must be new, I take it?"

His careful delivery finally registers.

"Ah, the room's not bugged. No need to keep that bit up."

I turn my mobile around to show the green **"CLEAR"** indicator on the security app I'd been fiddling with before he came in.

He slouches with relief. "You never know in places like this."

"Speaking of..." I point to his shiner. "What gives? I thought you were getting the white-collar treatment in here. Modified work release, fancy catered meals, contraband devices... the shite all the high-powered feckers get."

He huffs. "Not anymore. Things went south recently. It must've gotten *really* bad if the wild ace has come to call on me. What's the McKennon heir doing here, hmm? Has someone finally given you the king of spades?"

"No one's sent me your card to put you out of your misery yet."

"So who sent you?"

"Well, in a way, our queen of diamonds did."

His sickly pale face reddens. "What are you talking about? What have you done with my daughter?"

"Relax, Keeper. Whatever danger she's in is not my fault, I can promise you that."

"Kian, where the fuck is Lacey?"

My fingers tap the metal table, giving a low, ominous echo as I contemplate how I want to play this.

"Monroe Baron has locked Lacey away in one of his suites."

"She's..." His face works through the information. "She's with her fiancé, then? Big deal. That's where I thought she was. She's fine. I've spoken with her."

"Oh, you've spoken with her, have you?" My brow rises. "I have it on good authority that the last time you spoke with her was in front of Monroe himself. Not exactly a father-daughter heart-to-heart, now is it? She's been trapped for the past two weeks for simply dancing on stage during her bachelorette party at Rouge."

"She, um..." He shifts in his seat. "Her mother and I didn't think she could get into so much trouble at our own establishment, but she embarrassed Monroe from what I understand."

I nearly burst out laughing. "Funnily enough, neither of you knows half the trouble she got into. But now she's miserable."

He frowns. "She's safe in a penthouse suite. What more could a Garde woman want?"

I tug my hair in frustration. "Safe? Fecking hell, Keeper, you don't know a bloody thing, do you? How can you be the leader of a society without knowing a fecking thing that goes on in it?"

"Watch it," Charlie growls.

"Not only is Monroe himself a dangerous, abusive loose cannon of a bastard, a girl like Lacey can't be kept in a high tower all by herself like that. She's not a fecking fairy-tale princess. The girl *needs* to move about and be around the people she loves. Your so-called Red Camellia is wilting."

He cocks his head to the side and studies me.

"You know my daughter well, then, do you?"

Shite. I've shown my hand too quickly.

I bite my tongue, not sure if I should answer.

"Kian, look, I don't know what you want me to say. I see no harm in her being protected."

"She's not being *protected*. She's being jailed. You and I both know the difference. The gobshite wants to keep her there until their sham of a wedding day."

"And that's a problem because?"

I huff out a breath and decide to place my bet.

"Because she's already married, Mr. O'Shea. Or should I call you *Dad*?"

Scene 23

TWISTED GYVES

Charlie O'Shea's mouth drops as much as his broken jaw will allow.

"She's already married? To *you*? How the fuck did this happen?"

"Hours into Lacey's birthday, I invoked my right to our betrothal. I'm *sure* you've been worried sick over improperly breaking our contract without just cause, but no worries, Keeper. I've taken care of it and your honor is intact."

"This is insanity," he grumbles.

"Maybe. But so is marrying your daughter to that psychopath Monroe."

"You're a hitman, Kian. The fact that you don't think *you* are crazy is concerning."

"There are many different types of crazy, Charlie. Mine just so happens to be obsessed with your daughter."

I'm not supposed to know that Monroe is testifying on the O'Shea's behalf. Secrets are not only currency in the Garde, they're also a sign of trustworthiness. I won't betray Lacey by telling her father that she's confided in me, so I choose my next

"Monroe won't require a playing card to hurt Lacey, so why did you want her to marry him?"

"There were... extenuating circumstances."

"'Extenuating circumstances,' my arse. What does he have over your family, Charlie? If I'm able to find out what hold he's got, then I can bring Lacey back where she belongs. *Actually* safe. With me."

His cuffs clink as he gingerly rubs his face with his fingers. When he rests his hands back on the table, he lets out an exhausted sigh that leaves him sagging against the back of his chair. It's the most defeated I've ever seen the Keeper, even in the arrest pictures, court appearances, and mug shots that plastered the world's news.

It's unsettling and... interesting.

"What is it?" I ask.

"I never *wanted* my daughter to marry Monroe Baron." The words grate out and he clears his throat. "Marrying into your family was obviously the better choice for the O'Sheas, McKennons, and the Garde as a whole."

"But..."

"But apparently one of the families has it out for me. I suspect it's because I was trying to set my businesses on the straight and narrow."

"I could see how that wouldn't do you any favors. The Garde has never played it straight, even from the beginning. We're no better than the mob we tried to leave behind."

He concedes with a shrug. "Well, you figured it out before I did, then. Someone tipped off the police, claiming I'd committed fraud, extortion, bribery, trafficking... all of which was going on right under my nose here in Las Vegas, and I'd had no idea. Before I knew it, the authorities slammed me with racketeering charges."

"How could you not know what's going on in your own damn city, Keeper?"

"Once you try to go straight, enemies come out of the wood-work because they think you'll either turn them in or force them to take the high road, too. I protected secrets, but once I started operating aboveboard, they dried up along with my power to rule the Garde. The information used against me should've only been known by the Keeper and the men involved, and I had no clue about any of it."

"So the actual perpetrators are other Garde members... not you?" My brow furrows. "Who are the families?"

"If I won't snitch to the authorities, what makes you think I'd snitch to my enemy?" he sneers.

I raise my hands. "Alright, alright... it was just a question, Keeper. Don't get your clogs in a twist. It's not the McKennons who've put you here."

"Fuck you." He shakes his head.

"Look, Charlie, like it or not, you and I are family now. All I'm saying is, if you tell me those names, I can write them off as suspects. No one would risk bringing their crimes into the light just to pin them on you."

He stares at me for a long time, taking my measure, before he shakes his head. "If it comes down to it, I'll tell you, but only if it's for the good of the Garde. I'm sitting on that secret right now, though. Which is one of the reasons why I'm still in here."

"How so?"

"Ever since I was thrown back in jail under new trumped-up charges and forced to await trial here... the District Attorney has been pressuring me to testify against other families. She's threatened to throw everything she can at me if I don't."

"Huh, well the fact that she's taken this long is a testament to how little she has against you directly, right?"

Charlie nods. "That, but she's also waiting until a certain non-Garde judge can preside over the case."

"Fecking hell, how does she even know his affiliation? Or yours, for that matter?"

"Someone's been in her ear. She's embellished every possible charge you can think of, from petty theft to murder. Adding it together, I'm facing a life sentence... but she's seeking the death penalty."

"The death penalty?" My eyes flare. "Lacey doesn't know this."

"No, and I'd never tell her these stakes. She's been through enough, thanks to me and my dealings. I don't want to burden her with that, too."

"So to avoid life—and death—you broke our marriage contract and gave it to Monroe."

"I had to. Once Monroe's father died, making Monroe the new Baron, he came to me with an offer. One that was too tempting when I was looking at a lifetime behind walls like these. He said that he would use his knowledge as my financial manager to testify on what he can, but only if I promised Lacey in marriage. I lied to Lacey because I knew she'd try to refuse to marry the Baron unless I made you the villain and told her no one else wanted her because of me. I also didn't want her knowing I'm resorting to black-mailing a potential innocent for freedom I don't deserve."

"Blackmail?"

"The Baron's contacts in the Northeast have secrets on the judge. We'll only use them against him once the trial is in session."

"The judge isn't Garde." I point out as I piece it together. "So he has secrets even the Keeper doesn't know, but Monroe's non-Garde contacts do."

"Exactly. My attorney says Monroe's testimony will clear me of the financial crimes, and the blackmail should do away with the rest. Of course, that's only if Monroe decides to stop being an asshole and commits to testifying."

"So you bargained your daughter's future, her happiness, her *life* on a chance that someone who likely killed his own goddamn father would be honorable to *you*?"

"You think my daughter would've been happier with you than with the Baron?" He barks a laugh and it takes everything in me not to throw a right hook to blacken his other eye.

"I'd imagine she'd be happier alive than dead. Would the cost of freedom be worth it with your daughter's blood on your hands?"

"What the fuck are you talking about?"

"Did you know Monroe already had someone killed just to scare her into submission? At your own establishment, no less?"

The O'Shea's face pales, making the bluish-purple-and-yellow bruises even more pronounced.

"He did what?"

I'm bluffing, of course. All signs—but my instincts—point to me being wrong. The police have already arrested the victim's fiancé, making my hunch merely a conspiracy theory. But I'm not above telling a wee lie to scare the truth out of the Keeper. Besides, conspiracy theories are true more often than not when the Garde is involved.

"Before Lacey's bachelorette party, Monroe warned her not to get drunk and embarrass him. Then that night, a redheaded woman dressed as a bride—just like Lacey—was found murdered in Rouge."

"My wife never told me any of this."

"Did Moira not tell you? Or did you not call her like you haven't called your daughter?"

He huffs. "The security in the infirmary aren't as *understanding* about contraband phones. They confiscated my last one and I'm waiting for them to stop watching me like hawks before I send for another. I bet Moira's worried sick. Do you really think Monroe murdered an innocent?"

"I think it was a warning to Lacey to get in line. If he'd commit murder to scare your daughter, what's to stop him from murdering her if she gets in his way?"

"Dammit, this wasn't supposed to be like this. It was meant to be a marriage in exchange for a quick trial before the prosecutor could bring all these other charges. The Baron would give his testimony and I'd be free." The Keeper curses under his breath before meeting my eyes. "You... you have to get her out of there, Kian."

"I know. But I can't without starting a war with the Garde, not to mention one with my own wee wife. She'd never forgive me if she found out I kicked off a death penalty trial for you."

"She takes after her mother. That woman would stand by me at any cost," he answers without any humor in his voice. A fact, then. No doubt one that's been proven too many times.

As I rest my forearms on the table, the cold metal leaks through the fabric of my suit.

"So don't abuse that trust, Charlie. Tell me as much as *you* can about what Monroe knows, who he knows, all that he's planning to testify to, and I'll figure out how to get you out as quickly as *I* can."

He shakes his head. "I... I don't know. I wish I did. My lawyers and the families I trust have already searched. But any evidence of my innocence has been destroyed."

"You've found *nothing*? Jesus, Mary, and Joseph, what has your lawyer been doing while you've been rotting away in here for the past year, huh? If they couldn't find evidence, how can you count on Monroe to know anything at all?

"Along with the Baron's testimony, he also has incriminating photos on the judge. From everything my people have looked into, the judge is otherwise clean as a whistle. The pictures are blurry, but from what you can see, they're damaging enough to get him to override a jury if they find me guilty."

"And they're real? Did he tell you how he obtained them?"

He hesitates before answering, "As real as I can hope they'd be."

"Goddammit, Charlie, you did all this on a hope and a prayer? Bloody fecking hell." I slap the table hard, making Charlie jolt in his seat, but I don't feel an ounce of guilt over it. "The prosecutor is obviously grasping at straws and making threats she can't back up, so just let the trial happen naturally and have your attorney fight the good fight. I'm getting Lacey out of there and telling her it's over. War be damned. You're on your own."

"You can't do that!"

"And why the feck not?" I lunge forward, inches away from his head before I can stop myself. "Tell me why I should let *my wife* sacrifice herself for you and all these other Garde arseholes."

The son of a bitch doesn't flinch this time, but the impulse to murder him recedes as I take in the utter defeat in this once strong man's slack features.

"Because if it gets to the Baron that Lacey is no longer his fiancée and I'm still in here, I won't make it to trial."

He lifts his shirt, revealing bruises I've only seen after the worst of fights and a large bandage underneath his lungs. One of the most effective areas to strike if you're stabbing to kill.

"The Baron will *keep* sending attackers... until one day, he kills me."

Scene 24

THE WILTED CAMELLIA

"The Mass is ended, go in peace to love and serve the Lord."

"Thanks be to God," I mumble as I cross myself.

The final song begins to resound from the church organ, echoing inside St. Patrick's Cathedral in disjointed harmony with various lackluster voices singing off-key from the pews. As soon as it finishes, the congregants begin to file out behind the priests. I kneel with my hands folded in prayer until I see her coming up the aisle.

It's been seventeen days since I last saw Lacey, and our recent empty and hollow conversations were only made worse after my visit with her father yesterday. Or rather, since I said I'd have to tell her the details in person. *Again.*

I think that final dismissal struck a major blow to her confidence in our scheme and I'm afraid it made her lose confidence in *me*. Hopefully when I tell her what I can, I'll restore her trust.

Lacey's every bit the Garde's Red Camellia as she follows behind her austere mother with Monroe at her side. She's playing her part perfectly in a black and white dress with elbow-length sleeves and a skirt that flows from her waist to her knees. My eyes narrow at her short black lace gloves, an interesting choice and not her usual style, but my gaze drifts back up to analyze her features.

Being in isolation is sucking the light out of her, but she's poised with a lukewarm smile while her arm loops through his. The only way to tell that she's fecking miserable is her left hand fisted at her side and the fact that Monroe is crushing her arm against him to keep her close.

My eyes zero in on the contact and anger burns in my chest.

Strike four.

Logic says I should wait with my head bowed until they pass me, but at the sight of her barely holding on, my heart demands the rest of my body rise from my seat.

Monroe's not paying a lick of attention to me, smiling and waving at the rest of the churchgoers like he's campaigning. Counting on him to keep ignoring me and Lacey, I stride through the exiting crowd, steering toward the altar at the front of the church. My head is straight, seemingly not looking at anything else other than my destination, but Lacey's furtive glance flashes in my periphery.

I wind my way around passersby down the center of the aisle toward her, counting the pews between us as I go. My heart thrums in my chest. Every muscle tenses with the urge to throw her over my shoulder and flee with her. My fingers stretch at my sides, tingling even more with every footstep closer until we're merely rows apart.

Three.

Two.

One.

Her back straightens as my arm gently brushes hers. To onlookers, it seems as though I'm steering clear of people leaving their seats. No one else sees the way my fingers graze Lacey's soft palm. Or that, for a mere breath, her hand intertwines with mine.

She's mine again for a moment.

Then we both take another step...

...and she's gone.

I glance back just in time to see her give the confessionals a slight nod before refocusing on the cathedral's entrance.

Meet me in the confessional.

That was the last message I sent her this morning. She never responded, but I prayed like hell during the sermon that she would follow through with it. That one subtle look tells me she'll meet me if she can.

Once I get to the end of the aisle, I walk toward the votive stand and light a candle for my mother while I wait impatiently for everyone to leave. When the nave no longer echoes with voices, I cross myself and slip into the nearby confessional before drawing the long red curtain closed.

The hard wooden bench takes up half of the cramped space and the empty cubicle behind the priest's latticed window assures me that I'm alone in here. I should sit, but I'm a bundle of nerves at the thought of finally getting to hear Lacey's voice in person, feel her in my arms, and smell her sweet floral scent.

After only a moment, clacking high heels begin to echo against the marble. I frown at the uneven cadence, but I resist peeking through the curtain. Fifteen agonizing seconds later, the steps halt outside the confessional.

The curtain flies open and Lacey hurries inside before slapping it closed behind her. I tug her into me and all the worry, all the pent-up longing, releases as I finally get to hold her again. When she wraps her arms around me just as fiercely, the icy cold doubt that'd started to harden my heart warms into a puddle at her feet.

"Kian," she whispers and my chest aches at hearing my name on her lips for the first time in weeks. "I've missed you."

My heartbeat thuds and I squeeze her tighter, reveling in the softness of her loose strawberry-blonde curls against my cheek.

"I've missed you so damn much, *tine*."

We've texted or called every day since I last saw her, but feeling her in my arms is unmatched. Ironically, she's taken a liking to me much more quickly than if Monroe hadn't intervened. I have no doubt a flame would've ignited for me eventually, but instead of a slow burn, this adrenaline and secrecy have brought us together in a conflagration.

"I don't have much time. My mom and Monroe think I'm confessing my sins from Devil's Night. They were both too busy courting his favorite potential donors to care."

"Why haven't you been messaging me back? You can't leave me hanging when your safety is at stake. My people said Monroe got in this morning and didn't go up to the suite when he picked you up, but I was still worried."

She blows out a breath and the pungent smell of liquor wafts toward me, taking me aback.

"I know, I'm sorry. I should've replied, but when I had to change your name to 'Roxxy' again, it made me sad to see her name instead of yours."

Before I can respond, she kisses me and I groan into her mouth. Taking control, I grip her neck with one hand while cupping her head with the other. She melts against me, but it's only when I allow myself to fully enjoy her silken tongue against mine that I taste it.

The sickly saccharine sweet of sugar and booze.

It takes every ounce of willpower I have to break away from her.

"Lacey, have you been drinking?"

When she steps back to answer me, I rest my hands on her shoulders, unwilling to stop touching her yet. My eyes roam over her features, truly assessing my wife for the first time in weeks.

The combination of her makeup and the confessional's dim light hides her freckles, sharpens the shadows on her cheeks, and further bruises the purple bags under her eyes. Her sky-blue orbs are glossy and slightly disoriented as they roll dramatically at my question.

"Chill out. It was just a morning mimosa or three to take the edge off of having to be glued to a man I hate for hours. Nothing to worry about."

Uneasiness churns my stomach.

"It was more than mimosas. You smell like tequila."

"Jesus, didn't know you were a fucking bloodhound," she snorts.

"Lacey." I level her with a pointed look.

"Okay, maybe I'm a little drunk from my wild night in with my elephant friends."

"Lacey, this isn't like you. You're drunk before *Mass*, for Christ's sake. Talk to me."

"I'm *fine*, okay? Even better now that I'm here with you. I need you, Kian."

Her lips slam against mine again. Bloody hell, kissing Lacey has been all I've wanted to do every moment we've been apart. But the taste of liquor overrides everything, reminding me what's at stake.

She's going down a dark path that's hell to come back from. Her light is being smothered in that tower all by herself and I can't stand by another moment while Monroe tries to snuff it out.

When she falls to her knees and goes for my belt, I snap out of it.

"Lacey—"

"I'm on my period, so I don't want to have sex, but I can do this instead—"

"*Fuck*, do I want to..." I stop her with my hands on her wrists. "But I won't if you're going back to Monroe's suite. If we do this, you're coming home. Those are your choices. Fucking me in a confessional before you go back to your ex-fiancé isn't one of them."

As I pull her to stand, her lips poke out like she's about to pout. But at the last second, her face blanks and she sighs.

"What'd you bring me in here for, then?" Her lack of expression is worse than anger. At least her rebellious streak is sexy as hell, but this? Indifference is torture.

"You really think I only asked you here to suck my cock? We should talk about the things we haven't been able to discuss because we don't know whether Monroe's security has audio."

"Oh... that." She blows out a breath that trills her lips. "Yeah, when you left me hanging again, I had to stop caring. It was easier than disappointment."

Her pain is a punch to my stomach, but I couldn't tell her that her father was in the infirmary, or she would've lost her shite. I'd planned to confide in her afterward until I saw Charlie's nearly mortal wound and heard a grown man beg me to keep his secret to "protect his daughter." I know he made the deal to save his own skin, but I agreed because its impact on Lacey could be disastrous. Hopefully, when this is all over, she'll understand that I shielded her heart the best I knew how.

"I'm doing what I can out here, but I can only do that if I know you're safe. You look like you haven't slept in days and you've stopped texting me unless I threaten you. Are you okay?"

She sneers at me while she tries to tug away. "I'm fine, alright? I'm the *perfect* Garde wife. Set aside like a trophy on a high ledge. First for you, now the Baron. You guys better be careful or I'll jump off."

"Lacey," her name rumbles low and deep from my chest, where my heart aches for her. I tighten one hand on her wrist while my other drifts to her throat to force her to meet my eyes. "Don't talk like that."

Holding her like this has settled her in the past, but she fights back now.

"Why not? Oh, that's right. I forgot. I'm just a pawn in all of your games. I should just *wait* for one of you to push me off the ledge, right? You know, before I do something drastic like think for myself."

"Goddammit, that's it. This ends now." Still holding on to one of her wrists, I let go of her throat to pull out my mobile.

"What're you doing?" she asks, no longer tugging away from me.

"Messaging my friends. I'll get Tolie or Merek to cause a diversion outside and I'm taking you out of here—"

She snatches the device and slams it on the wooden floor of the confessional so hard that something crunches.

"*Fuck...*" My hands carve into my hair as I growl, "What the hell, Lacey?"

"You can't do that." She turns to leave, but I grab her hand.

"Give me one bloody good reason why I shouldn't throw you over my shoulder and carry you back home right now."

She glares at me and jerks against my hold, but when I don't let up, she takes a deep breath like she's about to shout.

I clap my hand over her lips and whirl her around inside the confessional to press her against the back wall, blocking her from her exit.

"If you scream, I'll fecking do it, I swear to Christ, Lacey. I'll carry you out in front of God and the Garde. I'll start a war just to get you to talk to me, goddammit."

She harrumphs behind my palm and rolls her eyes. When she seems like she's calmed down, I finally remove my hand and bend to her level.

"Talk. To. Me."

"Ugh, you know why you can't call it off. I don't know what the Baron has that exonerates my father."

Frustration roughens my voice. "Your father's a grown-arse man. He made his bed in that jail cell and then sold you to a monster for *his* freedom."

"You *stole* me for yours," she snaps, jabbing her finger into my chest. "Are you so different?"

"*Yes.*" I snatch her tiny weapon and use it to draw her against me. "You were supposed to be mine all along, and *you* were stolen from *me*. Now I'm losing you again and for what? A fecked-up scheme where someone framed your father so Monroe can pretend he has evidence that can save him? Think about it." My theories spill out of me, but I hope she catches every word. "Monroe's goal is to become Keeper of the Garde, the most powerful man in the society, and maybe even the country. Why would he help your father get out of jail when he's right where Monroe wants him? In there, he's Monroe's prisoner as much as the government's."

Lacey chokes a gasp. "No... no. H-he has to have evidence, right? My father said it would be enough."

"But did either of them tell you what it was?"

Her mind works over the information, but she's still slowly shaking her head.

The hurt on her face gets to me, and I ignore my own ache inside over the defeat in my wee firecracker. I brush the underside of her jaw with my thumb and gentle my voice.

"Your father made all the choices here, not you. As the Keeper, he scared the wrong people by trying to go straight and he wasn't able to keep the Garde's loyalty. Whatever pointed to his innocence has been destroyed, and all Monroe can testify to are the financial charges, not the others the prosecutor is trying to add on. You might've believed you could save him, but not saving him doesn't mean *you* doomed *him*. The Keeper doomed himself."

Her face crumples. "No matter how he got in there, if I can get him out, I'm going to try. Or I would've tried... but if all the evidence has been destroyed—" She stops midsentence and I tense as she realizes my mistake. "Wait, how do you know that?"

"How do I know about what?"

"About the evidence being destroyed? That Monroe can only testify to certain charges? That he was framed by the Garde? I don't know, take your fucking pick of questions, Kian. I've got plenty."

She tries to yank her hand out of mine, but I press it harder against my chest and squeeze her nape again.

Feck, this is it. I've got to tell her.

I lick my lips and brace myself for her reaction, which only makes my perceptive queen of diamonds flare her eyes.

"Who have you been talking to, Kian? Tell me right now, or I swear to God—"

"Your father, Lacey... I saw your father."

Scene 25

MADNESS MOST DISCREET

I analyze the smooth features of his face to see if there's a hint of guilt for keeping this from me. His strong jaw is set in his decision, but his brows pinch slightly in the middle as he studies me.

"You saw my father?" My free hand balls into a fist at my side and my legs vibrate with the need to dance, jump, fucking *flee*. The buzz I worked so hard for this morning nearly vanishes. "When did you see him? Y-yesterday? Was that who your meeting was with?"

When he nods, I try to recall every possible hint he could've given me during our hours of texting and phone calls.

"But... why did you have to wait two weeks to see him?"

A barely perceptible wince flashes across his face. So quick, I'm not sure if my tipsy mind imagined it.

"They wouldn't let me meet with him straight away. Jail protocol."

"Good God. Jails are so extra with their 'protocol.' But you could've told me what was going on."

"I couldn't. We weren't sure whether Monroe had audio-based security."

Something about what he's saying doesn't ring true, but there are so many feelings swirling around in this small booth—worry, lust, anger, betrayal, fear—that I can't keep my head on straight. I'm not sure which emotion will win out.

I swallow past the emotions stuck in my throat.

"What did he... h-how was he?"

My father refuses to let me visit and while the prosecutor sits primly on the case, twiddling her thumbs, I haven't been able to so much as hug him.

Kian's harsh face softens a fraction and his hand massages my nape.

"He's okay—"

"Don't lie," I hiss and try to shrug him off, but he doesn't budge. "If he's fine, why hasn't he called me like he said he would?"

Kian hesitates before answering, "He's alright, Lacey. His old mobile isn't working anymore, but he's going to get a new one. He told me to tell you that he loves you and that he's okay."

"He's... okay. He's okay," I repeat slowly.

I try to swallow again, but my throat doesn't cooperate and I cough instead. Kian squeezes my hand and his thumb caresses smooth circles on my neck as he tries to comfort me. To my surprise, it works.

"What did you guys talk about?"

"About his case, how he was framed—"

"So you believe he was framed now, too?" Hope takes flight in my chest for the first time in days and instead of shoving it down to protect myself, I let it soar.

"I do. Your father also gave me the go-ahead to use my own methods to learn who framed him and why."

Kian is really going to help me.

The past two weeks of isolation had begun to chisel away the belief that anyone was on my side. Relief flows through my veins now until the words actually register in my mind.

"Wait, why are you doing all of this? I mean, I'm grateful... but why do you care so much? What's in it for you?"

His eyes narrow with confusion. "You're my wife, Lacey."

I huff. "Alright, and why is that? Since you already know all my family's secrets, maybe you can finally tell me yours. You said you married me because of who I am when no one is watching. But what does that mean, exactly?"

He rakes his hand through his hair, blocking out most of the light that peeks through the confessional's curtain with his huge frame. It's a miracle he has any strands left, although I have a feeling he doesn't normally do this little quirk as often as he does it around me. I wish I had a better view now, though, because I don't think I'll ever stop loving the way his bicep flexes with the motion, testing the seams of his jacket sleeves, how the locks stand on end before they relax back into his perfectly tousled style.

He sighs, snapping me out of my daydreaming, and he nods to himself like he's come to a decision.

"When I was a wee lad, I thought you had to be in love to get married." His smile makes my chest flutter and I try to combat the feeling with a joke.

"That's funny. I thought you just had to be told where to stand at the end of the aisle."

He shakes his head. "Well, *I* imagined it'd be in a church like this one, and of course my wife was supposed to not only remember it, but she was supposed to *want* to be there," he chuckles wistfully.

A small smile lifts my lips. "How on earth did a romantic like you survive in our world, Kian McKennon?"

"I had my parents to model after. They loved one another so fiercely it caused our families to hate each other. Did you know that?" When my brow wrinkles, he continues. "My mam was supposed to marry Charlie O'Shea in a political marriage, but my dad stole her away the night before her wedding. He would do anything for the woman he loved."

"Even start a war between families, apparently." I laugh.

He shrugs. "Like father, like son, huh?"

My lips part at the admission, and my breath catches in my

chest. I want to respond, but I can't for the life of me find the words.

"Watching them made me believe love was something I'd have for myself one day. And then, five years ago, it all came together like fate—or my mother's design, whichever way you'd like to look at it. You were the one I was meant to fall in love with. But then one day she wasn't here, and neither were you."

My chest aches at the pain in his voice and my hand drifts to his face before I realize what I'm doing. His jaw muscles tic underneath the scruff beneath my fingertips, but he holds my wrist, keeping them there as he continues.

"Losing my mam, then finding out you weren't going to be mine... it sent me off the deep end. I found solace in the wrong things. Tried any vice that could make me forget. Funny enough, with all the damage I could've done owning casinos in Vegas, poker was never my weakness. My love for the game and the strategy centers me. I don't even gamble. I win and give everything back to the house. But liquor... that was my favorite poison. I tried to drown myself in it. Who cared if Kian McKennon never surfaced again? Certainly not Lacey O'Shea." He huffs a laugh. "It's funny to think about now since I stopped drinking because of you."

My hand drops from his face to point at my chest.

"Because of *me*?" My voice lilts at the end and my heart stutters to a stop as I listen.

He nods. "A year ago, my dad dragged me kicking and screaming out of the pit of one of my benders. Once I came to, he gave me a queen of diamonds card and a job. I'd needed something to care about that was bigger than myself to get sober. So you became my purpose. I was to study the Red Camellia. Learn you inside and out. In the beginning, I used your social media—"

"Oof, I hate to break it to you, but Roxy does most of that for me. If you think you know me from my social media, you're sadly mistaken. That Lacey is a completely different woman."

"Oh, I know." He chuckles. "I could tell. Professionally edited pictures. Perfectly curated for the masses. It was *her* social media where I saw the real you. In the background, you weren't this bubbly, vapid socialite. You were the quiet girl, the rebel, and the free spirit. The Garde may keep you caged, but you rattle the bars every chance you get. I've studied you—the *real* Lacey—for over a year."

He rests his hand above my head on the confessional wall and leans into me. Sweet, smoky amber fills my senses and makes my belly flip.

"You were my opponent and I analyzed you furiously until I knew your every tell. The more I found out, the angrier and more obsessed I became. This woman with a soft heart that she shielded from our harsh world..." He strokes my cheek and tips my chin to see the fire in his eyes. "This woman was supposed to be mine, but she thought that I wasn't good enough. It made me hate you even as I fell in love with you."

My eyes widen and my lips part, but he continues on.

"Then, on Devil's Night, I saw you dance for the first time."

"I... I never let Roxy post that," I whisper. "Dancing is for me."

"And you're incredible at it. The passion in your body, face, the way you moved with me. Feck, I needed more. I had your queen of diamonds card and I had my orders. I even tricked myself into thinking I could follow them. But you changed my mind with every touch. And then I got a taste of you."

"A taste?" I shiver at the thought of him feasting on me that night.

"A taste..." he murmurs low before brushing his lips against mine. It's a whisper of a kiss, but it sends ripples of pleasure down my skin. "I married you because of this."

"You... you married me because of a kiss?"

"Not *a* kiss. *Your* kiss. You kissed me first, Lace. You wanted me as badly as I wanted you and you went for it. The Garde tries to restrain that fiery strength inside of you... and I want to free it."

The air is too heavy around us and my heart races in my chest.

I search for something to relieve the tension and I try to huff out a chuckle.

"So a dance and a kiss. That's what sealed my fate?"

He frowns at my attempt at deflection and yanks my left hand up.

"What're you doing?"

"Making my point."

My brow furrows as he tugs at each finger of my lace glove, slowly pulling it off, and it takes me a second before I realize he's about to reveal my own secret.

"Wait..."

But he removes the glove in one fell swoop and holds up my hand. The silver band on my ring finger glints in the light.

"Even now, you rebel against the Garde so you can be mine."

His gaze is intense, but I can't look away from it, even as he unbuttons the top half of his shirt. He places my left hand over his warm, hard, bare chest before pressing his palm above the neckline of my dress, erupting goose bumps over my skin.

I hold my breath as his heart races underneath my palm, and my own sprints to match his pace. It's not until my back leaves the wall that I realize my body has leaned into his, trying to connect everywhere it can.

"See, you feel it, too, *tine*," he murmurs.

"F-Feel what?"

"This *cuisle*. The pulse between us that tugs us closer together. I felt it that first night and I could tell that you did, too. But if you feel this pull even half as much as I do, you should know why I stole you when I had the chance. *This*, more than anything else, sealed *our* fate. You say that you're a pawn in this game. But you're so much more. You're not a pawn. You're *my* queen, and you rule me, my rebel queen of diamonds."

He caresses the sensitive skin above my breast as his hand leaves my chest to dip into his pocket and retrieve his silver poker chip. My hand still rests over his steadily thumping heart, but he lowers it to hold between us. Curiosity has me tilting my head as he raises the chip to the light peeking through the confessional curtain. The number twenty-four and the words "to thine own self be true" catch my eye on the raised silver exterior.

"I thought that was a poker chip," I whisper.

"No, this... is a lifeline. This Alcoholics Anonymous chip has saved me countless times over the past year."

Guilt nags in my mind at every joke I've made to him about drinking or when I snapped at him for being worried about me. I want to apologize, but I'm hanging on his every word and I don't dare interrupt him.

"The day you became my focus was the first time in years that I didn't have a drink. I went to my first of many AA meetings and got this twenty-four-hour chip. It's the only achievement that's ever mattered to me because it was the day my life changed for the better and I never looked back. I dove into my new purpose and sobered up. Except for Tolie and Merek, all my friends left me. For the past year, I've become religious about this mission, you, and my sobriety and this chip have helped me through it all. But now..."

He takes a deep breath and places the coin into my palm. "I want you to have it."

The metal is warm from where his fingers have been. Gratitude and guilt war in my chest and I shake my head.

"Kian, I can't take this." I try to give it back, but he closes my hand around the chip again and presses it to my chest.

"It's no coupon book, I know." He chuckles. "But it's my gift to you. The only way I'm leaving with it is if you leave with me."

"I... can't."

"You have to get out of there. I'll figure out what evidence Monroe has on my own. We can't risk you going back to his suites. He's too dangerous."

"More dangerous than you?" It's meant to be a flirty joke, but neither of us laughs.

"To the world? No. To you? Yes."

"What do you mean?"

"With him, your life is in danger. With me? The world is. No one touches my wife."

His voice is pitched low and ominous. It should scare me, but it hits me right in my core and my lower belly flutters in response even as logic screams at me to get a grip.

"Monroe is dangerous to my father, too. If I leave without answers, my dad might never get out."

"And how far are you willing to go for this charade? Would you go through a second wedding? Sign an illegal marriage license? Fuck him? Have children that are supposed to be *ours*?"

"No... no." I flinch at every word and shake my head as my resolve begins to crumble. "Kian, stop."

"Lacey, no matter the outcome, if Monroe's alive, he'll have your father killed in the end."

"But if someone kills Monroe before the trial, there's no hope for my father, either!"

I slump onto the small bench and the longer I sit, the more Kian becomes a watery blur. I've only had his chip for a few minutes and already I'm clutching it like it holds all the answers.

"What am I going to do? I... I don't want to do this anymore, but I don't want to hurt my dad."

"Oh, *mo thine*, come here." His whisper sounds like "mu hin-neh." I don't know what it means, but his warm tone wraps around my soul like a heavy blanket as he gathers me into his arms. I press myself against him and shut my eyes tight to fight back tears, but eventually they win the battle.

Kian's amber and smoky, sweet scent comforts me as he squeezes me tighter. It's been so long since someone's held me this way, if ever. The closest I can think of is the time my mother taught me the harsh truth about what it means to be a Garde wife. I've been lonely in my reality ever since.

"Come with me, *tine*."

Those words. I'm desperate to give in. But...

"I can't." He resists when I pull away. "I have to do this for my family."

"*I'm* your family now, too."

"Maybe we could've been if things had been different." I swallow to keep going even though I hate every word as it burns my tongue. "But we're a stolen relationship and you took my decision to get married away from me."

His brow furrows as he shakes his head. "Your family did that to us both first. And yet you're loyal to them."

The truth slams into my chest like a physical blow.

"I... I don't know what to say. I'm sorry. I *want* to go with you. But doing that means my father loses his freedom *because* of me. You told him you'd use your own methods to find out who framed him. The Baron's never home, so can't I stay in his suite as a decoy until you've found out how to free my dad? If we try *everything*, then... then you can get me out."

"Promise?" he asks, his brow raised.

I swallow, hoping I don't regret this decision. "I promise."

"I'll work as fast as I can, then. But this?" He swipes his thumb underneath my eye, over the purple circles my concealer couldn't hide after so many drunk and hopeless nights. "This isn't okay, Lacey. The way you're coping isn't okay. I need you safe."

"I'll be safe. It's not like the Baron will hurt me. He'd be too afraid of the optics, so there's no way he'll harm my 'pretty face.'"

Just my soul.

Kian curses. "But if he so much as touches you—"

"I know, I know. Tell you where."

"*Immediately.* I'll give you a week. Respond to my messages and calls, and if you're not taking better care of yourself by next Sunday's Mass, I'm taking you home. Whether I have answers about your father or not. Got it?"

I wince and point to the shattered pieces on the ground. "But how will I message you?"

"I'll take care of it. I'd take care of everything if you'd let me."

"I know you would."

I inhale him one more time before exhaling slowly. This decision is nearly taking all the willpower I have. I want him to whisk me away, giving me the freedom I crave. But then my father will never be freed.

Whatever Kian sees in my face must finally convince him that I've made up my mind. He nods to my hand that's holding his chip.

"Keep that safe until you're back with me. While we're apart, see it as my commitment to you. I'm always with you and doing my damnedest to get you out of that pit."

The sincerity in his voice nearly brings me to tears again and I give him a watery smile.

"Thank you, Kian. This gift means everything." I tuck the coin in my dress pocket. "I'll keep it here. Whenever I can't wear my ring, they'll be side by side."

Possession and pride spark in his eyes, but a sliver of pain dims his expression. Is letting me go killing him as much as it's killing me to leave him? I blink back the remorse threatening to spill down my cheeks and I clear my throat.

"Can I, um, can I have a kiss before I go?" I chuckle nervously. "Not on the lips, though, so we don't get carried away again."

He encircles my neck and tips my chin up with his thumb as his mouth hovers over my forehead.

"Somewhere like here?" His warm breath tickles my sensitive skin as he whispers. Before I can answer, his lips caress down to my temple until he kisses the apple of my cheek with a featherlight touch that makes me shiver. "Or here?"

My hands clutch the lapels of his suit jacket to keep me steady.

"Anywhere else?"

I shake my head, even though I'm dying for him to give the rest of me that treatment.

"Shame." His accent thickens, making my core flutter as he whispers low, "I would've liked to kiss more of you before having to say goodbye. Love should be more than hushed conversations and stolen touches."

Love...

I yank him down and collide my mouth against his. His tongue dives between my lips, wasting no time, and he tugs me by the waist against his already hardening cock. I thread my hands into his hair and he groans into my mouth—

"Lacey?"

My mom's voice echoes through the church and a shock of fear straightens my spine. She calls again, closer this time, but I wait a moment longer, holding my breath until her high heels clack off into the distance.

I can't meet Kian's eyes when I finally whisper, "I have to go."

His lips brush mine again before he pulls away.

"I... I care for you Lacey. *Is tú mo rogha.* Don't make us regret you choosing this instead."

I swallow, unable to respond.

I already do.

Scene 26

CHANGE OF PLANS, NOT OF HEART

I put my glove back on as Kian helps me straighten my dress and hair. Once I'm ready, I give him a kiss that's way too short before slipping out through the curtain.

The sanctuary is empty as I walk between the pews to exit through one of the back hallways. I'll use the bathroom there so I can at least be partially truthful about where I went when my mother asks why I didn't answer her. I'd be shocked that I was given this much time unsupervised, but for all my mother's faults, she still believes in the sanctity of confession and Monroe was likely too busy preening for his sycophants to notice how long I was gone.

When I push the hallway door open, I hear the faint rustling of the confessional's heavy curtains on the other side of the sanctuary. I don't have the heart to watch Kian walk away from me, so I keep my eyes straight ahead and let the hallway door shut behind me.

Once inside the ladies' room, I'm tempted to splash my face with water, but I don't want to ruin the "no makeup" look that Monroe is so fond of. He has no idea it's far from effortless, requiring just as much product as my normal style. Instead, I touch up with the compact in my purse, send a prayer of thanks to the woman who created waterproof mascara, and take off my gloves to wash my hands with frigid water. I hold them under, rinsing my wrists to cool the fever in my body that spikes around Kian.

When I step back to analyze my handiwork, I study myself from his point of view and my eyes widen.

Underneath them are bluish purple bags that I nonchalantly slathered concealer over this morning. My cheeks are hollowed and it's not just an effect from the bronzer I used for definition. Being tipsy makes the red veins in my bleary eyes stand out.

I never wanted this for myself. Ever since I was little, I've wanted to dance. My father and mother indulged my dreams for a while until the day my mother broke it to me that Garde women don't have aspirations. We're there for the success of the men, the family, and the Garde as a whole. Since my father was the biggest success of them all, so much more fell on my shoulders to make sure I toed the line.

I was twelve and other than the stoic pain that seeped through my mother's hug as I cried, the only other thing I can remember is throwing up violently afterward. As if the heartbreak was a tangible feeling that I needed to purge.

The Baron's punishment is slowly draining everything from me. But being locked in the Elephant Room isn't the only thing that's killing me. It's my role in the Garde itself.

This society has exhausted me for years. I've endured it by painting over my pain with makeup and a wine-stained false smile. Despite the bright spotlight I'm in day in and day out, no one's ever noticed I've been slowly dying inside... but Kian McKennon could tell in the dark.

"I've got to get out of there," I mutter to myself before toweling off my hands and leaving the bathroom.

I decide to take a shortcut outside through one of the hallway's side doors, so I don't bring any attention to myself by exiting through the entrance. Once I navigate the church's prayer garden, I see the large gathering outside the front of the cathedral.

St. Patrick's is gorgeous, but it sticks out like a sore thumb. Its ominous, gray stone facade and tall spire are a dark beacon against Vegas's iconic flashy lights and bright, over-the-top colors. Against the sunny backdrop, the church sucks vibrance from the city itself, much like the group of loud, boisterous men gathered out front seem to do to their pretty, silent wives.

Many Garde members attend St. Patrick's, but they do so in waves. They'll not attend for weeks at a time, and then suddenly, the whole clan packs the pews one Sunday like it's Easter morning. The church grounds are considered neutral territory, so they fly in from all over to gather for Garde announcements or whenever they believe their social or political standing could benefit from acting the part of good and pious church folk.

But no matter the reason for their attendance, they rush from the pews as soon as the last hymn ends to congregate outside of the church and impress whoever they find most important.

Despite every muscle in my body trying to slow me to a halt, I enter the crowd.

Laughter bellows from the group of politicians and famous wannabes that the Baron is regaling with some story. As someone else begins to give his own spin, Monroe spies me walking closer and glances at the gold watch in his hand. He shakes his head slightly and tucks it in his pocket before giving me a disappointed glare.

Shit.

I push past the dread churning in my stomach and stand beside my mother to join them.

Her sky-blue eyes, just like mine, flare slightly when she sees me, but that plastic smile stays in place as she leans toward me.

"Where were you? You didn't answer when I called your name inside the cathedral and I couldn't find you in the bathroom."

"Confession went long, but then the stalls downstairs were full, so I had to use the one near the Sunday school rooms." My fib rolls off my tongue as easily as the truth, but my mother didn't survive as the Keeper's wife by being gullible.

Her eyes narrow as she assesses my face, but she finally nods once and whispers in my ear. "Whatever you do, don't say a word. Play the part, Lacey."

My brow furrows, and in light of Kian's revelation about our parents, I really study her as she turns back to the group. From our profile, we look exactly alike, but for the frown lines fighting against her Botox. Her faded strawberry-blonde hair is wrapped in a chignon and she's wearing a long black dress, just as she's done every day since my father went to jail.

She was his second choice, and yet she's stayed faithful to him this entire time. Was she ever happy? I thought they'd loved each other, but did they ever? Was it always a marriage of convenience and politics? I shudder at the thought and avert my eyes to face the group.

But as I begin to listen to the conversation, the reason for her warning soon becomes clear.

"When the judge revoked his bond, I swear he shit himself. The bastard deserves it though." A political pundit from one of the popular news stations laughs. I'm sure whatever happens here will be broadcasted tonight at eight pm, eastern time.

"He's been ripping people off for decades. It's good riddance, I say," one of the senators chimes in.

"I don't blame you," Monroe agrees heartily with the rest of the group.

They continue to drag the victim of their gossip through the mud, interspersing their ridicule with sports statistics and talks of weather, but the more I listen, the more I realize whose reputation is the casualty.

They're talking about my father.

My cheeks heat and when Monroe opens his mouth to say something else, I interrupt him before I can stop myself.

"He was framed, you know. My father didn't cheat anyone."

"*Lacey*," my mom hisses.

The Baron narrows his light-brown eyes at me. "You don't actually believe that, do you?"

"You *don't*?" I ask, tilting my head and darting my gaze toward the reporter salivating for a scoop even in his off-hours.

Monroe is supposed to testify *for* my father. If he continues to blaspheme the O'Shea name like this, he'll taint his testimony before he even takes the stand.

The Baron's face purples and his lips tighten into a razor-thin line. He's trying to keep his cool for the audience, but fuck him. If he thinks he can talk shit about my father right in front of me, he has another thing coming.

"If he didn't cheat those people, then who do you suppose did?" a Nevada senator asks. I can't for the life of me remember his name, but his son is an asshole who likely got away with literal murder last year when a girl went missing at his college.

"She's kidding, Senator." The Baron chuckles. "It's best not to take socialites too seriously when they decide to get political."

I cut a glare to Monroe before answering the question anyway. But I choose my words carefully now that all eyes are on me.

"I don't know who hurt those people. That's not my job. I just know they've got the wrong guy and if the authorities reopened the case—"

"You know nothing about the law, Lacey," the Baron hisses under his breath, but everyone in the group shifts on their feet. Wives dip their heads and the less evil men pretend to switch topics among themselves, giving the Garde's princess and the future Keeper privacy. But I make note of the ones who keep their beady eyes on us, soaking in the gossip and potential secrets like it's their lifeblood.

"Don't try to insert yourself in things you know nothing about," he reiterates for good measure, but it only pisses me off more.

"Don't talk about those things around me then," I warn in a low voice of my own.

"Oh, Lacey. Please *stop*," my mother whispers and digs her nails into my forearm, but I refuse to back down from Monroe's angry glare.

I've been around worse men than Monroe Baron throughout my life. He may scare me in private, but I won't let him disgrace me in public, no matter what's in store after this.

Still, I have to fight the instinct to shy away from him as he wraps his arm around my waist to pull me close and whisper into my ear. His hand squeezes my hip painfully and his cologne slithers over me, making me desperately wish I could have smoky, sweet amber flood my senses instead.

"If you know what's good for you, you'll shut the hell up. Or if you don't care about your own safety, at least think of your father's. Now laugh as if I've flirted with you."

The threat makes me shudder, but I try to keep a brave face as I follow his instructions. A giggle claws its way up my throat and I lightly pat his forearm.

"Oh, Monroe, you're so bad."

The playful tease satisfies him, and a twitch of his lips is my only warning before he barks a laugh, spurring the crowd to do the same.

The touch of a gaze warms my cheeks. It takes me only a second to find Kian leaning against the cathedral doors, his hands in his pockets. No one's paying any attention to him, and I hadn't realized he'd even stayed. His protective fury caresses me like a salve compared to the crowd's burning stares.

But I'm snapped back to the conversation around me when one of the politicians laughs with Monroe.

"You've got a firecracker of a fiancée, don't you, Baron?"

"Speaking of which…" Monroe's voice grows louder as he steps away from the group, tugging me with him. The reporter's eyes bug out and he points his phone at us like a revolver in a duel. "As many of you know, I have an announcement to make."

"Monroe, what're you doing…"

"My Red Camellia was a bit of a naughty girl, but she went to confession and repented of those sins today. Didn't you, my sweet flower?"

Disgust churns in my belly, but I keep my lip from curling as I nod.

"Perfect. With that in mind, I've decided to forgive her. We're going to be married in two days!"

"Two days?" my mother and I gasp. She remembers herself before I do and reapplies her smile.

My gaze catches Kian's as he steps onto the first step, his eyes ablaze. I can't look away as Monroe elaborates on how he's screwing up all of our plans.

"We'll have the rehearsal dinner tomorrow. Stay tuned for details, ladies and gentlemen. You won't want to miss it. Now my fiancé and I must be off. Lots to prepare for a surprise wedding."

He turns us around, forcing me to drag my eyes away from Kian. I silently pray more than I ever have in church that he'll figure out how to get both me and my dad out of this.

People snap pictures on our way to the limo and Monroe waves as we walk.

"Monroe?" my mother's voice lilts as she clips behind us in her heels. Once she reaches us, she grits out her objection too quietly for anyone else to hear. "A rehearsal dinner and a wedding in less than forty-eight hours? That's... that's so soon. And almost impossible to plan for with the amount of detail you've requested."

He lowers his voice so that only she and I hear, but there's no respect for his future mother-in-law as he answers her.

"According to that reporter out there, some royal prince is throwing a secret wedding this Saturday that'll be broadcasted internationally, then it's Thanksgiving. I learned in New York that my contacts and I can't wait for me to put this off any longer. It works out because, this way, the only news report we'll be up against is the fact that it's supposed to rain in the next few days. Not to mention I'm sure the O'Shea is desperate to get out after all this time. You'd think you'd want his name cleared as soon as possible." Monroe pauses and raises a brow.

My mom blushes in shame. "Y-you're right. I do. It's just not a lot of time—"

"Plan the rehearsal dinner tomorrow at Rouge, Moira. Should be easy enough. It's not an inaugural dinner or rocket science."

One of Monroe's bodyguards opens the limo door and Monroe all but pushes me inside.

"At Rouge?" my mother squeaks as Monroe walks around to the other side where another bodyguard opens the door for him. "But... a woman—" Once he slides in and the door is closed behind him, she leans into the limo and hisses. "But a woman was *murdered* there two weekends ago."

"Make it happen, Mrs. O'Shea. I'm thinking a masquerade theme for the rehearsal dinner. Should be fun."

Confusion wrinkles her brow. "A *themed* rehearsal? But Monroe, *marriage* is supposed to be the theme. A-and what time do you want to meet at the church beforehand to run through the ceremony?"

He swats away my mother's concern with his hand.

"No need. We've all been to a wedding before. I don't have time to go through a whole rehearsal. I just want the dinner party. All the biggest names have soirees leading up to their weddings. Plain rehearsals are blasé and don't make for interesting news segments. So I look forward to seeing what you come up with, Moira."

"But—"

He flicks his hand at his bodyguard. The man slams the door in my mother's face before she can finish her question, sparking anger in my chest.

When it's just the two of us left in the backseat, I slide as far away from Monroe as I can. Thankfully he doesn't stop me.

I search out the tinted window for Kian and find him stalking through the crowd toward the limo. But before he can reach us, we pull away from the parking spot and into traffic, leaving him in the dust. I don't know what he would've done if he'd caught up.

Would he have ruined the whole charade? A part of me wishes he would.

But my dad...

"The Baron Suites for Miss O'Shea," Monroe barks at the driver and pulls out his stopwatch. He grumbles before shoving it into his pocket. "You took long enough confessing. Now I'll be late to one of my meetings."

"Sorry," I whisper.

"Hmm. Are you happy about finally getting to marry me?" He presses the button to close the partition between us and the cab.

"Ecstatic," I answer dryly, refusing to look at him.

That was my mistake.

As soon as the window quietly *snicks* shut, pain slams into my lower abdomen. The sharp blow forces a gasp from me and I clutch my side, leaving my back exposed as I try to protect myself. When Monroe punches me again twice near my kidney, I cry out. My entire body tenses, worsening the agony, as I brace myself for the next strike.

"Look at me, Lacey."

Tears brim my eyes as I turn weakly toward my attacker, the man who was supposed to be my husband and, thanks to Kian, now never will be.

The Baron smooths back the dirty-blond strands that fell from the gel binding them to his head. His goatee has moisture at the tips of his whiskers from where he seems to have literally been foaming at the mouth. He takes a deep breath and shakes his head.

"I shouldn't have had to do that, but you brought this on yourself when you questioned me in front of my peers. You will never embarrass me like that again. Do you understand? This high-and-mighty princess Red Camellia bullshit ends with me."

I nod once reflexively. Pain still radiates from my lower back and I have to breathe deeply to think straight. I'm willing to agree to anything to keep him from hitting me again.

"Answer me!" he screams, making me flinch as his spittle lands on my face.

"I w-won't embarrass you."

"Good. Recently, I've had more innocent women than you killed for less."

"You... the woman at Rouge? That was you?"

He huffs a laugh. "Isn't it funny? In hindsight, it was stupid of me to order a hit on you, but your defiance made me act rashly out of anger. Now some random woman is dead and it's all your fault. She was supposed to be you, which is why I didn't bother showing up to sign the license the next day. Imagine my shock when your mother said you apologized for sleeping in. Thank God for my bodyguards' fuckup though, because they saved me from making a terribly short-sighted mistake. Killing you would've ruined *everything*, not to mention my chance at Keeper. Now give me your phone. I don't need you telling all your little friends lies about how I discipline my own fiancée."

His fingers motion for me to do as he says. I pull it out of my pocket and hand it to him, too stunned to disobey. But as he pockets it, understanding and fear shock through me, almost worse than the pain itself.

"But... but I have to have my phone. How will I talk to my mom? Roxy? What if my dad calls?"

"Too bad. You'll learn even pretty, spoiled brats have consequences for their actions. You can have it back after we get married. I trust you've already made arrangements for your dress for the rehearsal dinner?"

"Yes," I grit out through clenched teeth, hoping like hell I don't have to actually go through with any of this.

"Perfect. Congressmen will be attending, as well as some of my contacts from the Northeast. You'll need to be on your best behavior. Business deals are riding on this marriage. If they fall apart, there will be major consequences for all of us. But if all goes well and we show a united front, these men could put their name behind mine when I run for Senate here in Nevada next year."

My ears perk up. "Nevada? But you're from New York."

"Obviously. But I have a residence here. It's just a matter of paperwork and rubbing the right elbows. Then I'll make sure to expedite your father's case and testify for him. It'll look better for your father to have a senator in his corner. But all that is only if I win and only if you're the picturesque senator's wife throughout."

"But... but that'll take forever. My father has already been in jail way too long and the judge refuses to let him out until his trial. He needs to be freed."

"You'll have to think about how to be beneficial to this campaign, then. And know this..." He leans into my space, making me curl up tighter and bite my tongue to keep from hissing in agony. "If you fuck this up for me in any way, I will let your father rot. Your father may have been framed"—my eyes widen at the admission—"but, if you don't shut your mouth and open your legs when I tell you to, no one will ever find out whether he's innocent or not."

His other hand rubs up my inner thigh and I shudder. Evil leaks through his smile as he chuckles.

"Does my little virgin Red Camellia slut already crave me? You *are* a virgin, aren't you?"

"Of course," I answer automatically, my life at stake. But his eyes narrow.

"Come to think of it, I don't know why I haven't checked yet. Maybe I should—"

"We're here, sir," the driver's voice carries over the intercom, saving me.

The Baron curses and shakes his head. "Another time, then. Perhaps tomorrow night after the rehearsal dinner. Close enough to the wedding day. You're lucky I have business to attend to today."

I really fucking am.

As soon as the Baron's hand leaves my thigh and he exits his side, I snap my legs closed. My door opens before I'm ready and when Monroe holds out his hand, I take it out of sheer self-preservation, swallowing back bile when his clammy palm envelops mine.

Once I gingerly unravel from my seat, I stand beside Monroe. He smiles warmly for the people gawking at the limo and leans into me, his arm wrapped around my back and his fingers like small daggers in my waist.

"Kiss me, Lacey. Give them a good show. Your father's life depends on it. And so does yours."

As if on autopilot, I step up on my toes to press my lips to his. He pulls me closer, but thankfully his forked tongue stays in his mouth. When he finally releases me, he waves at the crowd like a damn celebrity, his ego made all the worse by the raised phones, no doubt snapping pictures and recording video.

My breath lodges in my chest until he finally hands me off to his bodyguards. It isn't until he gets back into the limo that my air releases. I'm a balloon on a string trying to fly away as the helium escapes, but still tethered to the three bodyguards who escort me inside the Baron Suites.

The bright lights of the first floor's casino float by in a blur while I concentrate on breathing through the aftermath of the Baron's physical and verbal blows. They play in my head like a horror movie over and over with every step closer to my gilded cage.

I don't know how much more of this I can stand for my father's sake, but the Baron might put me out of my misery before I have to find out.

Scene 27

ACE HIGH

Watching Monroe announce to the world yesterday that he's marrying *my* wife tomorrow night made me want to strangle the life out of him right then and there. I couldn't stop myself from going after their limo, and the driver's prompt exit was the only thing that prevented me from doing something foolish. If my plan doesn't provide answers tonight, though, I don't care about the Garde, the Keeper, or anyone else in this goddamn town. I'll steal my wife back before she stands at the altar with someone else.

Ever since Monroe pulled that fecking stunt with Lacey in front of his hotel, he's been out gambling, drinking, ogling, and schmoozing. I haven't heard from Lacey despite having texted and called her the moment I got a new mobile and it's driving me mad. But the contacts I've secured in the Baron Suites over the past two weeks have confirmed that she was safely dropped off in the Elephant Room by herself yesterday. It isn't enough to ease my mind, but it'll have to do until I see her tonight.

Three minutes ago, Lorenzo messaged the new mobile Merek secured for me, notifying me that Monroe was hemorrhaging money in my family's casino. The fact that the bastard is in my family's business right now makes me see red, but if he's here, then that means my men can get into position and Lacey is still safe. I told my employees to keep him occupied for as long as possible while I quickly made my way here.

The casino is abuzz with the cheers and yelps of winners and losers at every machine. The tables are just as expressive, full of "oohs" and "aahs" as the tourists gamble. Once I get to the high roller room, I nod at Lorenzo standing guard. He juts his chin in response before going back to assessing his area. His alertness soothes my racing heart for the moment and I enter the room with less anxiety than I started with, spotting my prey quickly.

Monroe has a scantily clad dancer from the casino floor on his lap. I'll have to triple her tips tonight for her sacrifice in entertaining this arsehole.

He reveals his hand to the table in the showdown between two other players. It looks like he's won, for once, and he claims the meager pot, scooping the chips toward his seat as he gloats. The arrogant glee on his face quickly dissipates as the players get up and throw their cards on the table before leaving him and the game behind.

"Come on! Another one!"

"Deal me in," I place the stack of chips I brought on the table and slide into the empty seat near Monroe before pushing a one thousand dollar chip in the center to place my blind bet.

The dealer begins to shuffle the deck while Monroe does a double take.

"Kian McKennon, I wasn't expecting to see you here."

"It's my family's casino, Monroe. Or did you forget?"

An onlooker at any of the other tables would think my smirk was about getting under another player's skin, but this facade is the only trick that keeps me from succumbing to the urge to break his nose on the table.

Monroe's flushed cheeks turn purple. The dancer in his lap tries to brush his hair back, but he swats her hand away.

"Get the fuck off me," he growls, tossing her to the side opposite of me before she can obey his command. She hurries out of the room, but my hackles are still raised when she's gone.

"Mind yourself, Monroe," I warn. "She's a McKennon employee. I don't want to have to throw you out. If the press learns you nearly assaulted a casino dancer, it will look bad for your political aspirations. And getting arrested would ruin that rehearsal dinner I've heard is happening tonight."

"Aw... is someone feeling left out? Did you want an invite to my party, Kian?" He snorts.

I shrug, ignoring his taunting tone. "Nah, I don't think I'll be missing much."

He frowns at my dismissal and waves away my concern before placing two chips in the center for his blind.

"Well I don't know why you're making such a big deal about a stripper then," he grumbles. "You won't actually call the cops, and politicians are caught with their pants down all the time these days. Nothing a little money and handshaking can't fix."

He smooths the lapels of the same suit he wore for Mass despite it being a full twenty-four hours later. In this town, you can find almost anything you need at any hour. Women, drugs, booze... everything except for fecking windows. It looks like Monroe has been partaking in the first three all night long and the last has made him lose track of time. The sun shines bright outside, but you wouldn't know it in here. Considering Monroe's wild, bloodshot eyes, he sure as hell doesn't.

"I knew this was your family's establishment, by the way. I figured you'd be out fucking some whore."

"No, Monroe." I suck my teeth and shake my head. Two cards land in front of me and I glance at them before raising and pushing more chips into the pot. "That sounds like something *you* would do. Not me."

"It's *Baron*," Monroe hisses as he calls, adding the same amount to the pot. "My father is dead, which means I get the title and the respect fair and square."

"Fair and square..." My face furrows in thought. "Interesting choice of words, considering the circumstances of your father's death. I know you're new to the game, Monroe, but respect is only given once you've secured an heir. At its core, the Garde values family above individuals."

The dealer discards the top card in her hand before placing three cards face up on the table. I'm careful not to make an expression while I watch Monroe's eyes narrow at the board.

"As soon as I marry Lacey O'Shea there will be no problem securing that. I plan to fuck her until her virgin pussy is raw—" He gasps and presses his hand to his mouth. A smile lifts his goatee as he asks in an exaggerated tone. "Oops, is that a sore subject? You know, since she was supposed to marry you? I'm so 'new to the game' and all. I'd forgotten."

He chuckles as he tosses chips toward the dealer.

My knuckles pop as they form into fists. I've been playing this game since I could talk and I've honed my poker face, but those countless hours of practice are barely holding back the rage building inside me.

Instead, I lie through a practiced smile and match his bet. "We don't want anything to do with a family who doesn't honor their agreements."

"Yeah right," Monroe scoffs. "You don't let a piece of ass like that go without regretting not hitting it."

Strikes seven and eight.

Including the wee show I had to see earlier, Monroe won't like when I make him pay for all his transgressions.

The dealer burns another card before laying a fourth.

Fuck.

There's no way I'll win this game easily, but if I get in his head, I could still come out on top.

"You know…" I move a stack into the center, feigning a strong hand by raising the bet. "For a wannabe politician, you talk like a fecking first-year at uni. We were engaged. Then we weren't. Now you're marrying her. Big deal. Not much else to say."

Monroe scowls and we both watch as the dealer discards the

top card before flopping down the final community card in the center. He shifts in his seat and I could swear the beginning of a smile twitches his goatee.

"I don't know how any of you thought that you could get away with that arrangement anyway. A McKennon marrying an O'Shea?" he barks a laugh.

"What's that supposed to mean?"

Monroe's pride mixes with the liquor and drugs in his system, loosening his lips. "The Garde would never allow the two reigning families to unite. Right now, there's a semblance of power among the rest of us. If you consolidated it, we would be mere subjects under your rule. They had to do something to stop it and the O'Shea had to be punished for overstepping."

My eyes narrow. I'd thought it was just a few players against the O'Shea, but...

"Are you saying the families were against the marriage contract he and my father brokered?"

Monroe nods and opens his mouth to answer, but whatever he was going to say catches at the edge of his tongue.

"Um, well, none of that matters now."

Dammit, he isn't drunk enough yet. I'll have to let him talk shite and hope he'll slip up again.

"You dodged a bullet anyway. The O'Shea girl needs to be house-trained."

Nine.

I reach for the chip in my pocket, but I remember too late that I gave it to Lacey as my fingers meet the empty pocket's silk seam. My jaw clenches and I breathe deeply through my nose to center myself. I hope Monroe knows what's good for him and shuts the feck up before I lose it and punch him in the bloody face.

"The O'Shea obviously wanted you instead of me," I counter. "So a fiery redhead is what you get. If you can't handle her, that's on you."

"I can handle her," he hisses. "She's just a womb. After she's done her part, I couldn't care less what happens to her. It's being Keeper that I want."

I bristle at the remark. "Ol' Charlie's got to croak first. Once he goes, *then* the job's open."

Monroe's chuckle digs a pit of dread in my stomach. "With as upstanding as our little organization is, it's incredible that we still rely on a man who's behind bars to guard their ideals. Who would've called that? The Keeper keeps our secrets safe, but he holds our freedom over our heads with them. Granted, we get the beautiful women, money, and power and while that might be worth it to some, the key is to get it all. That's the best part about a marriage arrangement with the Keeper's daughter. And in my case, I won't have to wait long after marrying Lacey to get it."

My brows rise slightly, but I doubt the drunken man can tell. "Do you have an in with the grim reaper, then?"

He chuckles again. "Let's just say I know one of his minions in jail, and he's been itching to get his hands on the O'Shea."

My watch buzzes on my wrist. I glance down to see the thumbs-up on my screen from the text message I've been waiting for.

"Fucking phones. Let me guess. One of your many conquests?"

"Something like that," I mumble and pull out my mobile to text Merek back.

> Do it. Tonight during the rehearsal.

"Women are so fucking annoying with their constant texting and calls. That Muñoz girl messaged Lacey incessantly yesterday. I had to turn it off."

My brow furrows. "*You* had to turn it off?"

Is that why she hasn't responded to my messages?

He huffs. "The bitch is always on her phone. I took it away from her after she tried to show off at the church. All she has to do is show up to the rehearsal dinner anyway. She doesn't need her phone for that. She'll be a piece of work to discipline, though, I can already tell."

My heart thunders in my chest as what he said finally hits home. He thought I was Roxana... *fucking* hell, that was close.

"When I get my inheritance and become the Keeper, she better straighten up. I'll have secrets to blackmail everyone she loves if she doesn't. She's proven that's the only way to get her to do what I want."

He finally turns over his hand, reminding me that we're playing a game in the first place. I'd been too wrapped up in trying to find answers and now this bastard has a smug grin on his face.

"An ace of clubs... and a queen of spades to pair with the queen on the board," the dealer declares.

A pair is hardly a guaranteed winning hand in a showdown, but it's no better than mine. Reading him was difficult with his drunken ramblings, but it paid off in the end.

"You O'Sheas and McKennons thought you could trick the Garde's system," Monroe taunts. "But once I'm Keeper, I'll have it all and you McKennons will have to answer to *me*."

"See, that's where you're wrong." I lay down my ace of hearts and my queen of diamonds sword side up.

"A tie," the dealer announces. "A chopped pot to split between the two of you."

"I don't want it all, Monroe. I always have my eye on *one* prize." My fingers graze my queen and ace combo that turns our game into a draw and I meet his frustrated frown. "I answer to one person and that sure as feck isn't you."

I push my half of the winnings to the dealer and nod to her. "Distribute them out to the others working on the floor."

Monroe purples with rage.

"Rematch!" he yells, but I'm already leaving.

"Don't you have a rehearsal dinner to go to?" I call over my shoulder. "Freshen up before you go. You stink."

"Name the time and day! I'll have my rematch."

I shake my head, not chancing looking at him. If I do, there's no way I won't murder him right here in my own casino. I only have so much willpower.

"I don't rematch in my own house, Monroe. One way or another, the McKennons always win."

Scene 28

YOU SHOULD SMILE MORE

"Stop fidgeting," the Baron hisses in my ear as we walk through the first floor of the Montmartre Hotel on our way to Rouge's casino entrance.

I'm not the one who reeks of cologne, perfume, and booze, but you don't see me giving you a hard time about it.

The words scratch the tip of my tongue, but ever since he dropped me off at the suites yesterday without a phone, I've had a lot of time to think.

This man tried to kill me—and *did* kill another woman—just because I'd wounded his pride with my bachelorette party. At this point, I'm counting myself lucky that he's only caged me in his suites. I want to do everything I can to help my dad, but now that my own life has been threatened, my resolve is weakening. As selfish as it may be, if Kian doesn't pull through quickly...

The thought makes me wring my black masquerade mask in my matching gloved fingers. Despite my fear, I've made sure to put on my pretty simple wedding ring under the silk fabric. Wearing the band is a huge risk, but after being alone, scared, and hurt for the past twenty-four hours, I've found strength in wearing this little secret.

Too much, though, apparently, because I accidentally snap the thin strap off my mask.

Oops. Guess I'm not wearing that anymore.

"I *said... stop... fidgeting.*" The Baron's not wearing a mask either and his annoyance at me is plain as day on his face.

He snatches me by my black trench coat sleeve and threads my arm through the crook of his elbow with a jolt that snags one of my heels on the carpet. I trip and clutch his forearm to stand upright. The sudden movement spikes a throbbing ache up the left side of my body and my teeth clench as I bite back the pain.

Thank God I decided not to wear the suffocatingly tight corset underneath this crimson, diamond-studded princess line dress. Without it, the lace-up enclosure in the back is more revealing and shows bare skin where the crisscrossing ribbons don't cover. They begin just beneath my shoulder blades and tie right above my butt, however there's enough fabric to cover the nasty purple bruise that's formed on my lower left flank. Even if there wasn't, I wouldn't have been able to survive trying to breathe past steel boning.

Once I get my bearings again, I stop fidgeting and leave my arm wrapped around his, but I refuse to apologize for a nervous habit that *he's* making worse.

This is what the rest of my life would've been like if Kian hadn't saved me. Invisible rebellions amid bloody and bruised losses. I have no doubt that Kian would *never* treat me this way. The only thought getting me through it right now is knowing that soon enough, I'll be with him again.

"I spoke with your father this afternoon."

The Baron's announcement makes me nearly stop in my tracks, but he drags me forward without pausing.

"You did?" I can't help the squeak in my voice. "I haven't heard from him in weeks."

"You wouldn't have. He's been in the infirmary."

Monroe delivers the news as nonchalantly as a weatherman reporting that it'll be "another sunny day" in Vegas.

"The infirmary?" Dread digs into my stomach. "Why was my father in the infirmary? Was he sick? Is he okay?"

"He is now. Of course, it was touch and go after the attacks."

"The attacks? What attacks?" My voice is nearly unrecognizable. Every lesson my mother has taught me about being a quiet, demure, Garde woman has leaped right out the window.

"You didn't know?" His head tilts to the side slightly as he frowns. "He was attacked a few weeks ago."

"A few *weeks* ago? But... but he said he was okay!"

Kian saw him. He said he was okay. Why would Kian lie to me? Or is Monroe lying to me?

The Baron frowns at me. "Who said your father was okay? I thought you hadn't talked to him."

My mouth opens and closes as I try to get my thoughts straight. I'm grateful for the years of Garde "training" that finally kick back in and offer an easy lie.

"I, um... I mean, he sounded okay when we spoke on your phone at the restaurant."

I have to get to the bottom of this. I've relied on Kian so much to help me get my father out of jail, but has he been playing me all along?

"Ah, well, your father's quite the performer, and he put on a show for you that night, making you believe nothing was wrong when he's had a near-death scare. Twice actually. Once before your little stunt at Rouge..." He stops to pull out his phone. "And once after. Two attacks, one right after the other, right in his cell. Almost as if someone ordered them. See look. I even have a picture for you."

He turns his phone around and every cell in my body freezes. My father fills the screen as he lies in a hospital bed. He's nearly unrecognizable in a patient gown with both eyes swollen shut, gauze wrapped around his head, and IV lines connected to him.

My breath hurts in my lungs. "Monroe... are you... did you...."

I can't get the words out and my chest begins to ache as if

Monroe's delivered a physical blow to it too, just like my back and stomach.

"Are you questioning whether *I* had something to do with your father's attack?"

There's no way I can answer with the bile that's threatening to come up my throat. All I can manage is a small nod.

"Well, then the answer is yes." He smiles and leads us around a group of tourists.

"But... I... I don't understand. We were supposed to get married."

"Were?" His eyebrow rises and I get my shit under control.

"Are. We *are*, but you're talking as if that's not the case. If my father dies in prison—"

"What? What will happen, Lacey? Do you know? Because you've been insolent and acting as if you don't, so let me refresh your memory. If he dies in jail before we get married, you're no good to me anymore." What he's saying is horrible, but the smile he flashes outwardly is what chills me to the bone as he continues, "You'll no longer be the Garde's bratty princess. The Keeper position will be up for grabs and your name will be on the chopping block along with your mother's. Without the patriarch in the family, and no marriage prospects, you and your mother's days are numbered. To the rest of us, with your father gone, you're worth more dead than alive."

Most of this would be true... if I wasn't already married to Kian. No one would dare try to extinguish my family line if they knew who my husband was.

If they knew...

I'm not sure how to use that information yet. It's a card that should be played at just the right time. I shake my head and hold back my secrets a little longer, hoping to hear Monroe's in exchange.

"If my father dies, the order will be in shambles. It'll take time to appoint a new Keeper. What happens then?"

"Well, it's good we don't have to worry about those details, right? Because injured is still alive, which means I have a lot of wiggle room to hang over both of your heads. It's what your father and I talked about today actually. I've reinstated his protection in there, at least until we get married. As long as I testify, he'll no longer face the death penalty, too."

"The *death* penalty?"

"Oh," he sidesteps another passerby, ushering me with his arm around me. "I see our Keeper has been keeping many secrets from his own daughter. Don't worry, Lacey. Just remember that if you step out of line, all *I* have to do is make a phone call. Once we get married, you can help me determine how long he'll stay unharmed by being a good Garde woman. Sound fair, wife?"

Hearing Monroe say that word makes me shudder. With Kian, it sounds like salvation, but with Monroe, I can already feel the mouth of hell opening beneath me.

My mind races a million miles a second, trying to figure out the next play as we approach Rouge's entrance. I want to slow down, mull over the bomb he just dropped, but Monroe doesn't give me time to think.

"Answer me," he hisses.

"Y-yes. It sounds fair."

"Glad we could come to an agreement."

When he picks up speed, I stumble again and whimper in pain.

"Clumsy drunk," he mutters under his breath, despite the fact that I'm tragically sober.

Just ahead of us, a Montmartre staff member opens a huge black oak door framed by a thick red curtain. It's the second entrance to Rouge and Monroe drags me along before steering us through it.

My half-baked plan is falling apart, but once we step inside Rouge, I'm still in awe of the work my mother has done in twenty-four hours.

It feels like two completely different parties in one venue. Mood lighting sets the tone for the elaborate banquet, where hundreds of guests mingle near Rouge's casino entrance. Closer to the club entrance, the bright lights of the stage darken the dance floor in front of it. A band plays and there are already so many people on the floor I could join right now and blend into the shadows. Did my mom plan that anonymity for me so I could let off steam during my last night of freedom? If so, it might be the nicest gift she's ever given me.

On the casino side, long banquet tables are piled with food while waitstaff carries around *hors d'oeuvres*. The round tables that used to be in front of the stage have been exchanged for high-top tables throughout the room. Acrobats intersperse through the crowd to stop and perform between guests. The tablecloths, drapery along the walls, and faux candles are back to crimson and silver accents, with a smattering of real rubies and diamonds glittering everywhere. In light of Kian's text messages about the origin of the Red Camellia, I now realize the shades and gemstones are no doubt meant to represent my family's color on my mother's side. But, Jesus, it makes for an over-the-top rehearsal dinner. There's so much going on with the masquerade theme it almost feels like no theme at all.

Monroe wanted to go all out on the party aspect of our wedding, telling my mom over and over about how much it needed to be a two-day affair. We didn't even have a "rehearsal" before this dinner. He only cared about having double the opportunity to schmooze in his honor. But if this was what he ordered my mom to do, I can't imagine how extravagant the wedding will be.

Would be... there's no way I can go through with that.

But what if I don't and Kian doesn't come through? What will happen to my dad, then?

The band ends their song, jarring me out of my thoughts, and the lead singer's voice booms over the microphone.

"Ladies and gentlemen, the future Mr. and Mrs. Baron have arrived. Let's give them a round of applause."

My stomach churns as all the guests turn around in their

masquerade masks to face the entrance. Some of them are pretty and bright, bejeweled with gems or elaborate petal-like feathers that match their ball gowns and tuxedos. Others resemble skeletons and clowns, and more than a few have macabre beaks reminiscent of the doctors during the bubonic plague.

When they break out into polite cheers and clapping, Monroe takes an exaggerated bow and I fight the urge to flee. Just as I have the thought, a waitress helps me shrug out of my coat, almost as if she knows I'm a flight risk. I glance around among the masked audience for Kian, but he's nowhere in sight.

And why would he be? It's an O'Shea event and we're supposed to loathe the McKennons. My heartbeat races at the thought that I'll have to go through tonight alone, and it's only made worse when the Baron whispers low.

"Don't humiliate me tonight like you did yesterday. There are backers, congressmen, and potential donors that I need to impress. These types of events are some of the few that enable the Garde to congregate on neutral ground and you're not going to squander my opportunity. You are to stand by my side at all times, remain silent, and be a woman in love. Got it?"

I am a woman in love.

The thought crosses my mind before I can really register it. It's only when Kian's cheeky smirk flashes in my thoughts that I realize what the words mean.

"Lacey... answer me. Your father's life is at stake." Monroe squeezes my arm and I hold back a wince.

"Yes. Got it. A woman in love. I can definitely be that."

But I can't be in love... I barely know the guy, right? He's a virtual stranger, my family's enemy, and a playboy in this criminal underworld. Just another man who thinks he can own me and cage me.

But everything I've experienced at the Baron's hand is exactly what my mother warned me life would be like. And I was taught that everything I've experienced with Kian so far is supposedly a fairy-tale fantasy. The reverent way he holds me feels so real, though, and my body calms with just his presence...

Oh my God... I might be in love with Kian McKennon.

My heart thunders at the revelation, but dwelling on it right now is dangerous. I try to ignore my racing pulse and focus on smiling for strangers, breathing in this tight dress, and my way out of this.

Despite concentrating on my showmanship for these guests, my head is on a swivel, still trying to spot Kian. But if he's here, I can't find him, and when we walk farther into Rouge's ballroom, my mother is the first person I see.

She's one of the guests who didn't bother to wear a mask, and her strawberry-blonde hair is wrapped tightly in a chignon again, so different than my relaxed, lightly curled half-up, half-down style. Her long, black ball gown is understated, and even though she's worn her mourning black since the day my father went to jail, it looks like she's dressed for a funeral tonight.

One of the congressmen the Baron tried to rub shoulders with after church is speaking to her with big gestured hand motions and she's nodding her head slightly as she seemingly takes what he says into consideration. She was once set off to the side, a pretty trinket to be admired and ignored as soon as she opened her mouth. But look at her now.

She's running my father's businesses as well as—maybe even better than—he ever did. Monroe has no respect for her, but she's been in the spotlight as a Garde liaison for nearly a year. Once my father is released from jail, will she go back to watching backstage? Or will he let her continue to shine? Which life would she want?

Which life will I live with Kian?

Once this is all over—*if* this ever ends—will he place me on a pedestal like a trophy? Or worship me on an altar like a goddess?

Or rule beside me like a queen?

A smile teases my lips because I already know the answer.

He's my wild ace of hearts and I'm his queen of diamonds. I have no doubt we'd rule side by side.

My mother waves us over and introduces us to the CEO of I Don't Know and Co. and the founder of Who The Fuck Cares. The Baron lights up, but I couldn't be less interested in being another asshole's stepping-stone into high society. They're only one word into the conversation and I'm already searching for the bar.

My mother frees me from the Baron's clutches. He lets go of me easily, too busy wooing a potential backer to worry about me.

But my mother seems concerned as she whispers through frowning lips, "Are you okay? What's been going on? The bodyguards were absolutely no help when I dropped off your gown today and you haven't answered any of my messages."

"Sorry, um..." I'm tempted to lie, but she and my father helped put me into this mess. They should at least see what it's doing to me. "The Baron stole my phone."

"Were you on it too much?" my mother asks with her head tilted in disappointment.

My jaw drops.

"Like *that's* a reason for one adult to steal another adult's phone?"

My mother at least has the decency to look abashed. Her soft ivory skin blooms into a natural blush, but even though she knows I'm right, she doesn't relent.

"You have to be careful with Garde men, Lacey. They're quite particular. When your father—"

"Did you know Dad was attacked? And that he might get the death penalty if he's convicted?"

Her eyes don't widen into saucers like I know mine did.

"You knew," I whisper, hurt twisting my chest. "Why didn't you tell me?"

Is no one on my side?

She sighs. "He called me on the automated line this past weekend to talk about Rouge. When he mentioned the attack, he said it wasn't that bad. He didn't want to worry you, honey. And the death penalty thing isn't a big deal as long as you do your job with the Baron."

"Not that *bad*? Not a *big deal*? Monroe said he nearly *died*, mom. And he might die anyway if he gets convicted!"

"Shh, shh." She jerks me behind an ice sculpture of a flower bigger than me. I clench my teeth again to keep from groaning at the sudden movement, and I swear I can feel them crack under the pressure. "Keep your voice down. Do you want the whole Garde to hear how vulnerable their king is?"

"Maybe they should know," I hiss back at her. "Then they can find out who's behind all of this bullshit and I wouldn't have to be the damn sacrificial lamb."

Her eyes narrow and the tension between us rachets up until she exhales a defeated sigh.

"I'm sorry, I'm just trying to help you the best way I know how. My own mother used to tell me to focus on the good and keep a positive attitude. So let's both do that? If we stay positive, everything should be fine. No one can be unhappy *all* the time." Her smile is brittle and it breaks to pieces as I shake my head.

"But what if we can have more than 'fine'? Wouldn't you want that? We're all focused on transactional marriages, but what about love? And happiness?"

My mother groans. "Get your head out of the clouds, Lacey. The Baron can provide something just as good as love. He has security. That's what your father has provided me and we've lived a very happy life together."

I shake my head. "You've really convinced yourself of that, haven't you? Even when your husband is in *jail* right now?"

Her lips thin. "Whether you like it or not, we're stuck in this, Lacey. There's no way out. As soon as you realize that, the longer we'll all stay alive."

A thick gulp chokes my throat and I shake my head.

"What if I want more than just 'alive'? What if I want to *live*?"

She reaches up and I stiffen before her cold hand rests over my cheek. Her brow wrinkles slightly as she studies my face.

"I saw you come in. You've been pirouetting since elementary school and you've had excellent balance your whole life. Years of dance have made you light on your feet, and yet, you were stiff and slow when he tugged you to him."

Her hand leaves my skin. The air that brushes over it is warmer than her palm.

"At least he doesn't touch your pretty face, right? You're alive, and sometimes that's the best we get. Be thankful for that. My advice? Try to enjoy the night. I turned out the lights above the dance floor so you and Roxana can have some fun, but don't embarrass the Baron. This is his night to make as many contacts as he can all in one place. Get a glass of vodka. No soda. Tell people it's water like we all do. Smile. Play the part of the happily engaged woman. Hopefully that and dancing will help numb whatever pain you have."

"Sounds perfect," I mutter through gritted teeth.

"Oh, before I forget, I was in the church today and I took another look at the tabernacle and the table it sits on. That altar is a little gaudy, isn't it? Maybe too much for a wedding?"

"Mom..." I blink slowly before waving my hand to indicate the extravagant rehearsal dinner. "You think *that* is 'too much'?"

She doesn't seem to get my sarcasm as she nods. "Do you think they'll let me move it to a side altar? Or maybe scooch the communion table to one of the annex rooms?"

"I don't know, Mom, and I don't care." I swat the air at her and turn on my heel to make my way toward wherever the hell the blessed bar is.

My mother huffs at my back before reminding me. "Make sure to dance with all the highest of society. It's your party, so I'm sure you'll be a hot commodity. Schmoozing with the right people is the best way to make the Baron look good."

"Just what I was worried about," I mumble before calling to her over my shoulder. "Tell Monroe I'm off to *schmooze*, then."

The room is packed, but the bar calls to me like a moth to a flame. It takes nearly all my willpower to stop myself from using my "Garde princess" status to beeline past everyone and go directly in front of the queue. I stand at the end of the line, shifting from one heel to the next.

Monroe was right. I *am* fidgeting more than usual. My nerves are electric under my skin and my stomach is in knots over not knowing whether I'll see Kian tonight.

I didn't realize how much I craved his constant messages, check-ins, and flirty jokes until they were gone. Even though I've refused to reply to him lately out of childish spite, he's been my salvation the last few weeks. I'd give almost anything just to hear one word from him now.

But he's nowhere in sight and waiting in the line only worsens my jitters. I'm out in the open here for anyone to talk to, and I don't have it in me to pretend right now. When I finally step up to the counter to place my order, the bartender gives me a perfunctory smile.

"What'll it be?"

"Vodka." Not even a hint of surprise lights his light-brown skin and he goes to pour it as if he's done it a hundred times tonight already. Seems like I'm not the only one ready to get wasted at this thing.

"Here ya go." He places the drink in front of me and I reach into my dress pocket for a tip.

But hard metal warms underneath my fingertips and it takes me pulling it out and flashing it in the light to remember what it is.

Kian's AA chip.

Scene 29

RUMOR HAS IT

My chest aches. The coin is likely silver plated, with little to no monetary value, but he gave it to me to inspire hope and promised that I can count on him. Not only that, he was vulnerable, trusted me with yet another secret, and confessed that he cares for me. It's the most precious gift I've ever received.

So why did he lie about my father's injuries? My mom said my father didn't want me to know. Is that true? Was Kian honoring my father's wishes?

My fingertips caress the number before I return it to my pocket for safekeeping. I switch it out for one of the hundred-dollar bills my mother ensured was in my pocket when she dropped off my dress and lay the cash on the counter with more resolve than I've had in... well, maybe ever.

"Actually, I'm going to go with a water." The man's black brows rise nearly to his hairline, but he doesn't say a word as he dumps the vodka from the glass. He untwists the top of a small bottled water, breaking the seal, and I trade him in exchange for the hundred-dollar bill and my thanks.

I sip my water before turning around to observe the party and assess how much damage this night is going to do to my morale.

Everyone is dressed to the nines, with women in ball gowns and men in their tails. Not everyone has a mask on, but it's kind of fun to see if I can identify the ones who do, although I don't think I'm having much luck.

The band starts up a new song and more people gravitate toward the dance floor. I'm dying to get some of my energy out, but I'm not sure how well I'll be able to move, considering the ache in my lower back and abdomen.

I've danced through pain before. Blisters, sprained ankles and stress fractures are nothing new. This injury is different, though. It doesn't feel like a "dance through the pain" kind of situation.

It feels like I might need to see a fucking doctor.

"Lacey!"

I shift toward the sound of my best friend's voice. A sharp cramp radiates from my lower back, preventing me from running and jumping into Roxy's arms. She has no such restrictions though, and she barrels toward me despite her tight black mermaid gown and wraps me in her arms with a strong squeeze. I bite my tongue to keep from whimpering, but she speaks over the small sound that leaks out anyway.

"Oh my god, please tell me you're not mad at me. I need you to not be mad at me. I know I haven't called or texted, but I was so stressed and I thought you hated me." She pushes away from me and tugs off her black masquerade mask before holding me at arm's length and pleading with big brown puppy-dog eyes. "Please say you don't hate me. Did I mention that this sweetheart neckline makes your boobs look fantastic? Also, please don't hate me."

I snort and lead us to the side of the room, away from prying ears.

"*Jesus*, Roxy. I don't hate you. I'm really glad you're here. I was afraid I was going to have to navigate this by myself."

"Yeah, girl. I'd never miss my bestie's wedding festivities. Although this feels more like a campaign fundraiser than a rehearsal dinner, no offense."

"None taken."

"And..." She lowers her voice to a whisper. "I'm kind of confused about why we're here."

My eyes narrow. "Why?"

"Well, um... Devil's Night. I thought something might've happened. Maybe a "Wish You Were Still Single" coupon got cashed in? I figured you'd want to be with... you know. Your mystery devil."

I glance around before lowering my own voice. "What do you know? Because I *know* you know some things. That so-called mystery devil told me. You haven't told anyone about him, though, have you?"

"No, oh God no. I would never."

She's acting like she'd never gossip about me and I huff at her bewildered expression.

"You know, it makes so much sense now. You used to be someone I could trust until my dad went to jail. After that, you never kept my business to yourself. And you're doing it now because the Muñozes are *McKennon* loyalists, right?"

Hurt crumples her face and I want to feel bad for her, but it's the truth. She's my best friend and we usually run away from confrontation, but I can't let this one slide.

"That's not true. I never told anyone about your little 'fuck yous' to the Garde whenever I was your diversion. I just leaked enough to the rumor mill to keep things interesting. This is different."

"Right, but a McKennon is involved now, and you were behind the scenes in his scheme from the beginning."

Her chin dimples as she frowns. "Come on, Lace. My dad made me. I had to."

"You had to betray me? Over and over again?" I think back to all the times my mother called to rip me a new one because Roxy had leaked something that reached an heir to a rival family. "You could've ruined our friendship, you know."

"I know, I'm so sorry. But my dad... I had to. You understand, don't you?"

I sigh. Because I do. I would do almost anything to free my dad.

"I get it, but I'd like to think I wouldn't betray someone I loved."

"Wouldn't we all like to think that?" A sad smile crests her red-painted lips. "I'm sorry, Lacey. I really am. But I promise I never did anything that would actually put you in danger. And I only ever shared enough to make you sound exciting."

"Oh, well as long as you made me sound exciting, all's forgiven." I roll my eyes and grin.

She gives me a theatrical wink and I can't help laughing. I've never been good at staying mad at my best friend and the ache of betrayal in my chest has eased a little with her apology.

But my brain begins to mull over everything she's said. She was trying to play all sides for the good of her family, like I am. I thought I was just a pawn in the Garde's game all this time. But what if we're all being pushed around and forced to play the board? And if that's the case, who's holding the pieces?

"So... how was it?" she asks, waggling her eyebrows the best her Botox will allow. "Rumor has it that Kian McKennon is huge."

Jealousy sparks until I realize she's only talking about his size. He's big, sure, but if women were actually talking about my husband, there would be one very deliciously unique feature at the end of his cock that would spin that rumor mill out of control. Instead of answering, I decide to shock her with a bigger plot twist.

"Hmm... before or after the wedding?"

Her eyes widen. "The... the *wedding*? Oh my God, you're *married*?"

"Shh, shh, shh, Rox, be quiet," I giggle nervously.

Thank *God* everyone is either dancing, eating, drinking, or mingling around Monroe. I might be the so-called bride, but he's the belle of the ball.

"Sorry, sorry. Where's the ring?" she whispers, and I place her fingers around my left hand to feel the band underneath my glove. "Oh, wow. Yup. You're fucking married. Wait, are you already pregnant, too? A two-for-one Vegas special?"

I snort. "*No*. Today should be the last day of my period, thank you very much," even as I say it, disappointment twinges in my chest.

"Bummer. Hey, at least you get to be wasted for your wedd...ing." Her eyes widen. "Lacey... what's going on? Why is this even happening if *that*"—she points to my left hand— "has already happened?"

I sigh. "It's complicated..."

"Complicated? Math is complicated. This is life or death." She grabs my hand. "We have to get you out of here, now. If the Baron finds out—"

"I can't, Rox." I tug back, hating the pure terror on her face.

"He will *murder* you once he finds out he's been played. I can't believe Kian has even let you near that monster."

I wince at her blunt delivery, but she's never been one to shy away from the reality of the Garde.

"There's more to this. Kian knows. He's helping me as much as he can." Even as I say it, I'm still questioning why he lied. I push the awful thought away and hold my best friend's hand. "Please help me ride this out until I can escape."

"But you can run away now—"

"Listen, the Baron knows something... important. I need to find out what it is. He's been holding the information hostage—"

"And now he's holding *you* hostage. Shit, I knew that '*Eat, Pray, Love*, kumbaya, taking time from social media to better myself' press apology was bullshit. Your extroverted ass isn't meant to be isolated like that. But it was all his doing, wasn't it? Look, I don't care what he knows, your life is in danger."

"I know. So help me live, then. I need to make it seem like everything's normal."

"Lacey... I don't like this—"

"Please? Seriously, I've been losing it in the Baron's suite all by myself with only elephants to talk to. I *need* you."

"Elephants? What the—" She shakes her head and holds up her hand. "Fine. Fine. I'll do my best to make sure everyone in the Garde knows you're a happy bride. But girl, you've got twenty-four hours before you end up as a case on *Dateline*. Or married to two men. Which would be totally cool if one of them wasn't the Baron and if bigamy wasn't also a fucking *crime*. I know you like to live life on the edge, but an orange jumpsuit would not mesh well with your hair, girlfriend."

I wince. "Trust me, I'm not looking for a wardrobe change anytime soon. I'm hoping that Kian can find whatever the Baron knows before it gets that far."

"What happens if Kian doesn't find anything? Or what if you use the Baron and he finds out about Kian? You know his reputation."

I shiver at the reminder and my mind conjures up the vision it's concocted of the dead woman who looked like me.

"I don't know. I can't think about that right now. I just have to get through each day."

"Okay... well, if you're sure about this suicide mission, I'll do what I can. Let my rumors run free throughout the Garde." She taps her chin. "Maybe I'll make up a bunch of different ones and see who the blabbermouth is."

"Pretty sure it's you, Rox." I chuckle as she frowns.

"Hey! The Baron might've put you in time-out, but that doesn't mean you can be a meanie."

"It's not *time-out*, Roxana."

Fear shocks through me as I turn around to see Maeve.

She's walking toward us, sipping the Garde woman's version of water. Her white empire waist dress and matching feather masquerade mask are angelic, though her mocking smirk ruins the effect. That smirk is a godsend though, because it's nowhere near the expression she'd have on her face if she'd heard any of the rest of our conversation and the heart attack I was about to have dissipates in my chest.

"Tell her, Lacey. My brother is just worried for your safety." She gives me a pointed look before turning on Roxy. "Lacey seems to keep getting herself in trouble lately and he's making sure both their reputations stay intact."

My cheeks heat. This poor girl drank the Kool-Aid, and I can't very well be mad at her for protecting her brother. I was trying to use her brother to protect my father before I realized it was a fool's errand.

"You're right, Maeve. Hopefully, your brother will find it in his heart to forgive me for my transgressions."

She doesn't get my sarcasm as she shrugs. "One can hope."

"Ugh, enough talking." Roxy rolls her eyes. "Let's dance. If we're going to have to stay here all night with everyone kissing the groom's ass instead of the bride's, I'm going to take her out on the dance floor myself and show her a good time."

I glance toward the growing crowd. I've got to hand it to my mother, the band is great and I'm more than grateful that she turned out all the lights above the stage so I can dance my heart out. There's a good mix of musical genres, something for everyone and we're in Vegas. As proper as people want to be, the more liquor and music that floods the system, the more even rich snobs want to twerk.

"Love that idea." I smile.

Maeve scoffs. "Everyone's too afraid of my brother, you know. Do you really think someone would risk getting on his bad side just to dance with you?"

I shrug and use the same words she did earlier. "One can hope."

She huffs a laugh. "That's like banking on it to rain in Vegas."

"Which, funnily enough," Roxy chimes in. "The weatherman reported that should be happening soon. So it's not necessarily the 'when pigs fly' scenario you're making it out to be. Come on, Lacey, let's go."

Maeve scowls at her before turning back to me.

"You haven't been asked to dance yet. You can't just go out there—" she stammers before she's cut off by a rumble that sends delicious shivers down my spine.

"May I have this dance?"

H is deep voice and Irish accent heat the back of my neck, warming my body inside and out. Maeve's eyes nearly pop out of her head as she stares over my shoulder. I already know who it is, and despite the fact that Kian lied to me about my father's health, his presence settles my nerves, like when my mind clears before I step out on stage.

When I turn around, Kian's there in an all-black tuxedo with his hand out, waiting for me. The only pop of color he's wearing is his red silk tie and a red devil mask. It's the same one he wore at Rouge, giving me delicious déjà vu, and my core flutters at the memory.

"Oh yeah, she'll have a dance, won't you, Lacey? You can't be rude and say no, right, Maeve?"

Roxy's a fucking saint. She's effortlessly forced Maeve into a corner with formality. What Garde woman says no to a man?

"I'd be delighted," I answer primly before letting him take my hand and lead me to the dance floor.

The previous song slows and rolls into a sultry cover of "Fire On Fire" by Sam Smith. I recognize it instantly when the lead singer begins to croon into his microphone. Strings carry the melody as Kian rests his hand on my lower back over the crisscrossing laces. The tips of his fingers sneak underneath one of the straps, touching my bare skin and making me shiver. As I place one gloved hand on his shoulder and hold his raised hand with the other, my heart thrums in my chest at the possession in his gaze.

Once the song begins to flow, we glide into step and begin our waltz. Normally, I would lean away from him at a slight angle, but not only would my lower left back muscles protest if I tried, but I also don't want to put any distance between us. I follow his lead, letting his body press into mine to guide my steps back, left, front, and right.

He moves us about in long, elegant, flowing steps into the middle of the floor. We're hidden from the rest of the party by the other dancers and as much as I've been craving being alone with him, the questions about my father still burn in my mind and I can't hold in my accusation any longer. My eyes narrow as I brace myself for yet another betrayal from someone I care about.

"You lied to me, Kian."

He jerks back as if I've slapped him. "Lied? About what?"

"Monroe told me my father was attacked. And that he might get the death penalty if he's convicted." As soon as the words leave my lips, understanding softens Kian's features and my heart twists. "So either you never went to see my father, or you lied when you told me he was okay—"

"He *is* okay now, and he told me to tell you that he was okay. He didn't want his daughter to worry about him. Once we figure out how to free your father, none of the rest will matter."

I scoff. "He has a lot of nerve telling me not to worry about him while also making me marry a monster."

Kian's frustrated huff flutters against my forehead. "I agree, but your father begged me to keep his secret. I didn't want to, but I'd hoped I wouldn't have to keep it for long. My plan was to tell you once everything was sorted and you were out of Monroe's— wait..." Kian's brow furrows above his mask. "Did your father tell him about us?"

My eyes widen and I shake my head. "I don't think so. If he

had, I *highly* doubt I'd be alive right now, let alone dancing before a wedding that can never happen."

"Good. Then he still trusts me to find answers."

"What do you mean?"

He meets my gaze again. "If your father didn't trust me, he might've used that information to bargain with Monroe. But he hasn't, which means that he's trusting me to free both of you."

"Should he trust you? Have you found anything?"

"I've been working with my contacts to find answers. I tried to update you through texts, but Monroe told me that he has your mobile."

"Monroe told you? When the hell did you see him?"

"This morning. The gobshite was in my family's casino. I went down while my men were working on figuring out how to get into his suites and I kept him busy until they texted me. One thing I did learn from Monroe himself is that multiple families were opposed to our marriage."

"*Multiple* families?"

Kian nods and his face darkens, the mask making him look more deadly than usual. "I think he was sobering up, so I couldn't get much out of him. But he made a snide remark that the families would've never allowed our marriage because we would have been too powerful against everyone. They wanted to punish your father for overstepping. This is more than a few people framing him for crimes they did. I'm afraid this is a Garde-wide conspiracy." His eyes dart around the room before he whispers even lower. "And we have no idea who's against us."

The song begins to crescendo and I raise my voice slightly. "Jesus, what're we going to do?"

"I have a plan in motion right at this very moment."

He spins me outward, and air hisses from my lungs as I use the muscles that the Baron abused yesterday in the limo. I stutter-step back to him, attempting to spin, but he pulls me gingerly and holds me in front of him with my back against his chest.

"Christ, Lace, are you okay? Did that bastard hurt you?" He

embraces me, cupping my bare shoulder with one hand while his other presses my hips into his, using his large frame to wrap around me and comfort me.

"Shh, shh," I whisper up to him and close my eyes, trying to block out the pain. He's forgotten to keep up the pretense of our dance, so I step from side to side to get him to sway with me. Breathing slowly through my nose helps center me before I speak again. "I'm fine, really. The move shocked me is all."

I want to sink into him, to give in to his warmth. His fingertips resting over my lower belly are dangerously close to the apex of my thighs. His other hand glides down my bicep in a protective caress and I lean against him with a moan.

"Fuck, *tine*," his lips murmur against my temple. "You can't be sounding like that right now. I'm barely resisting temptation as it is."

My eyes snap open to see if anyone is spying on us, but the dance floor is packed and they don't seem to notice anyone past their own partners. We're shadows in the dim light, thankfully, but still playing with fire.

"We should be more careful," I whisper before sucking in a breath and twirling around in Kian's arms

The move was intended to show that I'm okay, but once we reposition our hands to continue our waltz, all I can muster is a brittle, plastic smile. The swell of the song warns me that his touch is almost gone, weighing anxiety like an anvil on my chest and making it hard to breathe. I blink rapidly to keep dangerous tears from falling down my cheeks and I duck my head away from anyone who could see.

"Bloody hell," Kian curses above me before whispering against my hair. "You are not *fine*. Follow me after the song ends."

I nod quickly and barely contain my sniffle. His smoky sweet amber scent fills my nostrils, soothing me until the last beats of the song drum out into the crowd. Everyone claps and I slip into old habits as I do a modified curtsy that doesn't require me to bend too low.

Kian bows and kisses my hand, his eyes swirling with emotion as his warm breath caresses my skin.

"A pleasure, Miss O'Shea."

The sensual way he enunciates O'Shea makes my belly flip.

Just weeks ago, I fought against him saying "McKennon," but now I crave to hear my new name with his deep voice and accent again. I bite my lip to keep from smiling at the thought and his eyes darken as they flick to my mouth. He curses and I quickly exit the dance floor before he has time to even stand, making sure we don't get lost in each other again.

I try to gather my wits about me as I walk toward the group of D-list celebrities and politicians surrounding the Baron, but I also angle myself in such a way that I keep Kian in my periphery.

Maeve stands beside her brother and her harsh glare zeroes in on me. Her eyes narrow on mine, but something calls her back to the conversation and her face softens for her potential audience, ready to speak when prompted. There's no doubt in my mind that she hasn't even gotten a word in yet.

A few women actually take the time to congratulate me along the way, although I'm not sure how sincere they are. Every woman here knows signing a marriage license with the Baron could be signing my own death warrant. I thank them politely, mentally keeping tabs on the ones that are viciously gleeful rather than somber.

My mother leaves the group before I reach it, her face still plastered with a fake smile even as she grabs my arm to roughly steer me to the side of the room. When we're away from listening ears, she whirls around on me, fear and anger contorting her face.

"Lacey, what were you doing with him?" she hisses.

I'm surprised by the amount of emotion in her voice. She's not one to show it, even in private company, let alone in the corner of a ballroom with hundreds of Garde members and high society lurking about.

"What're you talking about?"

"You know exactly who I'm talking about. Kian McKennon. Maeve told me he took you to the dance floor. You're lucky Monroe didn't see you go with him or he would've had a fit. I couldn't find you in there to stop you without bringing more attention to your foolishness. What were you *thinking* dancing with him? And why is he here? He wasn't even invited!"

"H-he asked me and you told me to dance with other men—"

"Not Kian McKennon! Never a McKennon. They're our *enemy*. Their family is dying to be in charge. You know that!"

It's on the tip of my tongue to ask her if she knows why we hate them, but if she doesn't, I won't be the one to break it to her. Especially not when she's already pissed at me.

"It was just a dance, Mom."

She shakes her head. "It doesn't matter. Acting so foolishly the night before your wedding can only end poorly. I'm only trying to protect you."

"No, you're only trying to *control* me and you've done it my entire life," My voice is an angry whisper, and I can't dial it back as I keep going. "I'm the Red Camellia, the Garde princess, but all I'm good for is raising a man's status by lying on my back."

"Lacey, you can't talk like that and you can't be seen with Kian McKennon, either. It only starts rumors."

"Would it be so bad if I was with Kian instead?"

She scoffs. "For you? No. Not at first. But once those puppy-love eyes dim and you see him for what he is, another ruthless bastard like his father and all the rest, you'll look around and realize you have no one left because *your* actions got your father killed in jail."

My eyes widen and my chest caves in. "Mom... it wouldn't be my—"

"Be careful. That's all I'm saying. Whatever you're doing with Kian. End it. You don't want to sacrifice your father's life just to be treated like a whore. Once your beauty fades, you'll be set aside for a newer, prettier model. If you want to ruin your life, fine. You're an adult now and I can't stop you. But don't bring your father and me down with you. Now smile and pretend like you haven't potentially cost your father his life."

She drags me back to the group in a daze. Her warnings ring through my mind, drowning out all other conversations until the Baron shouts toward me.

"Ah, there's my dancing flower." He offers his hand and I place mine in his mechanically, letting him pull me into him.

Many of the men in the group wear masquerade masks. Devils, jesters, and various other creatures leer at me with disgusting, knowing grins. I don't know what Monroe's been saying about me, but I highly doubt my mother should've heard it.

The whiskers of his goatee poke the shell of my ear. My muscles tense and I try not to recoil as he whispers.

"Not a word. I'd rather forget you than hear you. Do you understand?"

I bite my tongue to keep from replying as I move to stand behind him and his sister.

"Now, what was I saying?"

I'm one thousand percent sure he didn't forget a word he said, but a man with a jester mask reminds him like he's expecting a cookie for remembering, and the Baron launches right back into his story.

I've lost track of Kian and a pit of worry gnaws at my stomach, until I spy Roxy. She's twirling her hair, trying to flirt with the bartender, but she catches my eye immediately. The bartender hands her a drink and she knocks it back before prancing to my side, only slowing down to mingle her way into the group. Once she reaches me, she whispers low enough so that no one else can hear.

"I saw you-know-who head toward the hallway. Do I need to do a little distraction? Like old times? These men are so much easier than your bodyguards."

I want to laugh, but I'm on the verge of tears after my conversation with my mother. The added burden that my father's life rests on my shoulders is making me buckle under the pressure.

Glancing around, I quickly find the hallway that she's talking about. I face the group again and analyze their posture and faces. My mom and Maeve are enthralled by whatever the Baron is boasting about now, and once again, I'm invisible beside my would-be husband. It's perfect.

I give her a subtle nod.

She winks back at me and mouths, "Showtime."

Scene 31

FRAYING AT THE EDGES

L acey's eyes flick to the hallway, where I wait for her in the shadows. I'm standing behind the bunched curtain the club uses during performances to keep the lights from interfering with the production.

The dressing rooms backstage would've been the better choice, but I didn't want to subject her to what was a crime scene mere weeks ago. Thankfully, attendees to parties like this are wholly absorbed with themselves and they haven't been paying attention to my comings and goings anyway.

Which has made for some interesting eavesdropping.

Everywhere I've been tonight, I've heard rumblings about New York and families in the Northeast. I can't identify everyone in attendance due to their masks, and I'm wondering if that was Monroe's intent all along.

Before this morning, I would've never guessed that he had more than the O'Shea's backing. But today, he insinuated that there were many families who were against our marriage from the start. Have his ties in the Northeast somehow helped him steal power in the Garde?

Fecking hell, I have to fix this. Lacey is in too much danger and too close to the problem to find answers herself.

I'm silently begging her to come to me when Roxana sparks a conversation with the group. I smirk at the sight of the men's frustration and the women's mortification over a woman speaking out of turn, but I know a diversion when I see one.

Lacey squeezes from the crowd and slowly meanders her way toward me. Even as my heart races to be alone with her, alarm bells go off in my mind at her careful gait. She usually glides everywhere she goes, her balance and dancer's body working with gravity and the air around her to make everything she does look effortless. But she's hunched tonight and her steps are too measured to be natural.

Something is very wrong, and I need to get to the bottom of it. She's sober tonight, so I know her deliberate steps aren't because of alcohol. I don't know what's happened in the past twenty-four hours, and that all-too-brief waltz gave me more questions than answers.

I shouldn't have asked her to dance with me, but goddamn, it felt bloody fecking good to have my wife in my arms again... until I realized she was in pain. Her suppressed whimpers nearly made me sick, and I can't part with her again without knowing what— or who—has hurt her.

She's finally close enough that I know she can see me, so I turn around to travel down the hallway until I reach the coat closet at the end. I slip inside before softly closing the door and it takes a minute for my eyes to adjust to the light peeking through the cracks in the doorframe.

Once they become accustomed to the darkness, I can make out the extravagant furs and long coats hanging in several rows. There's a metal chair between the first two clothing racks, but I pace impatiently in front of it, unable to sit still as my mind races.

Nausea taints the back of my throat at the fear that we'll jump into this godforsaken loop again. I'm going to demand she leaves with me. She's going to insist on staying. I'll have to agree, so she doesn't blame me as the arsehole who gets her father killed. Then my heart will break as I watch her leave and I'll go on worrying whether I'll ever be able to save her without making her hate me, too.

But this time is even more infuriating than all the rest. I'm potentially hours away from Merek texting me that we've finally got some answers, but I know nothing will be good enough for her until they're in my grasp.

I stuff my hand in my pocket and brush my fingers over the frayed edges of the queen of diamonds card there. Ever since my father made her my mark, I've kept it in the breast pocket of my suit. But I learned my lesson when I didn't have my chip earlier today, so I'm using it as a replacement to keep me calm for the likes of Monroe Baron. It'll wear the card even more, but I'm hoping it can hold out a wee bit longer.

"Hello?" Lacey's voice is muffled by the row of coats as she closes the door. "I-I can't see."

I emerge around the first layer of coats to retrieve her and wrap my hand around her wrist.

"It's me," I murmur so I don't startle her and gently guide her between the two rows with me.

When she's finally in front of me, the light seeping from the cracks of the closed door is bright enough to see her blue eyes shine with unshed tears.

"Christ, what has he done to you?"

"Nothing. It's just period cramps and it's making me emotional." She shakes her head, but her voice wobbles as she whispers, "Y-you said you have something in motion. Please tell me I only have to do this one more night. I don't know how much longer I can go through this—"

Before she can say anything else, I'm hugging her against me. Her sweet floral scent fills my nostrils as she wraps her hands around my back and clutches my suit jacket like a lifeline.

Fecking hell, I've known this woman for mere weeks and I'd already kill for her in a heartbeat. In fairness, it didn't even take that long. The world was in danger the moment she first held my hand.

"*Tine*, you don't have to do this at all. Come with me. We'll leave right now. I've got a man searching for answers this very moment. He should have some by the end of the night."

She pulls away from my embrace and looks up, her eyes glittering like diamonds from the moisture.

"So you don't have anything yet?"

My teeth clench and it's a wonder they haven't cracked to pieces yet. "I will at any second."

"But not yet." She breathes deeply. "Okay... okay, you don't have answers yet. But you will. One more night of lies. I... I can do that."

My chest caves in as my prediction starts to come true.

"You're coming with me. No more of this. You can't go back there."

"Do you *know* your man will find something?"

"I'm sure he will—"

"That's a no. Which means I can't go with you yet! Listen, I know you're worried for me, but I saw my father in that hospital bed. Monroe showed me his picture. I *have* to get him out."

"What if you're the next one in a hospital bed?" My voice quakes as I confess my worst nightmare aloud, but I try to hit it home with my suspicions. "I know the authorities think they've caught the suspect, but what if Monroe was actually behind that woman getting murdered here in Rouge? I read people. It's what I do and I'm bloody good at it. I don't think the case is as cut and dry as they say it is."

She's slow to shake her head, and she shudders in my arms. When she finally speaks, her voice has less strength, almost as if she doesn't believe the words herself.

"Th-that's just paranoia. The Baron won't kill me, but he will hurt my father, again and again unless we save him. My dad could die behind bars and I can't live knowing that I could've stopped it by being patient for just one more night."

"And you're dying *inside*. I can't live knowing I caused that. I feel like I'm losing you right before my eyes and I can't take it. I want you safe in our home. I can't stand by and watch this anymore."

"I-it's fine. We just need to be patient and before you know it, we'll be back in bed doing all the things you want." She tries to laugh, but I don't give in to her attempt at deflection.

"That's not what this is about." I grab the strands of my hair and pull in frustration as I try to get through to her. "I'm in love with you, don't you see that? Don't you *feel* it? Going back to him is killing you and it's killing me. Why do you keep insist—"

Creeping doubt of what I hope is true paranoia kicks in and I ask the question before I can stop myself.

"You don't *want* this. Do you? Do you want to be with Monroe?"

"What? No, of course not. I hate this, too! But please, see what you find in twenty-four hours. Hopefully, it'll be only one more night."

I bite my tongue almost to the point of tasting blood. The only reason I stop is because her hands cup my face and bring me down for a kiss. I grab her wrists and shake my head.

"No, Lacey. Now's not the time—"

"Please," she whispers against my lips. "I need this. Just one more kiss until I see you again. You're my freedom and I'm about to lock myself back into a cage. Let me taste freedom again."

I'd rather throw her over my shoulder and say feck the Garde, her father, and Monroe. But when my wife asks me for a kiss of freedom, I give it to her.

Her soft lips caress mine and I can't hold back anymore. Her tongue plays with the seam of my mouth and the touch is all we need to give us both permission to lose ourselves.

My hands glide down her sides and I'm about to pick her up, but she gently pushes my chest until the chair behind me touches my calves.

I settle into the seat and shove the flowing skirt of her ball gown up to help her straddle me. The fabric flows around my legs and her core heats my cock through my pants. My hands roam over her bare skin to wrap my fingers around her outer thighs and I tug her closer to me. She grips the back of my head, and her fingernails scratch my neck hard enough to mark me, reminding me of the new ink I have on my forearm.

For once, I'm letting her take command. She grinds against my cock and I thrust to meet her center at the same slow, rolling, deliberate rhythm she's set. Under her control, our tongue strokes are long and sensual, with more feeling behind them than we've ever had between us before. But there's something in it that feels... final. I'll savor this kiss as long as I can, but the world be damned if it's our last.

A rumbling sound stills us both. She leans away and as I stand, I grip her by the hips to gently pick her up and place her behind me in case someone comes in.

We wait several hushed moments until a group of women breaks into laughter next door, and my tense muscles finally relax.

"It came from the women's bathroom," she exhales and my fear leaves with her breath of relief. "Shit, that was close. I should get back—"

"*Now?*" I turn around to face her. "What if someone heard us?"

"It was those girls. Besides, with an open liquor bar, people are probably too drunk by now to know their names. I'll wait until we hear the ladies' bathroom door open and then I'll go too." She grabs my face and whispers harshly. "Listen, I'll be fine. I swear."

"No matter what you say to me, wife, I'm not letting you walk down the aisle with another man." My vow is more forceful than I intended, but I don't relent

She nods. "I... I won't walk down the aisle with him."

"Promise me."

"I promise. Only one more night."

"One more night..." I rip at my hair with one hand while the other balls into a fist. "Goddammit. I don't want to do this."

"But you will. For me. Won't you? Please? You being a part of this has been the only thing to sustain me. I can't do this without you."

"I don't want you to be doing this at all!" I hiss.

Her posture straightens and her lips tighten as she slowly takes one step backward, opening a chasm of space between us. For one brief moment, I lost my temper, and with it, I lost any ability to persuade her to leave with me. She's not giving in.

"I've got to go, Kian."

She doesn't kiss me goodbye this time and I let her leave before me. I can't go first because I'd be incapable of leaving her behind. But she doesn't have the same problem as she goes out the door without a glance back.

I collapse in the chair and yank at my hair, willing myself not to feel betrayed, to trust that she's making the right decision, and praying that Merek finds the smoking gun. After I've collected my breaths, I finally leave. The hallway is empty when I come out. But the ballroom is still bustling when I enter it.

My eyes are drawn to Lacey immediately, but her attention is fixed on Monroe, a placid facade pasted on her face so securely that I wonder if she'll be able to take it off again. Monroe's sister and Mrs. O'Shea wear similar expressions. The women in this ballroom didn't need to buy masks for the masquerade theme. They could've just used the ones they've worn since the day they were born.

While I watch, I get a bottle of water and mill about to avoid sulking in the corner and gathering suspicion. She never once looks at me. Every second away from her breaks off piece after piece of me while she shores up her defenses like cinder blocks. She's excelling at living this lie.

Maybe Lacey O'Shea is meant for this world after all.

My father slowly drifts over to stand by my side. Neither of us is supposed to be here, but there are too many people for the O'Shea and subpar Baron bodyguards to keep track of. I've already suspected these masks helped Monroe sneak in some non-

Garde member allies, but at least it's helped the McKennons scope out our enemies as well.

"You're staring," he reminds me, but I don't give a feck.

"I can't do this anymore, Dad. I need her back with me."

"Don't lose sight. If what you think is true, then we've been going after the wrong family for too long. Let this play out. Any news from your man?"

"Not a word yet," I grumble, checking my mobile anyway. There are no new notifications and I shove it back into my pocket. "Still nothing."

"Then be patient. You've waited a year for this woman. You can wait one more night."

I huff out a breath and scowl at Monroe behind my mask until Maeve's eyes catch mine. Trying not to bring attention to myself, I slowly turn away to face my father.

"One more night," I finally agree. "But no matter what, tomorrow, she's mine again."

Act 4

Scene 32

THEY STUMBLE THAT RUN

The Baron is scary quiet. He has been since we left the ballroom. As soon as he shook the last parting hand, he hooked my arm through his and locked onto me in a stiff hold. He hasn't let go of me ever since, not even to get in the limo or to *tap tap tap* on his phone the entire ride. I even tried to talk about the impending storm so many guests brought up all night, but he stayed silent. When we arrived at the hotel, he wrapped his fingers around my wrist and nearly dragged me to his suites. All without a word.

I'm fucking terrified.

Fear buzzes through me and I have to ball my hands into fists to keep from wringing them. The blood in my veins runs cold by the time we get to the Elephant Room and it freezes altogether when instead of dropping me off, Monroe stops right outside the partially closed door to talk to the bodyguards.

I busy myself by taking off my trench coat and organizing the room like nothing's wrong. As the minutes pass by, all two hundred and thirty-seven elephants stare at me like they're waiting for the guillotine to drop. But if I continue to tidy up and fake a good Garde homemaker routine well enough, maybe he'll get bored and leave with a simple good night—

The door slams behind me, making me jump. The hope that I'll be left alone drains with the blood from my face as I pivot on my heels to see the Baron standing in front of my only exit.

His mouth purses in a frown as his brown eyes study me, narrowed in thought. Moments pass by, and I can't stand the stifling silence.

"Did you, um... did you have a good time?"

He's had a lifetime of putting on a face for the crowd, just like I have. I should be better at reading him by now, but I'm thrown off balance by everything tonight. Literally and figuratively.

"Mhmm," he answers with a slow nod. "It was very... enlightening, especially near the end."

"Well, that's great."

"Yes, it is."

He stalks toward me over the marble and my heart thunders as he steps onto the gray elephant-shaped rug I'm standing on, too. He's not much taller than me, but he is bigger and the displeasure curling his lip as he looks down his nose at me makes me uneasy.

This was a bad idea. I should've left with Kian when I had the chance.

"H-how long are you staying in Las Vegas after the-um, the wedding?"

He huffs a dark chuckle. "Oh, I don't think you need to be concerned about that. I don't think you should be concerned about anything but yourself right now."

Shit. I need Kian.

"Wh-what does that mean?"

"It means... I had an interesting conversation with my sister right before we left. You see, she doesn't remember much about your bachelorette party. But when Kian McKennon asked you to dance, his devil mask sparked the neurons in her addled brain. It wasn't until you two danced that it all clicked into place. She claims that *he* was the one you danced with on stage the night of your bachelorette."

I shake my head slowly and try to laugh it off like it's ridiculous, but all that can come out is a raspy huff.

"It's a regular part of Rouge's show. I-I have no idea who that guy was, but Kian's not part of the cast. Why would it be him?"

A wide, evil smile stretches within his goatee and he laughs much more heartily than I did as he takes another step forward.

"I know, I know. I thought it was crazy, too. But I still have that picture on my phone. I got a glimpse of him right before he left, and you know? My stupid, sycophant sister might be right for once in her silly life."

"I—she has to be mistaken—"

"Don't lie to me, whore!"

He lunges for me, and I scramble backward, collapsing against the floor-to-ceiling window that takes up the entire back wall of the suite. My stomach flies up to my throat at the realization that only inches of glass separate me from a fifty-story fall.

Whatever he screams at me is lost as his fists fly. They collide into my stomach and I double over with a shriek that tears from my throat. As I cower away from him, the diamond studs on my dress scratch my arms. He grabs me by my ribbon straps and before the laces can unravel, he throws me into the glass coffee table, shattering it against my back. Burning cuts slice my skin and pain shoots up my spine. My vision dims as I try to breathe.

I'm curled on the ground, the stabbing glass needles more comfortable than moving anywhere else right now. All the while, he prowls around me, yelling.

I'm ungrateful.

I'm a whore.

I used him.

I'm pathetic.

With every accusation, true or not, he kicks my back, forcing me to uncoil and giving him space to kick my front, too. Agony ripples through my body, but not my face. Never my face.

Even now, when he's in a rage, he's thinking about optics, careful to bruise, not break. I'm a deceitful bitch, but he avoids my face because he trusts that I'll hide the evidence of his fury underneath my clothes. As painful as this is, he doesn't want to kill me. He wants to shatter my spirit into a million tiny splinters. He's on the verge of succeeding too, and I'm afraid even Kian won't be able to piece me back together.

Finally, he calms down enough to merely shout at my huddled form. I breathe in, spurring a cough from deep in my chest and I groan as it racks through my body. Agonizing pain throbs through me inside and out. My lower back is killing me and nausea churns my stomach.

He throws me against the window again and my whole body seizes in terror, bracing myself to go all the way through until I collide with a sickening thud. I want to crawl away, but he snatches me by my hair before I can even sit up.

His sneering face and wild eyes fill my vision.

"Maeve followed you when you sneaked into the coat closet like a fucking rat. She didn't go in, but she heard enough outside the door. Kian said he wouldn't let you—his *wife*—walk down the aisle with another man."

He tugs the glove off my left hand and shakes my wrist, glaring at the band on my finger. "It's *true*?"

Before I can answer, he snatches my wedding ring from my finger, cutting the skin on my knuckle as he rips it off.

"No! Please!" I choke out, making me cough more.

He tightens his grip on my hair before sitting back on his heels and shoving the ring in my face. "You actually *married* him, you stupid bitch? How is that even possible? When did it happen?!"

"I... it all happened so fast. M-my bachelorette. It's n-nothing. A mistake. H-he's o-obsessed with me and... and I let him pretend for a while. It's over. I ended it t-tonight."

The lies burn on my tongue, but I'll say whatever I have to in order to protect Kian from the wrath I'm experiencing right now.

"You Garde bitches are all the same. Always looking for the richest dick to fuck over. Let me ask you. Did you *consummate* the affair? Did *he* take what's *mine*?"

"I'm... not... *anyone's* to take." I put all my anger behind the last word, but it only exhales on a hoarse breath.

"Oh, see, that's where you're wrong, you precious *flower*. Have you forgotten that you are the *Garde's* Red Camellia? You've been bought and paid for. Plucked for my pleasure. Mine to do with however I see fit."

He grabs my pussy through the satin fabric of my dress and digs into my center, making me cry out.

"Whatever freedom you think you have in this society is gone. If you don't start obeying me, you can kiss your sorry father's freedom goodbye, too. I'll sic my men on him in jail over and over again until he's hanging on by a thread. I just need him breathing until you have my heir, then I can become the Keeper. And if you don't tell Kian McKennon that you're getting an annulment, I'll go after him, too."

I shake my head. "Y-you c-can't. He's too powerful."

The Baron barks a laugh in my face, making spittle fly on my cheek. "I thought you were at least clever, but it seems you're as dumb as the rest of them." He points to his chest as he boasts. "*I* garnered backing in the Northeast and the Garde to take down your father. *I* orchestrated your father's arrest. *Twice.* I cooked your father's books and used his own money to pay the police, prosecutor, and judge to keep him in jail. It's amazing what you can get with billions of dollars swindled from other people. Loyalty and betrayal with one transaction. Now I decide whether your father suffers or thrives with a single text. Do you *really* think I can't do the same to Kian fucking McKennon? He's a nobody in the Garde. No assets. No backing. He's walked around here like he owns the goddamn place, but he's a glorified hitman and *I'm* the one holding all the cards."

The walls cave in around me. A low rumble resounds from far off and it takes me a moment to realize it's thunder and not my chest. I breathe through my mouth to stay alive. But every word he says feels like a nail driving into my coffin.

Kian said he had support from families in the Garde, that he could find out how to help my father. And yet, he's come up with nothing. Does he have as much power as he thinks? Or have people turned on his family like they've turned on mine?

Could the Baron kill him?

It feels unbelievable, but even as I think it, my chest aches at even the tiniest possibility. I'm trembling uncontrollably and tears shake from my eyes to spill down my cheeks.

The Baron sneers at me and releases my hair with a shove away from him. "See, this is why I hate makeup. You look like a goddamn disaster. You'll clean yourself up, but first, we need to make a call."

My eyes widen as the Baron digs into his pocket to pull out two phones, his and my sparkling red-and-silver one. A sinister smile cuts across his lips and he holds mine up.

"I noticed that Roxana calls and texts you incessantly throughout the day. But then *Roxy*, with one *x*, texted you on the way back here. At first, I thought the different spelling was a mistake somehow. But now I've got a new theory..."

He presses buttons before holding the screen to my ear.

"Say hello, and nothing else, or I swear it'll be the last phone conversation either of you has."

The dial tone rings only once and my heart stops when *he* picks up. I lick my lips and swallow before speaking.

"H-hello."

Before I can say anything else, the Baron presses the mute button and Kian's voice comes over the speaker.

"Lacey, *finally*. Monroe gave you back your mobile?"

"Tell him it's over," Monroe orders and raises his other phone with a number on the screen. "Tell him right now. Or I'll have one of my men go after him. I nearly put your father on life support without even lifting a finger. Do you think I can't do worse to a lowlife McKennon?"

My heart cracks in my chest. The pain is worse than any of the injuries the Baron has inflicted yet, and the rapid whooshing of my racing pulse drowns out all my thoughts. Every dream I'd begun to have over a life with Kian snuffs out.

"*Tine?*" His accent thickens with worry and the word has me crumpling onto the ground as all the fight seeps out of me.

"H-he won't believe me." I shake my head. My tears wet the rug underneath me like I'm shedding my last few drops of hope.

"You better put on the performance of your life and make him believe you then. Warn him, and I'll take him out anyway. Your call. Your father and Kian's lives are in your hands."

The Baron unmutes the phone and when the cold screen touches my cheek. I know what I have to do.

Scene 33

HARSH LIES

Bloody fecking goddamn hell, we've finally got a breakthrough. Merek messaged me the news minutes after Lacey left the party with Monroe, and it was all I could do not to run after the limo and snatch her out. Instead, I sped from Rouge to the Baron Suites and parked within a block in order to have a getaway car.

The Baron Suites is no longer our establishment, but just as the Elephant Room has been virtually unchanged after all these years, the same goes for its staff. It's an oversight that's biting Monroe in the arse now because I know plenty of disgruntled employees on the inside. Ones that are eager to feck over their boss.

Early this morning, while Monroe was getting hammered and donating his fortune to my casino, Merek was able to procure a universal hotel key to break into Monroe's suites. That sham of a rehearsal dinner tonight was the perfect time for Merek and Lorenzo to go in, hastily install cameras above the entrance of each room, and search for the smoking gun.

And feck did they find it...

Monroe brazenly left laptops, hard drives, flash drives, and printed spreadsheets lying about in one of the offices in his suites.

Merek was able to download and take pictures of everything. Once he and Lorenzo got back to the McKennon Hotel, he sent file after file and photo after photo to my mobile. I've already skimmed much of what he's forwarded for my review. The bits I've read can topple this society's house of cards.

Turns out, Monroe was the linchpin in setting the O'Shea up. As Charlie's financial manager, he was in the prime position to take our Keeper down. He cooked O'Shea's books, stole from rival Garde members, and used the money to persuade the authorities to stack the deck against Charlie. But it wasn't just Monroe behind it. Many people, inside and outside of the Garde, not only knew about it, they helped orchestrate it.

It gave me peace of mind to know that the families my father and I have collected as allies over the past few years aren't on the list of traitors. Not even the Luciano, to my pleasant surprise. But for some of the members, I was floored.

According to their communications, Garde families had conspired to keep Lacey and me from marrying, and they pitted us against each other while supporting Monroe. According to one email, they believed that merging the two most powerful families would've turned the Garde into a monarchy rather than a semblance of a democracy. An O'Shea-McKennon union was too powerful a force.

They have no idea how fecking right they were.

I plan to make our enemies pay, but that will happen in due time. McKennon revenge takes patience and for now, I just want my queen of diamonds in her rightful place, ruling by my side.

To ensure she can't say no again when I insist she come home with me, I've already made the calls to her father's defense attorney, my contacts at the police department, the jail, and even local judges and district attorneys. Even at this hour, every one of them answered my call. I informed them all that if they don't let the innocent Charlie O'Shea out of jail by tomorrow morning, heads will fecking roll. It might take a few hundred thousand dollars to grease the wheels and get our leader processed that quickly, but I've got enough money and blackmail to make it happen, and I'll do whatever it takes to have my wife back in my arms.

With everything falling into place, Merek has ordered me to be on bloody standby. He surveilled the top floor for weaknesses in Monroe's security and now he's organizing a team to back me up when we break in to save Lacey. I'm supposed to wait for them, but thinking about her spending one more fecking second with a monster is agony.

Despite the impending storm rumbling toward the city and the occasional splash of rain on my forehead, I pace outside on a brick footpath. It may be in the wee hours of the morning, but the open-air plaza is still full of drunk tourists. They meander from all four directions, traveling to the Baron Suites, an O'Shea casino, an overpass that leads to the McKennon Hotel, and—with less traffic—one of my old haunts, the Elysian Bar. I take turns roaming toward all four as I impatiently wait to go inside Monroe's hotel and rescue my wife.

I check my mobile to see if she's called, but the only message I've gotten is from Merek reporting that the camera angled on the Elephant Room's living space is working. Once Lacey entered the room by herself safely, he switched gears and began to gather McKennon security to go inside with me. The lad's been working around the clock nonstop to get me answers and surveillance. As soon as he updates the security app on my mobile, I should have the feed, too, but it's killing me in the meantime not being able to see her.

Swiping through my apps, I look to see if it's finished updating, but my mobile interrupts me when it vibrates in my hand. My heart leaps to my throat when I see "My Wife," and her soft, sleepy smile fills my screen.

Excitement buzzes through me, and I can barely resist the urge to blurt out everything I've learned since we left the rehearsal dinner. But I force myself to wait until I hear her speak, so I know it's her. Once she does, I can't hold back anymore.

"Lacey, *finally*. Monroe gave you back your mobile?" I wait for her to respond, but she's silent on the other end. "*Tine?*"

Worry seeps into my accent, but she answers and it all melts away.

"Um, sorry, I had to get to a quiet spot."

"A quiet spot?" My brow furrows as I lower my voice. "Are you safe?"

"Oh, oh yeah, of course."

There's a hesitancy that slows her replies to a cadence I'm not used to.

"Really? Your voice sounds... off. Are you sure you're okay? I can come to you—"

"Actually, I-I'm not okay." Her heavy sigh makes my stomach flip. "We need to talk."

"You're right. Lacey, I found—"

"It's over, Kian."

My pacing halts in front of the bar and I crane my neck to peer at the top floor of the suites. There's no way I can see her from here, and all I'm met with is a droplet of rain that slaps against my forehead.

"What are you talking—"

"Th-this is hard for me to say, but I can't do it anymore. I've been on the fence for weeks. But I've f-finally come to a decision, and I can't risk it anymore."

"Risk what?"

"My father. My reputation. My inheritance."

"Your *inheritance?*" My hand rakes through my hair. "Oh, now I know you're talking shite."

Merek said that she was dropped off at the room by herself, but what if the angle of the camera was wrong? Or what if Monroe came back in after Merek began to organize breaking in to save her?

I lower my voice before asking, "Is Monroe with you? Just say yes or no. I have a plan—"

"No! He's not with me, alright? This is more about me than

him. Tonight I realized that being with you would mean sacrificing everything I have."

"What do you mean?"

"Well, you saw everyone tonight. After we talked, Monroe and I stayed for hours and I had a lot of time to think. It made me realize that people came out in droves to support my marriage with him. I don't want to risk losing millions of dollars by losing the Garde's backing. This silly puppy love isn't worth ruining my place in our society."

Her words started out as wee paper cuts, but as she keeps going, they slice deeper into my chest.

But something is... off. I wish I could see her face. I can read my wife like a fecking book, but behind a screen, she's always been somewhat of a mystery.

I tuck my hand into my pocket as I resume pacing. The worn queen of diamonds card is soft under my fingers, even as Lacey's voice gets harder. Still, I go with my instincts.

"That first night, you said I was the type of man you could love. Was that true?"

There's a pause before she laughs at me. "Of course not. I was wasted and having fun."

I slowly shake my head. "I don't believe you."

"Ugh, Jesus. Of course you don't. I've only been trying to tell you this whole time that I don't care about you and I want to be left alone. But you've only ever seen what you want to see, haven't you? You've conjured up a woman in your head that looks like me, and you even call her by my name, but she's a fantasy. Your little speeches about knowing the real me? They're bullshit." Her harsh scoff makes my head jolt away from the receiver. "You've convinced yourself that I hide behind a mask in public, but have you ever stopped to think that's just who I am? Or does that not fit the love story you've concocted?"

"So you mean to tell me that you're a shallow party girl like everyone believes?"

"Not necessarily a party girl, but I'm also not some head-in-the-clouds romantic, either. Sorry to disappoint you."

My hand leaves my pocket with the queen of diamonds still in my palm. I tug my hair around the folded card and glance up at where the Elephant Room is.

"Where is this coming from, Lace? Did your mam get in your head or something?"

"She didn't have to, but when I spoke to her tonight, she did help me realize what's important."

"What's important? Fecking hell, I won't hear this anymore. I'm coming up there—"

"No! I'll call the cops! I have enough on you to get you locked up for life. You're just a hitman, the Garde's bitch boy to stay on their good side, *and* you wanted to kill me at one point in time. What do you think the cops will say when I tell them what I know?"

Her threat makes my heart leap into my throat, but I call her bluff. "Go ahead and call them. I'd love to have a chat with one of my friends."

"Oh, I'm sure Monroe has a few on the squad, too."

I grimace because she's likely right. Monroe was making moves in my own city while I was singularly focused on getting Lacey, but my mind races as I try to weigh the odds.

"Listen, Kian. We need to call it, alright? The Baron has goals. He's going to be a senator, maybe even president, and he wants *me* by his side. Not only that, he can provide security, support, and get my dad out of jail."

"But, I know how to—"

"I don't care!" she cuts me off with a hoarse scream that sounds so painful it makes me swallow. "I. Don't. Care. You lied to me when you didn't tell me you were seeing my father, and you lied to me when you told me he was safe. For all that Monroe's done, he's never lied to me. Whatever you say now, I can't trust, and I... and I don't want to risk my father's life on some w-worthless drunk's word."

The accusation is a blow to my chest and I halt in the middle of the sidewalk as rain peppers the ground. Boisterous, late-night tourists duck into the buildings towering over us to escape the open sky like it's drizzling acid. They have to dart around me to avoid crashing into my motionless form. It's good they do, though, because I can't take another step and one tiny push could send me toppling to the ground.

"You can't mean that," I finally whisper, my voice rough with emotion as the faith I had in us finally begins to crumble. I slide the card into my pocket and shake my head in disbelief. "I... I told you that in confidence. You would use it against me now?"

Silence greets me and I think that my words might have hit home until she sneers.

"I've never meant something more. You were a daydream for me. Someone I could use to pass the days while I endured a punishment that *you* caused. I thought you could be my ticket to freedom, but you not only can't back up what you say, I don't need you anymore now that the Baron is letting me go. He's promised to give me everything a Garde woman could ask for."

A pouring sensation runs down my chest, as if blood flows from the brutal wounds her words cut into my heart. It isn't until I press my hand to my shirt and hold it up to a mist-covered neon light that I realize it's just rain mixed with sweat.

Still, I weaken as my emotions bleed out of me. I stagger backward to lean against a wall underneath an awning, barely stopping myself from collapsing.

Only hours ago, at the rehearsal dinner, I questioned whether she wanted to be with me or Monroe. And when I saw her wear her mask in front of the guests, it was so effortless and natural...

Have I been seeing what I wanted to believe?

"Being the Baron's whore won't give you what you want, you know. It only makes him rich. You owe that bastard nothing," the biting tone snarls out before I can stop it, but maybe if I spark that rebellious fire in her, she'll come to her senses.

"And you are nothing to me, Kian McKennon," she replies

coldly, calling my bluff in an instant. "You've screwed me over way too many times in a matter of weeks and I'm done with your lies."

"So what about everything that *you've* said? Were those lies, too? I wasn't lying when I told you I love you, Lacey. That doesn't go away. You can make me do a lot of things, wife. Love you. Kill for you. Die for you. But don't make me leave you."

There's a breath of a pause on the other end before she coughs into her mobile. Concern has my lips parting to ask if she's okay, but caustic words spit out from her, making me realize that she's tricked me again.

"The fact you think you're in love with me is ridiculous. We barely know each other. It's your obsession with love that's made you think some divine destiny is being played out. You're a McKennon and I'm an O'Shea. Your family is a sinking ship, and I can't go down with you. The Baron is on the rise and he'll give me the life I've always known *and* free my father. I can't be lost in silly dreams anymore. I have to face reality, and so should you. And the reality is, you're a lovesick fool, but you're not in love."

Each word is another painful slice. I clear my throat before finally answering.

"What I feel—what I *felt*... it wasn't ridiculous, *tine*. It might take longer than a few weeks to fall in love, and maybe that's where I went wrong. I had a head start and assumed you'd catch up. But if I was ever lovesick..." I carve my hand through my hair and tear it at the ends. "Well, you've cured me of it now, haven't you?"

She doesn't reply and I think she's hung up, but when I see that the call is still going, I try a different tactic.

"What're you going to do about Monroe? We're already married."

Her voice is detached and hoarse when she replies, "It'll be easy enough to get an annulment. All I have to do is show the video. Anyone can see that I'm wasted."

The video.

It dawns on me that she hasn't seen the rest of it yet. And an idea pops into my mind.

"You'd have to get the video from me to use it, you know."

"Right, um... okay. Go ahead, then. Send it. I'll get it in the right hands. With my father's name, we'll have an annulment in no time. I want to legally marry the Baron as soon as possible. That way, I can ensure my father gets out of jail and I can leave all this nonsense behind me."

I stare at the top floor, past the raindrops falling freely now, and nod even though there's no way she can see me. The ringing bell of an opening door beside me makes me step farther out onto the sidewalk to avoid getting hit by the person leaving. Rain dampens my hair and I'm so disoriented I glance over my shoulder to remind myself what building I was loitering outside of.

The low buzz of the Elysian Bar's bright neon cursive sign calls to me like a siren in the rumbling storm. I turn around to drift toward it, no longer caring if I crash into the rocks.

"I'll send it." My voice is just as dead as hers. "Let me know once you watch it. If you haven't changed your mind, I won't try to convince you again."

"Don't bother waiting by the phone. I won't change my mind. I'm a princess in the Garde, but I can never be your queen, Kian McKennon."

And with that, she hangs up.

My heart thuds in my chest like a drumbeat as I open the heavy wooden doors. The entryway is as dark as a cave, but I open the next set of doors, revealing the dim lighting hanging above the bar.

"Kian?" The bartender still knows me by name even though it's been over a year, but his black brows furrow, wrinkling his olive skin as he dries a beer glass. "What're you, uh... it's been a while. You sure you want something?"

"Just a minute, Archie." I peel off my suit jacket and hang it on the back of the tall bar chair before sitting in front of a video poker machine. "But turn this shite off, will you?"

Archie nods and flicks a switch behind the bar, killing all the video poker screens' garish lighting and effectively running off any patrons wanting to sit and gamble with a drink. Now that I can see without being blinded, I roll up my sleeves and open the video the chapel manager took for me on the night of the wedding.

With all the various jingles coming from the slot machines in the bar's obligatory casino floor behind me, it's way too loud to hear the video properly. But I still take the time to watch Lacey's mouth move as she recites her vows.

With her gone the past few weeks, I've watched this hundreds of times just to see her smile for me again. But there's never been an ache in my chest like there is now. I want to carve open my sternum, reach inside and cut out the very essence of what's causing me so much pain, but a man can't live without his heart.

My fingers hover over her face on the screen, wishing I could caress her freckled cheek as she grins. Anyone paying real attention can see that she's not completely in her right mind. I was lucky she humored me with the whole marriage scheme at all. She could've very well insisted on playing the annulment card soon after the hand was dealt, but something had stopped her.

Whatever it was, nothing's in her way now.

The realization hurts more than I thought it would when I started this entire scheme. I watch the video once more before sending it to her and then again right after, imagining that we're both viewing it at the same time. But once it's finished and there's no response, I glance around for the bartender.

He's on his mobile, and I wave my hand to get his attention.

People in the Garde don't realize how many men and women we McKennons have on our side, and Archie's one of ours. When the families turned on us and the McKennons were cast out, non-Garde members remained faithful. Being good to people pays dividends. The Garde only looks for allies in the rich, influential, and famous, but it's the people you help without any expectation that wind up tapping in when your back's against the ropes.

There's no one but me and Archie in here now, though, and

with all the whirling racket and flashing screens, studying my surroundings to center me just grates at my nerves.

I reach into my pocket for my coin, trying to find some last-minute vestige of self-preservation and self-control.

But it's gone.

I pull out the worn queen of diamonds card instead.

It's been folded and refolded thousands of times over the past year, and the creases are beginning to tear. The line I've formed horizontally across the center separates the queen of swords from the queen with the camellia in her hand. Two queens. One card.

I look at it so long my eyes become blurry and before I return it to my pocket, I try to flatten the card against the wooden bar. But even though I'm as careful as I can be, my hands are too rough. The card splits in half, severing the connection between the two queens. The last few threads of willpower I have rip away with it.

I fold.

As I stuff the two halves into my pocket, I scan the liquor behind the bar. None in particular call to me, not until I catch the Midleton Dair Ghaelach. I point to it when Archie gets off his mobile and check my messages one final time to see if I've gotten anything at all to show that the video has made a difference.

But there's nothing.

I silence the device and toss it in my pocket before nodding to the bartender. For the first time in three hundred and eighty-three days, I turn my back on all that I've worked for.

"Midleton, neat... and I'll have a double."

Scene 34

VIOLENT ENDS

Tears soak my cheeks and as the Baron pulls my phone away, the screen sticks to my skin.

His face twists in disgust. "Look at all that makeup." He flashes the phone in my face before wiping the foundation off on my Valentino gown. "You won't wear that whorish shit anymore."

I don't say anything. I'm defeated and drained. After all that I've had to endure from the Garde, the Baron, expectations, isolation... none of it compares to losing Kian. Lying to him snuffed out the last spark of energy I could muster.

The Baron texts on his own phone before frowning at mine. "That's weird, there's Wi-Fi up here." He glares at me. "Did you have internet service this whole time?"

My eyes narrow as I shake my head and he huffs.

"Well, it's no matter. I was going to get my bodyguards to turn it on, but since we already have it, hopefully we won't have to wait too long to see if Kian will follow through on his word."

Rain pitter-patters against the window behind me. The glass is cold on my back where the crisscrossing ribbons reveal my bare skin and I slouch against it. Part of me wishes the window's frame would give way, even as my stomach lurches at the thought.

The phone buzzes between us and the Baron barks a laugh.

"Ah, he actually sent it. Let's watch this disaster."

He grabs me by the hair, making me yelp. I hold on to his wrist as he drags me toward the couch where he plops onto a cushion and dumps me at his feet like a dog.

"You'll watch him take advantage of you, and you'll realize that this is the nature of our society. Your parents bought into it, as did their parents' parents, and you've enjoyed the perks up until you were called to play your part. Now it's time to step up and do your damn job. You have this fantasy in your head that Kian McKennon represents freedom and love. But that doesn't exist in the Garde and Kian's no better than the rest of us. He doesn't have the power to free you and he doesn't love you. He loves your money and your status. Fucking you is a bonus."

He snatches my head up and I hiss as he uses my face to unlock my phone. It works despite my grimace, and he presses the notification that's from "Roxxy."

"I should've known you'd do something crafty like this, you little bitch," he mutters more to himself than me and swipes the message.

My texts with Kian appear and fear shoots down my spine when I realize I can't remember the last time I deleted our messages as a safety precaution. Thankfully, Monroe is solely focused on the video for now as the wedding takes over the screen.

Thunder rumbles and rain pelts the glass and as soon as the video begins to play, Monroe falls silent for once. I'm captivated, too, so much so that the pain ravaging my body fades into the back of my mind while I drift into the faint memories that break the surface. The combination of drinking and whatever was in Kian's syringe makes our wedding hazy, but where I can't recall everything, the video fills in the blanks.

I'm standing across from him in one of the over-the-top midnight chapels that I've only ever seen the inside of on television. He's changed into a black suit and other than my runaway bride costume, nothing else looks out of place. The venue isn't gaudy or silly, and pretty red flowers—albeit fake—vine around the white lattice wedding arch. As I gaze up at him, I'm perfectly calm, with a blissful smile on my lips.

It starts with the priest asking if we have our own vows and rings. I wince at Kian and answer no. He only chuckles at the admission, so I return to sheer excitement as the priest reads through the traditional ones for me. When I repeat, "I, Lacey O'Shea, take you, Kian McKennon, to be my husband," I don't bat an eyelash and my smile is practically blinding.

At the beginning of the night, he was a masked stranger who had nothing to do with the society that couldn't care less about me. I was the woman who protected herself by hiding behind the mask that society taught her to wear. But by the time we stood before the priest, both of our masks were off. I knew it was Kian, and we held hands the entire time I pledged my life to him.

I recite each phrase happily, promising to have Kian and hold him from that day forward, for better or worse, whether we're rich, poor, sick, or healthy. I beam as I vow to love and cherish him until death. The emotions from that night flood back to me, overwhelming me, reminding me of the hope and freedom I felt marrying him. He was my escape from the Garde at the time, the answer to the peace and freedom I'd been craving.

When the priest turns to Kian to say, "Repeat after me," Kian shakes his head and shocks me.

"I've got my own."

As I watch, the pain my mind tried to trick my body into forgetting begins to slowly kick back in. I hold my breath, partly to stave off the ache any movement causes, and partly because I need to hear every word.

The priest nods and steps back.

Kian inhales deeply, seemingly gathering his thoughts before he clears his throat.

"I... I have wanted you, Lacey, from the moment your father promised you to me. When the marriage was called off, I mourned the future we'd never have together and I tried to forget. I lost myself for a while after losing you. But then my father gave me an opportunity."

He must've squeezed my hands because I glanced at them before I smiled up at him again. My fingers tingle now as if they remember better than I do.

"Tonight, I had a choice in how to use that opportunity, and I choose you. *Is tú mo rogha.* You are my choice, *tine.*"

Beside Monroe, my breath hitches in my lungs, and I try my best not to make a noise. In a society where so much is dictated for us, choosing your own fate is a powerful rebellion. But tears fall freely down my cheeks as I remember every time Kian confessed that he chose *me.* All he wanted was for me to say it back... but I never did.

"Even though we've never properly met," he lets go of my hand to reach into the inside pocket of his suit jacket and bring out a small silver band. It glints in the light as he slides it easily over my left ring finger. "*Cha robh dithis riamh a' fadadh teine nach do las eatarra.*"

"What does that mean?" I ask in the video as he holds both of my hands again.

A hopeful smile plays across his face. "It means that even though we've never met, there's still a fire that lights between us. I realized it tonight during our dance and again when you kissed me. You are *mo thine*, my fire. We were meant to be together and when two people are meant to be, no one can explain why the fire sparks between them, but it kindles all the same."

I gaze up at him, eyes wide and no doubt my pulse is racing. Even now as I watch it, my heart flutters in my chest, my body feels buoyant and airy, and it finally dawns on me.

He always talks about how he dreamed of love and knew it could ignite between us. And here it is, right in front of my eyes. We felt it flare in its purest form that night and the flame has only increased as we've gone through these trials together.

Even when we were apart, he encouraged me through text messages and calls, gave me peace during our clandestine meetings, held me when I was overwhelmed. He was vulnerable and trusted me with his secrets, even going so far as to give me a physical reminder of something that matters so deeply to him—his AA chip—to promise his devotion and protection.

I tricked myself into thinking all I wanted was the independence that Kian represented. But it wasn't just freedom I hoped for with him. It was love. And he's given me that and more from the moment we met.

The priest smiles at us both and the elderly women watching us sigh with dreamy smiles almost as big as mine and Kian's. I notice them now, but back then, I was too enthralled at the way Kian looked at me, like he couldn't wait to eat me up and worship me at the same time.

When the priest raises his hands, he announces, "What God has joined together, let no man separate. *Slíocht sleachta ar sliocht bhur sleachta!* May you have children and your children have children, and may the Lord bless this marriage for all of your days. You may now kiss the bride—"

Before the priest can even finish the words, I'm already lunging at my new husband to make out with him. Kian quickly catches me and cups the back of my head. Somehow, he continues the kiss as he scoops me up underneath my thighs. Once he's holding me bridal style, he carries me down the aisle, with one arm supporting my spine so he can massage the nape of my neck, the way he's done so many times since.

The screen becomes blurry as tears fill my vision. My fingers drift over the screen as it pauses on Kian grinning back at me—

The phone suddenly disappears from in front of me. Two crashes come one after another before I realize that the Baron has thrown my phone at the wall and the broken remnants have shattered onto the marble floor.

"You thought you could play me by marrying that fool? You'll ask for an annulment and you'll get it. I promise you that." An evil smile slowly curves across his face and my belly churns with nausea. "And if you need any more motivation to end it, I'm happy to report that Kian's already been cheating on you."

"What?" the word escapes on a breathless whimper as if he's punched me.

No...

"Today, during our poker game, while you were locked away without your phone up here, he was messaging one of his conquests. In fact, he left without taking his money to go meet her and refused a rematch. Who the fuck does that? Only a man about to get laid would ever think to."

"I don't even gamble. I win and give everything back to the house."

Kian's confession floats across my mind and I reach for the coin in my dress pocket as my heartbeat begins to slow to normal again. I know without a shadow of a doubt that he didn't cheat on me. He was working on finding answers to free my father. Judging from our conversation a few minutes ago and how many times I had to interrupt to protect him, he found some. He's been on my side this entire time.

At least me letting him go keeps him safe.

No matter what happens tonight, I trust that he'll do whatever it takes to free my father, and Kian will be safe from the Baron's wrath now that I've ended it. But I'm still imprisoned up here with Monroe. After that video... I don't think I'll ever get out.

I've been forced to pretend all my life. If the Baron kills me tonight, I want to live the truth out loud, at least once, before I go.

Kian loves me. And I...

"I love him." I shake my head lightly and clutch the coin in my palm as I meet the Baron's wide eyes. Lightning flashes through the window, highlighting Monroe's face as it purples with rage. "I love Kian."

As soon as the revelation leaves my lips, the Baron crashes in on me and yanks me up by my hair again. I scream and try to scramble for purchase against his collar. His brown eyes are wild with rage and his slicked-back dirty-blond hair has fallen out of place.

"When Kian is done using you, your father will still be in jail —or dead—and you'll have sacrificed his life and your fortune to be treated like the whore you are."

He twists my wrist, sending blinding pain through my arm before throwing me to the ground. I land on it at the worst angle and I feel a pop before a wave of agony pours through me. My vision goes dim again. Nausea overwhelms me and I purge the watery contents of my empty stomach on the rug next to me. But the Baron doesn't even let me do that in peace.

Mid-gag, he kicks me again, screaming and shouting that I've tricked him. That my father will never see the light of day again. That he'll murder Kian. He doesn't vow to kill me, even though it's the one threat I'm wishing for right now.

With each one of Monroe's strikes, I curl up tighter on the cold marble floor next to the window. He's beaten all the strength out of me, and a haze tunnels my vision.

Crashing thunder jolts me awake to find Monroe straddling my waist.

"No, no..."

His hands wrap around my throat, cutting off my feeble pleas. I kick and thrash, but even as I manage to suck in tiny sips of oxygen, the fight slowly leaks out of me. My legs fall limp, my face grows hot and tight, and darkness barrels toward me. When my mind taunts me that I'm going to die with Kian believing I don't want him, I give in and slip away.

It's a blow that hurts more than anything else. More than the Baron shaking me so hard that I slam against the marble floor. More than when my head crashes into the hard ground.

My mother's words drift across my mind with that final impact.

"At least he doesn't touch your pretty face..."

...but no one cares about a pretty face in a closed casket.

Scene 35

ORPHEUS AND AMOR

The lights from the slot machines behind me glimmer against the amber liquid inside my glass. My eye twitches from glaring so long at the drink that sits inches away from me. Sweat pricks the back of my neck as I fight every impulse to down it in one gulp so I can forget.

"The liquor's not going to drink itself, son."

I swivel in my seat to see my father brushing off rain droplets from his suit jacket. He pulls out the stool beside me and nods to the bartender.

"I'll have what he's having, Archie."

As if Archie was expecting the request, he's already pouring my dad a Midleton in a Glencairn glass like mine. When he drops it off, my father grabs it and swirls the whiskey before taking a whiff.

"Ah, it always smells so good when it's first poured." He tips it in my direction. "Now... are we going to do this or not, lad?"

His brown eyes take my measure like only a father's can. The Garde seems to have forgotten that Finneas McKennon is one of its most formidable members. His glare alone has made weaker men fold at the poker table, which is good since my father is

"Leave me be." I wave him off and return to my staring contest with the whiskey. But after a moment of silence I glance at him. "How did you know I was here?"

"Arch," his bushy gray eyebrows rise as he nods toward the bartender studiously cleaning glasses on the near opposite end of the bar.

I curse before calling out, "Hey, Arch!"

Archie turns around, like he hasn't been listening the whole time. "Yeah?"

"You call everyone in Vegas and tell them I'm on the ledge, or just this bastard?" I scowl at him, but he doesn't seem fazed.

"Called Merek, too. He said he's on his way." Archie smirks.

I roll my eyes and lean back in my stool to endure my father's lecture.

"You've got people who care about you, lad. Something the Garde won't ever understand."

"Grand. Now if only the woman I love did the same."

"I was afraid that was what this was about. Did she not like the new tattoo?" He glances at my forearm with a laugh. His joke lands hard on my chest and I rub the burn there.

"Feck off. She never even saw it."

"I'm just fecking with you, lad." He chuckles at first, but after studying me for a moment, he clears his throat. "I know this is a delicate situation, son, but the two of you have done well with the lot you've been given."

When I don't respond, he sighs and tilts his head at me. "Have you figured out why your mam and I decided that you and Lacey should get married?"

"For the good of the Garde," I repeat the phrase I've heard a thousand times by now in a detached tone. "Mam had the idea that our marriage could solve the Garde's divisiveness caused by the hatred between two families. Although, I found out tonight thanks to Merek's surveillance that many of the families weren't too keen on the idea. I've got a list of gobshites who conspired with Monroe to drive us apart and send the O'Shea to jail."

"Hmm." My father's face reddens with anger. "I'll have to see that list. We might need to assign cards to a few family heads sooner rather than later." He huffs before going on. "But in any case, that's the reason I gave the O'Shea. Your mam and me had another objective."

My brow furrows. "What was the *real* reason, then?"

"The greatest of leaders are the most reluctant. I could tell years ago that our Keeper was losing his backing among the Garde. The society has lost sight of the fact that we need people on the outside as much as we need them within. But you..." He points his whiskey at Archie's back. "You've amassed a following of both all on your own. You don't need the Garde and that scares the society more than any alliance between families. The thought of a leader in charge who actually wants what's best for everyone, and not just the elite? Now that's dangerous."

"If it's not what the Garde wants, why would you want me in charge?"

"Bah, don't be thick, lad. It was so you could change things! The old men are tired. Our ideas are tired, too. The new world, the new Garde, should be what we actually strived to be from the beginning, one of higher ideals. You and that wee firecracker of a wife of yours are our best hope to make sure all the harm we've caused is righted."

"But all that is gone now." I shake my head. "Lacey's chosen Monroe."

My father frowns and his voice is rough. "What happened? I doubt it's anything your wild card can't take care of."

"She's finished with me." I swallow and shrug. "Told me so tonight. She used me to help her father, and now she wants what Monroe can give her, status in the Garde. She said she doesn't want a worthless drunk for a husband. I thought she cared for me, but I guess my heart made it all up."

My father barks a laugh. "Maybe we're doomed after all if you really believe that load of shite."

"What do you mean?"

"I saw the two of you on the dance floor tonight. It was a mistake to behave like a dog and piss on her like that, son. But when you danced, it was bloody obvious that you're meant for one another. Two flames..."

"Kindled all the same," I finish. Hope lights a fire in my chest.

"I don't know what's gotten into your wife, but when something's wrong with your woman, it's your job to fix it. Love isn't for the weak or heartless. You might have to fight for it. Do you think you have the courage for the battle?"

I straighten in my chair at the question. "If my wife comes back to me in the end, how could I be afraid?"

"Now there's a good lad. Besides, you've kidnapped her once before and managed to convince her to fall in love with you in a matter of hours. What's the harm in doing it again? It's the McKennon way, after all." My father chuckles and lifts his whiskey in a toast. "Make your choice, but once you do, don't ever look back. It'll only hurt her if you do."

I glance at his raised glass before I study his assured expression. A confident smile, bushy brows slightly raised, and he's waiting for an answer he seems to already know. He never judged me for my vices or my addiction. But he was more worried than anyone about how much I could've lost if I'd kept on down that path.

My eyes narrow. "Did you know how I would play the queen of diamonds when you gave me the job a year ago?"

A knowing smile lifts his lips before he shrugs. "Come on, now, you know I'm shite at cards."

"Fecking hell." I chuckle as I settle into my chair.

He grins and tips the glass again. "So what'll it be, son?"

My dad believes in me. I have friends in my corner. I may not have my chip anymore to remind me of how hard I've worked. But I didn't achieve sobriety just for Lacey, I did it for me, too. I'll be damned if I lose us both now.

When I glance back at the untouched whiskey the draw is nowhere near what it was.

I push the drink away from me and stand from my chair before meeting my father's eyes. Pride replaces the concern that had crinkled at the edges.

"I'm going to get Lacey and change her mind. Merek said she was alone in the Elephant Room, but maybe her mam or Monroe said something that scared her off after we danced at the rehearsal dinner..." My words slow as my father's words finally click. "Wait, you said that you saw us dance?" When he nods, I curse. "Do you think Monroe did as well?"

My father's lips purse as he follows my logic. "If he did, he has a better poker face than we thought. But I watched him like a wolf the entire night, and he didn't notice, I'm sure of it. Although you, yourself, just said he has supporters. And then there was his sister—"

"*Fuck.*" I yank at my hair and reach for my mobile. "I've got to call Merek and—"

The device flashes in my hand and when I read Merek's name at the top, I quickly accept the call.

"What've you got for me?"

"Key, I've been trying to call you, man. It's Lacey," he speaks quickly and his careful tone makes me sit back down.

My jacket falls from my chair but my father catches it before it hits the ground. He holds on to it and frowns at me, but all my attention focuses on Merek's shaky voice.

"I was on my way to the Elysian, so I didn't see right away, but I got notified by the hotel's security that there was a disturbance reported on Monroe Baron's floor."

"Do you think he knows that we broke in?"

"I wondered that, too, so I checked the surveillance we put in tonight. But, Kian, after I thought Lacey was in the clear, he went back inside—"

I'm hopping off the seat and racing out of the bar, but I keep listening as I run.

"I only watched for a second before I called you. But I've seen that rage before. *Fuck.* I've already called 9-1-1. That's all I could do this far away. I can't watch while I'm on the phone, but if he hasn't already—"

"Watched what?" My heart stalls in my chest, but I push forward on feet that are way too slow. "Merek, what happened? What's he doing to Lacey?"

Merek's pause feels like a lifetime until he swallows and finally answers, "He's going to kill her, Key... if he hasn't already."

Scene 36

DEATH TO THE CAGED BIRD

Deep down, I must've known I would go back for her. There's no doubt why I chose to go to the Elysian Bar right across from the Baron Suites instead of crossing the overpass back to the McKennon.

Fecking hell, am I grateful for that decision now. It's pouring rain when I sprint across the plaza, and even though I've already called Lacey seventeen times, every one of them has gone to voicemail.

Thankfully, Merek has his head on straight. I hung up straight away after his last warning, but he texted that he's called the authorities and told one of the employees he befriended to leave a universal swipe key for me at the concierge desk.

There's no one behind the desk when I reach it, but the key sits there for me like a beacon. I snatch it up and rush toward the elevator.

Once inside, I use the universal key to unlock the top floor. When its icon lights up, I slap it and the "close door" button at the same time. I'd race up the stairs if I knew I could outrun an elevator up fifty flights, but I have no time to waste and this will have to do.

The music and the wait as I ride gives me a chance to breathe but I spend the time unholstering my pistol from underneath my shirt, pacing, and ripping my hair out. I glare at the blinking numbers as they slowly increase and I try to prepare myself for what I'm about to see. The entire time, my mind won't shut the feck up.

What if Merek had been able to immediately link my app with the surveillance... if we'd found evidence to free her father sooner... if I'd trusted my goddamn instincts and kidnapped her again instead of listening to her insist on being the fecking sacrificial lamb.

"*Fuck!*" I whirl around and slam my fist into the elevator's mirror wall. It cracks like a spider web, making my reflection as jumbled and broken as I feel.

I want to do it again, but I pull up my mobile and begin to text, instead. Only when blood smears on the screen do I realize that rivulets stream from my knuckles down the veins of my forearms. I can't be arsed to stanch the bleeding, so I swipe the screen clean on my black shirt and try to send out the message again one-handed, but Merek's text bubbles up on the screen.

MEREK

I'm on my way. I've called all your people and anyone who can help. Baron just left the room. Looks like he's leaving the premises, but paramedics should be there any moment.

My fingers fly over the keyboard.

How is she?

Instead of texting, he calls me and my blood turns to sludge in my veins.

"Listen man, wait for me or the paramedics, alright? You don't want to go in there."

"The feck I don't. You can see her on the camera, right? Is she alone? Is she okay? How badly is she hurt?"

"He... he strangled her. Once he started he didn't let up. He knew what he did, too, because he ran out of there like a criminal. She hasn't woken up yet..."

"Don't say it," I growl, but Merek's never been one to shy away from the truth.

"She's... she's gone, Kian."

I slam the mobile against the metal doors with a deafening *bang*. The device crunches to the ground as microscopic glass fragments explode in the air like sparkling dust. My feet stagger backward until the cracked wall stops me. The pistol clacks against my head as I tug my hair with both hands. All I can do is watch the numbers change, listen to the floors *ping ping ping* by, and try to tune out the jarringly upbeat elevator music that taunts my sanity.

Before the elevator slows to a steady halt, I lower my stance and hold my pistol out in front of me. As soon as the doors slide open, I barrel out into the hallway.

The *empty* hallway.

It's eerily quiet. The top floor is supposed to be full of various suites that Monroe uses as his residence here, with one at the very end being the Elephant Room. Merek said Monroe left, but Lacey is still here. Wouldn't that mean that *someone* should be on guard?

Not if she's dea—

"No," I growl under my breath.

Shaking my head, I rid myself of the thought before I run down the carpeted hallway. I go as fast as I can on light feet, careful not to make too much noise in case someone has been left in charge. Anxiety burns my lungs until I get to the door with the elephant sign next to it and I realize I've been holding my breath. My feet slow and I force myself to breathe past the fear lodged in my chest.

The door is cracked.

Nausea churns in my stomach as my fingers touch the metal. Heavy hotel doors don't crack open. They're too heavy. But the security latch at the top of this one has been lodged between the door and the frame. Whatever is inside... someone wanted it found.

Did Monroe know I would come for her?

I raise my gun with one hand and gently push the cold metal door with the other. It opens silently and once I get inside, my eyes dart around the room to clear it for threats.

The studio suite is just as I remember it from years ago, with a living space, queen-size bed, en suite bathroom, and a kitchenette. Elephants cover nearly every inch of the place in colors so bright they would hurt your eyes after too long.

It's in total disarray now, though. The glass coffee table is shattered, gold and silver elephant statues and figurines are strewn about, and panic begins to paralyze me when I can't find Lacey.

But then, I see her.

My blood runs cold even as my heart punches into overdrive from the adrenaline pumping into it. Lightning flickers through the window wall, outlining my wife's prone body. She's sprawled on the marble in front of the glass as if someone threw her into the window and she collapsed at the bottom.

"*Tine?*"

My voice is hoarse as I whisper, but I have a sick pit in my stomach that she wouldn't answer even if she could hear me. I trip toward her until I collapse onto the floor at her side, landing on the sharp diamonds that were ripped from her crimson dress and now glitter around her.

"W-wake up, Lace."

But her eyes remain closed. Her left wrist lies at an uncomfortable angle by my knee, clearly broken, and there's a red scrape on her bare left ring finger.

Fuck.

More cuts and scratches slice across nearly every inch of her arms, no doubt made by the broken glass coffee table behind me. Her gorgeous strawberry-blonde curls are now soaked by the blood pooling from the back of her head and they lie flat against the formerly pristine white marble. Her face is unmarred. Light-brown freckles stand out against her ghost-white skin, and her rouge-painted lips are parted. But as I sit here, counting my own inhales and exhales, her chest doesn't rise and fall with mine.

I saw a crime scene photo similar to this one only a few weeks ago. It was a nightmare then, but I'm living it now. I couldn't have stopped what happened that night. Tonight, though, after everything we've been through, my mind screams one truth.

The love of my life is dying... and it's my fault.

That realization is what finally jars me out of my devastated daze.

"Goddammit, baby. Wake up."

She's bruised and battered, and I'm terrified I'll hurt her worse if I touch her, but watching her die isn't an option. Even though I know how to knock someone out better than I can revive them, long-forgotten first-aid lessons kick in and I feel for her heartbeat in her neck. My fingers tremble and I have to will myself to stay still so I can count, but if it's beating, it's too faint to tell.

"You're not doing this to me, *tine*."

I lift her chin like I've done so many times before to get her sky-blue eyes to focus on me. Only this time her eyelids are closed, and I'm doing it out of necessity to get her to breathe for me.

Sitting up on my knees, I tug the neckline of her dress to fit the heel of my hand between her breasts. I try not to think about how her straps have been loosened and what all she could've endured. Monroe is already a dead man, but I'll need Lacey to help me decide how he goes, and that can't happen until she's been saved.

When I have enough space to start CPR, I press against her rhythmically so hard that I'm sure I'm going to crack her fragile body in half. I do several compressions before bending over her, holding her nose, and forcing air into her lungs.

Every push against her chest and every blow of breath feels more futile than the last. My own heartbeat races to the point of pain, and my skin heats with exertion. Sweat pours down my cheeks as I try to breathe life back into the woman who unknowingly saved mine. I shake my head to get the stinging salt out of my eyes until I finally realize it's not sweat. The droplets are hot tears falling like the rain outside.

After what feels like an eternity, my muscles begin to shake from despair, adrenaline, and effort. I slow down and take deep breaths to calm myself so I can feel for her heartbeat on her uninjured wrist.

When I hold her hand, a flash of silver falls from her palm and clinks onto the marble. I pick the coin up from the ground, but I don't need to examine it. I know it better than I know myself.

It's my AA chip. And Lacey held on to it until her final breath.

A low, mournful moan rumbles from my chest as I gently scoop my wife up to hold her. Thunder rolls and lightning flashes outside. Rain is a fecking miracle in this drought, but I'm begging for one of my own. One more breath from the woman I love.

All I get is her faint floral scent as her limp body rolls into my chest.

I knew how I felt about her months ago, but I fought it. I should've told her weeks ago, but I was afraid to scare her off. Yesterday I hinted at it to see how she'd react. And hours ago, I finally confessed that I love her without hedging my bets. Was it too late?

I've forgotten all the things she said when she tried to end it with me, but I don't care. They were lies anyway, and I only want to remember the truth. I love Lacey O'Shea and I know she loves me.

...loves.

Loved...

My heart cracks as thoughts run wild in my head and guilt pounds inside my chest.

I did this to her. If I hadn't been so goddamn selfish. If I'd only left her alone. If I hadn't tricked her into marrying me. If I'd refused to let her stay here. If I'd never asked her to dance in the first place...

My eyes burn and I hold her hand to my thumping chest like I did just yesterday. I rock her gently back and forth, back and forth, back and forth.

There's movement behind me and I barely register that strangers are talking around me like I'm a feral animal that needs to be calmed. Somewhere in my mind I know I make it worse when a tap on my back makes me snarl over my shoulder at them.

It isn't until someone speaks directly to me that I begin to fully understand what's going on.

"Sir... you have to let her go."

"*No.*"

The female paramedic jolts away from me at my growl, but she scowls and orders her team to keep moving around me.

Merek appears from behind her and kneels next to me, his brow furrowed with worry.

"Key, man, you have to let them near her."

"They'll take her away. She's... she's not breathing and if they take her—"

—what if she doesn't come back?

"I explained what I saw on the camera and they think they can help. But look at yourself." He points to the window and I reluctantly lift my gaze from Lacey's wet, spiky lashes to see myself in the glass. "They're afraid to take her from you, but they want to help her live."

Water has slashed across the glass. The tint combined with the storm has dimmed the Vegas lights, putting my reflection in stark relief. My eyes are wild with rage and sorrow as I huddle over Lacey in my arms. I'm cradling her head against my chest, careful not to touch wherever the blood is spilling from and my breaths rise and fall in quick movements, full of strain, fear, and life. Lacey's doesn't move.

"Let her go, Kian. If you let her go, she'll come back to you."

I nod slowly as I mull over his words. He says something to an

EMT, and when they reach again, I gently pass her off to two female paramedics. Once she's lifted from me, my arms feel light without her weight, but the air in my chest is too heavy to breathe. It takes every ounce of my willpower to stop myself from snatching her to me again, but I let Merek pull me back to get out of the way.

"She's not breathing," I murmur out loud again.

"We know, sir," the paramedic answers with more patience than I have right now.

"Let them do their job," Merek orders me.

I nod again, in a daze, as I watch them work furiously over her. They do chest compressions and CPR while checking her vitals. All emotion drains from my body, preparing for the worst. Mercenary logic fills the void and I welcome the cold that ices my veins. I barely recognize the harsh edge in my voice when I finally speak.

"Merek? Find Monroe Baron. Once you do, don't let him out of your sight. Do you understand? I've got a wild card I've been dying to use."

"Absolutely. He won't leave Vegas."

"I don't think he intends to. He left the door open for me to find her. He taunted me, but the bastard has always overplayed his hand. This was an act of war between families. The piece of shite knows that, but he thinks he's invincible and I'm nothing."

Something shiny catches my attention in the corner of my eye and I glance over to find Lacey's mobile on the ground. The screen is completely shattered.

Is that what did Monroe in? Did they watch the wedding video together? Was that the final straw that made him angry enough to kill her?

Mistake after mistake. Repeatedly I've fecked everything up a thousand times over. My dad might've orchestrated us getting together, but I... I ruined her after all.

"*Fuck!*" I yell and go to carve my hands through my hair. The one still holding my AA chip stops me, and I fist it in my palm.

I bring the coin to my face and steeple my fingers around it, partly to beg God to bring my wife back to me and partly because I'm unable to watch them abuse her body to do it. Hot tears blur my vision as they stream down my cheeks. I let the emotion flow from me as I pray to God harder than I ever have and I quietly beg Lacey to listen.

"Come back to me, Lace. *Please.* Come back to me, *mo thine.*"

As I rock in place, giving Merek the reins in finding Monroe and letting the paramedics fight for Lacey's life, I pray, and I pray and I pray... until *finally*... I hear the most beautiful words...

"We have a pulse!"

Scene 3F

YOU HAVE MY WORD

Harsh beeps pulse in my ears, making my splitting headache even worse. The satin sheets I'm wrapped in are soft, but they scratch against my skin. Red-orange light burns through my eyelids and I scrunch them tighter to block it out. It only drives the hammering sensation deeper into my skull.

Fine, I'll just open them instead.

When I crack my eyes, blinding pain stabs into my brain, and I cry out.

"Shh, you're okay, Lace."

Kian's smoky, sweet amber scent envelops me as he gingerly wraps one arm over my chest. His lips brush the shell of my ear as he whispers warm, comforting words, but I can only understand them once the agony subsides.

"You're safe, *tine*. You're home. He's not going to hurt you anymore. No one will ever hurt you again."

I try to thank him, but my throat is so dry, it only comes out as a whimper.

"Here." He shifts beside me until a straw meets my lips. "This will help."

My lips part to allow the cold, refreshing water to leak

between them. I lap it up greedily, and when he pulls the glass away, my eyes instinctively open to follow where it went. But that bright light crashes in, making me groan and Kian flies off the bed.

"I knew they shouldn't have opened these bloody things." Metal rings clatter against the rod as he violently closes the curtains. "Sorry, that shouldn't have happened. *Fuck*, none of this should've ever fecking happened."

With the light dimmed, my eyes flutter open again to finally assess my surroundings. Kian sits next to me on a silver comforter, shirtless and dressed down in gray sweats. His weight dips the mattress, and it takes me a second to realize I know this bed.

"Are we—" I clear my throat and wince. "Are we in your home?"

"Our home," he answers while positioning the straw at my lips again. I drink as he fills the blanks in my memory.

"We're in our suite at the McKennon. You went to the hospital after... after everything happened last night. You've been in and out of sleep most of the day."

"No wonder I feel like crap." I try to sit up but a shooting pain down my spine stops me. A hiss escapes my chest and I reach for the back of my head to feel where most of the ache seems to stem from, but Kian catches my hand.

"Don't touch it. You got a bad concussion and they had to stitch you up. It's best to leave it alone."

"A concussion?"

Exhaustion sags his shoulders and dark circles bruise the skin underneath his glassy eyes. His voice trembles when he answers.

"After I found you, I tried... I tried to save you. The paramedics said I kept your heart going until they got there. Once they arrived, they were able to bring you back to life. Do you... do you remember any of it?"

Almost as if my thoughts are trying to answer the question for me, memories knife through my mind while shame and guilt fill my veins.

"Kian, oh my God, that phone call... I'm so sorry. I didn't mean any of it. The Baron—"

"Shh, it's okay, Lace. I know." He rubs my thigh soothingly over the covers to calm me. It feels amazing, but all I can focus on are the cuts and bruises on his knuckles.

"Jesus, what happened to your hand?"

He glances at his hand as if it's the first time he's noticed. "I, uh, I lost a fight with my reflection. Definitely not the only thing I fecked up last night, though."

His hazel eyes glisten until a drop of emotion trails down his cheek, and he massages his eyelids.

"Fecking hell, you were apologizing, but *I'm* the one who needs to apologize. I'm sorry. So goddamn sorry. I've made so many mistakes. I should've figured everything out sooner. I should've trusted that you wouldn't say any of those things unless you were forced to. If I had—"

My heart breaks for the grief cracking his voice and making him falter. I use my thumb on my uninjured hand to swipe the moisture from his cheek.

"So many men demand respect by ruling with an iron fist, but they could be loved if only they gave us their tears."

"I'd give you everything to be given your love in return." He cups my hand against his cheek and kisses my palm.

I keep it there and lock my gaze with his as I make my confession. "Maybe we both could've been better. But honestly? I'd do everything wrong all over again if falling in love with you feels this right."

His jaw slackens, and he lowers my hand. "You... you love me?"

"I do." I smile and try to remember the words. "*Is tú mo rogha*. I love you, Kian McKennon, and I choose you."

He holds both my hands in his and his voice is rough when he speaks, "*Is tú mo rogha*. I love you, and I choose you, Lacey O'Shea."

"McKennon," I correct him with a small grin. His smile

makes my chest light and I go to touch it, but my left hand is stiff. My eyes flare at the sight of the fresh cast wrapping it.

"Is it... it's broken?" I whisper. "And... and my ring. Where is it?"

He cradles my hand, but his careful touch is in complete contrast to the rage on his face.

"I don't know where the ring is, but after I found you... I'm just happy you're alive. That piece of shite tried to kill you, Lace."

"But Kian McKennon wouldn't let him." I try to grin until a horrid thought crosses my mind. "W-what else did he do? I-I don't know what he did when I was out. What if he—"

"He didn't." His tan skin blanches. The words seem as hard for him to get out as they were for me. "They wanted to do a rap —a... a kit to see if he assaulted you. But I-I watched the surveillance myself. He didn't do that."

Relief makes me dizzy. "What did he do then? I hurt... everywhere. I'd hoped him punching me after Mass would've been the worst thing he'd do, but obviously—"

"He *punched* you after church? And you didn't tell me?"

"If I had told you, you wouldn't have let me stay, and I *needed* you to find answers for my dad, or it would've all been for nothing."

His lips thin, but he takes a deep breath. "I wish you had told me."

"I know. I'm sorry."

"It's okay. You did what you felt you had to do in dealing with Monroe. So will I," he murmurs as he begins to caress the inside of my left ring finger.

The move flexes his forearm, showing off a group of circles freshly inked there. His chest and back are tattooed in symbols and ornate designs, but for the first time, I really notice the ones on his left arm. On his bicep are two playing cards, an ace of hearts and a queen of diamonds. Fluttering soars in my chest at the realization, but the new circles on his forearm are still a mystery.

With my uninjured hand, I trace each tiny circle that makes up the oval... right where I—

"Did you get a tattoo of my bite mark on your forearm?"

He huffs a laugh. "I did. I told you if you marked me, you'd be marking me forever, wife."

"I didn't know you meant literally!"

"Fair warning, next time you scratch me, I plan to get those, too."

A laugh tries to fall from my lips, but I grimace at the thought that the marks on me right now aren't Kian's.

"I don't like that he left marks on me," I whisper. "I liked yours."

He squeezes my finger, and his face hardens. "You'll have mine again soon, I promise you. And you'll have justice, too. I plan to give the bastard back every injury he gave you and then some."

"What, um, what other injuries do I have? I mean, I'm glad I'm here, but with the way I feel, I'm kind of surprised I'm not in a hospital right now."

He sighs. "When Merek found out Monroe stayed in Vegas, I couldn't risk having you vulnerable to that fecker again, so I brought you here." He gestures to the bedroom that's been converted into a chic makeshift hospital room before continuing, "You have deep bruising to your kidneys, abdomen, and throat. A concussion and stitches in your head to match. Cuts and scratches from glass, and a broken wrist that will require surgery."

"Surgery? But what about dance? I need my hand for certain moves—"

"We'll figure that out. The rest of you needs to get better first, alright?"

Panic still flutters in my chest, but his encouraging smile comforts me as he strokes my palm. His warm fingers tickle my skin until it reminds me...

"Your chip? Do you have it? I held on to it..."

"I have it, tine. You kept it safe."

He shifts and pulls the coin out of his sweatpants pocket

before placing the chip into my palm and closing it. Remorse and rage cloud his face as he stares at my chipped fingernails. His jaw tightens until the small muscle pulses beneath his short beard. Finally he levels me with a determined gaze.

"I'm going to kill him. You won't be able to stop me—"

"Good."

His brows rise. "You... you don't have a problem with that?"

Instead of answering him straight away, I ask the question I have a feeling I already know the answer to. "Did you tell the police what happened?"

His lips thin, and he shakes his head. "I wanted to take care of this in-house. My police contacts know enough not to ask more questions, and your injuries made it easy to convince the paramedics to keep quiet. I believe everyone agrees that the justice system's methods aren't going to cut it this time."

It was what I expected, and with the anger raging inside of me, I'm grateful that, for once, the Garde's influence protects the good guys.

"Do you know how to get my father out of jail?"

He nods. "I made the calls last night. He'll be freed and have his name cleared any moment now."

I stop my head from jolting at the news just in time. "That was fast."

"You can do a lot of things if you wield the right secrets, and when it came to freeing an innocent man, truth, money, and blackmail were powerful motivators."

"Monroe said several families in and out of the Garde helped him frame my dad."

"I know, and they'll all pay for it, I assure you. I just need to know everywhere Monroe touched you and then he'll take a swim."

"Lake Mead?"

He's watching me for my reaction as he answers. "Would you... want to be there for it?"

I think over the question before I slowly answer, "McKennons are known for their revenge... and I'm a McKennon now, so..."

His eyes darken at my words. "I plan to use my wild card."

My eyes widen. "You only get one, though."

"If I'm ever going to use it, this would be the chance, and I'll have no regrets."

Kian's job is only referred to in hushed tones for both his benefit and for the ones who give him the playing card that orders a hit on an enemy. The only time he gets to call the shots himself is if he uses his one card. The joker. If the wild ace is using *his* wild card, Monroe Baron is already as good as dead.

I inhale and exhale deeply, letting the pain in my body fuel me to give him my blessing.

"Make him hurt."

A wicked smile curves his lips before he gently kisses my forehead.

"You have my word, *tine*."

Scene 38

BARON'S ROULETTE

It's been two days since Monroe Baron almost killed my wife, and as soon as I see my dad's text on my new mobile, adrenaline thrums in my veins. Apparently, the Baron bastard has the audacity to think he can crash a McKennon poker game and come out unscathed. He's always overplayed his hand, but I plan to call his bluff once and for all.

Roxana is visiting with Lacey, so I leave them both while Merek guards our suite. His presence gives me peace of mind so that I can make my way downstairs to deal with Monroe.

Once I get to the casino floor, I see Lorenzo standing watch outside the door to the high roller room. The lad proved crucial in helping Merek find evidence in Monroe's suite, and in an hour or so, he'll be enlisted for his biggest job yet. I have full faith in him that he won't disappoint.

He juts his chin at me, but his gaze stays vigilant as he fills me in, "When security behind our cameras told me that Monroe entered the casino I was going to lock him up in the vault, but your father gave me the go-ahead to let him come play. Mr. McKennon said you have plans for the asshole."

"I have plans alright. Anything else I should know?"

"He tried to take this inside..." Lorenzo subtly lifts his suit jacket to reveal a silver revolver.

I huff and shake my head. "What an eejit. Alright, stay sharp, lad. I'm ending this. Now. Don't let anyone in."

"Understood," he answers quietly as he follows me into the room.

When I get inside the high roller room, I point my thumb behind me to the door. The dealers and croupiers begin to immediately close up their tables and boards.

"Hey!" one of the patrons yells. "We weren't done!"

"Give them what they're owed. The rest is for the house," I announce, my tone making sure that the guests don't give any more trouble.

A few of them grumble, but they don't put up more of a fight, especially not after Lorenzo steps into the room and cracks his knuckles. A wee bit theatrical, but it does the trick.

Once everyone is gone and Lorenzo has closed the tall wooden doors that shut off the high roller room from the public, I travel to the back of the room and enter through the Red Room's curtains, where nervous energy thickens the smoky air.

Monroe's back is to me as he plays poker with my father and the families we trust like he isn't a dead man walking. Muñoz, Thomson, Milton, and Luciano aren't about to get their arses handed to them, but they still shift uncomfortably in their seats, a mixture of anxiety and bloodlust light their faces. My father, however, leans back in his chair, examining his fingernails, seemingly not a care in the world. He's been babysitting until I could arrive and the rest are thirsty to see McKennon revenge in action.

The leadership in this room has proven loyal time and again. They kept my marriage secret, and they weren't in on Monroe's plans to take down the O'Shea. I'll reward them in due time, but right now, I have business to settle in private.

"Families, out. Monroe stay." My voice is barely audible, but the men at the table hop up as if I'd shouted, abandoning their cards in the middle of the session.

Monroe's spine stiffens while the heads of the families leave him behind. As the Milton, the Thomson, and the Luciano pass me, wrinkles of disappointment mar the first two men's faces, while the last gives me a nod of respect. Before the Muñoz can get through the curtain, though, I catch his arm to stop him.

"With everything Roxana has done for Lacey and me over the past year, I'm forever indebted to your family. You have my backing in whatever you pursue."

"Of course. It's what the Garde was supposed to be all about."

"And it will be once Lacey and I become the Keepers."

Monroe's low scoff makes my fingers tighten into fists, but I'll deal with him soon enough. The Muñoz's black mustache twitches above his smile of approval before he exits.

As I turn to my prey, my father moves to sit by the door behind me. He settles into the chair with his hands resting on his upper thighs, casually revealing the gun holstered at his side. The man is pushing sixty but if anyone barges in to help Monroe, my dad will put a bullet in their brain before they can throw a punch.

"Ah, Kian." Monroe lazily swivels in his chair and smirks before pulling something from his jacket pocket. "I was hoping you'd come down. Thought it was time I paid you a visit."

He tosses a shiny piece of metal onto the poker table. At the sight of the wee silver wedding band, cool relief and hot rage duel for dominance in my veins. But when I meet the arsehole's gloating smile, it's Lacey's scratches on his face and neck that make my blood boil.

I knew she'd fought for her life. The sight of her chipped nails alone made me murderous, but Monroe wearing the evidence of her self-defense like a fecking badge of honor has me advancing toward him, barely registering that he's still talking.

"How'd you like the present I left you the other night? I thought she was a goner—"

My hands wrench him to his feet by his jacket collar and push him against the wall.

"You think you can touch my *wife*?"

Uncertainty flashes in his wide eyes before that arrogant attitude returns. His goatee outlines the downward trajectory of his lips like arrows as he frowns.

"It's Baron, to you—"

I slam him into the wall and enjoy the *crack* his head makes against the surface, just like Lacey's probably sounded against the marble. He groans and reaches for his head, and I have to stop myself from doing it again.

"How does that feel, *Monroe*? I wonder if you'll be able to take the same kind of beating that you gave Lacey. By the time I'm finished with you, you'll wish I'd used a bullet."

I shake him once more before letting him collapse at my feet. Energy is riding me, making my fury a tangible thing that wants to burst from my skin. I pace in front of him like a caged beast ready to fight.

"Why the *fuck* are you here? Do you have a death wish?"

Monroe's face contorts with anger as he scrambles up.

"Do *you*? You think you can treat me like this? You McKennons have always thought you were better than the rest of us, but newsflash. *I'm* the one who's in charge now. *I* run this city and I've come here to stake my claim."

I bark a laugh, I can't help it. "Oh, *you* run this city, hmm? How do you figure, arsehole?"

A snide smile lifts his lips. "I was afraid I might've lost my chance at Keeper when I lost my temper, but Lacey's still alive and I don't even have to hide my plans anymore. You may have the Keeper's daughter in your bed—for now—but after teaching her a lesson and showing her what happened to her father at my order, I have her right where I want her. Your sham of a marriage can be annulled in a second with the right judge. I will marry Lacey, and I will become Keeper. She may think she loves you, but she'll do anything to get daddy dearest out of jail. And because you're in love with her, that means you'll *both* do whatever *I* say.

With the O'Shea behind bars and his life in my hands, I'm fucking untouchable."

He ends his wee rant with a cheeky chuckle, but I can't wrap my mind around what he's saying.

What the hell? With the O'Shea behind bars? He's not in...

My eyes narrow for a brief second, but as soon as I figure it out, I blank my face. The people I've worked with have kept everything quiet for the O'Shea's sake as much as their own. No one wants the press to find out that an innocent man was kept in jail for a year on their watch. Which means...

He doesn't know Charlie's been freed.

I tuck that information away for later and jab the air between us. "You've always been one cocky piece of shite, but this wee stunt makes you a fool, too. I don't care how powerful you think you are in the Garde, you're in *my* casino and McKennon house rules apply. I want that rematch, Monroe. Right here and now."

I settle two seats down from where he was sitting and nod to our Red Room dealer. "Deal me in, Suzette."

She gathers the cards from the table to shuffle and I speak to Monroe without bothering to glance up at him as she works.

"Sit, Monroe. We're going to play for both right now."

"Play for both? Lacey and ruling the Garde?" Greed lights in Monroe's eyes. "Deal me in, too, then. If the great wild ace wants to barter with daddy's money, then I'm more than willing to win it all."

The bastard actually thinks he'll beat me. I'll remind him and the Garde that I'm not the one to feck with.

"Oh, we won't be playing with money. Every hand will have an immediate payout, but Lacey and the Keeper position will be in the pot. Best of three will win it all in the end."

He eyes me warily, some of the arrogance leaving him as he sits down. "Fine, then. If you want to make it interesting, let's *actually* make it interesting. Starting bet, one of the McKennon holdings."

My expression remains neutral at his blind bet and I make my own. "Grand. I'll have your right arm, then."

"My..." Monroe's dirty-blond brow furrows with confusion. "My what?"

"Your. Right. Arm. Every time you've touched Lacey or said something disrespectful about her in my presence, I've made a tally in my head. Each round, we'll bet something new. If I win, I'll remind you where you laid your perverted hands." I point at his right arm. "You held a death grip on her when you went to Mass. So if I win this hand, I'll get to take that out on your right arm."

He shifts uneasily in his seat. "And if I win?"

"I'm a fair lad. If you win, you get to do the same."

"How do I know you won't kill me whether I win or lose? Or have one of your men kill me?"

"No one will kill you in this casino, Monroe. I can promise you that."

And I can. Despite the fact that my hand flexes underneath the table with the urge to split open its healing cuts on Monroe's smug face, I have no intention of killing him here, or even today, for that matter. Lacey and I will make any decisions as final as life or death together.

"And outside?" he prompts.

"I can't control what others do out there. But in here? Anything off the table is now on. Truly no-limits."

Monroe's narcissism clouds his judgment once again and an evil smile lifts his cheeks as he snatches the opportunity like the true gambler he is.

"Alright then, your losses, McKennon."

We're dealt our two cards and I assess them before making my bet. "I'll call. Your tongue. You've talked shite with it several times."

His eyes flare and he laughs. "Okay, then. I'll *raise*. Call your man in here."

My eyes narrow, trying to figure out his next play, but I do as the man says out of curiosity and I call for Lorenzo.

"Yes, sir." His deep voice is swallowed by the curtains muffling the sound in the room as he enters.

Glee lights up Monroe's face. "Do you have my revolver?"

I don't take my eyes off Monroe, but Lorenzo hesitates in my periphery.

"You can answer him, Lorenzo."

"Yes. I have your gun."

"Excellent," Monroe slaps the table. "Here's my proposition. You were a fighter back in Ireland and your fists are your weapon. It's hardly fair for me to play without one of my own. So then my bet is *your* arm, but if I win, I also get to play roulette... with my gun."

My muscles tense and I sense my father doing the same before he bellows a laugh. "You must be mad, boy. There's no way my son will allow a gun to a fistfight—"

"Grand. Fair is fair."

Monroe's smile widens at my answer and my father curses behind me.

"Kian, lad—"

"I said do it." I tilt my head toward Monroe. "Lorenzo. Give the man his gun and continue to stand watch outside. I won't have him thinking I didn't play fair."

My heart thuds as Lorenzo slowly does as I commanded, no doubt wondering if I've lost it, but I show no emotion. No matter what happens to me, my dad will make sure this prick doesn't live long outside of our casino, and Merek will keep Lacey safe. If losing a game of poker is how it ends for me, well, that'd be as fitting an end as any for the wild ace.

Lorenzo places the gun in the center of the board, but it's snatched away before Monroe can grab it.

"Hey!" Monroe calls and I turn to find my father spilling the bullets into his hand before pocketing them and handing the gun to Monroe.

"Can't be playing roulette with more than one bullet, now can we?" my father points out.

Monroe's lips purse. "There's still one in there?"

"Check for yourself, lad." My dad swats the air as he goes to sit in his chair near the door.

Monroe frowns at my father's back before placing the gun on the lip of the table, but I lean over and push it into his chest.

"Put it away during the game. I don't want you cheating. We both know how much you like to do that."

"Fine," Monroe grumbles as he sinks his gun into the waistband of his slacks rather than returning it to the holster.

He's no doubt disappointed he couldn't get a rise out of me. But inside, my heart thunders uncontrollably as Suzette lays down three cards.

I have a shite hand, but you never play your cards. You play your opponent. Lacey has a better poker face than this fecker, though, and delight flashes over Monroe's expression before he blanks the emotion from it.

We place our next couple bets until Suzette lays the fourth card.

Jesus, Mary, and Joseph, this isn't good.

Monroe chortles. "Raise. Another McKennon holding. Say, Kian, how will your daddy like you gambling away his businesses?"

"I'm not like you." I shake my head as Suzette places the final card. "I don't play with other people's money."

He harrumphs, but I tune him out. I know I'm losing this round, especially when Monroe raises for yet another McKennon holding. I bluff and bet in kind. There's no way I'm folding to this motherfucker.

When we make our final bets, Monroe's eyes flick from his cards to the back of mine and he wiggles to sit straighter in his seat.

"Showdown, McKennon. What've you got?"

I turn my cards over just as he does and his smile carves across his cheeks.

"F-flush beats ace-high," Suzette stutters as she points to Monroe. "Mr. Baron wins, Mr. McKennon."

The poor dealer must be at her wits' end with these stakes, but I keep a level head as Monroe stands and pulls his gun from his waistband.

"So what's that for me? Two McKennon properties, your right arm, and your tongue." He spins his revolver and points it at me. "This might be a quick game."

I twist to stare him in the eyes, but otherwise, I remain stock-still. His forehead creases at first as if he's puzzled by my lack of emotion. On the outside, I'm channeling the part of me that used to not give a shite about living or dying.

Inside, though, I'm not as ready to meet my maker as I once was. I've made a lot of mistakes in my life, and putting Lacey in harm's way has been the worst. I would love to live the rest of my life earning her forgiveness, but Lacey will be safe no matter what happens to me, and—like I said—fair is fair. I proposed this game and I agreed to these stakes, so I'll be damned if I let this fecker see me flinch.

He shakes off his confusion and exchanges it for a malicious grin as he pulls the trigger.

Click.

Spin...

I hold my breath as he fires.

Scene 39

ACE OF HEARTS

*C*lick.

Having a gun pointed at me is never a pleasant experience, no matter the circumstances, and when the gun clicks empty twice, every tense muscle in my body relaxes.

Frustration and anxiety have Monroe cursing through gritted teeth as he examines his revolver.

"Put it up and sit back down, Monroe."

"Don't be so flippant," he hisses but obeys my order. "This is a six-shooter. You only have so many chances before you run out."

"Actually, every time you spin, there's a one-in-six chance, but who's counting?" I let myself relax a wee bit before I face the dealer again.

"Another hand, please, Suzette." I point to the silver wedding band in the center of the table and announce my bet. "My blind bet is the ring you stole, Monroe. Lacey's been wanting it back."

He scoffs. "*That's* what you're betting? What a waste. It's worth nothing."

"If my wife loves it, it's worth everything."

His face sours at me as Suzette sends the cards we've already played into the discard pile and waits for him to place his bet.

"Fine then, Roulette Face."

"My whole face, or is there a particular part you're fond of..."

"Shut the fuck up, Kian. You're making up your own goddamn rules, so I get to make mine. I said your face and that's where I'll aim after I win."

"Grand." I nod to Suzette and she quickly deals out our new hands. I study my cards and wait for Monroe to place his preflop bet.

His face is mottled with frustration. He's almost too easy to read, and when he places a low bet—my black Audi, of all things—I play in kind despite the fact that I've started with two kings.

As the rounds go on, he begins to fidget and grumbles under his breath, "This is ridiculous."

I ignore him and bet his back and thigh for his behavior with Lacey in his limo. Even though she kept Monroe's abuse a secret from me, I let her off easy because she was protecting her family. Monroe won't get the same treatment after hurting mine.

Suzette lays the last card and my heart leaps in my chest.

Feck yes.

When I meet Monroe's wide, twitching eyes, I can barely resist a smile.

"Your *left* arm."

His gulp is audible and I take great satisfaction in knowing he's thinking about the fact that he broke Lacey's.

He mutters his raise without any power behind it. There's no use putting effort into a bet he's going to lose.

Suzette's tan cheeks are sickly pale as she waits for us to turn our cards over for the showdown. It's a rarity that I have to mete out punishments or go "old school" with families in the Red Room. But it's been twice in a month that she's been subjected to it.

When we reveal our cards, she visibly sighs.

"Full house beats a pair of fours. Mr. McKennon's win."

"The house will comp your next vacation, Suzette," I murmur. "You can take your family and go wherever you want. You deserve a break after dealing with all of this."

Monroe snorts loudly, no doubt attempting to act less stressed than he is.

"You act like you run this shithole. Hey, McKennon!" He glances at my father. "You let your son dictate your casino?"

"Of course not." My father laughs and I smile too at our wee inside joke.

"What's so funny?" Monroe sneers.

"*My* casino." I snatch the ring and pocket it in my suit jacket before rising from my chair. "Now stand up."

"What?" Monroe's eyes widen and his body stiffens as I grab the roulette rake from the table behind us.

"Which part was hard for you? Stand up? Or that the McKennon Hotel and Casino is mine? I bought it years ago from my father and I didn't use the Garde to do it."

"What?" Monroe's jaw drops and I can detect more than a hint of jealousy in his voice. "How is that possible? You couldn't have had your inheritance yet."

I tap my palm with the wooden rake before signaling him to stand. He follows my order without even realizing it and backs away from his seat as I answer him.

"Some of us capitalize on what we've already been given rather than wait to be handed what we think we deserve. I've used my connections and resources to pave my own path. I don't need the goddamn Garde. *You* need *me*."

In one swift move, I lash the rake across his upper thighs. "That's for touching her thigh in your limo."

A guttural groan coughs from his throat as he doubles over. When he stumbles, I whack him across the back, and a sharp screech rips through the room.

"That's for wrapping your arm around her and forcing her to smile for you."

He yelps as I drive a kick into his lower back, where Lacey still has a nasty dark-purple bruise. I toss the roulette rake to my father and yank Monroe up by his hair, remembering the way her pretty strawberry-blonde curls were in total disarray as I cradled her in my arms.

"G-get off me, McKennon!"

"What's wrong, Monroe? You thought you could lay a hand on my wife without consequences? Don't throw the punch if you can't take the hit, motherfucker, and don't cast bets you can't pay out."

He flails at me, but I grab his left arm before it can make contact with my face and twist it behind his back. The move helps me force him to stand and I shove him into the wall face-first. He wriggles fruitlessly and I tighten my grip as I explain his fate.

"When the doctor read out Lacey's injuries, I made a note of each and every one." I shift my weight and feel Monroe's forearm creak underneath my hand. "And now, I'm going to give you everything back tenfold."

"No, no, don't, please—"

"You have followers, I hear. I don't know how I missed that, but after what I do to you, they'll know good and bloody well what will happen if Lacey McKennon is harmed in any way."

I use my body weight as leverage and yank Monroe's forearm into an unbearable angle. A loud *snap* crunches underneath my hands as I break his wrist where he broke hers. His high-pitched scream pierces the air around us, but it's dampened by the Red Room's heavy curtains. I throw him to the ground, where he wails and rolls around on the carpet.

Did Lacey cry nearly as much as this eejit? I doubt it. The girl has likely pirouetted through a recital on broken toes. No doubt this posh fecker sobs at a paper cut.

After a few more minutes of listening to him blubbering, I smooth my lapels and sigh with a shrug at Suzette.

"While we're waiting, I'll have a seltzer water, please, if you don't mind."

She nods hastily, fetches a bottle from her minibar underneath the poker table, and hands it to me. I thank her and unscrew the top, breaking the seal to take a sip of the cool, refreshing bubbles before addressing Monroe again.

"Play again, *Baron*? Best of three, right? Or would you like to call it a tie? Of course in the event of a tie in a McKennon casino, the house wins."

"Fuck you, McKennon," he sniffles and grumbles as he staggers from the ground.

"I'll take that as a yes to playing again, then." I motion to Suzette to proceed. She takes the cue and retrieves all the cards before shuffling for the next round.

Monroe snivels and whines as he holds his broken wrist to his chest and plops into his chair.

"D-deal me in, bitch," he stammers as he curses.

"Hey, arsehole," my father calls out before I do. "Don't go disrespecting our staff, you understand? Mind yourself, or I'll be avenging Suzette's honor if there's anything left after Kian's done with you."

Anger welts red blotches on Monroe's cheeks, but he at least has the good sense to shut the hell up.

"Your bet, Monroe?"

His eyes narrow. "You think you're so fucking invincible, but Charlie O'Shea isn't. If you and Lacey don't get an annulment, there's no reason for me to keep O'Shea alive in jail. Do you think she'll be *in love* with you when she finds out this stunt you're pulling got her father killed?"

I chuckle. "Is that your bet? We can decide that one right now. Go ahead and call your man. See if I care."

Monroe goes for his mobile, but he pauses. "Wait... why *don't* you care?"

I tilt my head and lift my shoulder in a shrug. "Well, when was the last time you spoke to your contact in the jail? A lot can happen in twenty-four hours."

Monroe's pale face blanches. "What did you do?"

"Let's just say you no longer have the upper hand over me, Lacey, *or* Charlie O'Shea. In fact... if the O'Shea were to, I don't know, be freed and have his name cleared after your suite was broken into while you were at your rehearsal dinner... I'd say you don't have any power at all."

His jaw drops and sweat beads on his brow at my revelation. "The Keeper is out of j-jail?"

"Sure is." I grin and tap the poker table. "By the way, I'm raising and betting your bollocks."

"My... what?" His face scrunches before he spits. "I didn't fuck your whore, McKennon!"

I slam my hand on the table, making Monroe jolt. "You called her a 'womb,' you piece of shite. It's fair play. Call her a whore again, though, and I won't keep up this ruse of a game to make you bleed. You're lucky I play by the rules." My glare still burns at Monroe, but I take the sting out of my voice with Suzette. "Deal us, please."

She distributes the cards deftly and Monroe tries to hold both his useless hand and his two cards.

"Do you want my help, Monroe?"

"Fuck you."

"Suit yourself." I have to push down my rage as I bet his throat. Remembering Lacey's raspy voice and the fingerprints on her neck will make it hard not to kill him if I win this round.

"Head," Monroe repeats for his preflop bet. He's shaking in his chair, rattled and no doubt trying to figure out his next move now that his advantage is gone. I wonder if the cocky son of a bitch has realized yet that he's playing his last game on borrowed time.

Suzette takes that as her cue to flop the community cards and we continue the rounds. I place my bets with his punishment in mind, but for every one of Monroe's, he just grumbles and repeats "head."

I doubt he knows it but injured and pissed is actually his best poker face yet. No matter what card Suzette places on the board, I can't get a read on the man. I have a good starting hand of a king of spades and a jack of clubs, but it's no guaranteed winner. When

Suzette places the last two cards on the table, though, hope rushes in my veins and my chest aches.

An ace of hearts...

"Who could've guessed the wild ace had a heart?"

... followed by a queen of diamonds.

"Only for his queen of diamonds."

"Head," Monroe barks again, but I swear there's more hope than usual in this one.

"Mouth," I reply.

"*Mouth*? I never punched her face."

Rage heats my cheeks. "I know you didn't strike her face, but you forced her to kiss you for a photo op, you goddamn bastard."

"Oh yeah." He chuckles. "I blocked that out of my memory. It was like kissing a dead fish. Your whore's already put out for you, though, so tell me... is it the same when you fuck her—"

I surge from my chair so violently that it falls backward.

"Kian! Mind yourself. You're letting him get in your head, lad."

Monroe grins as my chest rises and falls with breaths that I'm barely keeping under control. I pick up my chair and set it on all four legs before sitting back down. He laughs boldly and a sick feeling churns in my stomach as realization settles in.

He thinks he has a winning hand, and I...

I'm not so sure.

"Your cards, gentlemen?" Suzette asks.

For the first time ever, I'm slow to turn over my cards. I've never cared what I played for before, but now that my life with Lacey is at stake, I've got everything to lose.

I reveal my king of spades and jack of clubs and glance over to see Monroe's nine of clubs and eight of diamonds.

Suzette's posture relaxes again. "Straight with the ace high beats straight with ten high. Mr. McKennon wins—"

"No!" Monroe lunges from his chair and tugs his gun out of his waistband. "*I* will be the Keeper! Lacey is *mine*!"

My eyes widen as he aims and slams his finger against the trigger.

Click.

Click. Click.

Click. Click. Click...

Click.

"What the fuck?" Monroe shrieks and gapes at his gun with shock. He keeps his broken wrist against his chest as he jabs the barrel in my direction. "You... you cheated!"

But I'm as stumped as he is.

"*I* cheated? *I* won, and yet *you* tried to empty your gun on me—"

"Like *I* knew you would," my father interrupts as he stands beside me. "The Barons have always been cheats and thieves." He hands me the roulette rake before he spills the bullets from his pocket onto the table. All six of them. "My son didn't cheat, but *you* just proved that you would have."

"Leave, Suzette," I calmly command as I level my glare on Monroe. She sprints out of the room without a word.

As soon as she leaves, he moves, swinging the pistol in a wide arc toward the side of my head. I'd laugh at this eejit, thinking he'd be faster than me, but I'm too angry. I catch his gun and wrench it from his hand. The bastard tries to throw a punch as I toss the revolver to the side, but I effortlessly sidestep his arm and his missed right hook lands him on the roulette table. He wobbles as he backpedals away and flips a chair over to stop me, but I leap over it and land closer than I started. His eyes widen at our closeness, and I use his shock against him to shove the roulette rake against his neck and drive him into the wall. He nearly trips and his hands flail at the rod, but I keep us both upright by hooking the rake underneath his jaw, cutting off his airway.

"This is for trying to strangle Lacey to death."

His face purples as he pushes the rake. Even with both arms, this sack of shite wouldn't have been able to stop me. With one broken? There's no fecking chance. The rod chokes him and he wheezes to breathe. When he realizes fighting the rake is futile, he claws at me instead. He catches my forearms, but my training has me moving before I'm conscious of it, and I stretch away, putting me out of his reach.

"Is this how she made the scratches you show off now? No one else wears my wife's marks and *lives*, arsehole."

His bloodshot brown eyes widen as he finally understands the gravity of the situation his ego and fecked-up decisions have trapped him in. Lackluster kicks try to make contact with my shins, but they only cut off his airway further. Tears streak down his face, carrying his confidence and arrogance with them.

"The moment I found out you were behind sabotaging my marriage, you were a dead man walking. Every touch after that was another wound added to the final tally. This was always going to be your fate, Monroe Baron. How painful it would've been was up to you."

"Y-you said you wouldn't k-kill me. Wh-what h-happened t-to *honor*?" he gargles. His eyes bug out as I push harder to shut him up.

"I said I wouldn't kill you in my casino, and I played our game fair and square. But you tried to cage my queen and snuff out her light. I'll let her tell me how she'd like to proceed. In the meantime"—the smile that forces its way onto my face draws a shudder from Monroe—"I've got just the cage for you."

On that final note, I lean my body weight behind the rake and into his windpipe long enough to make him pass out. When I let up, he plops to the ground and I slam the rod into his head once, not hard enough to kill, but hard enough to crack the thing in half and give him a concussion like Lacey's.

"Good night, Monroe."

I toss the two halves of the bloody rake onto the table. One clatters and the other rolls along the felt surface, flicking and trailing blood over the deck the dealer left strewn about in her haste.

When I step back, I take the ace of hearts from the last hand

and stuff it in my suit jacket. I stare at Monroe, waiting for him to wake up, even though I know he's down for the count.

A throat clears beside me, snapping me out of my paranoia, and I turn to find my dad holding out a joker card with smeared blood on it.

"You sure about this, lad? It's your one card."

"I am," I accept it without hesitation. "I'll have the backing from the queen of diamonds to do it as well."

My father chuckles. "She's a firecracker, that one. Do you need that card as well?"

I shake my head with a wry grin. "I've still got the one you gave me that started all of this."

His laugh rumbles at the reminder and he points to the broken roulette rake. "Less blood this time, but you'll have to buy more of those if you're wanting to go after the rest of the traitors."

"I'll do whatever it takes to make sure no one gets between Lacey and me again." I huff a mirthless laugh. "If roulette rakes are the only McKennon casualty in my revenge, then so be it."

"I don't blame you. You want cleanup?"

I nod. "Fetch Lorenzo and bring him in here."

My father disappears from my side and the bouncer appears at the door in seconds.

"You needed me, boss?"

To his credit, he doesn't look squeamish in the slightest, maybe even a wee bit hungry for the bloodshed. He's coming around nicely. He'll be perfect for this next job.

"Get a cleaning crew—Garde, not casino. Keep it discreet. Detain Mr. Baron in the vault while Lacey recovers. In the meantime, get me a barrel, cement, and ready my boat. When Monroe laid a hand on my wife, he decided to take a long swim in the middle of Lake Mead."

"I..." He clears his throat. "I saw what the bastard did to Mrs. McKennon."

My heart soars at hearing my wife's new last name on

someone else's lips for the first time, but the rest of his sentence makes me scowl.

"And?"

His face hardens. "The lake is too good for that asshole."

"I agree, but trust me, I'm not done. And neither is he."

Lorenzo smirks before leaving to follow my order. As soon as he's gone, I study Monroe and stuff the bloody joker into my pocket. I snag a poker chip with the least amount of crimson stain on it and flip it in my hand while I speak to my enemy's unconscious body.

"The house always wins, motherfucker."

QUEEN OF DIAMONDS

The night is misty with rain, but thanks to the covered flybridge on Kian's yacht, I only feel the crisp wind on my cheeks as we float over one of the deepest areas in Lake Mead. The storm that started three days ago began to let up sometime last night after Kian came home from his poker game with Monroe. I don't know what the stakes were, exactly, but Monroe lost, and that's why we're here.

Kian's warmth seeps through my trench coat as he lightly grips my shoulders from behind, and I lean back against his chest. He's been downstairs helping his men, Lorenzo and Merek, with the details. I stare at the barrel sitting at the edge of the deck and resist shuddering at what we're about to do next. It needs to be done.

"Thank you... for everything," I murmur.

"I would do anything for you, *tine*."

He kisses me lightly, just above where my bandages were removed this afternoon. The pain is minimal with extra-strength ibuprofen, but he's still treating me like I'm made of glass. The parts of me that hurt—my arms, neck, throat, back—are appreciative.

But where I *ache*? I need more.

His smoky, sweet amber scent has driven me crazy ever since I've been back in his suite, and yet he refuses to touch me beyond cautious caresses. Now, even the slightest brush of his skin on mine makes me shiver with desire. I plan to end my torture as soon as possible, whether he thinks I'm ready or not.

"Are you in pain?" His voice is full of concern, mistaking my trembling. "You can have the other drugs. It won't bother me." He tries to pull away, but I latch on to his forearm—right over his new tattoo—to keep him close.

His question makes me gravitate to the chip in my pocket with my injured hand. He hasn't asked for it back and I don't want to give it up, but I feel guilty keeping it.

My decision made, I try to hand it to him.

"Oh no, that's yours now." He pushes it away before digging into his own pocket and coming up with an actual poker chip. His arm stays around me as he flips the chip in the air and leans me slightly with him as he reaches to catch it. "Monroe got this one for me. It's a new chapter. You can keep that one. This will remind me of what's important just as easily."

An appreciative grin lifts my lips as I return the chip to my pocket. I squeeze it for good luck before asking the question that's been on my mind since this morning.

"What happens after tonight?"

"What do you want to happen?" His voice is gentle, but tears spring to my eyes as my fingers try to make a fist around my cast, reminding me of the broken wrist that I was told today may never properly heal, even with surgery.

"I... I want to dance."

"Feck, Lace." He strokes my cheek. "Then dance. What's the point of being in charge if we can't chase our passion?"

I raise my cast. "But the doctor said—"

"The doctors can feck off. Together, we have more money than God. We'll get you the best surgeons."

"But what if that doesn't work?"

He gives me a pointed look. "I didn't think my *tine* could be stopped by the likes of a mere injured wrist. We'll do whatever it takes."

My chest feels airy and light with his promise. I hope he's right, but even if he's not, I don't have the energy to fight his resolve, nor do I want to. It's enough to give me courage for the rest of the night, though, and I hang on to it like a raft.

He must sense it, too, because he cups my cheek and exhales heavily before finally asking.

"Are you ready?"

I nod once. "More than you know."

His lips quirk up. "Let's go down, then. Lorenzo and Merek positioned the barrel at the edge for us and promised to give us privacy. They'll head off in the tender to scout the area and make sure we're alone on the lake."

He wraps a soft blanket around my shoulders and over my head to protect me from the rain. As he guides me down the winding, narrow staircase, he reassures me one more time.

"Unless this lake dries completely, the concrete on the bottom of the barrel should bury and secure it in the sediment below."

"And the rest of the world will think he ran away after almost... almost killing me?"

He grunts his assent. "The Keeper protects many secrets, but the wild ace keeps the worst ones. I know which families have ordered hits on others, and after breaking into Baron Suites, I also know who went after your father. Monroe will disappear and no one will question the narrative we spread because they know that if they do, their own involvement will be exposed. They don't want to tumble their house of cards or be anywhere near my—or your father's—wrath." He smirks at me. "Besides, they'll learn soon enough that my wee firecracker of a wife is formidable on her own."

I smile at him and accept his offered hand. By the time we reach the deck, Lorenzo and Merek are already hopping into the small boat that accompanies the yacht. They drive off so quietly that there's barely any sound or wake in the water. The lights on the tender's bow and stern flicker the farther away they go until darkness swallows them completely.

It's just me, Kian, and the soon-to-be dead man.

"Ready?" Kian asks again and I squeeze his hand in answer.

He leads me to the barrel that sits on the edge of the glossy wet deck and removes the metal lid. Inside, Monroe sits scrunched with tape around his hands and over his mouth. His brown eyes are black and shiny in the dark, begging Kian for forgiveness, as if my husband is the only one who has a say in this. Kian has made it clear that I'll be ruling by his side once my father's role as Keeper ends. I have no doubt that this is the first of many decisions we'll make together.

Kian's voice deepens with cold rage as he gives the monster his final sentence. "Monroe Baron, you attempted to snuff out a fire before we had the chance to kindle it. You nearly extinguished the light in my life before she had the chance to blaze. You've tried so hard to be the water to our flame, water will be your end."

I can barely make out Monroe's question as he enunciates behind the tape, "Who put the hit out on me?"

"I did." Kian pulls playing cards out of his suit jacket pocket and reveals his bloody joker card. "I'm the wild ace and this wild card is mine to do with as I please." His gaze locks onto Monroe's. "It's a reward for my service. No reprisals from Garde families, no tipping off any authorities, no grudges. One free kill." He juts his chin in my direction. "Not only that, but I have the support of my queen of diamonds."

Monroe tries to swivel away as Kian stuffs the joker and the ace into his breast pocket. My husband then turns to me with the two halves of a worn queen of diamonds card.

"Any last words, *tine*? Once you use this card, it'll be played. You'll no longer have the order over your head."

My heart pounds in my chest at the sight of the card that was meant for me. I've only heard about this part of his job and I certainly never thought I'd be joining in. But I didn't want to miss this. I'm a McKennon now, and McKennon revenge is exactly what I need to make this right.

I take the card and use the dim light of the moon to analyze the two queens. One wields a sword and the other holds a red camellia.

"You designed this for me, didn't you?"

Kian nods in my periphery. "The queen of diamonds is also the queen of swords. She's a compassionate leader and a symbol of change. But she's ruthless when she needs to be. She's always been perfect for you."

The compliment gives me the courage to remove Monroe's ring from my pocket and step closer to the barrel. He yells angrily at me, but his scorn is lost behind the duct tape. Even on the brink of death, he glares at me with hatred and disrespect. He has no idea that I'm the one who choreographed his last breaths.

After a deep inhale and exhale, I swallow past the pain in my throat and try my best to mask the hoarseness in my voice. I don't want to let this bastard's last thoughts be satisfaction that he hurt me.

"You tried to ruin my family. You nearly killed me and you took the life of an innocent solely because your pride was hurt. You are everything that's wrong with the Garde, and those ideals will die with you. But Kian and I will thrive."

Despite Monroe fighting against his binding, I tuck both halves of the queen card and his ring into his breast pocket in front of the ace and the joker. As soon as it's done, Kian begins to ready the diving equipment and hands me the mask. Monroe is so confused by our exchange, he lets me fit the goggles and mouth-piece halfway over his head before he starts to thrash again.

Kian ignores Monroe's attempts to get free and plops the rebreather onto the man's bound hands, before tapping the device once.

"This heliox tank will allow you to breathe at greater depths. The lake is deep enough here that an ascent without proper decompression will kill you before you reach the surface. With the low water temperature at the bottom, what winds up killing you will be a contest between hypothermia, pressure changes, the amount of heliox in the tank, and your willpower. I'm betting the last one gives out first."

Monroe's eyebrows shoot up at Kian's wicked grin, but it's me who gives the final decree.

"Monroe Baron, you isolated me knowing that it would slowly kill me inside. Then you beat me and left me to die. In your final moments, I thought it fitting that you finally learn what it feels like to be trapped."

When I rip off the tape covering Monroe's mouth, merciless satisfaction stirs in my chest, sparking what is no doubt a slightly unhinged smile. That, more than anything, seems to scare the shit out of him and he lets out a bloodcurdling scream.

Kian uses Monroe's wide-open mouth to shove the mask the rest of the way over his petrified face and fit the regulator between his lips. He tries to writhe out of the barrel, but his efforts are useless since Merek and Lorenzo cemented him to the bottom.

Once the mask is on properly, I crash the lid on top of Monroe's head and Kian snaps the latches. Muffled screams reverberate from the tin, but I have faith that Lorenzo and Merek have ensured no help is coming.

With the barrel clasped shut, Kian kicks the edge, toppling it overboard. It bobs for a minute and my heart pounds at the fear that it won't sink. But as Kian begins to embrace me from behind, Monroe's screeches grow more frantic and harsh banging slams against the metal as it loses inches to the lake that consumes it.

Once the water starts flooding into the metal, it fills quickly. Soon Monroe's shrieks become garbled until the lid of the barrel finally dips below the surface and bubbles float and pop in its place. I watch them swell, burst, and swell again, hypnotized by Monroe's doomed attempt to stay alive.

"This is just the beginning." Kian's chin rests on top of my head and I feel it move as he warns me. "Monroe had a lot of families that supported him. Our fathers couldn't figure out the truth on their own because there were so many people who had the same lie, it was nearly impossible to sort out fact from fiction. We'll have to decide how to punish the ones that tried to destroy us. I personally want at least a dozen more barrels right beside Monroe's."

Power flows through my veins. Whatever I decide, I know Kian will make it happen. He's proven that he'll not only go to battle for me, he'll start wars.

But do I want that?

I bite my lip before shaking my head. "That can't happen if we want things to change. The way the Garde treats women, its own people, and those they consider beneath them is horrible. I want to change that."

"Let's change it, then."

I glance up at him. "Really?"

"Yeah, really. Once the Keeper position falls to us, we won't stand for the shite that has had family conspiring against family for decades. Snakes like Monroe shouldn't be able to slip into our house unnoticed. Your father has plenty of secrets to take them all down one by one and cut them off at their knees. I wish we'd sent Monroe's sister down with him, though. She was a right cunt in all of this. Hell, maybe your mam, too. No offense."

I follow his glare to the slower-forming bubbles on the water.

"They're both products of their environment," I answer, my heart rate increasing at what it will mean when those signs of breathing stop. "My mom got worse while my dad was away. Now that he's back home, she won't feel the immense pressure of keeping us alive. And as for Maeve... without a Garde-approved marriage she'll neither have power nor access to her complete trust fund. For her, that'll be worse than anything we could ever physically do to her. Power is what they all care about. If we take that away from them they'll wish they'd died instead."

He chuckles. "The new era of McKennon revenge. Fates worse than death, catered to the sinner. That's the kind of punishment I can get behind."

Quiet settles around us and I face the water again to find the bubbles have disappeared.

"Does that mean what I think it means?" I whisper.

"Depends. He's hundreds of feet down, so his exhales could be taking a longer time to rise. But his rebreather only has an hour of helium and oxygen, less if he hyperventilates. Hypothermia could get him before that in as quick as thirty minutes if it's cold enough."

"And then he'll be gone," I whisper.

"If he's not already."

My pounding heart slows. We stand in silence while listening to the lake gently lap at the boat. The weight of years of turmoil, stress, and fear drifts away with the current, and I take a full cleansing breath for the first time in ages.

Scene 41

SAY THE WORDS, TINE

After a few more minutes, Kian takes my uninjured hand in his and wraps his arm around my waist to help me up the slippery stairs to the bridge. The navigation panel there is full of screens and faint red, green, and yellow buttons that glow against the window. He gets behind the controls and flicks lights on while I sag into the co-captain's chair next to him.

It's dim enough inside now to ensure we're not a noticeable beacon in the middle of the lake while also giving us visibility in the room. It's nearly pitch black beyond the window, giving me peace that we're alone. But as I glance out onto the water, my reflection in one of the side mirrors catches me off guard.

My aches and pains reached their peak bruising yesterday. Some of the scratches have begun to heal as well. I woke up this morning and the red spots underneath my eyes had disappeared, too, thank God. But *his* fingerprints are still there, dark and ugly in my reflection.

More than anything Monroe did, those are the bruises I hate most. Kian's fingerprints were a morale boost and helped get me through the worst of my time locked away. Once they fully disappeared I had a mini meltdown, and I've wanted them back ever since.

Monroe's bruises, however, make me nauseous and the overwhelming need to get rid of them shocks through me.

"I want them gone," I whisper.

I'm already unwrapping my trench coat when Kian glances up from the controls.

"You want what..." His voice drifts off. Whatever he sees on my face makes him jolt out of his seat and he leaps toward me to cup my cheek. "Lace, what's wrong?"

My *cheek*. He used to calm me just by gripping my neck, but he's been afraid to so much as caress it.

I need more.

"Please, Kian." My voice is frantic as I shuck my coat and toss it to the side, popping off one of the buttons on my tunic dress with the force. Now that I'm free of the fabric, I can't stop myself from scratching at my neck.

"Lacey, stop it," he growls and snatches my hands.

Emotions flood his face as he locks his eyes where I clawed myself. Rage, anger, guilt... but I don't want any of that. Anxiety is crushing my chest and I can't help the pitch my voice has risen to.

"I need these gone. He's gone, but his bruises aren't. Please, make them go away. I can't have them on me anymore. He can't be the last one to mark me."

"Shh, *tine*, calm down. It's alright. I'm—" He swallows as his eyes dart over the bruises. "I'm sorry I let this happen. If I'd gone up there when you called—"

"Stop! I don't need sorry. I *need* these gone. Please. His... his marks, his touch. I can't stand it. I need yours."

"*Fuck*," Kian growls and carves his hand in his hair. "I'm not fecking doing the same thing he did."

"Do something, *please*."

I don't know what the hell has come over me. All I know is that even though Monroe is likely either dead or dying right underneath our boat right now, I won't be completely free of him until the marks he left on me are gone, too. My eyes brim with tears and I'm nearly hysterical before Kian rips off his jacket and picks me up by my thighs.

He carries me to the captain's chair and sits with me straddling him, raising my dress to my hips where his hands grip my upper thighs. I hold on to him as he switches off the overhead bulbs, leaving only the outer safety lights. We're cast in darkness but for the glowing LEDs around his chair and the buttons on the navigation panel.

I'm almost afraid he won't be able to see the bruises well enough to erase them, but as his eyes home in on one specific area, my heart skips with anticipation. When he gently wraps his hand on my nape and brings my neck down to his lips, I finally begin to feel peace.

He sucks hard at my skin, just underneath my jaw. That area doesn't hurt at all, and the tentative way he's increasing pressure feels like he's testing me for pain. As he marks me, he cradles my tender neck, preventing me from moving it at an odd angle. His tongue joins in to caress my bruising flesh, springing tingles of pleasure throughout my body. I moan and grab on to the back of the captain's chair as I grind against him.

My breath hitches as he finds where Monroe's hands were. Kian's movements are more wary now, and he begins to suck so gingerly that I don't feel it at first. But as he increases pressure once again, his mouth becomes deliciously painful on my skin while still managing to leave my sore throat muscles alone.

"Is this what you need, Lace?" he whispers as he drifts down. "You know what to say if you want me to stop. Say it for me once, and tell me you're mine."

"*Is tú mo rogha,*" I whisper as I press his head against me, telling him I can take more. "I'm yours."

"And I'm yours."

His mouth moves about my neck as he clasps his lips around each and every bruise left by Monroe's fingers. Kian's sucking bites, licks, and kisses are gentle and possessive as he leaves marks of his own. The ones that I crave.

While he's being so careful with me, I'm the opposite. My uninjured hand yanks a handful of his hair every time he tries to let up. I want him to be ruthless.

He nips me below my ear in retaliation, but it only elicits a moan from me and I shift on top of his hardening cock.

"Do you think you're in charge, wife?" he whispers against my neck. "Because you are. You have me, Lace. I'm yours. Take what you need from me."

I let go of his hair and try to unzip his pants, but my broken wrist makes it difficult. When I whine my frustration, he jerks his zipper down and releases his cock from his boxer briefs. I quickly stretch my panties to the side so I can be skin to skin with his bare shaft.

The metal barbell at the end is warm but cooler than my aching hot core, and I shift to rub my clit against it. When the ball hits that little bundle of nerves just right, I cry out and Kian curses against my throat.

Even though I'm not wet enough, I take him in hand and fit him at my entrance before I shove myself down. My channel's resistance makes me whimper and he growls underneath me.

"*Fucking* hell." His hands drop to my waist as I try to move. "*No.* You're not fecking ready."

"I don't care," I hiss back, but he stops me from riding him and I grunt my frustration.

He captures my lips in a kiss, distracting me as he nimbly unclasps the front of my tunic dress until he's unbuttoned me completely and the fabric drapes around us.

"What're you doing?"

Instead of answering, he tugs down my bra and leaves my lips to lave my nipples. His warm, velvet tongue is nirvana and I hold his hair like reins to latch him to my breast. He takes it in his mouth and swirls around my pebbled areola before using the same hard suction he applied to my neck.

His hand on my upper back guides me like it would in a dance, and he uses the control to get more of a mouthful while his other hand travels to my center. I'm fluid in his arms as he flicks over my sensitive peaks and plays with my clit. When he bites and clamps his teeth around me, creating new marks that are just ours, pleasure sweeps through me.

"Oh my *god*."

A gush of desire flows from my core to drench his cock. He murmurs a curse against my breast before settling back against the headrest, leaving cool air in his wake.

"There it is, baby. *Fuck*, I've needed you."

"I've needed you, too, Kian."

Reaching between us, he wraps his fingers around the base of his cock to help coat it in my arousal. When he's as wet as I am, he slowly thrusts up and down, setting our pace and he eyes our connection greedily.

"Goddamn, look at us, Lace."

While grasping the captain's chair, I lean back to admire his shaft glistening in the dim light as he eases in and out of me. His strokes are long and sensual, and they glide his piercing over my G-spot, giving me full-body shivers with every inch.

Keeping one hand around my waist to maintain our rhythm, he splays the other across my lower belly.

"You'll take my name, Lacey. Stolen or not, you'll be a McKennon."

"I'll be a McKennon," I whisper with a small nod as I slide down him again.

"You'll have my child... or three."

"I want that, too. Wh-what else?" I ask.

"We'll live life our way."

"Our way," I whisper in agreement, invigorated by the promise.

He teases my clit once before his hand leaves my stomach, making me mewl my frustration. I want to come so badly and I need his tongue, teeth, fingerprints, cum inside and out. I need *him*. I want it all so I can forget that I was ever away from his arms.

His fingertips, warm and damp with my arousal, return to grip the back of my neck. He squeezes lightly, stealing my breath before he kisses me hard.

And finally his pace quickens.

It's a dance we're still so new at together, but God, do I love him as a partner. He protects my neck from moving too much even as he pounds into me at a blissfully hard and fast pace. I meet him stroke for stroke, using my thighs to rise and fall on his thick cock. His piercing slides along every inch of my sensitive channel, hitting my G-spot with each thrust.

He kisses me and we mimic our dance below with our tongues and lips above. The motion gives me what I want in no time. When the ecstasy becomes too much, I collapse against his chest, suddenly weak with the need to come. But he slows down right before I begin my ascent.

"No, no, no..."

"Say the words, wife, and I'll let you come."

The words. It only takes a second before I realize what he's asking for.

I wrap my hands around his neck and kiss him fiercely before I whisper against his lips.

"*Is tú mo rogha*, Kian."

He growls into my mouth and his voice is rough when he replies. "I choose you, Lacey."

I expect him to lose all control and pump into me with wild abandon to get me to come, but he doesn't. Instead, he makes me realize there's more to us, just as he's always done.

We lock eyes as he moves in slow, deliberate thrusts. Emotions well within my chest, threatening to break free, made heightened when he sucks my neck again. It's painful, but I fucking love the rush of it. My skin begins to ache and just when I'm about to use my safe word, he lets go and slams into me one last time.

Sensation floods my veins and my orgasm sends me spiraling. I scream his name as he rolls underneath me, hitting that spot where I need him most.

"Kian!"

"*Fuck*, Lace."

He pushes my hips down, pressing his piercing deep inside me to completely fill my channel. As he holds me to him, he rocks inside me and jets of cum coat my core.

We cling to each other and emotions throb in my veins. When my breaths stop racking through me in heavy pants, I whisper against his neck.

"I love you, Kian McKennon."

He shivers underneath me and pulls away to look into my eyes.

"I love you, too, Lacey McKennon."

He grips my hips to steady me as he reaches to switch on a dim light. It moves the mirror that started all of this and he tips my chin to the light.

"Is that better, *mo thine*?"

Monroe's fingerprints might still be there, but I can't see them past the dark purple and red already blooming over every inch of my neck from Kian's lips. When his fingers drift along his possessive marks, I meet his eyes in our reflection.

"It's perfect."

He points to a screen on the navigation board. A quarter of the monitor is full of numbers and calculations, while the rest shows where the boat's security camera has been trained on the deck. Thanks to the moon and the lights from the boat, I can see the smooth, placid water where we sank Monroe.

"Still no bubbles," I whisper.

"Nope. And the right side of this screen shows the levels left in the heliox tank. He hasn't used it in almost two minutes. Which means... we were in heaven while he was sinking to hell."

My small smile grows wicked at the thought. "He's gone."

"He's gone," he repeats as he turns my face. His dark gaze makes my chest flutter and his fingers are featherlight as they graze my neck.

"No man will ever mark you again."

428 ❦ GREER RIVERS

"I'm yours," I answer without hesitation.

He grunts his approval and shifts underneath me again. I hold on to his shoulders to keep from moving and I'm about to ask what he's doing when he pulls out a flash of silver from his pocket.

"You asked what happens next. I know something we can do."

"What's that?"

He cradles my injured hand in his before securing my wedding ring on my ring finger.

"You got it back," I gasp.

"I did, and I never want you to take it off. Marry me, Lace. Again. I want the world to finally know you're mine and I'm yours. And I want *you* to admit it, too."

His eyes glitter from the moonlight behind me and my heart skips a beat before I kiss his lips.

"Yes, Kian. Make me yours. Forever. I want to marry you."

"I have one condition, though. You remember when we were texting and I bet that I could prove you weren't afraid of me?"

"I lost and... and you said you'd save it for a rainy day." A smile lifts my lips and I glance out the window where the rain falls gently on the lake. "You calling on it now?"

"I am..." His lips curve into a mischievous smile and mine can't help but do the same. "But it's going to drive your mam fecking mad."

Epilogue

Kian

There was a time when I thought I'd never see Lacey O'Shea walk down the aisle toward me.

But here she is, my beautiful bride, gliding toward me in St. Patrick's Cathedral, all smiles with her gorgeous blue eyes sparkling back at me. Half of her strawberry-blonde hair is braided in a crown, tied with a red silk ribbon. The other half flows in loose curls behind her shoulders, showing off her low neckline and all the fading bruises I gave her on my boat last week.

Everywhere Monroe touched her, I left a deeper mark, and since then, I've given every inch of her the same treatment. That night, she'd wanted me to choke her like I'd done before, but I wasn't having it. Instead, I stayed close to the surface of her fair skin so I wouldn't reinjure the muscles in her throat while I erased the marks another man made. As soon as I see mine on her now, I smirk and she gives me a coy smile back.

Moira O'Shea was appalled when Lacey arrived at her dress fitting with the purple-and-blue evidence of my possession. She was already on the fence about meshing modern wedding practices with traditional, like Lacey and I wanted—not to mention her daughter's choice in groom—but seeing my hickeys was too much for the woman. She tried to put off the wedding, but my bride wasn't having it and insisted on the following Saturday—today—or not at all.

Lacey had already verified in front of a judge that our wedding license is legitimate. In the eyes of the law, we've been married from the moment I tricked her into it. So this is for the Garde, not us. Lacey was ready to call the whole thing off, but she and her mother allegedly compromised with a high neckline that matched the rest of the Irish lace on her long, flowing dress.

But when I proposed, I cashed in on the bet we made and told her not to cover my marks when we got married. I wondered if she'd be bold enough to defy her mother, but I shouldn't have doubted my fiery bride.

Moira's in a bloody state, though. From her aghast expression and reddening cheeks, it seems my wee firecracker didn't warn her that she was going to make good on my bet. Another rebellion against the Garde from my queen of diamonds, with many more to come.

Fecking hell, I love her.

Once she arrives at the altar, her father kisses her on the cheek and she smiles brightly at him.

The O'Shea is finally home with his name cleared and the true perpetrator of the crimes has mysteriously vanished. Most believe Monroe went on the run after being found out for framing Charlie O'Shea and nearly killing Lacey. Everyone else is keeping their fecking mouths shut, no doubt worried sick while waiting for the O'Sheas and McKennons to enact their revenge.

Despite everything I've done for the O'Shea, the arsehole scowls at me before "giving Lacey away." I couldn't give two shites what the man who tried to sell his daughter thinks, but thankfully, I don't have to address it.

He leaves her beside me without incident and sits next to Moira, whose dark red and silver dress matches the silk ties and maid of honor dress in the wedding party. I wish my own mam was here to sit beside her, but I know she's watching from above, pleased as can be that her son finally found his dance partner.

As Charlie stretches his arm along the back of the pew, he nods to my father standing behind me as my best man. It's mad to think that just a month ago, we all hated each other with a passion and blamed our woes on one another. Color me a romantic, but I believe love can overpower even the darkest of histories. Of course, a mutual thirst for revenge helps, too.

Lacey hands Roxana her bouquet of red, pink, and soft white camellias. I clasp my bride's hands in mine, careful of her wrist in its cast and I take in the fading marks my lips made on her slender neck.

"Don't look at me like that," she whispers under her breath with a shy smile.

I lean in, brushing the shell of her ear with my lips as I speak my filthy thoughts just for her.

"Like what? Like I want to fuck you in front of all these people and God himself?"

"Kian!" she hisses back at me and her freckled cheeks turn a delicious rouge that I want to nip.

But the priest clears his throat and I step back to stand across from her with a savage smirk.

"Sorry, Father. Please, proceed."

He frowns in disapproval. Maybe he did hear me, then. In fairness, he might be right to judge me. Fucking my wife isn't a sin, but the way I go about it is.

The priest goes into his litany of rituals and Lacey and I are unable to take our eyes off one another as we follow them, ignoring the hundreds of Garde members in the audience.

I'll admit, it was a power play to invite every family head in the Garde to attend our wedding. With the huge guest list, those that tried their damnedest to keep us apart can see how many support us in—and outside—the society. We are a force to be reckoned with.

It's been hardly over a week, but I'm sure many in the audience believe they've dodged a bullet and maybe even gotten off scot-free, but Lacey and I have just been biding our time. Once she and I have a child, Charlie O'Shea has promised us both that he'll make the unprecedented decision to step down from the Keeper role and give it to us. We'll take on the secrets of the Garde and ruin those who tried to destroy us. It's a long con, but I'm a patient man. I had to be to wait for Lacey. And hell, if all goes well right after this, I'll have a McKennon in her tonight.

The priest gives me a pointed look and Lacey's suppressed giggle tells me she knows I've been daydreaming about us again.

"The rings? I announced that the couple has decided to exchange them prior to the vows."

"Ah," I turn to my father for the rings and catch Merek and Tolie behind him, smiling their support from ear to ear. I return one of my own until my father deposits both of Lacey's rings into my palm.

When I face Lacey again, she has a silver band for me.

"Repeat after me," the priest begins and I focus on Lacey's sky-blue eyes as I take her ring finger.

"With this ring, I thee wed, Lacey."

Her eyes round at the sight of the emerald-cut red diamond I've added to her simple silver band.

"Kian..."

I was expecting a joke about how over the top it is, especially after I made fun of her first one, but she gazes at it in reverence, and pride expands in my chest.

"Your turn, *tine*," I murmur.

She inhales deeply before taking my left hand and easily fitting the thicker wedding band on my ring finger.

"With this ring, I thee wed, Kian."

"And now for the vows," the priest prompts us.

I keep hold of Lacey's left hand as I face my father again. He, Merek, and Tolie still grin like fecking fools as they give me their ribbons.

Lacey receives Roxana's and lightly tugs the red one from her own hair. I take mine from the inside of my coat jacket, and together, we hand all six ribbons to join with the priest's. Combining old and new might be unorthodox for St. Patrick's of Las Vegas, but it fits Lacey and me perfectly, and the priest was happy to oblige.

We cross our hands between us, with my left gently holding hers on top and our right hands underneath. The priest gathers the various shades of silver, red, and green and wraps them around our joined hands like an infinity knot. Once we've been fastened together, he places his hands over the binding.

"What has been bound together, let no man unbind. What God has joined together, let no man separate."

With my bride's hands securely in mine, it truly feels like it's just the two of us.

I stand straighter and lightly squeeze her hands, careful of her cast. Even though this wedding is for the Garde, now that we're in front of everyone who thinks they matter, I want them to know how important *she* is.

"Lacey O'Shea, from the moment you were promised to me, I knew you were mine. Outside forces tried to separate us, but as I've said before, *cha robh dithis riamh a' fadadh teine nach do las eatarra*. A fire lit between us when we'd never met before, and we've proven that nothing can keep our two flames apart.

"I'll have you. I'll hold you in sickness and in health. We'll live, we'll thrive, and we'll fight to keep those flames burning. You're the love I always believed in. You're my queen of diamonds, and I'm your ace of hearts. Here to fight your battles and stand beside you when you want to fight your own. *Is tú mo rogha*, Lacey. You are the one I choose."

Her eyes glitter with happy tears by the time I finish. When the priest turns to her to have her repeat after him, she interrupts him.

"I-I've got my own this time, actually."

Even though my poker face is one of the best, I can't stop

myself from splitting into a broad smile. My wife is full of surprises.

During our brief rehearsal earlier today, she never mentioned doing her own vows. Granted, I was quite preoccupied with scoping out the back rooms of the sanctuary to pay proper attention.

The priest waits for me nervously because she went off-script, as if I would stop my own wife from saying how she feels. I cut a glare at him in response. He's a Garde priest and a McKennon supporter, but that sexist shite stops now. My wife is my equal. My partner in crime.

She ignores the priest and lightly clears her throat.

"Kian McKennon, I didn't know who you were when we first met, but the rest that followed, I couldn't have gotten through without you." There's a pang in my chest at the harsh reality of her words, but she keeps going and I don't dare stop her now. "You held my hand in the shadows and led me into our light. You are the man I want by my side. To have and to hold. To raise a family. You said, '*is tú mo rogha.*' I remember when you taught me that phrase."

My brows lift slightly and my cock twitches at the memory of the moment I taught the phrase to her as her "safe word." A smile forms on my lips as my heart races to hear what she says next.

"Those words mean safety to me now, just like you do. I want to live my dreams by your side. I'm your diamond, but you have my heart. Now and forever."

My chest swells and I lean in to kiss her, but the priest throws his hand out.

I glare at it and rumble low, "Get your hand out of my way, Father, or I'll break it. What God has joined together, let no man separate, yeah? Nothing comes between me and my wife."

The priest's eyes widen and he yanks his arm out from between us before blurting to the congregation.

"By the power vested in me, I now pronounce you husband and wife. You may—"

Just as she did during our first wedding, I kiss her before the priest can finish. Her tongue teases the seam of my lips and I encircle her waist with my arm to bring her closer. My hand cradles the back of her head to gingerly tip her chin up so I can get an even better angle.

The organ rushes to play and the crowd stands and cheers. When Lacey wraps her arms around my neck, I lift her in a bridal carry and rush to the side, completely bypassing the aisle.

"Mr. McKennon, that's not where—" the priest calls, but my father laughs beside him.

"Let it go, Father. The lad's on a mission. Also might not want to go back there for a while, if you know what I mean. Rest assured, if they break something, we'll add it to the tithe tenfold."

"Got that fecking right," I mutter, making Lacey laugh against my lips.

I back into the annex room door that I found earlier today, pushing it open to dip inside. I can't wait any longer for her.

Despite the fact that she was a rebel about the Garde's archaic rules before marriage, she put her foot down after I proposed to her on the boat. She refused to have sex with me again until our wedding night, and although I managed to bend her rules a wee bit, we didn't break them. It's been barely more than a week, but it's felt like a goddamn eternity.

"Kian! The guests! The reception. We have to go mingle." She giggles.

"Oh, you and I are going to fecking mingle, Lacey McKennon. You told me we had to wait until after our wedding. Well, that was our wedding, wife, and I'm not waiting another second."

I push aside the vestments and robes that were hastily stacked on the communion table. Mrs. O'Shea made the church move the altar because it "didn't fit with the aesthetic of the wedding." I thought it was a ridiculous ask then, but I have to admit, I'm grateful for it now.

Once there's a spot for Lacey, I set her on top as gingerly as I can manage with the desire riding me right now. I dive my tongue into her eager mouth and spread her legs to fit myself between them.

"Kian, God, I've missed you."

"It's your fault, *tine*. I would never torture you so brutally, but now *you're* going to pay for making *me* wait."

Before she can protest, I kneel in front of her and push her long, flowing dress up. My mouth waters at the sight of her bare pussy already gleaming for me.

My voice is rough, "You're not wearing panties underneath your wedding dress?"

She smirks down at me. "Let's just say I had a feeling where this night would go."

I grip her arse underneath her dress and pull her forward for my feast.

Her thighs drape over my shoulders as I swipe my tongue up her center, already damp with arousal. My thumb massages her clit, but I use my mouth on her entrance, soaking it with my own spit to get her ready for me. My wife sits on the communion table, and I dine on her like she's my last fecking supper.

She cries out and tugs my hair, sending pleasure-pain shooting down my spine and straight into my cock.

"Jesus Christ, that feels so good."

"Go ahead and pray, baby. You're going to need it."

"How do I already want to come? Oh my god, you were right. It was too long to wait."

My tongue twirls around her clit, making her moan my name and her thighs tense against my ears. I shove my tongue as deep as I can inside her core and curve it up while my thumb works her clit furiously.

But when her voice pitches higher and her dancer's legs begin to tighten around my head, I rip myself away from her.

"Kian! What the hell?"

"That's what you get for denying me." I smack her inner thigh, making her hiss and glare at me as I stand. "Now you'll get no mercy from me, wife."

I quickly free my cock from my slacks and her eyes widen. The barbell I know she fecking loves is already glistening thanks to the precum weeping from my tip.

When I glance up, she's licking her greedy lips with all her focus still on my cock. I wrap my hand around her nape and capture her gaze.

"I have half a mind to make you get on your knees and apologize properly, but I've missed your sweet pussy for too goddamn long."

On the last word, I shove into her cunt in one thrust. She's already drenched from my mouth and her own arousal, so I don't give her time to adjust to my size or my piercing, and I pump into her at a fierce speed. Despite my threat, I'm careful with the rest of her, making sure I don't reinjure anywhere that's tender even as I drive into her already swollen pussy with long strokes.

She hooks her arms around me and scratches my nape with her uninjured hand. When her pussy begins to flutter around my length, she tries to tug me closer with her stilettos on my back, but I spank her just below her arse. She mewls her submission before relaxing around me and I smile wickedly as I fuck the rebel out of my fiery wife.

"Say it, *tine*." I kiss her neck where I've marked her so many times already. "Say it for me."

She doesn't need her safe word, but she knows what I'm asking for anyway.

"*Is tú mo rogha*, Kian. Always."

A growl of approval rumbles from my chest and I drive into her so hard that the table slams against the wall with every pounding thrust. She cries out my name over and over until her pussy squeezes the fecking life out of me, setting us both off.

She moans my name before biting my neck above my collar like she's trying not to scream. Her fingers squeeze my suit jacket right over her tattooed bite on my forearm, and I lose my rhythm entirely.

What should be pain becomes instant euphoria and ripples

through my body straight to my cock. On my last thrust, I shove into her, sealing myself inside her tight pussy as I fill her with my cum.

We've talked about getting pregnant right away. The doctor said once she has surgery on her wrist and recovers, it will take her a while to be at peak dance performance. It was Lacey's idea to try for a baby in the meantime.

I splay my hand over her lower belly and whisper into her ear. "If fucking on a communion table doesn't get us pregnant, I don't know what will."

She laughs against my neck and pulls away to kiss me. I remain locked inside her, making sure all my cum stays where it needs to.

"I'm up for trying again and again until it works." She giggles. My cock jolts at the sound, making her pussy contract in kind and we both hiss at the pleasure before I reply.

"We'll try again and again and again. Whether it does or doesn't work, I'll still kneel to worship this sweet cunt to show your body my appreciation." I brush a chaste kiss over her lips before I meet her eyes. "But no matter what happens, you're following your dream."

Her eyes light up and a hopeful smile lifts her freckled cheeks. "You're part of that dream now, too, you know."

"You're bloody right I am, and I'm following you every step of the way."

"Don't follow. Walk beside me." She smiles and pulls at my tie, tugging me closer to whisper against my lips, "I love you, Kian McKennon. *Is tú mo rogha.*"

"I love you, too, Lace. I chose you then, I choose you now, and I'll choose you every day from here on out, *mo thine. Is tú mo rogha.*"

~ END ~

Also by Greer Rivers

<u>Conviction Series</u>

Escaping Conviction

Fighting Conviction

Breaking Conviction

Healing Conviction

Atoning Conviction

Leading Conviction

<u>Tattered Curtain Series</u>

Phantom

A Dark, Modern Phantom of the Opera Retelling

<u>Standalone</u>

Catching Lightning

An Enemies-To-Lovers College Sports Romance

Join my newsletter and receive a FREE copy of A Tempting Motion, an enemies-to-lovers, office romance short story

Thank you for reading!

Please consider leaving a review on <u>Amazon</u>, <u>Goodreads</u>, and <u>Bookbub</u>! Just one word can make all the difference.

Be a Dear and Stalk Greer Here

You can find all things Greer here

Acknowledgments

Hi! If you're new here, this is one of my fave parts! You obviously don't have to read these many pages of praise, but you can if you want to! Hell, you might even be in it. But the tl;dr version is: if I know you, I am thankful for you, more than you'll ever know.

First, and almost foremost (sorry, the hubs is always my #1), thank you READERS! The dream makers, the spicybooktokers, and the Boss Ass Bitches! I know your time is precious, so to have you spend it on something I wrote is a true honor. Let me just tell you that you make an author's world go 'round. Hanging out with y'all is why I do this and I love hearing from readers! All you beautiful words of affirmation people who reach out to me to tell me pretty things: You rock my world with your encouragement and I'm truly so surprised every single time someone says something nice about my words. I wouldn't be able to pursue this dream without y'all so thanks for making my dreams come true!

The wonderful team at Valentine PR: Thank you so much for all that you do!

To Cat at TRC Designs: You did it again with this cover. You are such a wonderful hooman and I'm so excited for all that your future holds! Thank you for putting up with me! You are an angel, my frand.

Many thanks to Ellie McLove, my editor at My Brother's Editor: You are a master puzzler and I am so grateful for you as my editor and my friend!

To Claire, my newest Irish friend! Thank you so much for all of your help and guidance with these characters! I'm so excited to see what your own author journey holds and I can't wait to read the rest of your Irish mythology fantasy (if you're not Claire, check out Claire Wright, she's the bomb.)

To the lovely team at Bitesize Irish: I've truly enjoyed learning my ancestors' language and I appreciate all that you do to keep the Irish language, culture, and history thriving.

To Lo: You are a light in the bookish community and I'm so glad to have met you! Thank you for all of your help!

To Rouge's alpha and beta readers:

A.V., Whitney, Carrie, Serenity, Kristen, Blanca, Randi, Heather, Ashley, Rosa, and Mandy:

Y'all. This time was chaos. I know it. You know it. And I'm super appreciative that y'all don't send me glitter bombs in retaliation. Thank you so much for being on this wild ride!

A.V.!!! My beautiful friend who's been with me through thick books and thin, (let's be real, mostly thick). Thank you so much for always being so kind and ready to read. Your feedback is everything I need and I love that you make me a better writer with every book. I can't wait to read your newest books!!

Thank you betas for telling me pretty things. I love you all and I'm so appreciative of the friendships we've developed. My favorite things about y'all reading this book: the excellent music expertise and suggestions, being on the same wavelength, seeing some of you in Vegas 2022/2023 and some of you in Denver 2024, Vegas sunsets, poker and dancing expertise and insight, encouragement, critique, requests for bloodthirstier revenge, and play-by-play emotions that made my day.

Moral of the story: I've made some great friends with all of you and that means everything.

Thank you Bre and Carlie! I'm so grateful for y'all every day! It means THE WORLD to have y'all in my corner, and I can't thank you enough!

Thank you to Below Deck for giving me inspiration on a mafia-style yacht ending.

To KK: You are amazeballs and ily. This year has been really fucking hard on both of us and I'm glad you've been in my corner.

To Rachel: One day you reached out to encourage me and then we never stopped talking. It's been the best and I'm so thankful for our friendships and Zooms!

To my OG BABs/Dinner Divas: Katie, Sydni, Liz, and Lauren: As I'm writing this I am SALIVATING over the thought of eating SG's salsa macha torta al pastor fried tofu under the gorgeous weather and patio deck. I am SO EXCITED. It's been amazing welcoming the cutest little baby into our group, dancing the night away at the most amazing wedding.

To my wonderful family, my momma, sisters, BIL, and 2 precious baby angel face nieces, Baby J and Sweet P: Your support means everything. I've been blown away with how wonderful y'all have been and I'm so thankful for each of you. Menee never stop sending me snaps. Those girls mean everything to me. BG I WILL take you up on that wine date now that I have zero pre-orders to fulfill. Momma, your party in your new home on Sunday is going to be the bomb and I can't wait to bring charcoots. Once again, I *never* expect y'all to read my books, but if you do, I hope you at least enjoy them!!

To my dad: I've always wanted to write an HEA for someone who has struggled with addiction and worked for their sobriety. It is one of my greatest sorrows in life that I couldn't help you with yours.

To Maria: I firmly believe that when everyone is born we should be assigned a therapist and I'm so grateful I lost my mind at the perfect time that I got to have you as mine.

Athena, you crazy bitch. You've been very quiet since I wrote Phantom in your honor and there were *plenty* of times where you could've acted wild. Thank you for chilling out enough to put me in remission, bestie. You rock.

And finally, to the hubs: This was a wild one. Two hundred more hours than normal and not that many more days. It was super hard and stressful but I truly couldn't have done it without you and I wouldn't want to. You are my "Mighty Alpha," first reader, last reader, all the readers in between, co-writer, business partner, co-owner, manager, TikTok approver, cliff jump pusher/catcher, favorite encourager, IRL book boyfriend, best friend forever, and the love of my life. Thank you for telling me you like Kian/this story the best. I hope I keep this streak with every new MMC. Your pretty words fill me up and give me the courage to do all the scary things in this world. Admin walks and plotting with you are two of my favorite things and quite literally keep me sane. As always, I am so incredibly thankful for you believing in me 100% and taking hugenormous leaps of faith with me. You've saved my life and you've changed it for the better. I wouldn't want to spend a moment of it without you. Thank you for making every day an HEA.

Love,

Greer Rivers

All About Greer

Greer Rivers is a former crime fighter in a suit, but now happily leaves that to her characters! A born and raised Carolinian, Greer says "y'all," the occasional "bless your heart" (when necessary), and feels comfortable using legal jargon in everyday life.

She lives in the mountains with her husband/critique partner/irl book boyfriend and their three fur babies. She's a sucker for reality TV, New Girl, and scary movies in the daytime. Greer admits she's a messy eater, ruiner of shirts, and does NOT share food or wine.

Greer adores strong, sassy heroines and steamy second chances. She hopes to give readers an escape from the craziness of life and a safe place to feel too much. She'd LOVE to hear from you anytime! Except the morning. She hates mornings.